To date, Tomas Leander has produced four other westerns, three dramatic novels, one collection of short stories, and three plays. He lives in Sweden.

Tomas Leander

FLATLANDS

AUSTIN MACAULEY PUBLISHERS™

LONDON * CAMBRIDGE * NEW YORK * SHARJAH

Copyright © Tomas Leander 2022

All rights reserved. No part of this publication may be reproduced, distributed, or transmitted in any form or by any means, including photocopying, recording, or other electronic or mechanical methods, without the prior written permission of the publisher, except in the case of brief quotations embodied in critical reviews and certain other non-commercial uses permitted by copyright law. For permission requests, write to the publisher.

Any person who commits any unauthorized act in relation to this publication may be liable to criminal prosecution and civil claims for damages.

This is a work of fiction. Names, characters, businesses, places, events, locales, and incidents are either the products of the author's imagination or used in a fictitious manner. Any resemblance to actual persons, living or dead, or actual events is purely coincidental.

Ordering Information
Quantity sales: Special discounts are available on quantity purchases by corporations, associations, and others. For details, contact the publisher at the address below.

Publisher's Cataloging-in-Publication data
Leander, Tomas
Flatlands

ISBN 9781685621070 (Paperback)
ISBN 9781685621087 (Hardback)
ISBN 9781685621100 (ePub e-book)
ISBN 9781685621094 (Audiobook)

Library of Congress Control Number: 2021923282

www.austinmacauley.com/us

First Published 2022
Austin Macauley Publishers LLC
40 Wall Street, 33rd Floor, Suite 3302
New York, NY 10005
USA

mail-usa@austinmacauley.com
+1(646)5125767

First of all I want to give thanks to Jesus, my Lord and Savior. Without Him nothing is possible. Thanks also to my agent, Rev. Lars Borgström for his gallantry using the post and the telephone, and his wife Rachel for occasional peek toward my text. A special thanks also to my dear friend, the computer wizard, Berthold Nilsson, the guy who helped me fix the cover picture of the book, showing a section of the country side of South Montana with the branding fire and the cowhead, and the stream in the background. Last, but not the least, my gratitude goes to Austin Macauley Publishers. I owe you all for what you have done.

I

"Let everything that has breath praise the Lord. Hallelujah!" Psalm 150:6

One late afternoon a few miles short of town...

Rocking and careening rhythmically at an even pace, like a liner far out on the swells of the wide ocean, the heavily loaded stagecoach in a flurry of hooves in a wake of slowly dissipating smoke, rumbled its way forward across the flat brush country. As of yet, neither mountains nor hills were about. The coach was delayed by more than an hour, and this was more a rule than an exception in these days. It was, in fact, so habitual that people around never reckoned with anything else. The teamsters faulted the time-table, claiming it was too tight, whereas people along the trail, including the majority of the passengers, had their own explanations, blaming the teamsters, alleging they were perpetually drunk and sleeping on the box. Others claimed the horses were lazy. These folks, however, these currently seated down there in the battered burgundy plush with a fragrance of lavender about them, appeared to be different, the teamster thought to himself. He'd swapped a couple of words with them when they changed horses at Indian Junction where they'd climbed outside for a brief interval to stretch their limbs and inquire about time while enjoying the sun shining on them in walking a lap around the vehicle, before they again clambered aboard. Upon being asked about it, they'd even denied it being dusty there in the murk. Nor did they mention the horsehair stuffing erupting from a splayed seam in a seat. Classy people by comparison, in their best mourning black, like they were dressed for church, the driver thought, chuckling to himself. Perched alone high up on the spring driver's seat of the high-wheeled wagon, you have a lot of time to think. And dream. It was different in those days, a number of years back, when the coachmen were doubled, but things changed when the authorities started to notice holdups and Indian assaults became less frequent. This route hadn't experienced a swoop of any kind in more than two years, and then it was unlikely it would happen again. That's the way the authorities in Cheyenne reasoned, those at Wells

Fargo, educated dressed-up people, dexterous folks with crafty solutions when it came to the math. It is different with me old harmless gaffer, he often thought. I don't vaunt. I don't have skill with words and can barely write my own signature, and have never lived in a luxurious fashion, but I'm not touchy and have never gone in the way, and I've tried, for all my tumbled image, to do right and not vituperate, he reflected where he sat perched on the driver's seat, chancing a sidelong glance down at the loaded short-barreled Kentucky rifle with its worn mended stock of fruitwood, where it stood in its weather-cracked scabbard, one designed for just that purpose right beneath the seat, within easy reach with its pipe pointing to the featureless skies. But he knew he'd done what he could to persuade them, but failed in repeated efforts. As for himself, he had a couple of days back, from his high place on the stage, spotted two reds some miles downriver. They'd been sitting on their haunches, paddling their canoes along the shoreline. Nearsighted as he is, he could make out no details, but he assumed they'd been Sioux or perhaps Crow.

The wonky clip seat creaked under him and whimpered under his heavy and unwieldy body each time the wheels hit a solidified rut. Every once in a while, he experienced a sensation of being dormant. It came with the loneliness. In a little less than thirty or so minutes, though, they were supposed to roll into Sioux Falls for another swap of horses and an hour-long break with something to eat, a couple of beer, and a few words with the driver of the stage headed in the opposite direction.

With the wagon creaking faintly and the iron-bound hickory wheel's rasping in their cutting ruts in the loose uneven ground, the four-in-hand, a spry team of matching bays, changed gait, fading into a labored short-gaited walk. Incited by the teamster's piercing whistles and the cracks of the long whip, they snorting with mouths working strenuously, sucking long scoops of air and with dustpurs sifting up from their fetlocks, climbed up the barren height with edgy tread at an easy pace, their backs and brawny hindquarters in rhythmic flexion, their breaths rifling in and out with their mouth's moving while working the seeping froth, bobbing their heads by every step, the long bridle reins quivering alongside their sweaty flanks. It wasn't often he let his whip out. He didn't have to. These horses were massive and showed as of yet no sign of tiring, no he could perceive no diminution of their power. They looked almost like real good and spry cutting horses, he meditated, and they pulled well together. Yes, pretty good passable horses he'd had for the most part, and they'd seldom been footsore.

They'd all but topped out the elevation, and a desolate hidden length lay ahead stretching on as far as he could overlook to the north, and to the west. This was to him a familiar territory. No ranches nor habitations of any kind there was to see, with the exception of two droopy abandoned homesteads apt to thump to the ground with chimneys licked black by flames, and with sections slanted away in every direction, grown with moss and lichens, unsupported as they were. There they stood these one-room shacks and dugouts as havens for bats and owls with glassless windows and rooftrees sagging and half prolapsed with brush starting to grove inside them, partly burned down by Indians in past times, their sagging and rotten boards littered with arrow shafts, and rifle-balls gray with oxidation, and cracked pottery, and glassware and ruptured glass in myriads fallen from their sash in their own devising. They were seldom old, these fall-ins. The holding pens for the most time stood intact, as did the outhouses. Neither grazing livestock nor stray cattle there was to see about them, despite it was an open unfenced pastureland with the best growing dirt in the county. No, there was only wilderness, rattlesnakes, moose, deer and other antlered game, pumas, rabbits uncountable in the evergreens, wild pigs and you know not what other animals, and carrion birds out on the prowl. The country looked these days merely like it were haunted, he mused, although he'd heard there were those who had their eyes on it. Last week in an upland copse, he'd passed by a couple of fallow deer that had descended a creek to look for water. They stood with strained ears looking at him as he trundled by. He foresaw they were escaping, and hence he slowed down his pace a little when approaching on them, but they didn't escape. Instead they remained drinking, and in hearing and watching him appearing they just sharply flung their heads upward, one then the other, and watched him long and featureless in the manner of cattle with their muzzles dripping while keeping watch on him all the time uncertainly during his passing, then they anew dropped their heads to the mossy still-cool spring water where it was issuing out of the swampy ground of the underground stream, and jaw to jaw they'd resumed sucking deeply again. It was indeed a beautiful sight, yes, indeed a peaceful scene, he thought while picking up pace. This meant they didn't frighten him. But why should they frighten him, an one-eyed and ungainly coach driver with a sour back and aching elbows, he thought, grinning to himself humorlessly.

Holding the bridles loosely, slapping occasionally the flanks of the horses while rocking slightly with the wagon's motion when it skewed about, he turned his head and with eyes stinging and wet by the constant headwind looked out the arid flatlands in all directions to see if there was perhaps any sign of people around. It was a wind-scoured terrain with shadows growing long upon it. One day or two of wetness and it all would turn green again, he meditated. He'd seen it do before, many times in the past. He watched the country about for any hint of movement, but there was none. Hence, let alone he had a creepy sensation of being followed, and the feeling didn't abate, he kept on driving, cutting for signs meanwhile.

He'd gone a quarter mile or perhaps a little more when he a little further on might have heard an outcry from somewhere about, or he might not have. He thought he'd had. He also had an unmistakable sensation of somebody lurking close. Sensing his pulse speeding up, he with growing unease turned his head in all four and gazed out for a long time, but there was nothing to see, nor anything to hear but for the breath from the horses and the wheels groaning against the axles. Else there was to perceive nothing of consequence. Just cauterized grass and withering flowers. Lives running out. Bargaining with himself he at last pulled the rifle out of the scabbard, and clutching it tight in his hand swung it upward and then stood it upright with the buttstock down between his knees. After near forty years on a coach seat, starting back in those days long since gone, the olden times, the times twenty odd years back when they used mules to pull, and before four-in-hand became general and when the seats were uncushioned by any upholstery, those times to which he often harked back, he'd learned two devices. Watch your rear, and never whip on a tired horse. Holding the bridle reins in his left hand, he with the other for the purpose of shading sight, readjusted his worn brown Stetson hat, and once again checked behind him, then took a final look around, as if he'd a portent of something, his face shining with sweat. He then bent over sideways, and trying to look forward and down at the quivering bridle reins and muscled necks of the horses and not to at the same time, reached out his hand for the long whip, closed upon and clutched it, and with an upward motion snatched it from its place right beside the wonky seat, his eye set to the frontrunners. He raised the whip upward, and sensing the wheels of the wagon drifting slightly and sidling a little in the loose ground, he gave some cracks in the dusty air, and in a voice hoarse and urgent incited the horses with some joyous acclamations, some of which humorous from time to time, according to people who had overheard them. In his own opinion, all ancient teamsters used to acquire a pretty broad repertoire of them with time.

The country now was changed into a dense forest interspersed with coppices holding different types of trees, hardwood mostly, when the horses now slowed their pace significantly, and with a good amount of force started climbing up the elongated butte at a labored walk. Perched on the squeaking bench the coachman let them tread their way upward in loose bridles following the rutty trail with rapid rasps of hocks, the gear squeaking in the stillness. They had walked it many times before, they knew the way, they always tried to suit. That is, in his experience, the way horses are by nature. Listening to the constant breath from the horses and the trundle of the wagon's wheels, he raised his head and squinted up toward the skies where the reddish sun showed on and off, and where white clouds were drifting in from west, eastbound with no water in them. Sitting so, spread-legged with his head aloft, twitching the bridles, rocking slightly with the vehicle's motion, and singing and whistling quietly to himself, he studied them carefully with gross attention while they rapidly sailed from left to right, looking as if they might be speaking to him, his eyebrows raised in astonishment and eyes red-rimmed and watery, watching them carry so light on the heaven, and build images of all sorts, towers, faces of humans and animals, yes, all kinds of illusions and silhouettes of things he couldn't decide which. This was a habit he'd adopted long ago, it was kinda pastime. He watched the clouds how they rapidly came together, how they remained for a short while and then drifted apart as quickly as they had encountered, and within short vanished ephemeral, leaving no traces of where they'd been, like passing fugitives there high above, guests and strangers like the rest of Creation, doomed to perish here and perhaps arise later some other time, some other place, he pondered while watching them until they got dissolved or went out of his sight, marveling at how hastily they went by. It is like life itself, he meditated. Nothing stays the same.

He never observed the masked rider behind the curve where the road leveled out, because his eye was still watching the skies. Right when he topped the rise with the wood dense on either his side, he heard the bang though, a single report, one that vanished almost instantly in the otherwise stillness with no hills or rocks about to build up an echo. With an expression of sheer surprise, he experienced a release of tension in his arms as the bridles felt maddingly heavy in his hands and he sensed his hands stiffen, and the grip about the whip soften, and his chin sagged and the whip got out of his keep and the gun slanted down, and he experienced a spinning sensation inside him as he, as though torn down by some invisible underground force, slammed back, the power of the impact all but tearing him off the box. Soon, though, he re-caught his equilibrium, and while struggling to maintain his seat he the while tasted a sudden warmth on his tongue as he caught in the impromptu pain from where the rifleball had struck when the shot clattered out. So intense the pain was he could scarcely bear it, and he registered the sudden great warmth from the red viscous blood that slowly pulsated from his abdomen in its seeping downward, and he comprehended that a firearm must have been discharged from a close proximity. And he did also apprehend the agonizing whinnying from the horses as they braced their feet against the ground so as to gain traction picked up speed, and running now at will wildly with none to herd them with the huge wagon lurching awkwardly behind. Feeling giddy and breathing heavily through his mouth, having a faint awareness his life was passing, he for a last time snapped his head to the side for a second look, then he sensed his firm doubled hold on the bridles slacken. Limp and helpless he slouched and sagging clawed for handhold, groping for whatever purchase might present itself, his fingers contracted into a tight claw. Knowing there he would never make it, he by gradual increments of his head ultimately slew sideways, and headlong in an acceleration he fell off the springy seat without no sound coming from off him. He plunged down and slammed into the ground with a solid thump so heavily that his brachium broke flush under his weight with a cracking snap, the way it sounds when you crack a branch, and had he also an odd feeling in his shoulder that something had given away, and he lost sensation in his legs. Expelling a long breath, taking in the pain in the shoulder, he lay face-upward with his back in the dirt with knees splayed, coughing gutturally, the clumsy vehicle, now far ahead of him, on the verge of stampede. Other than this he apprehended nothing for he wasn't clearheaded, and in the ensuing moment he went into a darkness and lost consciousness.

    No sooner had the masked rider come alongside and reined in the bumping equipage and gradually brought it to a wobbling complete halt than another five companions materialized from its wake, sawing their mounts about in a cloud of drifting dust that slowly leaned upward. With his smoking rifle across the bow of the saddle, touching his horse's sides with his heels, one of them advanced upon the coach and haltingly closed into. He reined in the horse and slanted the brim of his hat down to hide his eyes, then snatched open the door and in the bright of its opening took a brief look inside the dark interior. Sitting diagonally across his chest was a shell belt. Panting, opening the door wider, looking from one to the other while pointing his firearm at them, he with grim determination with broken voice brusquely instigated the horrified people in there to step down, his voice loud in the otherwise hush.

    The first to make her exit was a twelve-year-old girl, one incredibly pallid, elvish-looking and wide-eyed with smart features under her black dusty bonnet, cuddling tight against her a little white and quivering snub-nosed dog, her right hand set to its nose so it wouldn't cry. They were both paralyzed with terror and panic. Shortly after she'd ponderously climbed out of the half-light and had descended, and when on the ground she drew a ragged breath and with eyes recoiled from the brightness of the sun began walking aimlessly, her light head shaking in disbelief, her features contorted in anguish while the dog, that was rife with fear with eyes wandering about crazily with tongue lolling out, still in her arms started to flounder and yap while urinating vehemently on her striped dress. On the spur of the moment her some years elder brother took advantage of the racket and somehow forced his way out of the coupe, and silent and catlike rounded the wagon and squirrely dashed off with unsteady straightness, and took after a short rush protection behind a nearby wind-tattered willow thicket. From his refuge he could see nothing but the horse's feet sidling and stepping. Then things happened quickly, things that should alter his world for ever in the space of a heartbeat. Huddled up behind the thick growth, he heard one report coming outrageously hard, and some seconds later one more accompanied by curses and harsh ribald words, and tramping of horses. Next two shots consecutively got squeezed off with purposefulness. Offensive gunsmoke was hanging in midair and somewhere in the middle of it he discerned the voice of his mother for the very last time, and he heard the men calling to one another, their words muted by the distance. He felt his heart strike and his tongue swell, his mouth all drained. He didn't dare, however, to get himself out of the thickets to see what was happening. His head was numb and his white shirt wet, and he was sweaty under his arms. Yet he felt cold.

What about his folks? Where they dead? He felt feeble and tired, but fought hard to keep his stay. After sometime the sounds grew fainter.

"We'd better get goin'," a raucous voice grunted sulkily as he dug his heels into his horse's flanks, his words muffled under the dusty bandana. "Let's get goin'!"

"Yeah, let's get the hell outta here!!" another horseman exclaimed while eagerly reloading his gun.

"Where's the kid at?" a third demanded disapprovingly, his voice smattering like thunderclaps in the otherwise stillness when turning his dancing horse out into the rut packed wagonroad again and stopping it sideways in it.

"He might of went…To hell with im, let's get it done, an' then we set off!" a shrill and nasal source-less voice oddly high-pitched shouted over the clang and chink of bridle metal.

Sometime later, it might have been fifteen minutes, the sharp thunder of pounding hooves had died away in the late afternoon, and there were no more windy riffles of harsh voices, nor was there any crying and shrieking from his mother. They had receded, and there was no sound from her at all. The boy with a stunned look in his face crouched with his jaw hanging, shivering in his shirtsleeves, continued with wonder to peep between the leaves of the willows until a long time after the horses had disappeared from sight, and there was nothing left to hear but the silence of nature, the soft and regular thrashing of the wind through the trees, and the unconcerned tweet of the songsters, and the occasional snorts of the team that now was standing inert with heads down in an odor of sweat and manure. One frontrunner stood listlessly pawing at the ground with a forefoot, jerking fiercely its blazed long head up and down, its mouth pleated back from the teeth as though it were petulant or angry at the gnats, or just keen to get started, the others standing with their heads declined, their long tails swishing and flanks in a constant quiver against the intrusive blue flies. With huge eyes he'd watched it to happen. All of it.

It was in the last of the day's light and high above, shielded from sight, a big red-headed woodpecker was heard tapping a hardwood stem by the roadside, the irregular thuds echoing and reechoing from one side of the road to the other. The riders, six in number, had long since in a single file set out in a haze of gray lingering gunsmoke. Neither laughing nor crying was to be heard anymore. The drone of noise was now transformed, had ceased altogether, and all he wanted as he willed himself up was to know what had befallen his father and mother and his little sister Hannelore and Mathilde, her beloved dog. Soon he found out, stepping about knock-kneed with no aim. Feeling a pressure inside his head, and realizing now he was bereft of quarters, he while chancing an eye at his dead kin on buckling knees, hauling up his pants at the waist as he went with his curly light hair riffling slightly, crossed without stopping his way downhill toward the coniferous trees. Feeling his legs getting shaky, he with a slice of his flattened hand swept his trousers in the back and exhausted sank down on a decayed stub sheltered from the wind, and sat and rocked back and forth, kicking his feet and rocking without cessation, twisting his body, his heart in palpitations. As if perhaps to conjure up some memory that he turned in his mind, he commenced crooning lowly with his lips so clamped his teeth did scarcely show, the vivid final part out of "Symphonische Etüden," a piano work by Robert Schumann, a piece he'd started to rehearse on his own piano not long ago. Overhead lay the black night sky and to the east a halfmoon phosphorous hung cocked on the cloudless neutral firmament. Around him a vastness. The wind had abated altogether, and above him there was a steady whine of gnats, and in the greenery the crickets without intermission had commenced their endless sawing away.

Some hours later the evening found him sitting in solitude shivering with chattering teeth in a white moonlight, holding his head with both hands so as to make his teeth stop chattering, hearing inside it voices and sounds he would be feeding on the remainder of his life. High up in the trees the smallbirds were gathering and soon quieted as the last daylight vanished and the ground went cool, and the calls of the cicadas took over entirely. What waited was the cold night and the advent of the night sounds and the night animals. It might have been ten at night or midnight. He didn't know. He'd dropped his timepiece somewhere. And his hat also.

The wire delivered to the sheriff's office of Sioux Falls had been unmistakable. The coach had set out from Black Creek on time. But for some reason it never emerged in Sioux Falls. The issue already was subject to speculations, and solemn faces already were coming together in town. The coach was due to appear at six on the previous afternoon, but it didn't. It did not appear at all. It was as if a wake already had begun in town, Jeff O'Halloran, vice sheriff of Sioux Falls, thought, after having read the wire at seven in the morning following. Douglas Kimble, his hefty foreman, was told all about it some minutes later when he chewing on a cheekful of tobacco lumbered his way to the office. Obliging voices had told him the news, and advises were delivered. It normally took him five compact minutes at the most to make it from his home to the office, but today it had taken at least the double.

Focusing the badge that sat pinned on the sheriff's vest one lady said with a loveless anticipatory smile, "Sheriff Kimble, you've to do somethin' 'bout it, you hear, cause it ain't likely 'em murderin' thievin' buggers turn 'emselves in…Draw a posse!! My three sons gladly join the search!!"

Another, a paunchy man in street clothes and jaws knobby by tobacco, a local merchantman, brawled in a higher voice, heard over the other, "Ride out there an' figure out what happened fore it all gets off track!!"

A third voice of a stout little man with a thick matted beard and leather breeches and hard top dismally added in a high-pitched querulous voice, "Yeah, right…get down to hardpan…That's what we are payin' you for, right…?"

"Yeah, sure we'll try to figure it out. O'Halloran is ridin' out there first thing!" the sheriff rumbled reassuringly in his dark baritone while bullying his way unhindered through the throng, and limping just a little, mindful of every step, zigzagged his way through the crowds. Deep inside he had a feeling people in town were taking advantage of the situation, taking all chances they had to patronize and plot against him. He knew his position was disputed, that his chances to get reelected next year were substantially reduced. He slowed down a little and looked about helplessly and spat his chew of tobacco into the dirt, then quickened his pace somewhat while wiping his mouth with the sleeve of his shirt. Within a minute he ascended the steep and gritty wooden stairs that creaked slightly under his weight and pushed the door of the low-ceilinged office open, his face flushed. With his head slightly bowed to clear the entrance he stepped inside and slammed the door shut after him. Outside there was a burst of voices as a convocation of people was assembling before the weathered wooden door.

"Oh, my God, huh! Those damned boots ain't made for walkin', that's what I've always said…Em are like pyrosis and anthrax…" he puffed out deep-voiced. He snatched off his Stetson hat and hung it on the wall peg just inside the door. He cast about in the gloomy office, near lightless but for a lit lamp that stood on the deputy's table.

"Mornin', Jeff, I reckon yo've heard about it already," he went on without turning to his vice sheriff, his voice not raised above a mutter.

Jeff O'Halloran straightened himself and dried his second mug of coffee and contemplated his boss, who with steps cracking loud with a heavy shuffling stride was walking in his fraying buffed boots to the cookstove where there was still a glow of coals. From the sooty kettle, he sloshed up for himself a mug of the strong perking brew, then with a woeful look on his face, like he were weighing some dark problem, carrying it in his booth hands with the contents lapping sluggishly, walked toward and around his knocked-about varnished writing desk. Gingerly so as not to spill, he set the mug down, and easing his large frame downward subsided heavily in the wooden swivel and sat looking back at his deputy interrogatively with his face tensed and eyelids puffy, his belly tight under the red-checked shirt and open vest, his fingers restlessly drumming on the edge of the desk.

"Pretty hard to escape, ain't it?" the deputy after a moment of thought replied earnestly, a cigarette in his right hand. The sheriff blew on his coffee then took a long thirsty drink. He lowered and stalled the mug and raised his head and looked at his deputy above the mug's brim, his hand quivering a little.

"Look…" he commenced, his tone a little fret, "People in town are afire. I figure it would be a good idea you ride out to see if you might find out somethin.'" he went on, his voice gaining strength. Without waiting for an answer he sipped his coffee reflectively and pushed back the seat, arched himself stiffly and rose with pain and stood and brought the mug to the stove, scuffing his heels along the plain hardwood floor while glaring covertly at his deputy in his passing him. He made a halt and looked back at him where he sat on the edge of his scratched desk smoking, one leg dangling.

"An' yo' do the paperwork when I'm out, right" he replied with perfect sarcasm, their eyes meeting briefly. The sheriff produced no answer. The deputy took a last draw and with smoke issuing out of his nostrils reached across the desk and stubbed out the cigarette in the wooden ashtray. The old timepiece ticked from its corner. It chimed 7.30 a.m. He said while looking across at it, "That clock yon'…Does it tell the right time…?"

"It never does," his foreman replied in an undertone of melodramatic chagrin. With dull loathing he added, as if talking to himself, his voice barely audible, "It always is at an obstinate age…like my kids back home."

Nodding assent Jeff shifted his gaze down to his polished high-heeled boots and crossed them before him. After a while he pushed himself off the desk and stood and stretched, then crossed to the plank wall along which the gun rack run, the rowels jingling when striking the dirty unevenly planked floor. He reached up for his rifle and with a doubled grip upon it took it off. Hefting its weight in his right hand and turning it to bring the muzzle down he went back to his desk where his gunbelt hung slung over the chair back. By rote he broke the rifle open, and holding it to the light of the lamp for the better light there with his left eye closed altogether peered into and checked the chambered round, then levered the breech shut in one quick movement, and cautiously put the gun down on the desk and let go of it. He retrieved the gunbelt from where it hung on the chairback with the five-shot Colt in it. He adapted the belt, jerked it tight and buckled it around his contracted middle and when done he drew the Colt from the holster and broke it up and checked the cylinder to make sure there was a full round chambered. Once he'd reseated the Colt back down into the oiled holster, he resumed his rifle by the stock and hefted it in his hand and got it off the desk then took another couple of steps to get his hat, put it on left-handed and stood ready. His foreman now was situated at his desk with one foot propped into an open drawer, some paperwork scattered about on the desk before him. He looked forlornly at his deputy who with one knuckle touched the brim of his hat to exit. Nothing more was said as the vice sheriff so equipped with purpose made it for the door with the rifle swinging low at his side. Without turning or looking back he opened and with slow tread went outside and silently let the door to behind him. Sheriff Kimble expiring reclined and sat in the quiet for a long while and looked after his deputy, listening to the clock's ticking, his eyes red with tiredness. Deep in thought, he scratched his three days' worth of grizzled stubble. He was slightly drunk and raging with thirst. Suddenly his face got stiff. Ponderously he straightened himself up. He'd spotted something on the desktop. He watched it with disdain. It was moving. Spread-fingered he raised his hand above it and let it hang in the air motionless for a while. Tight-jawed, with a low outcry, he with full force slammed his hand down on the desktop and then removed his hand. With his lips pursed he meditated the crushed fly, then with an oath swept it down in one clumsy go.

 The better part of an hour later Jeff O'Halloran reined in the great black stallion, and it stood, champing at the bit. Sitting high in the saddle he looked about the range. A scrubland grown with bramble and juniper leaned in the wind. Patting the horse's shoulder he addressed it friendly so as to calm it, then slacked his hold on and dropped the reins on the saddle. He pushed the hat back on his head. There was a long minute while he glassed the country about with his cavalry field binoculars that sat at chest level to hang by its thong. Gazing across the distance he pressed them into his eyes and adjusted the focus, spinning slowly the cylinder in his fingers. He kept on scanning. Windswept reaches. Nothing moved out there with the exception of the rolling grass. After a while he lowered the glasses and passed them back over his head. He collapsed them then re-bagged them in the saddle. He let his shoulders slump and caught at the reins with one hand and assumed them. He incited the horse forward with his shanks, and when he'd got it going, he set spurs to it and put it forward at a slow canter.

It was good daylight and all night things gone when he caught sight of a pall of smoke and a branding fire licking in the wind, and a half dozen or so drovers on the plain roping Hereford cattle at some distance off the wagon trail, and some hundreds of young cattle grazing or starring motionless with innumerable gnats shimmering before their eyes, slat-ribbed yearlings mostly and new calves with laddered ribs, some deployed, others grouped, some of them lying in the dry luxuriant grass as if hiding out. Neither of the herders paid him any attention, or hadn't they spotted him. Some two miles ahead of him he at the same time distinguished a stagecoach coming bouncing in his direction at a hard gallop, trailing a wake of dispersing dust. The stallion under him snickered softly while pricking his ears back and forth, tossing his jet-black head. He drew rein and halted in the middle of the trail, awaiting the vehicle's hovering into view. Some minutes later, the teamster with a boot up on the brake for the purpose of applying it, angled up before him, and hauling on the bridles slowly brought the wagon to a rumbling halt working the brakes, the horses with whitish slobber seething in their teeth, tossing their heads as the wagon eventually in a squeal of wheels, covered with a fresh coat of mud, rolled to a swinging stop well ahead of him. The young driver, a smallish denim-shirted square-hipped figure, poised high up on the seat, wreathed in dissipating smoke, slacked the bridle reins and collected them in one hand, and blinking rapidly peered down at him through the powdery dust while making a curt gesture of salute. He then immediately recognized the rider in the saddle beneath, and he shaded his eyes with an arm to see him better. He looked upset, his wedge-shaped pallid face contorted with horror and despair when he excitedly shouted, his words coming erratically, all but lost in the wind, "Jeff, 'em are out there! I'm sick with pain at what I saw! Damnedest thing I've ever witnessed...Whew...Shot to death, five six miles out...on a ridge...yo'll see 'em..."

Jeff waited for the driving wind to clear the dust, then moved another step forward and queried the coachman how many they were lying out there, his voice no more than a windy riffle. In the coach a man sat peering out at him, silent and suspicious. The driver shouted back he was scared shitless, and hadn't taken a tally.

Facing the wind, alert to any disturbance, he some quarter of an hour later set the horse. Sitting in the saddle he with the bridles doubled in his fist kept the tramping horse stationary by a twitch, looking back the way he'd come. There was no shape of movement anywhere, no nothing. A ways out obliquely ahead of him, some quarter of a mile or better away, he could in the ensuing moment observe a phalanx of scavengers massing, wafting mutely in descending circles, conniving and flapping apart, riding on an updraft with awry necks, nine or ten of their kind as of yet. With his heels he goaded his fickle horse forward by fits and stops.

Astraddle the saddle, sitting slumped with both forearms across the pommel, he looked down at the dead bodies where they were lying in the dirt, half turned his way, in a narrow shadow cast by the wagon. They were shot cleanly just below the heart, looking past him in a fetal crouch just outside the stage where it stood with the door out-flung. Their jugulars were severed by some animal's claws and fangs, the white cartilage of the gullets and windpipes visible. About them valises and possibles bags were deployed and torn open, and clothes in tatters and canvas covers scattered about. Among them zigzagging was a grid with imprints of high-heeled boots. The four horses, interbreeds between cutting horses and wagon horses, standing their wired together with heads hanging down, as if in teamwork levered their heads and without applying any visible strength simultaneously took some occasional small steps forward then stopped short and stood with their sides heaving, their withers quivering against the rioting flies. After sometime the horse farthest back, one standing on the left side with its croup aslant and tail whisking without intermission, swung its long head and with ears cocked looked back at him as if to see what went. Noticing it was prevented from actually seeing him, due to the blinds it wore, it with failing enthusiasm soon looked away again and gave a shake of its head. In a little while it bowed up and nickered then took a sidestep and turned its head back at Jeff another time, so anxious he could hear its breath. He pulled his hat back and boosted himself up in the saddle the better to see, then eventually let go the reins and patted his horse's neck while addressing it friendly, and then thoughtfully, processing his options, with studied slowness with two fingers reached and felt for his shag pouch of leather in his shirt's breast pocket. Struggling a little with it, he reflectively dredged it up backhanded and caught its leather straps up with his teeth, and shucked his offside leg backward out of the stirrup and slung it over the horn of the saddle to ease his seat, then got him a paper from another pocket. He cupped it with his fingers and sprinkled shag onto. With some twisting motions of his fingers, he deftly rolled himself a cigarette then closed the pouch and by feel restored it and removed his hand from the pocket, and crooked in the back licked the paper and folded it shut neat and perfect. With the unlit cigarette partway to his lips he stalled it there and crouched. He sat listening in concentration for a while to the distant yaps from the coyotes that now were growing fainter as the day accrued, and after yet a while receded and were to hear no more. He reached to and from inside a pocket of his jean trousers by feel, fumbling distractedly with his fingers sought and at once retrieved a match from the box, but it wouldn't come and it was awkward getting at it, and he had to pull the matchbox halfway out. He slid open and picked out a match then shut and let go the box, and turned a wee bit in the saddle so as to have the wind behind him, then struck the match to the heel of his boot, once and once again and sat and looked at it flaring up yellow with a woosh. He cupped the light in his hands and got the cigarette afire then sucked the match out. He flung the twisted and sooty residue from him and straightened himself up in the saddle and took to smoke in long thoughtful pulls, sensing the smoke gripe his trachea and lungs as the horse meanwhile swerved to nibble at whatever of the little blowsy burnt grass there was for him to crop. Sons of bitches, he said to himself in a quiet voice as he leaned to the side spit out a tobacco flake. The dead bodies lying out there before him under the shadow of the coach, were already partially defiled with rags twisted about and strewn all across the area. Having sat in that manner for a lengthy interval, smoking slowly, contemplating what he would do next, he unlimbered his leg back then gripped the horn for support. He put weight to the left stirrup, and slowly, with his hands cupped on the saddle, stood down on stiff legs. He looked at and dropped the glowing butt, and trod it down with the sole of his boot. Looking about him, he adjusted the gunbelt that sat about his waist, and in a saunter sought his way, crossing to where the stagecoach stood with red dust settled over it and door widely open, his long shadow bouncing thin and oblique beside him. Once there he stepped abreast of the coach and peered inside, certifying the coupe being empty, making sure nothing and no one being missed. All he could detect in there was a closed book right underneath one couch on a place where the daylight fell in. He read Madame Bovary by Gustave Flaubert. He stood back and retreated some paces then turned and went away leaving the door open. He retraced his steps and proceeded toward and once again stood and sickly looked down at the corpses, his searching gaze moving from one to the other. This was more than he could stand, he thought to himself. "May the Lord have mercy on their evil souls...'em must have their punishment for it...I take it from here," he said to himself semi-loudly as he started walking again in the slowest of walks past the remains of the dog where it lay on its side soaked with blood, sorry-looking and partly eaten with guts protruding, perforated and partway delineated with heart visible and fur bedraggled, looking as if someone with malevolent will had lashed a bucketful with something stinking over it, and all of a sudden he felt nauseous, and his belly rumpled, and for a while he thought he was starting to air his paunch, so he retched and stood for a long minute in an aching curl. Pumping out low coughs, he got erect again and with slow tread made it back to the horse and got the canteen and lifted it up from where it hung by its strap over the saddle's horn. With a skirling sound, he loosed the tin screwcap, raised the keg and tilted it and put it to his mouth, and bending his neck backward swigged down a long drink. And another. He trickled some water between his teeth then leaned and spat, and trying to get facts in summary looked furtively about him at the roadside growth of young pine. Nothing moved save the horses where they stood somnolent with heads down and tails whisking. Thoughtfully he fitted and slowly screwed back the cap of the keg, then absently shook it in his hand to gauge the reminders. Three good quarts left. Holding it by the thong he absentmindedly went back to the horse and resumed the keg to the saddle, and removed his hand and swung around and stepped away from the horse by the expedient of taking a closer look at the surroundings.

A while later he was back at the dead girl. He nudged his hat a little more backward on his head and once again looked down at her where she was lying stiffly on her back, twisted at the midsection with one leg doubled under her beneath the coach in a strip of sunless blight, her head at an angle and arms out-flung to the sides almost like she'd been crucified. Her white hosiery were torn, her pale throat with larynx exposed as if he coyotes had eaten on her. Her sightless eyes, void of reflection, were widened and centered toward him, her hands brittle and passive, blue-veined and milky. A small thin girl with a sunken belly, a light hair and comely face, shot in the upper chest. Her both parents were lying a bit away from her, face down in their arm's crooks with wide puddles of congealed blood beneath them.

After sometime, having so shiftless walked with slowness from one victim to the next, he squatted on one knee studying the terrain as a faint call of cattle far off brought there by the winds penetrated the air. Prints of shod hooves underfoot, a wide set. He stood again and looked off south. One of the hindmost horses whinnied long and lashed out, fidgeting from foot to foot, tossing its head as though it wanted to depart from the others. He again shifted his attention back to the dead people and stood and thought. And looked about. At a certain point of his examination, he began feeling he now had to act in some way. He felt like the dead girl's eyes had ranged up on him and were pursuing him all the time, and he couldn't bear meeting her gaze anymore. With slow tread he sauntered out of the wagon's shade and down the hill. He looked around and down at the ground. There was nothing there to see but hoof-prints in the long light of the day's accruing, some of which entirely wiped out at places by the steady blowing where the wind had got at them. He looked skyward. Over the sides of the hill a ways out to the west, two vultures, brute-faced and taciturn with great burning eyes smelling the rotten scent, were sailing low to the ground just as the sun was coming back over the ridge. With no sound coming from off them they, as though disturbed by something, with wings immobile ascending headed for the brushline halfway up, then got out of sight for a moment, then reappeared where they just had been. His gaze pursued them following a winding route among the tall sagebrushes. It was known to him this was old Indian hunting grounds, a country unscathed and with a plethora of wild life, whitetail deer, moose, pumas, wild pigs and bear, black and evil-looking, and rattlesnakes crawling with tongues slithering in and out, testing the air, antelopes, it all in these times claimed not only by

Indians in wickiups, but also by Anglo settlers in the fat and flat open country with small herds of cattle and grass to the stirrups, and trappers in floppy caps of lynx and buffalo robes and buckskin boots, and hair grown half-way down their backs, dwelling in low shacks up in the mountains on rocky grounds where the walkpath ends, toting obsolete muskets, living poorly in one-room log cabins. It was a country claimed also by driving cattlemen with expanding livestock, some of which retired warriors from the war. Driven away from a country they once had inhabited since the government had went into rebellion with them and put them there, were Indians as well. They were now living short of food in reservations, Crow and Sioux, angry-looking men with dead black and unforgiving eyes, former trophy hunters in buckskin leggings, looking for game to catch, short of food, let alone the grounds yielded enough meat to carry them through the winters. Yes, times change.

Raking through the thick brush he'd not gone far before he some minutes later, in a clearing below, came about a young boy sitting in silhouette in a trapezoid of white sunlight on a withered and mossbacked downed log of spruce, bareheaded, his face turned away from him. From his hovering site – an ideal vantage point - he at a certain point in a sunless bright also caught the sight of a couple of brown and worn calfskin boots weighed with mud, and with a myriad of fissures in them protruding from a pair of faded mud-stained breechers. Some crows croaked in the vicinity. Some others with clarity answered a quarter mile out. Else nothing there was to rip the relative silence. With his thumbs thrust in his shellbelt, he with slow tread made his way downhill, perceiving before him in his coming a spray of smallbirds rising from the brambles in a great upheaval and bursting up against the sky in a rising babble with wings flapping frantically until losing definition by and by until only their motions were faintly discernible. Matching these sounds with the setting, he paused for some seconds, waiting and listening for other sounds, watching for movement and cutting for signs, but there were no other sounds coming forth than those from the seething of the wind. Neither down in the clearing did show any reaction. He gave a cry, his voice echoing hollow. Then it was quiet. Neither budged, yet the stretch wasn't distant. Without breaking his stride, he started down again on the soft ground through knee-high ferns and past rotting tree trunks, and didn't halt until he stood next to the scuffed and badly sutured low-heeled boots. His eyes wandered upward from them to the lying man until making a temporary halt at a mop of stringy silvery hair. A furrowed big face stiffened with a raised mole underneath one eye cavity. Green horseflies fluttering and swarming, creeping and crawling about over one another in the oblique lightfall. By fits and starts he went closer for a better view, taking in the entire scene while he did. It seemed like he were lying where he'd fallen by the log bedded in a thicket of greasewood and crushed and beaten ferns in the same attitude death had found him. The ground about him was moist and darkened with blood, his jaw slightly ajar, the few tobacco-blackened teeth he'd left partially on display as if he smiled with his dry lips drawn tight. The sole of his right boot had come loose as though somebody had cut through it with a knife, the front of his checked sweat-darkened untucked shirt sitting tight across the paunch soiled with drained blood. He appeared to be dead, yes, lying on his back, eyes slotted and unblinking, his both gore-blooded hard-calloused hands folded together one across the other over his breast, the weather-crested, mole-spotted face waxen gray, roiled-up mucous vomit with something unidentifiable in it, and tobacco sauce partially drained about his mouth and seams of his lower face. It was the coachman. He recognized him by the look of him, yes, he remembered him clearly. He was shot squarely in the stomach, his shirt, sticky with blood, partially thrown-up in the front and stuck with burrs and dirt. He squatted at his side and struggling with the studs he undid them and pulled the front wide. The shoulder looked to be wrecked. Yes. The shotwound in his stomach was still red. His thorax didn't heave. He watched him long to see if he was dead, and he held his hand over his mouth feeling for breath. He didn't appear to breathe. He got to his feet and called out a hello. Looking down at the teamster, waiting for an answer, puzzled as to how he come to be there, he went on watching him for a long time to see if he had indeed passed away, but nothing occurred. Apparently, he hadn't been dead long. His body was not yet quite cold he certified when he squatted to his heels beside him another time, palpating his pulse. He couldn't feel the blood pumping. No, there was no bloodbeat, no, not the slightest trace of any. His eyes searched the fingernails of the dead man to see they were scratched with earth underneath them and black to the quick as if he'd crawled on his hands. He raised his face and craned his neck and looked a little further out toward the kid. He was still sitting immobile, like he hadn't noticed his presence at all, his lean fingers lacing themselves on the knees, his fair head bent like in though as if in a state of catatonia. What he didn't know was that the kid several times had asked himself about his own name, but he couldn't tell it. So blank was his mind.

"How yo' doin', son?" Jeff began friendly, swatting at some gnats when treading with caution his way toward him so as not to frighten him, then halted and bended to hear what the boy would answer. He didn't reply though, nor did he show any inclination to. Nor did he look up. Instead, he looked disconsolately away while rubbing now and again an insect bite on his left forearm. Jeff tentatively held out his hand before his eyes and shoved at it with the heel. The boy shied. Bow-backed standing, unsure how to comfort him, Jeff gingerly reached out his hand across the small distance there was between them and put one arm around him. The kid shivered somewhat, then sat as before, looking like he'd lost his tongue, not moving a twitch, his mouth tight, his eyes staring vacantly down the country as it seemed at nothing in particular. Having figured a minute, waiting for the boy to speak, Jeff circumspectly subsided at his side and sat there for a while with his boots together and hands on his kneecaps. After sometime he inched a little closer to the boy's position so close he sat flush against him. They sat side by side for a long time, Jeff holding his arm around him. They sat in that manner until he felt the boy didn't shiver anymore, and at a certain point instead stretched out his right leg and nudged a stone with the toe of his boot and pushed it over, then drew back his foot and kicked at another stone then shifted awkwardly and withdrew his leg again, his face showing no expression. Jeff crossed one leg over the other and turned to the boy at his side and said while reaching out for the boy's hand and finally finding it to feel it was cold and moist to his own.

"Listen, son…I figure I know…what you've gone through, but you can't just sit here, 'cause if yo' do…" He interrupted himself. He couldn't finish his line, because the words failed him. He looked straightly at the kid to see whether he'd noticed what he'd said or not, but his eyes gave no sign he had, nor did they turn from their point. Instead, he withdrew his hand and went on looking steadily ahead down the country. As though he was awaiting somebody. In realizing he couldn't get further with him, Jeff uncrossed his legs and pulled himself upright and rose stiffly to his feet. He reached about in his pocket and brought forth his cigarette makings and adroitly rolled him a smoke, glancing when crossing the paper against his tongue and licking it and folding it shut once in a while down at the boy to see if he might perhaps budge or say something, but he didn't, nor did he show any inclination to, and once he'd got the cigarette ready, he put it in his mouth and hunched his shoulders forward to fire it up, and did then flung the match away. So standing he took him a greedy draw and another, and touching in his fingers pensively the smoothness of the cigarette, he sat down hard again, contemplating what he should do with the corpses. He quickly made the decision to haul them into the coach and bring them with him to town. He realized it would be a painful experience to the kid, but after he'd given the matter a second thought, he could see no other option.

II

After most of an hour later, a motley convocation of different people, gathered there for no other purpose, watched the coach when it wobbled to a gradual stop outside the funeral home with the black stallion tethered to it, falling in behind. People of all ages stood grouped in packs, some in tears, some smoking and talking in subdued voices, others just staring like mutes at the macabre cortege. It appeared as though the whole town mourned.

Pulling his weight against the bridles, Jeff slowed the equipage to a stop and halted. Relinquishing and gathering his hold on the bridles he applied the brake, and arranging the bridles in his both hands cast about for the pole at his left where he tied them. He stood up and stealthily climbed down. He stood for a short time by the sidewalk, waiting for the kid to crawl down from where he was sitting with a stricken look perched on the high seat. Seeing the kid did not move, he went off to the front door of the parlor and tried the massive lacquered black oak door to find it bolted. He rapped it hard and waited while looking about, watching two riders go past the hotel and out of town. The boy now had slumped back in the seat and appeared to be sleeping. During the ride Jeff on several occasions had offered him water to drink as much as he would, but the kid with lame shakes of his head had declined. He sighed and bolted again harder until his hand hurt then waited. Out on the street people were moving. A woman called for a kid. A horse carriage pulled up and stood in the sun that shone heavily in the east. On the front porch of the opposite house a man in a cattleman's togs and an unlit cheroot stub clenched in his teeth was standing looking across with interest, one hand hooked about a post, his slitted eyes almost invisible under the brim of his slanting hat. He nodded at the deputy, and the deputy nodded back. A mule screamed from somewhere, and outside the coach depot two young orderlies in a whirr of blue flies were backing two restive front wheelers into harness.

After a time, there was the play of a key in the lock and the door swung open, and appearing out of the semidarkness was a tall black-rimmed bulgyeyed gaunt, almost emaciate man in the late middle of his life with a withered leg and a mauve heart-shaped and very clean-shaven long-nosed doleful face and thin mustache and black oily and dyed thin hair, all slicked back and flattened to the skull, making him look under-fed and older than he actually was. He had a troubled look on his face where he stood squinting at the light. Rumor had it he had Indians in the bloodline. Standing rigid there with his fingers clutched about the door's knob, blinking like he weren't quite awake, raising and lowering his forehead, he looked at the deputy and the vehicle and at the deputy yet again the way one looks at somebody trespassing. He was wearing a rather elegant sartorial smooth worn three-button wool dandruff-dusted black funeral outfit of a glossy sheen, looking like it had been pressed with an iron too hot, and braces hanging down the sides, and shineless black low-cut shoes. He had shaving soap on his chin and a pill of blood underneath, one that hadn't as of yet congealed. He eventually let go the doorknob and haltingly took a half step outside. Poised there, looking out, fidgeting restlessly from foot to foot, he tinkered nervously with his black bowtie that askew sat knot by his thin neck with shaving soap on it. Blinking again he looked steadily across at Jeff then past him, and across at the stage, raising and lowering his head, then at Jeff again with a wan smile. Finally, he cleared his throat and managed a pitiful nervous chuckle, his protruding larynx jumping up and down. "Thanks for comin' by, Jeff, but what's this all about?" he despondent-looking queried in a thin quivering voice, sounding genuinely worried, starring incredulously at the huge vehicle where it stood in front of his driveway, then again, as if he was having trouble making sense of what was, looked aloft at the boy then across out the street at the packs of people who were regarding them with strained attention.

"Ain't come just to say hello, Mr. Petersen," Jeff croaked, touching the brim of his hat. "No true is I've four dead people for yo' lyin' in there," he declared harshly and motioned with his chin in the general direction of the wagon.

"Four dead bodies, eh…" the mortician repeated softly, rubbing his hand over his mouth, his eyes wandering halfway out the black walls. He repeated it to himself as if making sure he hadn't got things wrong, "Four dead bodies, eh…?" His throat almost caught and he sighed mournfully then smiled appreciatively.

"Yeah, that's what I said," Jeff confirmed, shifting his weight of body while looking severely at the man before him.

"Four?" he echoed and clasped his hands together, trying to digest what he just had heard. "Godamighty," he said and smiled again.

"Look, can we bring 'em inside?" Jeff forthwith wondered with an effort to appear patient.

"You know who 'em are?... From around...?" the mortician inquired with voice tense and quiet while taking yet a step out from the shade of the doorway.

"Well, according to their baggage the man's from Boston. That's what his doctor's case says... Robert Süsskind M D....When it comes to the lady an' the girl, I don't know. Haven't checked their baggage thoroughly yet, uh...There's another one too...the coachman."

"I see...But we have to get 'em in earth pretty soon...Can't wait long, can't wait long," the mortician stuttered defensively, rolling his eyes heavenward.

The kid, apparently tired of sitting perched subject to the gross attention, had in the meantime begun his climbing down, and was now with firm aggressive strides waddling around the vehicle as though in trance with eyes down-slung and cheeks jammed and shoulders hunched against the light breeze. Muffled voices got heard around, speculating as to who he was. Jeff noticed the undertaker was looking clandestinely in the direction of the boy, so he forestalled him, telling him the kid had got a shock, and that he somehow had escaped the slaughters out there. Out of consideration for the dead people, there was a short debate between them to the effect of which way was the most convenient to bring them inside. They lastly got agreed on the rear door.

Once the dead bodies were laid to rest, covered-over with their arms at the sides inside the windowless funeral home, Jeff and the mortician lingered a while in the sepulchral quiet in a thick funk of polish and disinfectant and an indistinguishable medley of something else, then spent a brief moment in the square shaft of light in the doorway saying their farewells, the mortician promising to make them look the best he could. "Didn't you say the man was a doctor, Jeff?" he asked solicitously, his voice subdued.

Jeff halted in mid-step. "Yeah, I did."

"Haven't you heard about some doctor settlin' down in town?" the mortician wondered, rubbing a hand roughly over his eyes.

Jeff stood watching the door, hat in hand. He slowly turned around and said tiredly while raising his gaze and looking at the stoop shoulders of the man before him, "Well…uh…there's been a lot of talkin' for some time, but most talkin'. Not much has happened." He thought for a short moment, then put on his hat saying, "I'll promise I'll consider it. Thanks for remindin' me… Now I better get goin' to check on the boy an' 'em horses." He turned and started toward the door.

"Alright Jeff, see you," the mortician grunted and stepped aside to let the deputy through, then went to and closed and with a hollow metal sound bolted the door carefully from inside then retreated into the dim interior, walking in a stooped and shambling gait, his tread hollow on striking the oiled floor.

Humming something with his legs dangling, hands in lap the kid was settled on a handcart that stood parked along a walkway outside a low-built coffin storage. As though he wished to protect himself from the painful sight of watching his own folks being carried inside, he sat with his back turned to the stagecoach. Jeff halted and stood to look at him. It didn't seem like he was bothered by the chill in the air. Neither did it look like he'd made any association with those recently taken inside and himself. He did not pay them any attention at all. It was rather like he'd smudged them out of his mind. Coughing into his cupped hand he just straightened when he heard Jeff approach him from behind.

Without breaking stride Jeff made for the coach and climbed up on the box then reached out for and untied the bridles and released the brake. He gave a yea-up and clapped the horses into motion and turned the vehicle around then slowed some while he told the boy to climb aboard and join him up there. He obediently did. During the short ride to the livery stable, he leaned to the side and looked into the kid's eyes, hoping to find any kind of expression in them, but he couldn't detect any. It was like he shunned eye contact. All there was to see about him was just profound tiredness.

By the time Jeff was in the funeral home the ranks outside had thinned and were crowding in on him in a scuff of bootheels and clink of spurs. Some drunken voices in the throng was screaming, and there was a seething with surmise and hate engendered in the air, demanding reprisal. Already a secret was out, saying the dead bodies belonged to a doctor and his family from the east coast who was due to set up in town in the near future. Jeff immediately recognized the pimpled young man in cowboy outfit and hat at a jaunty angle cocked over one eye standing swaggering in the middle of the street, a bottle of beer in his left hand. He took a swig out of it, raised it in the air then took a couple of unsteady paces toward the vehicle while shouting out in a loud trumpeting voice with a hill-folk drawl as the hum of conversation resumed, "Listen, Deputy!! We know very well who 'em are, yo' hear…?! We've heard it, yo' hear…?!" he went on smacking his lips. Jeff pulled up and stopped the wagon.

"WE know….Who are WE..?" he demanded.

The cowboy sat the bottle to his lips for another swig, arrested it though in mid-air and held it hard by the neck as though to strangle it, then brawled out, his tongue thicker from shouting, "Go on…Ask for yo'self, ask Raw in there!!…They were waitin' on 'em!!" He pointed at the hotel.

"Joshua's right!! The hotel's waitin' 'em!!" another raucous voice shouted out and placed himself next to his brother in fraternity.

Jeff, anxious now to get the kid off the place, shouted back, "Alright, thanks for informin' me…Now yo' just step aside so we can journey on, will yo'?"

"Yo're welcome marshal!…We didn't mean to cause trouble!" the pimpled declared helpfully.

Half an hour later Jeff checked with the hotel-keep who confirmed the cowboy was right. The dead people, recently taken to the funeral home, were indeed Doctor Robert Süsskind and his wife Christa and their youngest daughter. The boy who escaped the massacre was the doctor's only son, Wolf, lacking about a month being sixteen. The doctor, living in Boston, Massachusetts, was planning to settle down in Sioux Falls as per coming Monday as a general practitioner.

Very soon it got apparent any further interrogation with Wolfgang Süsskind would be meaningless and lead nowhere due to the boy's inability to communicate. The doctor of town came to see him in Mrs. Penn's apartment where he spent the night sharing room with Jeff, a precautionary solution looked upon as a recommendable move, suggested by the doctor, a long-jawed and very thin bespectacled 83-year-old veteran with careful fingers and all but fifty years in the branch. According to the physician, the boy was currently suffering from a serious mental disorder induced by the trauma he recently had experienced and, as he put it, it's extremely urgent the patient comes to see a specialized doctor who soonest possible introduces a regimen for the future treatment of the young erratic man, who might need assistance for a long period ahead, maybe several years of competent surveillance. This interpretation of the circumstances seemed to have made deep impact on Sheriff Kimble, who first thing in the morning following, started to rummage through the possessions of the murdered family in pursuit of name and address to some individual in Boston, one somehow related to the family, some person who might get handy with practical arrangements such as the burial, the division of the inheritance and last, but not the least, the taking care of Wolfgang Süsskind, the only survival, who currently had shut the world out as a means of protection.

It demanded a great deal of cajoling and persuasion from Jeff O'Halloran to get the dumb and inaccessible kid into the stagecoach, headed for Boston some days later. The coachman got informed on the matter, and promised benevolently to assist when a transfer came upon along the route. Five days after the massacre of his family, Wolf left Sioux Falls at 6.15 a.m. During his entire stay in town, he had been carefully supervised by the local physician who had come to see him twice a day at Mrs. Penn's residence. According to the doctor the boy was beset by periodic staccato coughing against which he'd got treatment. Apart from that, his medical condition had undergone neither deterioration nor improvement. On the doctor's 15-minute-long sessions the young patient was provided to process the horrible event. His closest related human appeared to be his some years older sister living in Boston, who, although cracked by learning about the tragedy, expressed her will to help her junior brother in whatever way possible. It is true that all communication with the sister so far had taken place by means of exchanging wires, and as a consequence of this the messages were scant and concise, but not void of emotions when coming to the sister. At the beginning things went relatively smoothly with the exception of one crucial point, the motive. Why had the stagecoach got subject to an attack? Was there any motive? How many were the highwaymen? What had they taken? Was the attack planned? The remains of the dead family offered no clue whatsoever, but, like Jeff pointed out, the reason to that was obvious, because no human being now alive, could tell what their belongings hold, except perhaps for the boy's older sister in Boston. There was a slight possibility she knew, but if she did not, then it was unlikely there would be someone else around who did. Possibly her mute brother, Wolf, but he didn't talk, and consequently he was of no help in the coming investigations. A lot of detective work now was lying ahead of the two sheriffs of Sioux Falls.

It was in the interval between night and day, not much past daybreak, and the crickets had ceased. Sheriff Douglas Kimble sat tilted in his office, studying morosely the coming day, his hands folded on the desktop, a quart bottle of whisky nestling in solitude before him. On the air about him was an odor of old urine and fecal matters. Throughout the night he'd slept and waked and slept again. Coughing fits that had become more and more frequent. Brought from his reveries, he rubbed his red-swollen eyes and slid back the wooden swivel and stood with difficulty, his eyes slowly adjusting to the dim light.

The sheriff's office of Sioux Falls, Wyoming, was situated in a detached, almost square mortar building in center of town, and built sometime in the early 1840's. A drunken camaraderie of cow drivers from local ranches had spent the night in custody, merged at random, sharing the four ironbar-doored and windowless custodies, all of which supplied with a hard bunk bolted to the wall and one battered straight-back chair of hardwood. Other than this there were no other fixtures. Sounds were heard from the gratings indicating the occasional detainees had stood up of their bunks and had begun to prepare themselves for a quick departure, well knowing a long workday in the saddle lay ahead.

Heaving a sigh and steadying himself heavily with one hand, the sheriff stood and rigidly ransacked the outdrawn drawer of the scratched oaken writing desk. Being the center of attention certainly was a role he didn't appreciate very much nowadays. Since that stagecoach incident he hadn't got much sleep, and as if this wasn't enough he now was hangover to boot. He belched and without expecting the stench that followed let go a fart then grabbed and took up the brass ring of door keys. Sorting them through he walked clumsily, shuffling his feet like a man bored into the jail section, slapping his right hand against the gratings for balance. He turned the key and in turn unlocked the wrought iron gates. When standing outside the last grating, he heard the outdoor open in a squeal of hinges, and male voices coming from the office section. The sheriff flinched and quickly opened the last gate and motioned for the captives to step outside and into the office so as to retrieve their personal stuff. He then told the three newcomers, young drovers from a ranch a long ways out, to unload themselves. No sooner had he done, before his vice sheriff walked inside and slammed the wooden door shut behind him. Neither of the former detainees were now on the area. Sheriff Kimble noticed the men turned to his assistant when seeing him appear. Uncertain as to who should take command, Jeff threw an asking glance at his foreman. When noticing Kimble avoided eye-contact, he took three long steps inside and took charge demanding the men to tell what brought them there at that early time of the day. He recognized them all since before. They were all reliable and hardworking cowhands. The three men looked at one another as Jeff meanwhile with slow tread started to walk deeper inside the room, his hat still on. "At daybreak we come upon a dead drifter stringed up in an oak tree up 'em mountains!" the oldest of them began telling, looking steadily at Jeff, who right in that moment placed himself on the edge of his desk. Jeff with his leg dangling slightly gave a nod to this while noncommittally glancing at his foreman who now stood by the filing cabinet flipping a sheet, his rounded back turned to him. "You heard the man, boss? You heard what he said..?" Jeff asked in his direction.

"I heard 'im, alright" his foreman snorted angrily, raising his face. "More work...never ends..."

"Alright" Jeff went on turning again to the nearest cowboy who stood blinking with his eyes anxious to be of help, his brethren hanging on every word, nodding affirmatively to what was said.

"Why were you up in the mountains that early in the mornin'?" Jeff inquired thoughtfully and stood. For the purpose of rolling himself a smoke he by feel groped for the sheaf of cigarette paper stuffed into his breast pocket.

"We were up there collectin' some stray yearling heifers, yo' know...The boss told us yesterday to do," one of the others declared with great zest, his compeers nodding confirming.

Groping for his shag pouch Jeff said, "Your boss, eh...Nelson, ain't it...?"

"Yeah," the men confirmed.

"You haven't seen 'im before some time?" Jeff wondered broodingly.

"No," the men nodded simultaneously.

"A regular suicide," Kimble grunted from his desk and yawned.

"That's what we thought at first, but...uh...when we rounded the guy, we saw he's shot in the back. Pretty many shots!" the oldest drover declared triumphantly.

Jeff turned to Kimble who rubbed his eyes, shifted, looking blankly in front of him.

"Alright" Kimble grunted after a while, "We ride out there an' bring 'im in." He glanced at Jeff, gave a shrug then forthwith added, "So the doc can examine the corps." He placed his square hands on his knees and lent back, the swivel creaking underneath him.

"WE ride out…? So you're goin' out there with me…?" Jeff asked, his voice full of disbelief.

"No…yo' go…an' bring Petersen with you," his foreman corrected gloomily.

"Alright, sir," Jeff said, now ensconced behind his desk. "Alright."

They sat in silence for a while, it might have been minutes after the drovers had left. Starring down at the scarred top of his desk, Jeff thoughtfully smoked his cigarette down and then crushed the butt in the ashtray, and then slowly climbed to his feet.

Wondering gazes followed Jeff and the mortician when they without sharing many words left town right after the shops had begun to open some half hour earlier. Jeff was riding point, ahead of the wagon, Petersen in black shiny hardhat and in his starched funeral outfit with its black jacket that just covered his buttocks, following drag a few paces behind him on a buggy with an empty cheap pine burial box jolting and rattling on the bed. Some of the onlookers were country folks, now flocked to town for their weekly shopping.

When quick out of town and out on the open pastureland that spread out itself in every quarter with longhorn cattle standing on it with the horizon quivering far out in the raising heat, the men in a slow acceleration put their horses into a steady trot. The northerly wind had now much abated in their faces, and the skies were clear but for a reef of red to the north. Soon they had glide into and were part of the landscape. It hadn't taken a long time to get Petersen alerted, and before long he had the vehicle ready, very anxious, as it seemed to pull away. Letting out a short chortle, without looking at the deputy, Petersen had said when they were about to leave, "Jeff, I begin to think there's somethin' odd to this."

With a sweet musty smell of death, oblivious of their arrival, the dead body hung featureless like a wraith from a hemp catch rope wholly to sight, scrawny-looking and heavily stubbled with his hands secured behind his rear under a long-armed live oaken branch, his shapeless bloated and blackened face grinning toothless as though in pain, and jaw sagging with tongue partway out. A man of middle years perhaps, clad in rags. One socket was empty, the eye eaten by birds, the other eye shriveled and partially started out and protruding, as though destined to fall down. Apart from that the body gave an impression of being reasonably intact. Sitting in his saddle, leaned forward a little with his lower arms propped on the horn of the saddle, Jeff studied the shape of him long. He thought he'd seen him before, yeah, he'd a vague memory of him, but he couldn't place him. Somehow, however, he recognized the structures that made up his face. Slowly he stood down of the horse and turned to the mortician. "Have yo', speakin' out of insight, any lore of how long the thug's been dead?" he demanded, forking his hat backward and looking up treaded his way toward him. He rounded the corpse and while moving slower went back to where he could see its rear. Once there he stood to inspect it with scientific interest as the surrey rolled upward with wheels drifting slightly in the mud where the ground was so soft that the wheels at places sank past the rims and finally stopped. The mortician bounced off the driver's seat and stood down and arranged the reins to the harness as the deputy repeated his question. Petersen, as though his wind was knocked out after the short ride uphill, whined as he standing back with a myopic habituation and brows drawn together in concentration regarded the dead body with great concern, examining it from every angle, his face reddening. "A swarthy character...eh a wop...eh...two, three days at the most might be a feasible truth," he panted badly winded, watching with fascination and disgust, fanning meanwhile his sweaty forehead with his black narrow-brim hat. He'd hardly breath to speak. The hanging man grinned at them, exposing the few yellow tusks he'd left. "You've seen 'im before somewhere?" Petersen inquired barely audibly, his eyes shifting from the dead man to Jeff and back, on his face a suggestion of joy.

"You bet," Jeff grunted. Fishing about for a match, he went on. "Claimed to be from New Mexico...Hidalgo County...a knife fighter. Rode with hackamore and a Mexican saddle with brass trim and a patchwork repair."

"You talked to the man?" the mortician wondered curious as he whipped around, regarding the deputy interrogatively.

Jeff smoked thoughtfully, studying in the meantime alternately the dead man's nice-looking mud-streaked veal-skin boots and the multitude of horse tracks underneath and about him. Nothing there was to hear about in the hush but the horses crop the grass. After some while he said, "First time I saw 'im in town he kicked up a rumpus. He'd to borrow the kitty and then he alleged there were cheaters around the poker table in the saloon."

"Wasn't he right 'bout it…?" Petersen asked while taking a sidestep, sounding jollied by the subject, his breath now steadied somewhat.

Jeff turned and started slowly his retreat toward his horse. "Hadn't time to find out," he said. "Had to coop 'im. He couldn't hold his liquor…'em guys were near to kill 'im, you know, an' the followin' mornin' he left town in a rush by first light."

The mortician looked about matter-of-factly then said, shifting his weight, "An' now yo' watch 'im hangin' here in the end of a rope…" Swatting at a fly he stooped for a closer look at the shabby brown hat where it was lying under the hanged man. "Yeah," he grunted to himself in disbelief, "sometimes life is hard to figure out…"

One brief moment later the mortician bow-legged awkwardly and slightly bent to one side with prim steps followed Jeff uphill to get the buggy to take it down the packed clay ground with wild roses and wild-berry bushes growing in plenty. He raised one hand to shade his eyes and looked down the clearing to estimate whether it would be possible to bring the corps down without jeopardizing the vehicle.

The dead lax body feetfirst lurid slammed to the ground with a muffled thud. Jeff with his thumb and forefinger tried the edge of the wooden-handled hunting knife with which he just had sawed off the noose of the lasso then humped bent forward some and balancing a little to keep his stand wiped the blade on his knee and held it up for a brief inspection, then underhanded straight-armed it down to Petersen who stood by the horse, his hand birdlike outstretched to claim it circumspectly and sedulously pack it away. Crouched, flailing a little to keep his stand, Jeff grabbed the pommel and for better balance set his left boot in the stirrup then chucked it out and with a measured jump stood down of the horse and stood, expelling a long breath. The dead body lay in a motionless heap underfoot, reeking and stained and beginning to swell with rope-scorched neck, mouth half agape, the face unsymmetrical, the bristly jaw bruised and swollen. Old tracks and clumps of horses in the mud. They approached him in an instinctive tandem. After a quiet moment the deputy, forward bent to see the dead man's face better, asked the mortician to help him roll the thug over to make it possible for him to closer inspect the holes in his back. Nodding his acquiescence the mortician did, the arms of the thug flapping out to the sides when they did, almost as though in a suggestion of protest. "It ain't no way to say how many holes there are," Jeff announced and wrung back the bloody and soiled crude flannel shirt. "The shooter was pretty close to 'im...No cartridge left behind either," he added and squinted toward the sun.

"What if they shot 'im somewhere else an' took 'im here afterward?" Petersen suggested, frowning with an anxious cadence to his voice, chewing his lip while jauntily closing in for better vision.

Absorbing things Jeff thoughtfully weighed his words for a short while, then while clearing the body of the cord and coiling it as it came said that he'd no way of knowing surely, then coiled the lasso the rest of the way and then backhanded thudded it into the wagon's bed. In silence they afterward in collaboration raised and hazed the limp yielding body down into the coffin, the mortician weak but able and with eyeballs like eggs and mouth shut almost dropping his end, faltering and whining a little out of the strain, the dead thug waving his arms while they lifted him. As if in some simulation of protest. Petersen stood back, turned to the deputy and said that "everybody deserves a coffin even if he don't get to Heaven." Jeff said nothing, just nodded his agreement. All there remained to do now was to put the lid over the dead thug and hoist the box up onto the wagon and press it inboard. In the dead man's pockets was nine dollars and fifty cents in small bills and coins. And two thirds of a tobacco plug. Otherwise there were no items of importance. Why hadn't the murderers taken all there was in his pockets? Jeff reflected while they put the lid on and pushed the box the rest of the way inside until they got it clear of the tailgate. They made their withdrawal, and two hours later the old doctor came to the funeral home to examine the corpse in the casket. It did not take him long to see the neck was broken. After that nobody was never to look at the dead thug anymore, nor was anybody ever to ask after him. He was one of those whose name we never will know, and was now of no use to anybody, not even to himself, the doctor said dryly, eyeing them earnestly above his half-moon spectacles.

III

At the stagecoach depot eight days later…

The young lady bore the impression of another part of the world far off from this godforsaken area of the West. She looked to them the way of a woman who has lived all her life in a big city. The dialect above all, but also the gait, the motions, sophisticated, controlled, articulated, and the apparel, bodice-tight, long-neck Victorian style, elegant, gaudy outfit all the way from the hat with the sip ribbon under her chin to the mahogany-colored half-boots of veal with heels that barely touched the bottom of the high-banked ruts of the hard-packed thoroughfare, dotted by hoof prints and horse dung.

Once down on the street she a bit haughtily thanked the occasional co-teamster and stood and looked about. Having no clue as to which way to assume, she with a rapid movement with a suitcase in her left white-gloved hand and a violin case in the other, perked her head up and turned to the elderly weather-beaten man with no front teeth and seams stained with tobacco juice, sitting next to the driver on the coachman's seat, closed into some and managed, stuttering keenly as a wagon passed in a rumble, "The…marshal eh, excuse…where can I find his office, please?"

She felt that this was to her a foreign site with much tension in the air, something exotic but also threatening. Whatever it was, she sensed it, it was obvious, so obvious she literally could touch it with her hands. The weather-beaten haggard-looking old-timer, towering on the box above her, let out a light chuckle while peering down at the distinguished lady standing laterally of him by the muddy front wheel. Eyeing her and her luggage searchingly, he cagey bit off a solid plug of the tobacco pigtail that sat in his left hand and commenced chewing as though it were succulent meat, and for a time it appeared like he would shirk the inquiry, but so he didn't, though. Considering his answer he slid an inch or two on the box, making the iron springs squeak under the weight of his massive body, then he reached out and clutched the wipe to his right and pulled it up from the stand, then twisted around in the seat and pointed with the top point of it while leaning slightly into the woman and leaned to the side to look closer imparted very friendly in his tone, giving her a quizzical look, the driver to his side sitting meanwhile motionless and noncommittal, looking into space, packing his pipe.

"Right south, missus…Couple of minutes past Clarke's hardware store…yo' can't miss it, see." The lady nodded her head, and he nodded back and lifted his hand in parting. She turned sharply, and with her baggage, not too heavy, purposefully began moving her way on stiff legs past the beginning of a two-story house that was as of yet not completed, avoiding rutted wheel tracks to make the going easier, every step so prim, monitored by the driver who went on glaring, taking meanwhile in the discrete redolence of expensive French perfume she bore in tow until she'd walked all but halfway to the saloon, her heels churning up mud in the process, her eyes squirreling about, studying the shape of the foreign town. The lady's awkward walk arose a lot of interest and curiosity from the locals, some of which now standing with a frown looking at her until she was by and had receded in the same indistinct shape by which she'd came, and faded out of sight, the long state-of-the-art trailing in the clay. Two old women with tawed featureless faces at the second-story windows of THE LADIES' EMPORIUM she caught watching her in the violet light, as meanwhile a couple of whoops went up from some kids in their teens and lower twenties just by. Who was she? A high-class whore arriving at this hick town, a pockmarked plump-faced young man suggested, his voice hoarse with emotion, and some others joined in enthusiastically. It seemed to her as if the whole town had observed her advent. Younger kids were gathering on either sides of the long street, watching her with eyes shining expectantly and with looks of wonder, and looks of awe. Leaned against doorframes adults were calling among them in amplified voices and clipped words. Lunging in its kennel a mutt witlessly growled and slapped tongue from somewhere up the street corner. Another answered from inside the wheelwright's shop, and in the light from the doorway of the cooper's shop a small man with a long-spouted oilcan in one hand was standing rigidly by himself looking at her out front with an amused expression, a cigar clenched between his teeth. He kept on looking at her until she was by. Then he took out the cigar and looked at it briefly, then put it back between his teeth and sucked in a last draw, watching it glow and fade, then flipped the butt out into the dark and turned about and limping went back in. Near-sounding voices of men and faint piano music was coming from the saloon and filtering outside. No, she was none of them, the lady where she uncertainly made it forward on the newly wetted-down street. She was immigrant-looking, she did not belong there, she thought to herself as she carefully regarded what was happening on either her side in the decreasing light from the descending evening sun.

One of the shopkeepers was about to close the doors, and sounds of horses were approaching from behind at a small distance, near-sounding now. Thinking a lot of thoughts, sensing a shiver passing through her, she walked on, not slowing her pace, and don't turning to look at either side. Looking straight ahead she now had but eyes for her trajectory and didn't look at them, or anything else.

A bit away up the long street a little roan mare somnolent with head descended and half-shut eyes stood tied to the rail by the barber's shop. When she'd picked up the scent and perceived the lady she craned her neck and doubtfully eyed her advent. She snickered nervously and tossed her head, and with the flues of her nose widely open bucked and kicked one hindleg, then making her body for the sole purpose of launching backward in attack began backtracking as if preparing herself to thrash in agony, ears flat against the head. From the saloon that cast light onto the street got heard a bawdy din. The lady, thinking the intimidated mare might be primed for another and harder lash-out, ably wriggled, her eyes widened in horror. The occurrence attentively got subject to observation by the mare's master, who just exited from the barber's shop, cigarette in mouth, putting a hand to the hilt of his gun that hung down his leg then withdrawing it. A respected citizen in cowboy togs, the proprietor of a ranch in the county. Bill Buchanan. With a certain amusement he canvassed the strange lady with his eyes as he flipped a glowing match out across the hard ground into which there 'd come no rain in four weeks, then slightly touched the brim of his Stetson hat, and cigarette in mouth while exhaling friendly said when they'd come abreast, "Howdy, ma'am…It was a narrow squeak, eh." Their eyes met. She panted, conflicting emotions fighting within her while she hard-pressed to preserve dignity haughtily said in response, so eager to talk it all but took her breath, her voice a little tightened, "Marshal's office, please."

Buchanan shot her a keen eye, soon collected his wits and responded helpfully while tapping ash off his cigarette, "Just keep on walkin' ma'am…couple of minutes…past the church with the bell tower. Bear to the right an' yo'll see it…a flat-roofed tile…"

Sending a stealthy look his way she said thank you and turned sharply and retook speed with edged steps sliding in the mud. Looking after her across his shoulder out of idle curiosity the rancher in an amble gate started toward his waiting horse as she meanwhile heard the door of the barbershop squeaking and a cowbell rattling and another cowboy stepped outside and leisurely stood, legs a little apart. From somewhere a child's crying, and from the smith's shop a clank of hammers and a wraith leaning billowing out from its chimney. She began to feel woebegone of the entire situation, this gauntlet-running, these wry glances, these speculations.

The shadows were growing longer, and from the corner of her eye she in the encroaching darkness perceived yet another man sweeping with a broom with big sweeps of his arms, and yet another, one very thin at the waist and square-shouldered, standing leaning against the saloon's front with a flaring match stalled midway to his mouth, watching her intently for the way she would go. In order not to convey her feelings, she found it best to ignore them all though. She kept walking with undiminished speed, sensing anger and hurt coming up. In the saloon someone still was pounding on the piano. The same tune. What have I let myself in for? This wasn't the first time she was asking herself that question the last days. Nevertheless, she seemed to have noticed an encouraging almost supporting glint in Buchanan's seamed face. Or was it just an expression of sheer conceit? She was far from being sure. What if she'd whet their curiosity? Just one day or two, a week at the most, then she would be gone, anyway. As soon as the authorities had done their job, she would climb that stage again.

Seeing now the street was all but empty save for herself, hearing the music from the saloon coming louder now, she shrugged cheekily and began, hurrying against the fading light in the direction general of the sheriff's office, thinking about what she would say to him, her gait now somewhat more dignified. At the square some of those inside the houses opened their doors, kids and women mostly, and stood to look after her questioningly with interest until she'd went out of visual range. She discerned them, their outlines, and she sensed their glances, but she paid them no mind.

There it stood lastly, sketched in the partial obscurity, the flat-roofed brickwork house with a bullet-riddled plate over its door saying MARSHAL, printed in faded carefully shaped black letters, the half of it illumined by the last sunbeam of the day, its contours by and by taking shape as she drew closer, increasing her gait.

At the setting of the dying sun a few minutes later her journey was over, one that started in Boston more than a week ago. Jaded, careful of the steep gritty steps polished by traffic she while watching her boots straight-backed gingerly, mindful of every step, climbed the short flight of stairs, each foot placed exactly in the middle of every squeaking step, and made it for the wooden door. Her cheeks were flushed when she stamped the mud from off her boots and while trying to keep her breath even reached out an arm. Just one tap at the door of the office shouldn't appear to be sufficient in breaking the animated colloquy between the two lawmen of town. Hence she tried again, five solid whacks, and stood away from the door to listen and wait in the windy darkness, her garments snapping in the huffing wind. She had begun to imagine an empty office when she at that precise moment heard a voice half lost from inside. Teetering she crammed the knob downward to make her entrance and yanked the restive door open, raising a boot and fetching it a good kick with the toe, feeling suction of stale smoky air from inside when the door gave. The interior was scantily lit up by three carbide lamps equidistant placed in the shabby den. It took her a good time to locate the two men huddling behind their desks looking across at her, waiting, one of them holding a half-rolled cigarette in the fingers of his left hand. Within time they materialized though and gained structure one by one behind a pall of sour pipe tobacco. There suddenly became a lengthy gap in their conversation, everybody looking at the other. She with diffidence and faint steps with dirt grinding under her feet in a rustle of garments made it forward in the soft yellow lamplight toward the desk that appeared to be the marshal's in charge. Once there she made a halt.

"Afternoon, ma'am…Yo' don't have to knock before enterin'…Is there somethin' I can help you with?" Sheriff Kimble wondered in a flat low drone, a quill in one hand and a paper in the other, his face in half shadow. His eyes were narrowed in suspicion as he carefully ogled at her baggage, now collected in one hand, the wooden door standing ajar behind her. Noncommittally she shifted while studying him back. The stove ticked with flakes of soot on it quivering with the heat. All else was quiet save the clicking from a clock in a corner. "Yes…well…actually I might as well introduce myself…" she stuttered, her breath now even. Looking her up and down the sheriff cleared his throat angrily and drawled out, "You might as well put down your stuff, ma'am…"

Smiling uncertainly she forthwith obeyed, thereafter continued while taking some tentative steps in his direction, her voice quavering somewhat when saying, her eyes grief-filled, "I am Birgit Süsskind…daughter of Doctor Robert Süsskind who got viciously killed in that stage ambush…eh, twelve days ago…My greatest wish is to see the attackers tracked down and convicted soonest possible in a court of law… I just aim to see justice done…"

The sheriff, tired-looking and dumbfounded, re-pocketing his matches in his shirtpocket, shot a furtive glance in the direction of his deputy as if he wanted to say: Take command! I'm heading home. Noticing this, the deputy cautiously, so that the cigarette wouldn't leak, put it down in the ashtray and groped for his chair's armrests. He jacked his chair back and half stood as if he might approach her, but didn't. Instead he sat back immediately, shifted weight, the swivel cracking. He looked back at the woman, establishing the fact that her eyes were moist, and that her underlip was shivering somewhat. She was none of the regulars around, no none of the indigenous clientele. Her looks as well as her accent displayed an origin from overseas somewhere. The sheriff in charge grabbed the armrests and stood, and lumbering in a limp went past the lady, crossed the floor and grabbed the handle of the unpainted door and with the toe of his boot let it back, kicking it shut. He gripped a cane-bottomed wicker chair from off a corner and brought it to his deputy's desk and with a gesture of hospice offered it to the standing lady, then checked the time by the clock he wore in the breast pocket of his vest.

"I'm Douglas Kimble," he growled and with a nod to his deputy informed sulkily, "This is my assistant, Jeff O'Halloran…Please, be seated, ma'am."

The lady with a sweep of a hand by habit arranged her dress in the back against wrinkling and carefully sank down in the ramshackle upholstered chair that creaked ominously under her weight. She placed her feet one beside the other and discretely wiped her forehead with a white lace glove, then, looking like she were concerned with something, slowly peeled them both off and laid them down in her lap and then sat almost like someone called to account. All of a sudden Jeff felt a certain sympathy for the fragile and vulnerable being, sitting there opposite to him without moving a muscle, the half of her trapped in the gloomy light of the lamp that shone from the desk. She was now alone in this world, five, six years apart from him in age, he thought to himself. From its corner the old grandfather's clock ticked.

"May I offer you something' to drink…Miss Süsskind?" he said softly as he finally met her gaze. "Coffee…whiskey maybe? I take it yo've been travelin' long today…"

Her eyes cut across the smoky office. Unadorned barren walls but for a couple of wrinkled drawings showing mugs of people wanted by the law, and a yellowed map of the state of Wyoming. Shifting she said, "Coffee would be just fine, thank you…By the way…I have made no arrangements for my lodging…Is there perhaps an hotel or lodging house around?"

Jeff glanced at his foreman then said, "I'm sure my hostess, Mrs. Penn can come up with something' for you, ma'am,…there are always vacancies, yo' know…well, not that fancy, but I reckon 'em will supply yo' needs." He got silent and looked across at her so as to provide her space to answer, but she said nothing in response.

Some moments later Jeff crossed the floor and placed a brimful jug of tepid black coffee in front of her and a plate with buns that he weighed in his hand for a moment and then uncertainly tendered her. He still was contemplating her exposed position. After sometime he said, "As for the killin' of your folks, I consider the best for you ma'am would be, eh…well, if we go back to the day of the crime bein' committed. You are free to interrupt me whenever it suits you."

Raising her coffee to drink she said, "I appreciate that very much, deputy. As you understand I need immediate action." She lowered her gaze and drank her coffee sippingly.

"Yeah…Can't say I blame you for that," Jeff responded silently, scratching his right sideburn. He went on frowning, pondering how to put his words in order not to upset her too much as he took a quick trip along the memory lane. Shiloh. Gettysburg where his brother fell. Episodes from the war. He was living in a post-war situation and that's the way it always gonna be, he was often telling himself. Often the memories kept him awake at night. First of all I need to go for a slash, he thought, and excused himself, leaving the position behind his desk for a short while, thinking of whether he should exclude the most horrid foibles in the investigation of the coach ambush so far, or if he should not. Basically he wasn't sure how to tackle this situation. No, he was rather far from.

Eventually he retook his place at the desk. The buns that were given to her didn't sit there anymore, and her coffee mug was drained. Within short the darkness would have thoroughly occupied the semi-lapsed office. He reached out for the box of matches that sat centrally on the table. He slid it to him, pushed it open and felt about for a match. When he'd found it, he removed the chimney and after a while got lit the candlestub of the lamp that was standing on his left side. He stood and watched the shadows inside the room as he shook out and flipped the remainder of the match toward the ashtray, then put the chimney back into place. The lady looked at him as if she would perhaps say something to him.

"Well," he said speaking before she did commence, somewhat lingering as he laid the box of matches back where he'd taken it, "The crime took place on the 15:th of August, and to be quite frank I'm afraid the investigation ain't showing much so far…An' 'em tracks are I' colder by every day. Fact is…we have no motive whatsoever, no serious suspect. Hard facts, but that's the way it is."

Miss Süsskind faced up to him and looked away again. She looked down at her idle hands, folded together in her lap. "I suppose you are still working on the case, "Mister…O'Halloran…Or am I wrong?" she said after a while, eyes downcast, her voice so low he could barely hear her.

"We are workin' on it, alright. All we've got right now is a dead body lyin' at the parlor. It's pretty hard for 'em to preserve him…due to the warmth. Much thunder in the air an' so forth for one thing, and moreover, we have no idea as of his identity. A pretty slovenly individual, and we ain't even sure if he's involved in the actual holdup."

They sat silent for a little. Although giving the impression of having been listening carefully, the lady with slow increments of her head seemed to snuggle down successively in her awkward position. Jeff kept on watching her on the sly where she sat trapped in the lamp's yellow beam. Ash-blonde, reddish hair, rolled up and arranged in a heavy knot. Oval pallid features. High cheekbones. There was something aristocratic about her, something different that appealed to him, something fresh, undestroyed and still forlorn. As if she sensed he was watching her, she slowly raised her head, looked him deeply in the eyes and said gravely, her voice trembling a little, "You see, up to now I've had, let's say an anticipation…something to stick to, a clue or whatever."

He slammed open the bottommost drawer of his desk and propped his right boot on it. He exhaled profoundly and said reassuringly, sitting atilt, "We are far from havin' dropped the case, ma'am."

Clearing his throat Sheriff Kimble screwed the lid of the inkwell shut then edged some papers square and tapped them against the desktop once, then pitched the papers into the desk drawer and slid the drawer shut. He clutched the worn armrests and scooted the chair backward and heavily rose to his feet. He stretched. Up to now he hadn't taken part in the conversation, nor had he betrayed any reaction. He had just been sitting deeply reclining, listening. Lopsided he took a few strides up to the gun rack where his hat hung from its peg. He took it down and put it on. He pouted his lips carp-like, saying, "We'll let yo' know if we come up with 50 sometin' Miss Süsskind…Yo' see, it ain't that easy…Like my assistant said, such as it looks today, we don't have much to go on."

The door got open and a young boy stepped inside, one of Sheriff Kimble's many kids, a freckled blond, obese and large-footed precocious with a calm state of mind.

"Hello, Jeff," he panted in the direction of the vice sheriff, offering the unknown lady a shy glance. "Are we gonna do an outing some day, Jeff…?"

"Sure Buster, any time. It's been a long time…We'll see next week."

The kid had in mind the fact that they occasionally used to practice at the makeshift shooting range right behind the livery stable, where they executed target shooting by penetrating tins and old Arbuckle coffee boxes. The boy loved watching and practicing.

"Alright" his father snapped, anxious to come off duty. They hastily exchanged their farewells and made a hasty exit, the sheriff giving the lady a quick look in his walking out. After the brief gap in the conversation Jeff continued suggesting the lady they met on the following morning, continuing discussing facts, and the lady agreed. Jeff stood and said, "I suggest we ask my hostess about a den for you. I reckon you bein' exhausted, ma'am."

"Eh, when do we ask her…I'm really very tired, you know?"

"Before lights out," Jeff replied, and continued, "We go there right away."

Within seconds she stood uncertainly. She was looking forward to something substantial to eat. And if possible a good night's sleep. The deputy reached across the desk and lifted the chimney and snuffed the wick of the lamp's candlestub. When he'd done he turned to the lady where she stood with her face averted, looking as though she was about to say something. He was about to ask her what it was that she wanted to say. Noticing she stood and sobbed to herself, seemingly frozen in place with her fingers pushed to her eyes, he abstained though. Nothing he would say to her would matter anyway. After a while, unsure of himself, wondering if it was alright to address her or not, he took a deep in-breath and inquired her how she was doing. She replied between sobs that she had a wish to wake up next morning to see things were like before, and that she was, from now on, determined to live on with a great loss, and an unbearable past, one she would never be able to escape, and she felt like the only one on earth. Jeff answered that he was sorry for her loss, but that she wasn't alone. After all she'd one sibling left.

The town of Sioux Falls, Wyoming, was a friendly place with one long main street and three shorter that dead-ended. The town was set up in a couple of months in the late 1840's, the idea mainly initiated by a half dozen of cattlemen, the boss of which being Wayne Seay, a local rancher. He was head and chairman of the Cattlemen's Club, a legendary institution, regulating most of life in town, and in the area as a whole. Mr. Seay was also known because his alleged tendency to lash his wife, a former prostitute and half-breed from Oklahoma, the beating mainly induced by heavy drinking. As to the amount of people living in town, it was rated to 566 according to the latest census held in 1866, staged by Mr. Seay. A County Bank with two employees, one manager and one bookkeeper, one shyster, a general store with a long wooden bench running the wall right outside it where the veterans used to sit talking stories and studying the by-passers and the horsemen and the horses they rode, a school, two churches, one Baptist and one Presbyterian, in none of which Mr. Seay never had sat foot. Standing a little by itself was a jailhouse and marshal's office, a saloon and hotel combined with a billiard parlor. There was also a sundry general store, a smaller food store, the other buildings with different kinds of shops scattered in every direction with the livery stable southernmost at the edge, completing the picture. Saving but for the marshal's office, all houses were woodwork. At the other edge of town, not far from the Presbyterian church, resided Mrs. Penn, a needlewoman and also the widow of the former Presbyterian Reverend, the first ever in the history of town. She was a somewhat absent-minded but considerate lady with precarious health and arthritic hands in her late seventies, dedicated to her mission of offering shelter to needies at her rooming house. Right now, Birgit Süsskind from

Boston belonged to this category, and it didn't take much for the old lady to realize that fact. Without too many questions on that late hour, Birgit had got herself some place to stay for a couple of nights, all included. After a brief supper with the vice sheriff Birgit said good-night and went to bed early. Over breakfast the following morning, Jeff suggested an outing to the scene of crime, just the two of them.

The groom at the livery stable offered Birgit a nice five-year-old bouncy bay, one near fifteen hands, a shapely powerful and smart-looking mare with no cinch marks on her, newly shod, well-groomed and rested and keen to get started. She hadn't been on the road for the last couple of days, the stable boy confided to the deputy with a sneer when alone with him, watching him saddle his black stallion.

With her quite recently purchased hat hanging in a leather strap on her upper back, Birgit had the appearance of a genuine Westerner with all the appropriate outfit, a leather-banded Stetson hat, pretty good threadbare denim and a checked coarse flannel and a vermilion choker and high-heeled good boots with no spurs. Evidently, she had earlier in her mind prepared herself for this occasion to come up, and Jeff within minutes found out that she indeed had been looking forward to this ride, to review the scene of the act, the surroundings, where nearly her entire family got extinguished. The only survival, her brother, Wolf, was still in a mute state due to the massive shock. People involved in the case, some of which competent people, had recommended the boy must be left out of unpleasant inquiring for yet some time. It's important we give him time to come to terms with his past, they reasoned.

Jeff fitted and pushed the Winchester into the saddle's boot, then adapted and tightened his gun belt around his midsection and buckled it shut, then let go and mounted up. Without a word he caught up the reins with both hands and booted his horse ahead, casting a backward glance at Birgit where she sat a good horselength behind him, her face composed in a serious expression. Within short she started her horse though and gained momentum and fell into step, and soon the riders were sitting on the horses shouldered side by side, the morning sun that was well up, wearing hard upon them. A slight desultory wind from far out the prairie was the only means of disturbance in the otherwise peaceful morning, the air humid and sticky. Astride their willing mounts the two riders sat in silence and listened to the occasional snorting of the animals and the rhythmic clapper and seething of the hooves, some eyes watching them, some heads shaking with displeasure and talking quietly among themselves in seeing them ride out of town and successively disappear from view. After sometime Birgit's eye cut away to the left. "You are heavily armed," she remarked cheerfully, breaking the lengthy lull, stirring the almost sabbatical tranquility.

"Yeah. A necessity out here," Jeff responded and remained quiet for yet a while. "That's bothering you, ain't it?" he said and turned his head to her for an answer, but there wasn't any. He went on with a light grin, "If we are lucky, we might stumble on 'em Crow."

"Have you ever encountered the…Crow?" she after a while demanded, trying to appear casual.

"I sure have. A couple of times, although not latterly. We never came to blows, though." He got silent, then continued, "We are wise enough to leave 'em alone, and that seems to go for the army as well. As long as we don't bother 'em and they have enough to eat, there's no fear."

As if she wasn't sure what to say she made a face to show her disapproval, then shrugged and wiped some beads of sweat off her forehead. Kicking the flanks of his stallion with his heels, Jeff said, "If it comes to a confrontation, there's only one thing for you to do – ride on."

Judging what she'd just heard she looked off and about her, looking like she had in mind to produce an answer, but a quick glance and equal quick smile was the only answer she gave him. After another while she asked him if he'd met any Indians recently. He said he hadn't in a long time, despite they are known for generations to live not far away up in the mountain forests.

They rode on in the tall dry grass across a flat open country with nowhere to hide. After another half hour they reached the bottom of a hollow, and the landscape changed all together. Overhead clouds went in from northwest, obscuring the sun so gradually they took little notice. At an almost dry creek surrounded by a dense growth of willows and shrubbery they riding slowly shoulder to shoulder agreed on resting the horses and shape a fire, making themselves some coffee. They sat the horses there and dismounted, one, then the other. Freed from bridles and bits the animals stretched out their necks and started grazing among some low cedar trees. To the north a dark head of weather was making up. Jeff smoked. Far off was to hear a distant spat of a firearm being discharged. She turned toward him and shaped her mouth to speak, but he forestalled her, saying that it sounded like an old Ballard caliber 50. He also shared this place were claimed to be haunted. At least is this what the old chiefs of the Crow Indians believe, he told her.

"You got that association when hearing the shooting?" she demanded uneasily after some afterthought.

As though he hadn't heard her, he said, "There's a cattle ranch in the area. Runs by Clifford Fisk. Cliff's alright. Not the dangerous sort," he explained reassuringly, and keeping a roving eye around, he added there's a lot of quarry galloping about, deer, moose, rabbits. Eventually his narrowing eyes started focusing a handful of vultures, circling with wings locked, high up some five hundred yards afar. His gaze followed them for a long time until they finally landed on a mountain crest. Far out to the west a lightning flared soundlessly.

"I'm afraid a thunder's ragin' within an hour or a half," he after a while declared, looking at Birgit noticing the commotion he was causing, certifying she didn't look that brash any longer. By hearsay she knew what a thunder meant out West. She almost started panting and her eyes commenced flickering. She tried to collect herself. Without saying anything in response she twisted loose the stopper from off the waterkeg that she'd taken from its place right behind her and now was holding in her hand, and with circumspection swigged some water down.

"I don't like it either," he went on, looking full at her, noticing her reaction. "We'd better move on. But first we gonna find out what alerted those vultures."

Some four to five-hundred yards out Jeff reined in his horse and stood in the stirrups watching the scavengers, four in number, drifting off downwind, looking time and again back at him as if to see what he would do. At the horse's forefeet, not far from a chipmunk hole, was lying in a ripe scent the ropy remains of a flyblown colt, a carcass, a week old, maybe two, eaten to the bones with shreds of hide and black horsehair hanging off of them riffling in the wind with tall grass about, flattening and standing up again. Having located it, Birgit with a certain reluctance made some lame efforts to accompany him to the carrion, but suddenly relinquished and halted, and looking in a different direction sat waiting with her hands resting on the horn crossed at the wrists, her face clouded, and by the time they sometime later turned the horses and retook the ride, she looked real nauseous.

Just before noon, the wind had come up and a storm arrived so rapidly they could watch it coming across the skies.

"There's a cave in the mountain a couple of miles in that direction!" Jeff howled, nodding his chin out at the rolling flatlands, taking meanwhile a steady grip of the brim of his Stetson, pushing it forward down his sweaty forehead then kicking the horse's flanks. The horse took a prance and jumped ahead at a smart canter. A light drizzle had just started to wet the ground, and thin cracks and sporadic lightning was to be heard further out northwest. No dust was no longer coming up from the cracked hard ground revealing their presence. Just a damped slosh from the hooves of their mounts was to be heard, and that was all. Kicking her horse into a run, Birgit was soon following, anxious to catch up, the collar of her shirt turned up almost to her earlobes against the wind and the whipping rain.

The place of refuge was a deep cavity in the hill, hollow enough to welcome the two soak riders. Another hole, a reserve exit, was dimly to be seen far off at the end of the cave with rain spattering inside, making it able for the air to blow straight through. The place was well known to people around, and a perfect asylum for ranch hands in the district. Alongside one of the walls a long-funneled fireplace was installed as well, one built out of handkilned brick that got very warm even at winter when the storms blew down from the north and white wind-whipped snow reaching well up to the horse's knees was covering the country, as was a considerable heap of dry fair-sized firewood, dry sapling trees and kindling placed nearby, stored there for the coming round-up. Some chunks of leftover wood there was as well. On just such days it all came well at handy.

After having managed to lit, after four tries, the fire, built out of some saplings already topped out and limbed, they fanned and coaxed it with their hats. Sniffing the smoke, seeing the stove warmed quickly, they divested themselves of their coats and hung them to dry near the fire. Jeff returned to his saddle that he'd stood just inside the cave's aperture. He lashed open the saddlebags and from out them removed a skillet and crockery and what victuals they'd brought with them, hardboiled eggs, ham, floor and coffee, tinned fruit.

"I hope yo're hungry," he grinned half an hour later as he carefully tasted what he had accomplished. "We've two canteens full with water as well. And coffee."

Birgit, appearing semi-nauseate, lingered with her answer then said she could use a drink of water right now. Hopefully that would make her feel a little better, she added, her voice very low.

"Right. Help yo'self," Jeff said, rubbing his neck.

In a strong smell of food, ready to stab the cooking, they sat down to eat at a satisfactory distance from one another, Birgit on a flat stone and Jeff on another next to, one that reminded them of a king's throne. He had been there a couple of times before he confided between chews, offering an apologetic glance as he saw the amused expression in the young woman's still pale face. They continued eating, neither speaking a word. All of a sudden, she half turned to him and firmly watching him flung the question he long had awaited, "Did you, or did you not call a dragnet when first learning about the attack?" She said she wanted to know.

"Well, I made a proposal, but it got rejected. He claimed there wouldn't be enough candidates to swear the oath. Claimed 'em tracks bein' too cold after twelve hours. The teamster on the next tour was the one to report. Then I rode out to remove 'em bodies. That's about as far as we've gotten, I guess," Jeff said, studying his boots.

"Who claimed the tracks being too cold?"

"The sheriff did. Kimble."

She nodded thoughtfully, but said nothing.

After they'd done eaten they sat in the murky light for a while resting themselves, huddling and cradling their tin cups of coffee, waiting for the rain to slacken, their heads just inches apart, Birgit savoring every word of what she had just heard. She stared at him incredulously, her eyes moist, tears not far off. "Do you think…they suffered…before death?" she finally asked, her voice tightened, removing a tear with a touch of her hand.

"No," Jeff said. "Death must have been instant. That's what the doc said…and that's what he stated in the death certificates. They were all shot in chest or back…the driver in the stomach, severely wounded, bled to death slowly. This is what we know."

Birgit now was looking rattled. Unwieldy organized jurisdiction in combination with legal amateurism. What other outcome is there to await out in the waste? That's what she thought to herself. A couple of blacksmiths, a handful of sales-clerks, a couple of carpenters, a cooper, a cartwright, a druggist, a couple of barbers, a tailor, one hardware store, a saddler and harness maker, a cobbler. Out of town just ranchers and farmers and settlers none of which legal professionals, the nearest lawyer in Casper, the judge in Cheyenne.

She frowned when she thought of New England and Heidelberg, where she was born, Massachusetts, where she was brought up.

Outside the cave things were back to normal. The rain had petered out and the wind had receded with the skies spread low, and no thunderclaps were to be heard anymore. Finding its way into their temporary shelter a sunbeam now was falling in aslant through the crevice, enlightening their features, and at the other end of the cave there was to see a shifting patch of light, and outside the birds had taken up their singing. At a certain point Jeff said, "Yo' know…there's one thing I don't understand, uh…it's the coachman. I spotted 'im in the woods dead, not far from your brother. I can't figure out how he'd happened there so far away from the coach with a hole in the bum, an' bag an' entrails halfway out."

Birgit craned her neck and looked at him, her forehead puckered. Finally she said, "Someone must have dragged him, don't you think?…He couldn't have beat his way into the woods himself…or…?"

Jeff wiped his plate with his last chunk of bread then dried his tin mug at a last gulp then said as he tipped out the grounds, "I've no idea…I couldn't see no drag marks…I looked for 'em, but there weren't any…"

Birgit didn't respond. She was thinking about her brother Wolfgang. She frightened he'd gone into a darkness from which he would never return.

Jeff lit a cigarette with a brand from the fire and sat and smoked, and when they finished their coffees and emptied the grounds onto the fire, they rinsed and gathered their plates, cookware and cutlery then relegated them to the saddlebags and tightened the straps. Jeff extinguished the fire with the soles of his boots, then kicked some mud upon it. When he'd done and the coals were transformed into ash and cracked like eggshells when he stepped on them, they took up their saddles and blankets and went outside and caught the wet horses, bridled and saddled them and mounted up in a hurry and commenced their ride homebound. Heard out on the smoking plains was distant call of cattle and cry-outs and whistles of two men horseback driving them, partly closed from sight and faintly visible against the dark skyline. Of other living beings there was to note none.

"We've been out now 'bout four hours," Jeff growled at a certain point, twirling the bridles in his fingers, approaching her meanwhile, "Tomorrow at eight they're gonna bury that saddle tramp hangin' out there. There's no way they can keep 'im no longer, you know."

"Why not?"

"He's already half-rotten. It's a big risk keepin' 'im, doc said."

"Eight o'clock tomorrow morning. Is that what you said?"

"Ah-ha."

"Will you be there?" she said casually, trying to hide her curiosity.

"That's part of my duty," he said and slipped a grin to her and then went forth, "I don't look forward to it, though. We don't even know who he is. He ain't from around here…that we know for a fact. We sent out some drawings on him, pretty bad pictures, you know. We got nothin'. I reckon 'em pictures were too bad, that's what I think."

"You mean that they were not very much alike him?"

"Not if you ask me, and that was the sheriff said too."

"So you don't know for whom you are having a burial?"

"No, we don't ma'am."

Holding the bridles in one hand with the grips relaxed, they rode on in silence for some minutes seeing thin skeins of wildfowl overhead, the horses treading on at slow trot. Straining their necks, they both fell to watching. After a lull of quietude Jeff passed Birgit a glance sideways and said, "It's pretty funny, you know. His picture hangin' on every sheriff's billboard all over the territory."

"Yes, it certainly is," Birgit agreed absentmindedly. She then turned slightly to Jeff and asked him if they worked hard at the case. Long about answering, he replied they were.

They trotted along in silence until a timbered cottage of rough-cut logs chinked with clay and gray smoke issuing in thin almost vertical wisps from its chimney, caught their sight in a clearing of a grove. It was a coach station and street side pole with the sun falling upon it, roused to a frenetic frenzy. At the entrance of it was standing, bracing himself leisurely with one hand against the low door's lintel, eyeing them in a sort of wonder with a pervasive look, a very tall and lank man in a white wedding suit with a bottle bulging from the jackets pocket, and a red carnation at the lapel, and a paisley ascot at his neck. The passengers had climbed out of the coupe of the wet, recently swabbed stagecoach, a new-looking vehicle with varnished panels, and stood now lined-up shoulder to shoulder stretching their legs. One of them, a woozy and stagger-footed with an inquisitive air, pulling at a cigar, stood holding a massive gripsack in one hand. No doubt a salesman of some kind, he at least had the look of one, Jeff thought, as they slowed the horses to a walk. Four sweaty and tired horses were in the process of being swapped, the fresh ones waiting by the paddock harnessed, a Negro flunky right behind them to herd. An entertainment-group of some variety, people celebrating some occasion, maybe a bridal procession, more or less had seemed to occupy the entire cottage. Jeff pulled the horse to stop next to a full-bearded owl-faced middle-aged man in a dust-laden top hat and hackneyed nearly worn-out blue denim, having the appearance to be a coachman. He was adjusting the harness of the fresh horses and standing there so close to him that Jeff was quite sure of having seen him before.

"Howdy," Jeff said touching the brim of his hat with the forefinger of his right hand, the other born on the saddle's horn.

"Howdy," the other one shot back in a drawl and stood in silhouette, tying the bridle throatlatch. A bird sang pitiably from a nearby tree. "Yo're the sheriff, huh…?" he went on, eyeing him with a suggestion of joy on his face, as if wondering what he was supposed to do.

"Who are this people?" Jeff wondered, his tone akin to amusement. Birgit's bay had halted beside Jeff's and stood snorting, ears clipping back and forth, Birgit astraddle it, watching wonderingly. The teamster looked at Birgit, and at Jeff and at Birgit again, then said, "It's some vaudeville group, I figure. That's what 'em tol' me anyways." He leaned to the side and spat on the hard ground. "Who is that young lady yon'?" he inquired with a curious glance at Birgit, who oblivious of the rude question only had eyes for the assembled people. Ignoring the driver, Jeff's eyes began focusing on a slightly sober disguised youngster who in that shift had bowed out of the roadside pole and with great clarity of intention had advanced on Birgit's horse where he made a halt and stood straddling to the left side of it. He looked at her and at Jeff. Suddenly he lunged at her horse with a raw laughter. Fearful the horse gave a jerky start forward and stood fractious, slinging its head. Birgit pulled back at the reins to prevent it from bolting.

"Come here, fellas!!" he brawled spraddle-legged in the direction of the entourage. "I wanna watch our beautiful visitors dethroned from their mounts!!" he howled drunkenly.

Intimidated by the commotion the horse cried out and bowed up, tossing its head. Birgit frantically leaned low over the horse's neck, pulling the reins to keep her seat, fighting not to fall off. In the middle of this rumpus yet another shape materialized from an inner nook, a bosomy matron-looking woman in wedding dress and rolling breasts, and mascaraed puffed eyes and skin hanging in loose folds on her neck and ringed hands fat as cushions. Reflexively Jeff freed his feet from the stirrups and stood on plain ground. Feeling for his gun to assure it was in easy reach, he approached the rioter who was groping for a weapon of some sort. "Keep your hands still!" he ordered, his voice semi-loud. Avoiding Jeff's eyes, neglecting the request, the other was still digging as though in an effort to produce some means of assault. As Jeff never could recall having ever seen him before, he couldn't figure out whether or not the man's outfit was his regular. Right now the man was standing before him in a pirate's equipment, and having him just a few inches away, he appeared to be one-eyed. The socket looked empty, no eyeball, nothing but a grayish dry structure above the high cheekbone. Jeff watched, his lips clenched into a grimace. Framing him the man wheezed, his voice barely audible, "I will get you killed, yo' bastard! Yo' ain't comin' here askin' no goddam' questions! You gonna die you piece of shit!" He looked mad. Jeff noticed the glimmer of something in the man's right hand, and barely had he the time to ward off the furious attack. The man seemed berserk, and for the first time his one and only eye had a straight focus on Jeff. As if he'd just vanquished a foe. Surely this is gonna be a settlement face to face, Jeff thought. The other guy had made up his mind. Either he himself or Jeff was the one who was to be carried off the stage. Swiftly Jeff reached to his hip and seized the grip of his gun and pulled it free, coincidently cocking it one-handed. He levered it and stalled it at waist level. The half a dozen headed crowd, seconds earlier headed for the center of the event, now froze in mid step. Everything about was quiet. The only sound audible was the incessant Wyoming wind.

"Look at me straight" Jeff hissed, his teeth gritted, "and drop that knife before I bring yo' down right where yo' stand!"

Scarcely had he pronounced the order, before it was obeyed. With a muffled clank the knife touched down right in front of Jeff's boots.

"Don't take 'im seriously, marshal" the coach driver said in a semi-loud voice from his position right behind Jeff's back. "He's crazy always was, always will be. A badman, that's what he is…a blackguard…"

Jeff kept on gazing at the one-eyed as he heard some voices from the motley crowd murmur their opinion.

"He sure could deserve a flogging…He ain't human. Do us a favor, marshal, bang the devil out of 'im!" one suggested in a toneless voice.

"He's perverted, a loony!! God damn 'im!!" the barmy matron shouted in a singsong tone, moving her eyes searchingly around, her whiskey-husky alto heard above the rest.

"Come here!" Jeff said, addressing the one-eyed. "Bend down an' pick up the knife, an' give it to me."

"Didn't know you're a lawman, sir…didn't see that shield at first. Sorry," the other one said miserably.

Jeff fitted back his Colt to his recently oiled holster and felt it slither down just smoothly, then bore down and took up the knife by the hilt and went back the same way from whence he'd come. He stuffed the knife into his saddlebag while watching meanwhile his rear. Addressing his antagonist, he then continued, "If I ever see your face around again, I gonna arrest you. Yo' understand…?"

"Yes, sir," the other answered, starting in his direction, moving one foot slowly after the other, looking like he were engaged in some deep speculation, eye narrowed. He hadn't gone twenty feet when he suddenly halted.

Jeff slowly turned around to face him, said while walking toward him, "Where do yo' come from?"

Squinting he replied that he was from outside Butte, Montana, then with a slight tic at the corner of his mouth added he was raised on a homestead. He bent his head down as though in obeisance.

Jeff made a halt in front of him. "How ol' are you, sonny?" he demanded while looking squarely into his heart-shaped face.

"Twenty-one."

"Alright. What's yo' name?"

The young man contemplated the inquiry for a brief moment before answering while looking from one to the other with his only eye. "Smuts…Jimmy Smuts."

Jeff shifted the weight of his body from one leg to the other. Looking levelly at the man standing before him he said, "How come yo're one-eyed?"

"Lost my eye at an Injin Uprisin', Sioux in paints, scalp hunters…'em bastards tortured me an' killed my mother coupla years back, strapped her to a wagon wheel right after the sun had gone down an' set her afire by lamplight…uh, tried to, but it didn't catch…uh, she just got charred. When they saw she still was alive…an' had…pissed herself, they separated her skull into two with an axe with one single blow. I got so scared I shat my guts out. For a while I figured 'em heathen might perhaps flay her of her skin, but 'em didn't." He got silent for a while as if thinking, then leaned and spat, then went on with his breath soaring out, "I watched it, 'cause 'em bastards forced me hold the camphene lamp while watchin' 'em cut her heart out…I never will forget her shrieks an' her eyes when she looked up at me, but there was nothin' I could do to salvage her, an' she knows it. Jimmy, she shrieked, an' 'em devils imitated her…" He got silent and swallowed, then went forth, "She was a decent good woman, my mother…never harmed nobody…soft hands…"

Noncommittally, nodding austerely, Jeff studied the young man who was looking as though he was thinking hard. After a while he said, "How come 'em didn't kill yo' as well…?"

The man shrugged, spat and wiped his mouth with the back of a hand, then said, "Maybe 'em wanted for me to suffer for times to come…'em red bastards ain't easy to figure out…All 'em said to me was to rouse the fire."

"How' bout yo' father?" Jeff inquired, not taking his eyes off him.

The man, seemingly surprised at the question, answered lingering, "Ain't never seen 'im…He got stabbed by a lunatic in a knife fight long before I was born. None knows by whom."

"Alright Smuts, remember what I said…By the way, why are you dressed like that?"

There was flicker in his eye and he said, "I'm an actor. Well, you know how it is…yo've to live…Now I've none to care about my life, but myself, but I've got friends, yo' know, orphaned by the war," he went on with precocity, shifting from foot to foot.

"So that's what you are…the whole bunch…actors, eh?"

He hesitated a little, then he replied, his voice barely audible, "Yeah…and we have a she-bear in a cage and two apes with us as well, you know." He made a sideways gesture with his chin.

"Is that a fact, eh?"

"Just look around, and you'll see 'em."

Jeff noticed that things no longer were that tense, so he relaxed, having a glance at Birgit, who sat in her saddle holding the saddle's horn hand over hand in a steady grip, her horse's fear somewhat assuaged.

"Yo' alright?" he inquired, raising his head, focusing her.

"Yes, I am alright, but let us move on, please."

Her request immediately was followed by a hard-won smile. Without an answer Jeff turned toward his horse and approached it with slow boot-tread and swung himself onto the saddle. He looked about while catching up and stretching the reins in his right hand. He cast a quick sideways glance at Birgit and gave a nod to the teamster, then they chucked the horses up and turned them out, and without looking back left the place at a rapid trot.

"Sorry, honey!!" the voice of the fat lady echoed behind them in an urgent tone. "Sorry for havin' delayed your ride marshal!" she shouted after them, her fat jowls trembling.

From a thicket a ways out, a dove called. Else nothing there was to hear in the stillness, but the horse's measured breathing and the steady clops from their feet.

IV

Late on the same afternoon, in an eagerly longed for softly falling rain, Jeff O'Halloran and Birgit Süsskind, slouched in the saddles with the bridles slack in their hands approached Sioux Falls from northwest, the horses walking slowly side by side. As the groom wasn't seen anywhere, neither inside, nor in the proximity of the stable, they had to unsaddle and see to the horses themselves. They dried them and rubbed them down with a handful of straw each, watered them and fed them with hay and half a bucket of oat split up in two equal parts.

After finishing the chores with the horses in the holding pen outside the stable, Jeff took his rifle and the bag with what was left of the provisions, and stiff-legged, not feeling that jovial, sauntered away, headed the short way for the sheriff's office. Two shopkeepers in the process of bolting their doors, raised their hands in greeting then stood and looked at him interrogatively in the period of his passing. After having once again scrutinized the place of the coach massacre without having found anything of value, he had to rummage through the belongings of the victims one more time to make sure no mistake had been committed, by him, or by someone else. A list of the possessions of the victims was issued by the sheriff and himself and undersigned by both, but there was one object, besides a valuable one, according to Birgit, that not had been recorded, at least not as far as Jeff could recall. Birgit had excused herself alleging tiredness, so they exchanged their good-byes, after having agreed on a thorough rendezvous at the cluttered office first thing in the morning ensuing, after the burial, which was due at eight.

The tomb was ready since predawn to receive the simple board coffin manufactured by a local carpenter. It was placed on the body of the black ancient open hearse, now trundling to a stop, laboriously drawn by a likewise ancient blackish mare of enigmatic extraction, now standing in the bleak morning sun in complete silence. Besides Jeff not many had flocked around the cortege, just the regular assortment of professional mourners.

From their elevated site up on the dead carriage, the mortician and the local preacher, both clad in black, simultaneously bounced to the ground. The mortician motioned for the six assembled pallbearers in tight-fitting black shiny suits to take down the coffin and place it on the ramshackle biers. Everybody on the barren graveyard supervised their movements in silence, Jeff almost admiring their teamwork. Six elderly gentlemen about the same age, focusing on the same task, all dressed alike. In the middle of this process Jeff noticed that the old jade in front of the hearse, up to now immobile, thoughtfully turned its pike head toward the gate of the graveyard. Something evidently had caught its attention. It was Birgit approaching the picture in the same outfit as she had when entering town on the day before yesterday, same hat, gloves and pumps, her hair arranged in the same way, her stride resolute, her posture straight and erect. As opposite to Jeff, she appeared to be thoroughly rested, her feature though as always restrained, severe, yes, downright solemn. Some of the folks next to the mortician started to whisper between themselves in hushed voices anxious to get as much information as possible within shortest possible time before the starting of the holy ceremony. The preacher hushed, his hair blown askew in the slight breeze. When Birgit finally stopped in front of the assembly, the preacher announced a hymn before the discourse. When the hymn finally was out-sung, the young preacher recited some verses from different parts of the Bible by way of conclusion, deploring the fact that the dead man in the coffin was unknown to them, but not to the Lord, because to Him nobody is anonymous, his voice broken into snatches by the wind. At last they sang again and the preacher, walking in a stiff dignity, went graveward and said a prayer and left over the ashes to the grave until the day of resurrection.

As they left off Jeff put on his Stetson and with his hands crossed before him at the waist turned to Birgit, saying almost in a whisper, "Didn't expect you comin'.'"

"Well, I didn't feel like it at first…but I reconsidered, you see."

"Glad you did," Jeff said as the coffin sunk deeper.

She leaned into him and admonished gravely, "Take off your hat."

"Sorry…I forgot myself."

"He wasn't involved in…the slaughtering, was he?" Birgit demanded as they slowly distracted themselves from the gravesite, Birgit blessing herself with the sign of the cross. Jeff cast a quick glance at her, certifying when she'd caught up to him she almost came up to his shoulder, he being far above average length.

"You refer to…this wretch in the grave?"

"Yes, I actually do."

"Well, we have no reason to suspect, he was…Not so far anyways. You remember what I told yo' yesterday…He got hanged, I cut 'im down hangin' out there. No horse around, nothin' to sit or stand on, no drag marks as far as I could see…He hung pretty high, had been dead for at least forty-eight hours, most certainly more."

The rest of the company was left quite a long bit behind. Jeff and Birgit now had left the graveyard and were headed for the sheriff's office side by side in silence contemplating facts until Birgit broke the calm and turned to face him. She let the anticipation build for some while before proceeding calmly, "As for the horse…I mean, isn't there a possibility that someone came upon the dead body before you did, and then took his horse and simply rode off?"

Meandering with his thoughts, he clandestinely studied her face then answered, "A small possibility, but pretty unlikely, I would say. Yo' mean, just ride upon 'im hangin' in that remote site without contacting the law and just grab the horse and simply ride away with it? Well, yo' know, it's a serious crime to steal somebody's horse out here and everybody knows it. I've called aloft some men for it…No way, I don't figure that happened…And as a horse never go away from his owner by himself, there's just one possibility left – someone killed the man for some reason and took his horse with 'im, knowing it would take long before someone found the corpse…That's what I think…And moreover, the poor bastard was shot from behind…"

Birgit, now in deep thought, gave no answer, just nodded her head in acquiescence to tell she'd understood.

The beautiful yellow gelding that belonged to Wayne Seay, stood resting outside the saloon, the bridles nonchalantly flung around the gnawed and bitten wooden bar. Through the half open door of the sheriff's office with the paint-flaked sign above its door, not far off, a voice sought its way to outside the street. It was the burst voice of the deaf telegrapher, a recluse always clad in black with a pomaded hair licked backwards, available around the clock, no family, no close friends, evidently no relatives, never seen leaving town. Jeff and Birgit in tandem haltingly went closer to the half-open door, stepped inside the smoky semi-dark place, Jeff doing his best assuming a casual expression, whereas Birgit's approach appeared more expectant.

Douglas Kimble was sitting in his swivel chair that cracked under his voluminous body, every crack giving emphasis on his words when speaking.

"Mornin', Miss Süsskind, Jeff," he said with a grin that didn't light up his seamed and haggard-looking features.

The rancher immediately turned around to face Jeff and asked, almost relieved, "How was the burial O'Halloran?...Not so many people there, eh...Half a dozen or so when I rode by, not much, eh...?"

"Well, in that case you have to double that figure, I reckon," Jeff shot back, looking blankly at the rancher standing there tall of stature before him. Seay's eyes now were engaged in watching Birgit, still remaining just inside the open door.

Kimble, anxious to take control of things, quickly snapped, "The young lady is Miss Birgit Süsskind, daughter of the deceased Doctor Süsskind."

Keeping a straight face, the rancher turned to Birgit.

"An' the gentleman's Wayne Seay, the big shot in this county," the sheriff went on announcing, facing the rancher squarely.

"Save us from your sarcasms, Kimble!" the rancher fired back.

In an effort to be efficient and take control, Sheriff Kimble said, facing his deputy, "Alright folks, we now have some reason to believe this stalemate's loosenin' up."

Jeff, now seated behind his desk, returned with a shrug what he just had heard. With a motion to the telegrapher, Kimble went on, his voice raised significantly, "Tell 'im, Arnold! Tell Jeff here an' Miss Süsskind what yo' just got."

"Why don't you just show 'em?" the other responded meekly with a sign at the piece of paper in the sheriff's right hand.

"Alright, see for yourself," Kimble said tersely with address to his deputy.

Jeff stood and walked to his boss and took the telegram from his outstretched hand. He looked at it. It was wired all the way from Lexington, Kentucky, where a sheriff claimed to recognize the just buried drifter. According to him his name would be David Snipes, charged with manslaughter and involved in a bank robbery in Lexington. His description was said to be sent out all over the territory, the wire said further.

"David Snipes, eh," Jeff repeated slowly. "That was not the name he used when I saw 'im in the saloon 'couple of weeks back...He used to play a lot," Jeff went on delicately, giving the rancher a quick glance. Nobody in the county was unaware of the sheriff's, Mister Kimble's, maybe greatest foible, together with the booze. Jeff knew what the slight commotion prior to his arrival was about

"What name did he give you?" the rancher asked with an engaging smile.

"Kershaw...Jimmy, I think."

"Did you buy it?"

"No way. I know his sort...Said to be from New Mexico wheres... That's what he said."

Birgit, still just inside the doorsill, offered a mug. Jeff motioned for her to walk inside and take a seat at her usual place.

Seay now was pacing around the office, his spurs ringing and echoing against the dirty floorings, his purple red bandana constituting a striking contrast to his tanned weathered features. "Alright," he growled. "It looks to me you guys have got yourselves somethin' big to work on. The county's holdin' its breath waitin' for results, that's all I can say," he went on snarling at Kimble, still behind his desk, now appearing to be engrossed in some paperwork, sitting with his forehead creased in concentration. The sheriff exhaled audibly, answered without raising his gaze, "It ain't that easy, Wayne. In fact, we have not much to go on. That wire don't change much, if that's what you mean...an' what makes you think that thug's involved in the crime?...That's what you believe, right...?"

The rancher made a sudden stop and with both hands on his broad hips spit out, his lips tingled with anger, "It ain't exactly my job to think. It's yours and..." pointing at Jeff, "yours, and you'd better start workin' seriously on this case...Within a year there'll be a sheriff's election in town...I don't believe I need to say more. People around are waitin', they wanna' see action."

Without a further word he nodded and reeled around and stormed out and made for the saloon where Cattlemen's Club was due to have a meeting at ten.

The two sheriffs of Sioux Falls listened carefully as Birgit Süsskind began her narrative. Before them were standing sheet coffee-mugs, half-drained, the stale buns already gobbled up. At a certain stage in her description Birgit asked the question everyone in the room had been pondering over almost from the moment she had entered: Where is my father's violin?

"Miss Süsskind." Sheriff Kimble said after a short pause during which he packed his pipe. "Did you see your father when he left Boston headed for Sioux Falls?"

"Yes, sir. I did".

"Did you watch him load the violin?"

"Of course I did."

"Well…in that case I understand you're concerned, ma'am." He raised his face and continued, lips pouted, "You know…we have looked through their stuff and we found no violin…sorry to tell you that."

"Why have you searched through their belongings…in the first place?" she wondered not without irritation.

Kimble frowning on the question, as if confronted, at once shot back in a note of slight reprimand, waving a hand impatiently, "It's routine, Miss Süsskind. We're facin' a homicide investigation, maybe a culpable one. Four people dead out there," he added with authority and handed over the list of items. "Yo'd better see for yourself. As yo' can see it's undersigned by myself and Jeff here, which means we both were present at the inventory." He shifted and went on, "I have to make clear that the items remain here until we're finished, or the crime's solved…Hope yo' don't mind, ma'am. And as for the fiddle, it's replaceable, Miss Süsskind."

A sudden flare of anger crossed Birgit's features. "If you allude at my father's Storioni violin, a precious artifact from the eighteenth century, it is NOT replaceable, Mister Kimble."

The sheriff looked at her while trying a strenuous smile, then announced apologetically, "I'm not that good at music…how 'bout you, Jeff?"

"'Bout the same, I reckon," Jeff replied, casting one sweeping look in the general direction of the jail section. He was now sitting on the edge of his desk. Nodding toward a custody he went on saying as he faced Birgit, "All items on the inventory stand in there. You are free to go inside an' search it through. It might help us wind up the case."

Birgit, already on her feet, slowly approached the stale den where a great part of her past was gathered in a gunny sack, mumbling as if talking to herself, something to the effect, her father's pocket-watch was missing on the inventory list.

Sheriff Kimble already stood next to her in the dusty cell. She had just recognized the clothing and the footwear of her dead relatives, the same outfit they wore the last time she saw them alive when leaving Boston. All of a sudden, she felt like she now was on her way to lose control, as if being on her way into a mental turmoil. Jeff, up to this moment still lingering outside, began to wonder about the awkward silence when he heard Kimble brawl from the inside of the semi-darkness, "Jeff!!...Yo' out there?!"

Ignoring the clumsy behavior of his boss, Jeff took a breath and joined the two standing in the hovel, where Birgit now stood bent forward with her hands on her knees as if ready to throw up right away with eyes closed, cheeks pale, slightly shivering. She showed no reaction when Jeff emerged. She half-stood in that position, constituting a person in deep agony. After having watched the immobile woman in her despair for a lengthy while, Jeff suddenly became aware of the presence of a fourth individual watching the scenery, and behind him now yet another. Sheriff Kimble's chubby son and his bony sister, both just gawking. Yet the whole attention was caught, although temporarily, by the young white and brown dog that accompanied the two brats. There was a moment of relief, the tension somewhat removed. Birgit got erect, initially showing a serious face, her eyes on the young intruders, then with a careful look at Jeff offering him an apologetic, although forced smile. Sheriff Kimble, up to this moment looking like he was not quite sure how to handle the embarrassing outburst of the young woman in front of him, now had his focus directed toward the sniffing dog that just was about searching through the entire space, stopping and starting again with random inquisitiveness, tail wagging, shaking itself every once in a while. In spite of the basic gravity, everyone present had some problems keeping up a straight front, except for the sheriff. Irrespective of this fact most tension in the air seemed to be killed off just within seconds, and Birgit retook control of her despair. Jeff seriously doubted whether the kids had been noticing something, and what if they had? Being unfriendly addressed by their parents most of the time, these kids were familiar with grievous events, and they turned to Jeff increasingly paying him almost daily visits, most often furtively. Their father did not ever let on about it, at least not to Jeff.

"When will we go out practisin'?" the boy demanded, giving Jeff a glance of expectation, simultaneously awaiting his father's reaction on the sly.

Without awaiting Jeff's answer, his sister immediately exclaimed, "Jeff, let me come with yo', please!"

Sheriff Kimble, now fed up with the unplanned setback in the course, didn't wait for Jeff's reply. Instead, he pointed at the door and advised harshly his descendants to go home, his jaw-muscles in hard tension, then with an excusing eye at Birgit, hoisted up his almost new denim around his voluminous midsection and lumbered out from the inhospitable closet.

When back in the office Birgit more or less reluctantly retook her seat and said in the direction of Kimble, "By the way…there was no money among their possessions? No clock, no jewelry?"

Kimble now with obvious amusement, returned by saying that what they now had to face was a murder of robbery. "That's the only motive we can think of, Miss Süsskind. Have you some other motive in mind, then let us know. Just tell us. We are open to every option. We didn't know nothin' 'bout your folks, haven't seen 'em alive. Nothin' whatsoever."

Jeff, remaining to now silent, watched the watery eyes of his foreman and asked, carefully watching Birgit's reaction, "Did your parents have any enemies as far as you know?"

Seemingly startled by the direct inquiry she said after a brief while, her voice quivering somewhat, "It's just what I have been asking myself, you know. I really don't think so."

"Have they been out west…before?" Jeff asked.

"Papa has, not my mother."

"Yo' sure 'bout that, Miss Süsskind?" Kimble fired back from behind his desk, scratching his bristles.

"Yes, I'm quite sure."

Jeff now noticed how striking pale Douglas Kimble was. When at work he spent most of the time in his office, and off duty, he wasn't much outdoors. Quite a lot of liquor, and also quite a lot of time playing cards at the saloon, although he never touched the subject, but both activities were on the increase, a fact that had got even more obvious to Jeff recently. Sounding interested, Jeff inquired, addressing Birgit, "Who did play that violin? Was it your father or your mo…?"

"My father did," the answer came with alacrity. "In fact, he was a cellist, as well. My mother used to play the piano."

Sheriff Kimble let out a whistle and raised his shrubby eyebrows as if in admiration, half-sitting in his swivel, both hands folded behind his solid neck, the chair lamenting under him.

Discreet footsteps all of a sudden occupied the attention of the both sheriffs. A black-dressed male materializes slowly in the door standing on the doorsill, neither in nor out.

"Eric…Come right in!" Sheriff Kimble boomed, motioning him in with a cupping motion of his fingers, as he with an elucidating whisper to Birgit went on, "The mortician…Eric Petersen."

Birgit remembered him from the burial some hours ago, the emaciate man, about sixty. She'd heard that kids in town used to poke fun about him asking among themselves: "Listen! Why is Mister Petersen so popeyed?" The reply to that quest always was: "Because he has been watching so many corpses."

Snatching his topper from his head to reveal a black hair carefully slicked back and holding it in both hands before him, the mortician advanced circumspectly inside in a slight limp as though he had a damaged popliteal tendon. He stood just inside the slippery threshold looking about him, as if someone he knew might be there. Having once got Birgit in sight, he with purpose stepped in her direction and stopped right in front of her. He stretched out a birdlike hand, offering her a limp, dry handshake, his features somber.

"We met at the burial in the mornin'…I'm the mortician of town," he went on as though she had already forgotten his face, "Name's Petersen."

Birgit managed to find a smile, responded, watching him with inquisitiveness, "Well, Mister Petersen, I assume you already know who I am…my name is Birgit Süsskind. Nice meeting you, sir. I guess you were the one who handled the arrangements, isn't that correct, sir?"

"That's correct, I did ma'am," the mortician confirmed meekly, his gaze a bit wild. "I really have to extend my condolences," he added, now standing facing her, studying the floor, hands folded low in front of him, legs slightly apart. There was some long seconds of hesitation in the air until Birgit eventually took a forward step toward him, saying, her eyes focusing her hands that sat together before her, clasped together as though in prayer, "By the way, Mr. Petersen, when you laid…them in their coffins, they didn't have their clothes on, had they?"

The mortician gravely shook his head, no.

"I can understand that, because they are hanging in that cabinet at this moment bloody and dirty, separated from the rest," she replied bleakly with a slight motion of a finger.

Sheriff Kimble, until now passive, but carefully listening, interfered by saying, "Matter of evidence, miss uh, ma'am! As 'em bodies were unidentified, at least formally, it's routine out here…an' I figure it's the same all over this country, to keep their clothing in custody as evidence, an' that's why we keep 'em here, but from now on, you're free to take 'em with you whenever you wish…Furthermore, they were thoroughly examined by the coroner…We are talkin' 'bout a homicide, remember…we have to straighten things up, right?"

Birgit's face hardened instantly, and she stood with jaw clenched, her eyes deliberately shunning the sheriff. Icily she responded, "Yes, that I can understand, but how were they dressed…in their coffins?"

Looking at Sheriff Kimble the mortician forthwith elucidated, "In a special white shrouding manufactured by Mrs. Steinberg, a seamstress in town….Ordinary sheetin' one might say…sort of dress. Dignified outfit, really."

Birgit looked puzzled in hearing this, but refrained from asking anything further about it.

"By the way…talkin' 'bout somethin' else," Kimble went on with a slightly amused expression in Petersen's direction, "By what I heard from Buchanan's boys the other night, it ain't unlikely busy in the closest future."

"Why's that?" the mortician wondered expectantly, facing the sheriff.

"'Em reds are said to be on the warpath, at least what 'em boys said…Well, I don't know, just overheard."

This fact brought the conversation to a contemplative halt. Everybody in the room, save for Birgit, remembered the latest Indian raid in town on September last year, at dawn, most people of town still in their beds, many asleep, taken unawares. The woody smithy got to ashes. Just some iron-items were all that was left. Same with one half of the barbershop. All burned down except for 'em outer walls. It took only a couple of minutes, Kimble remembered. "Seven casualties 'mong the citizens," Kimble reminded, eyeing his deputy and the undertaker, his hands clasped together behind his neck.

"Yeah, I remember every single of 'em…" Petersen chimed in somber-looking, still standing at Jeff's desk, hands low folded in front of him, his hat resting on the desktop. Jeff eyed him. He couldn't recall ever having seen him in any other garments. He always wore them, like they were an uniform or regimentals.

"You can never be enough prepared for 'em bastards," Kimble growled and stretched for the sooty enameled tin coffee pan, placed in the very center of his desk. He half-filled his mug with the remains of the nearly cold contents. With an apologetic eye at Petersen, he at once demanded, "Sorry, Eric, you want some?"

"No thanks…had a cup before I went here," the mortician replied sadly.

"Just in case," Jeff chuckled from behind. He'd just got up and was standing stretching. Yawning he took a few strides while taking a long look out through the small grated peephole in the wall that faced the street and barely let in any light at all. As time went by, he got increasingly aware of the fact that he spent so much time indoors. Basically this was not the way he wanted things to be. A real man shall be out most of the time, and another thing: "Don't live in a thrall to others an' wear yo'selves out, boys. Yo're all I've done well, an' I want for yo' guys a better life," his father often had said to his two sons. Which implied a real man ought to be a rancher, Jeff and his brother had reasoned. That sure would be the optimum. Work for yourself. Be your own boss. Not as a cowboy or wrangler working for miserly pay, no sir, a rancher…This was, and had always, since that day, been Jeff O'Halloran's number one dream. But sometimes our decisions have no alternatives. The war came in between, and things changed from one day to the next. Nearly thirty-four and still day-dreaming, he thought, standing by the dirty hole, resting his lean frame on the gray-green shutter, without taking any attention to the hushed voices just a few inches away from him. He heard them, didn't listen though. What is this for a miserable way of living? He asked himself rhetorically, eyes closed. No family, not even a woman. Just myself and old Mrs. Penn from whom he rented a tiny den, one too soft bed, a commode, a water pot, a bar of soap, couple of towels, a shaving soap, razor, a mirror where he could watch his paired image, seeing himself growing older faster and faster, his life sort of wriggling out of his hands. I gotta get out, journey on, he said to himself every evening when in bed…This can't be life…I have my horse Ty, my only adherent in this world, a friend I dote upon, I've my saddle with roll and blanket, a rifle, a single-shot Springfield, the same one I hunted with as a kid, a couple of five-shooters, cartridge belt, two Stetson hats, one black, one brown, four pairs of denim jeans, two pairs of boots with spurs, a black suit, only used once, a couple of bandanas, four shirts of various colors, two winter coats, a pair of deerhide gloves, two saddlebags. Quite recently he purchased for his stallion a brand new snaffle, and soon, real soon, he had in mind to buy himself a real good heavy coat for the winter. One of the old ones was a gift from the war. A very young confederate cavalry man from Virginia offered him his coat before breathing his last. He thought about the war every night, the memories from it picking at him like knifes.

"We're after all…Americans both…this is crazy…" he'd whispered before his gaze bent inward. Jeff very clearly remembered that moment, used to think on it from time to time.

Suddenly he frowned. From his position behind the minimal aperture overlooking the bank, he watched someone coming in an uneven gait that was half walk and half run. It was the hearing-damaged telegrapher, Arnold, with two printouts in left hand, the other arm hanging dead down his side. Limping he directed his steps in great haste in the general direction of where he himself stood. He half turned and announced with address to the three assembled, "Someone's comin' in for a call."

The muted conversation now had come to an abrupt ending, and all heads were directed toward the open door where the messenger now was standing, breathing heavily from his opened mouth as though he'd been running a long stretch, his alert eyes slowly adjusting to the semi-darkness.

"Sheriff," he addressed in a strident voice, "here I've got another two wires for you."

Kimble, already on his feet, crossed toward him and snatched the wires without a word, scanned one at a time, then said struggling a little with the words, "This wire says our buried fellow's been seen in Waukesha, Wisconsin…He's name's Mark or Matthew Blake…It's all it says…An' the other claims his name's David Sniper…The wire's sent by a lawyer in Lexington, Kentucky. He raised his head and looked at the others who were watching and waiting. He continued, "Listen…haven't we heard those names before? Sniper and Kentucky?"

Without waiting for a reply, he swung around, went back to his desk, rounded it and jerked open the topmost drawer. Standing bow-backed he flipped through the piled papers till he finally came upon the same message that the telegrapher had delivered to him some hours earlier, where the sheriff of Lexington had claimed the same: Sniper, David. In the latest, there was no mention of either manslaughter or bank robbery, just his name, the same name. Wisconsin? Had he been operating nationwide? Jeff said he couldn't figure this out. He therefore ordered the telegrapher to go back to the bank and send a message to the judge in Casper, asking for advice.

"I will…right away," the telegrapher replied, rubbing nervously the back of his neck above his shirt collar, searching Kimble's gaze as if he wanted his opinion. He got none, though.

Petersen, now beginning to feel time drag on, waiting for the most proper opportunity to appear, and looking like something just had occurred to him, reached for an envelope in the inner pocket of his black suit and with his black heels scuffing the floor covered the few steps that until now had separated him from Birgit, and handed it to her, his head cocked a little to the side. It was a document of modest format. Initially he had been anticipating to push her aside and bring it over, but eventually he began to forget the idea, when he started to realize that he would be leaving the premises before she did.

"Well, Miss Süsskind…Hope you don't mind, but…"

"Oh, forgive me, Mister Petersen, I think I understand what you have just produced….I won't open it here. Can it wait until I'm back in my temporary shelter? I will review it and then I contact you…if that's alright with you, sir?"

The mortician took a few backward half-steps, let out a light chortle and said, "That'll be just fine…just fine, ma'am…it ain't that urgent."

With a light bow of his neck, he then took up his hat from where he'd placed it on Jeff's desk and without handshakes turned away from her then said good-by to the two sheriffs, and made for and went out through the already open door. He made a halt and looked up and down the street. Up on the heaven the sun stood at the zenith, and a hot day was to be expected. To all appearances yet another Indian summer day was in the making.

V

The inhabitants of Sioux Falls followed with unflagging interest the well-tended buggy where it in a slow progress rolled its way forward along the rutty main street in the late afternoon. The beautiful chestnut mare, the magnificent harness, the well-kept vehicle, the man on the driver's seat with bridles and whip in his gloved right hand, the left casually resting on the left knee, it all defined a captivating sight.

When in front of the unpainted livery stable the driver pulled up the horse, and collected the bridles in his both hands. With a try to bring about an agile bound, he with great caution lowered himself to the ground, and accurately on stiff legs, struggling a little with the reins, made it the short way to the dusty horse and attached them to the harness while making a wry face in the process. Being in the middle of this, he out of the corner of his eye noticed the groom showing up from the inner nooks, headed for the equipage on reverent steps, aiming to bring the act to an end. He was forewarned. Like always. The day before, the sheriff had went by to announce the judge was due sometime late on the next afternoon.

The two men in front of the stable did not swap more words than the situation insisted upon, and when in agreement, they split up in different directions, the groom with the mare by the snaffle into the stable, and the black-dressed official with regular steps with his gripsack in hand, leaning in the westerly wind stalked his way to the reserved accommodations at the hotel. Although the man didn't display himself long, the event soon was brought to everybody's knowledge, and speculations took shape. Even the pudgy dog resting in the shade of a handcart right outside the general store, for once seemed a bit alerted and rose his cheek from the ground, and his tail started to move, saluting the stranger. What the citizens of town did in fact not know about this well-groomed guest was that he was always doing his best to hide the fact that he was disabled and therefore forced to drag himself along on an artificial leg, one that constantly galled the skin of the remaining stump. The reason behind this was that he had undergone an carcinogenic episode, and as a consequence of this was forced to watch his steps and furthermore routinely survey and bind the wounds that at times got reopened. Hadn't it been a lot better him being wounded in action during the war and for that reason had got crippled, he used to ask himself in his darkest moments of self-hatred. But fact is he got exempted from military service. He still fretted over this fact and couldn't get it out of his mind. Still he was biding his time though, thinking things would improve. But there were no signs so far pointing in that direction, quite the reverse. His tendency toward self-isolation grew more and more profound, and lately he had often come upon himself cherishing suicide plans. The careless jump from the buggy no doubt had taken its toll, and now he literally looked forward to some privacy on purpose to inspect the stump. However, he was somewhat inspired with some hope after having been examined by a young physician, one specialized in internal medicine a couple of months ago. He asserted him to be a diabetic, and for that purpose prescribed some medications and gave him some instructions as to what kind of food he must avoid etcetera. So far not much had improved, though, he thought to himself as he slowly walked his way in a slight limp down the street with the dog still at the heel.

From the hotel attendant, a boyish Irishman with a searching gaze, he received his key and got escorted to his room. He didn't have to use the key though, the door already being unlocked. He entered and made the door to and flung his little travel-bag on the bed of the frugally decorated chamber, his regular. He slid off his gloves and tossed them on the bed then hastily removed his dusty black coat and Stetson hat and flung it all onto the bed in a flourish. With quivering fingers he untied the belt that sat tightly around his slightly protruding belly, his hands shaking feverishly, then pulled down his trousers and hunched down on a stool that stood placed right in front of the huge mirror. Nothing but a thin gauze bandage covered the stump. Sitting there with the black trousers around his ankles, he realized that his fears really had come true. The stump was heavily wounded and a fresh and massive bleeding displayed, one most likely induced when hitting the ground, dismounting the wagon. He remained in that position for some while as he considered his next move. Slowly he raised his head. "I'm dying…a slow death…that's what I'm doing," he said to the mirror, his teeth gritted. "It's like a broomstick up my ass."

He now got lost in deep thoughts, deliberating alternatives when looking into the mirror at his image, a middle-age circuit judge who had a long time ago crested his career. Shortly he had three different alternatives, he thought, out of which one didn't directly concern his main problem, but indirectly. Right then there was a bang at the door. He got motionless. After a rather long while of silence there was one more bang, one more urgent. From his current position, he couldn't see the door but through the mirror. He knew the door was still unbolted and the key put into the right pocket of his coat. He decided not to answer, he simply couldn't. Why run the risk at getting caught with his trousers down? He gave a roar to the mirror, "Who is it?"

"It's me…Sheriff Kimble…You're alright judge?" A high cracked voice.

Sheriff Kimble. That's about what he had anticipated. That man had made a weak impression on him. A spineless character, no backbone. Will never raise gumption. They had met a half dozen or so times at the very least. Moreover, he had got his suspicions increased when realizing that Sheriff Kimble was keeping his deputy outside things. "I can't open right now!" he roared to the mirror. "I arrived just minutes ago. Can it wait an hour or so…?"

A brief quiet ensued, then he heard from the corridor, "I see, sir. When would it be appropriate for you?"

The judge exhaled. He quickly dug up his golden watch from out the pocket of his vest. It showed 17.39. He half-turned and countered out into the corridor, "Seven thirty, at the saloon!!"

"Alright," sounded the suppressed voice from outside.

One and a half hours left, the judge told himself and rose and with a stalwart hold about the pants waistband awkwardly with edgy steps made it to the bed, his footwear swishing steadily. He clasped open and guiding his fingers into he started to rummage through his gripsack. Hopefully a splash of Scotch would make him feel a bit better. His well-manicured thin fingers took a firm grip around the neck of the bottle and pulled it out. He twisted the cork and re-caught his hold on the bottle's neck. The yellowish savory fluid would be beneficial to him and help him kill the pain and raise his spirits, at least for a while, a couple of hours or so. First a quick wash, then a nice dinner before he went to see Kimble. He raised and put the throat of the bottle to his lips and took him a good swig. The food at the hotel wasn't that bad…on the contrary, he thought to himself, shivering and smacking his lips. But right now, first of all, he had to figure out how to bandage his ulcerous stump. Squinting he looked around the modest single-room then drank a second time and stood with the bottle lowered. The ultimate answer to that question lay stuffed in his bag. He simply had to spend his white spare shirt.

Just a couple of minutes prior to the appointed time, Sheriff Kimble entered the saloon and bullied his way to the table where his deputy already was seated. The sun was close to setting and the premises, smelling of kerosene, tobacco and sour sweat and horse were half-filled with the usual selection of decent breadwinners and craftsmen, the usual frequenters of the only hangout of town. A handful of cowboys and backwoodsmen, most of whom single-people sat grouped around a round scratched table engrossed in a poker game, a cloud of tobacco smoke ascending over their heads. Now and then there is a glimmer of a match and a brief succinct conference. Otherwise, stillness prevails.

From his place at the very back of the locality, Jeff already had distinguished three shadowy individuals, all unknown to him arriving there about the same time as himself. They were all rigged out in cowboy garment and wore a deep tanning, one of them, probably the oldest, one with ferrety eyes, wearing a disheveled full beard, a long greasy hair hanging down the even greasy collar of his dirty tartan shirt, judging by his behavior, seemed to be the headman. His two companions, just as slovenly, appeared to be twins, and the more Jeff went on watching them on the sly, the more it got obvious to him, that they were in some way mentally retarded. Their goofy laughter didn't quite reach the same level of rawness and brutality as those of the older, but evidently the older one in any case was allowed to have a substantial impact on the twins. To Jeff it looked like they were worshipping him. Having surveyed the trio for a about a quarter of an hour, Jeff could establish them having had their conversation running without any interruption ever since they appeared. They wore firearms and a half-emptied whiskey-bottle purchased from the bartender when entering sat on the top of their table. When Kimble had showed up, the older one got alerted and shot some harsh words in the direction of his compeers and then went back to their private talk. Whether Jeff was recognized by them or not, was beyond his judgment. As for the twins, they didn't know him, Jeff reasoned to himself. He doubted them even having seen him beyond the smoke screen in the scantily lit-up room.

After having exchanged some words with the bartender, a native of town, most often grumpy-looking, Kimble motioned toward Jeff's table, jeering a little. From where he was sitting Jeff had a reasonably fine look-out over the area, fronting the entrance of the saloon. Kimble, arrived horseback, pushed down his stocky appearance in the scarred wooden chair. There was a faint reek of stale booze about him, and he was panting a lot and answered to Jeff's frown with an apologetic gesture, his lips pressed together in a closed smile.

"Need some exercise, deputy…Ain't no breach of law, I hope. Wife an' kids kinda blame me all the time. Allege I'm growin' heavy, you know…Kinda humps me…" He searched the deputy's eyes for reassurance, but got none.

"Any object in particular?" Jeff wondered, doing his best not to sound curious. Judging by the sheriff's body language, his inquiry didn't seem to have been appreciated.

He shrugged and snapped out, "Just 'couple of hours horseback, that's all…Needed to be alone and reflect some…don't you have that…need? His words came stolidly.

"I'm thinkin' all the time" Jeff answered with an unintentional edge to it. To be honest he wasn't in the mood for small talk.

The untidy trio at some tables distance now had become more muffled, but still Jeff couldn't help flinging a furtive glance in their direction. Quite unexpectedly the three companions rose to their feet and filed outside and out into the street. Two other men, well known to everybody around, stepped inside navigating themselves toward the bar. Wayne Seay and his factotum, Reuben Lindsay, a pockmarked lean and round-shouldered broncobuster, born in the saddle, a man having the reputation of being cruel, but also fair. Laura, the black chesty waitress, placed a coffee mug in front of Jeff. He at once cuddled it and went on watching the scenery, mug stalled in mid-air. Somehow he sensed trouble looming. Sheriff Kimble looked at him with his watery eyes. He was far from being sober, but that didn't hinder him from catching Laura's attention ordering right out, "Gimme a Scotch, Laura!" and with an explanatory address to Jeff, "It's gonna help me clear away 'em cobwebs."

"Any particular cobwebs, yo've in mind, sheriff?" Jeff countered flashing a comforting smile not trying to camouflage his disgust with his boss. Kimble, hesitating before turning to his assistant, snarled, "Why don't you order a drink for yo'self?…Always strained, eh…just for the hell of it, right?"

Jeff shrugged and looked back at him, "No way, I ain't…I'm just on duty. Like most of the time," he replied, his tone of voice sharpening.

"Who's handlin' most of that goddam' paperwork?" the sheriff spit out.

The last thing Jeff now needed was an argument with his boss, although he considered it worthwhile to clear the air a bit. Laura now had returned to their table and was now standing by the sheriff's side, glass and a bottle of Scotch in hands. Routinely she poured out about six centiliters of the eagerly longed for fluid that Kimble without ceremony drained at one greedy gulp. Within seconds the sheriff kind of started to sweat and Jeff now began to fear the worst considering the fact that the judge was due to appear any minute. As for the paperwork, Kimble claimed that he and the judge had an agreement that specifically implicated that he, the sheriff, should be the one to handle it. Jeff asked, "When did the judge give you the authorization to take care of the post and all paperwork? I haven't seen that written somewhere. Have you, boss?"

Kimble's mind now was racing. He sat back ordering his thoughts. "It ain't written here…don't fret…You've the right to back me up."

"When it's alright with you," Jeff chimed in, "Meanin'…when you need my assistance, ain't it so…?"

"Don' taunt…you hear…" the sheriff answered, his voice cracked, in some way feigned, Jeff noticed. They sat in silence for a time, the sheriff's slack face avoiding contact with Jeff who also noticed that his boss had started to talk even more thickly. Jeff almost felt a tinge of empathy for the poor bastard right now. They weren't close him and his boss, would never be, but nonetheless. There was something repugnant about him, Jeff couldn't figure out what it was, an odd sensation, that's what it was. Most often nowadays Kimble's eyes were burning from liquor. Jeff rubbed his neck, asked matter-of-factly, "Listen, boss, did the contents in that bottle provide you the ability to clear away those cobwebs so yo' can help tackle matters? Remember what Seay said yesterday…'bout re-election, eh?…Every step, every move from yo' are carefully watched from now on…You oughta think 'bout that, boss."

"Come on Jeff, don't talk…so much, don't exert yourself so much, dammit! I don't give a…damn…"

"Maybe you should" Jeff advised crossly with defiance as Kimble meanwhile tried to push himself upright in his seat, grimacing as if racked with pain.

"Why don't you just go look after…that…Boston titbit, eh…to get yo' a new slant on things?" he deadpanned… "Don't you think…I've seen the way she looks at you, ol' boy…?"

Suddenly a commotion stirred at the bar. Jeff looked across the room to notice the three strangers now back inside the saloon were involved in some arguing that now had escalated. Without being privy to any details, not distinguishing every word, he managed to discern spread remarks that got harsher by time. Expressions as "hussy," "whip ass," and "bastard" were frequent, making it obvious some people around were at variance. The chatter from the other guests gradually had muted and knowing looks and comments were flung in the direction of the gentlemen at the bar desk. Wayne Seay was so drunk he barely could stand erect, a predicament he shared with his dialogue-partner to his left. The gloomy-looking man standing on his right side, Reuben Lindsay, his foreman, hadn't uttered one single word so far. Jeff knew the man had a reputation for being patient, to a certain limit, though. Lindsay wasn't a man of many words, merely one of action, a man with a stingy punch. Now he was standing at the bar desk appearing casual, one boot propped on the brass footrest, his both arms resting on the desk, hands folded together as though in prayer, the brown Stetson pushed back, taking in every single word said next to him, accumulating all, forgetting nothing, his face as expressionless as always. The bulky character to Seay's left was the owner of a small ranch about an hour's ride from town. Jeff hadn't seen him around so often recently, and for the moment he couldn't recall his name. The man in question now lunged at Seay. Lindsay evidently had foreboded that movement to occur and stung like a cobra so fast nobody actually didn't see it happen. They just heard the roaring. With an unbelievable suppleness he turned some sixty degrees, grabbed his antagonist by the wrist and twisted it till the man bellowed in pain. Neither Jeff, placed far off, nor someone else, closer positioned, was offered sufficiently time to react. Focusing his adversary with his black eyes, Lindsay hissed between clenched teeth, "Go to your rental, pick up your stuff, get on your horse and leave town…Don't linger, you hear?" No strong language. No oaths.

"You take sides for 'im Lindsay…Didn't you hear you' boss offend me?" the other spat out in agony, recoiling and floundering about like he might topple, blood trickling from his broken nose, Lindsay riveting on the spot.

"I ain't deaf," he answered bluntly, his voice gaining strength. He went on lowering his voice, now somewhat scratchy, "You heard me, I'll handle 'im later on. Right now it's about you an' your future well-bein'…Listen, I say this for the last time: Check out an' leave town."

When he'd said this, he turned back and faced the bar and sought the eyes of the barman then slid his cup forward for more coffee.

Sheriff Kimble, sitting perplex, appearing sober, made no sign of joining the pack. Instead, he put a bold face on it, watching how brilliantly Reuben Lindsay took care of things. From experience Jeff knew Kimble's presence would make things worse and even start a riot.

"Wayne don't say much, eh," the sheriff said to Jeff, breaking the tense silence, "Just standin' tumblin', his lips movin' but I hear nothin'…too far off, I reckon…"

"Right. That's thanks to Lindsay," Jeff said cautiously. "If he ain't been around, we sure had got problems."

"It ain't over yet," Kimble said and composed his face into a stern gaze. Jeff didn't answer, just continued studying the party, all the while keeping an eye at all the people around, who sat like rooted to the tables. With the intention to smooth things for Kimble, Jeff inquired, "How 'bout the judge? Wasn't he supposed to show at eight?"

The sheriff looked long at the bar desk, hesitated before turning to his deputy, "Seven thirty," he corrected and directly went on, "You mean…it's Lindsay, who've set Wayne right?"

"Yeah, that's what I mean. Don't you agree…?"

"You may have a point there," Kimble admitted, his gaze turned inward watching Lindsay taking his boss by the arm to take him out of the smoky room and away to the livery stable. The assembly with the Cattlemen's Club was over for this time. Around the tables people had already started to express their admiration for Reuben Lindsay's tenacity. For a while it brought the town to a halt.

The poor hotel room rapidly got lit up by the ascending sun. Jeff O'Halloran pushed open the unbolted door, his boss right behind panting in his neck. Yet another man was following in tandem, his mouth wide open with curiosity. It was the hotelkeeper, and trailing behind him, the part-time employee, an elderly Negress with a sad and frowning face, her eyes so widened they looked all pupil. Outside the shut window, in the pinnacle of the Presbyterian church, two painters had just forgotten their whereabouts, and looking as though they couldn't credit what they really witnessed, squatted with their squinting glares focused on the man on the made bed lying in fetal position directly on the knit white spread. Under his left armpit a derringer was sitting in its holster. An unscrewed leg prosthesis at some distance away from the body directly caused curious attention. There he lay, the circuit judge, mutilated, maimed, exposed, devoid of every sign of dignity, dressed in his underwear and white shirt and black bow tie, the trousers flung on the floor, next to the prosthesis. A lengthy moment of silence loitered. Eventually there was some suggestions as to open the window, but it got turned down by Jeff, now more or less forced to take charge. As for his boss, the man hadn't so far uttered one substantial word. Instead, he had begun to show evident signs of nausea, and had difficulties standing straight. Finally Jeff was the one to break the stillness by saying, looking meanwhile at the black hotel hand, "You found 'im, Miss Jackson?"

"Yes sir, I did." She looked gravely at the man in the bed then at Jeff then back at the bed while sucking in the reek.

"When?" Jeff continued asking, shifting legs.

"Just a few minutes ago, sir."

"Alright..." Jeff said. "Let's take it from the beginning. Tell what happened."

After a quiet moment she answered, her voice quavering slightly, face scrunched inward, "Well, he didn't come down for breakfast...at seven, sir."

"Alright...an' what was your reaction to that?" Jeff countered, again taking in the sight. The Irishman raised his hands in a stopping movement and joined the discussion, announcing gravely, "I suggested he had overslept... or maybe he hadn't got enough sleep at night... Just let 'im get enough sleep, then he'll get down... that's what I said, you know... We couldn't imagine somethin' like this."

Studying the hotelkeeper's boots that had been cut down to shoes, Jeff went on questioning, his face clouded, "Was he out last night?"

"No, sir, he wasn't," the hotelkeeper assured helpfully.

"Did he order anythin' from you?"

"He did not, sir."

Jeff nodded imperceptibly as he digested this for a brief while, then proceeded, "So...he did not...to your knowledge, leave this room, right?"

"He did not, sir," the Irishman confirmed, his eyes a bit wild now.

Jeff looked askance at Kimble just in time to see him remove his Stetson and wipe his forehead with his fingers and then wipe them on the leg of his denim. He then looked down at his hands, flexed them together, looked up at the hotelkeeper and asked, "Listen, Mister O'Rourke, when was the last time you saw the judge alive?"

"At his arrival…here…by five or so last afternoon."

"How do you know he's dead?" Jeff demanded serious-looking.

The man, perplex now, as if trying to gain some courage, cast a furtive glance at Sheriff Kimble before answering, "To me it's pretty obvious. Yo' can see for yo'self, can't yo'. He don't breathe…"

"We'd better fetch the doc," it came from Sheriff Kimble, now somewhat bucked up, slowly headed for the door.

Jeff didn't answer. He instead approached the body and stood looking down at it, inhaling the mixture of nasty smells that stack in his nose. A nauseating sensation all of a sudden came upon him, and he tried his best to knock it down.

"Listen Jeff, I go get the doc," Kimble repeated from the door, his tone harsh.

Jeff thanked the hotel staffers for their cooperation and dismissed them, then stood deep in thoughts. Realizing this case now appeared to have taken another turn, he said without turning, "Come here, sheriff, we fetch the doc later. Just come an' look!"

Reluctantly Kimble got nearer. Jeff got the impression his boss was having the intention to dislodge the corpse in some way, as if he were discontent with its current position, so he therefore got forced to hamper him in the action.

"Don't touch 'im!" he lashed out. "Look at 'im, sheriff. Tell me what you see, don't touch!"

Kimble's bleach eyes, now even somewhat moist, focused the nestled dead body where it lay with its eyes wide open almost looking up at him. In an effort to pluck up his courage Kimble certified, "He's murdered, strangled…now I see 'em bruises, Jeff." He stepped past the body, half-squatted and studied it from another angle, then sank until eye-leveled with it. He then straightened laboriously and staggered abreast of his deputy, said in a murmur one barely audible, "This is a homicide, Jeff, that's what it is."

The old doctor straightened his lean upper body after having swiftly examined the corpse. He took off his golden half-moon glasses and turned to the two sheriffs standing next to side by side and firmly disclosed as he stroked a bony hand along his silvery beard, "He has been dead for eight to twelve hours." Without taking his eyes off the sheriffs he proceeded, "Sticky air, the sun hours high, thunder underways, window closed, well…all this is the answer to the fragrances around, and besides…well he has emptied bladder and bowels as well. Some nasty individual has caused this to him. That's all I can tell you, gentlemen. Asphyxiation. He's smothered. No nightly struggle did precede death, though. You may bring Petersen whenever it's convenient to you…I can't do anything for him, I'm afraid."

He retrieved an antique pocket watch from off his left vest pocket and looking at the face of it said, his low-pitched baritone having a solemn character to it, "I declare him dead at…12.15 p.m." With a quick glance at the dead man on the bed he added, "He's conveying all signs of strangulation, and I will make out a post mortem statement, right away."

"Meaning, you produce it an' give it to…us right on, doc?" Sheriff Kimble asked in a try to get in charge.

"Yes, that's what I mean, Mister Kimble," the doctor confirmed and placed his doctor's case onto the foot side of the bed. He opened it but soon clicked it shut, realizing he hadn't the proper form with him, well knowing the authorities being very particular when it comes to formalities in cases like this. He again fixed his gaze upon the two ill-matched men waiting at bed-side, and stood for a moment as if thinking of whether or not he had missed something, then proceeded, "Come by my office around five, and I'll have your certificate ready, alright?"

The two sheriffs then watched the doctor put on his hat and walk out. Jeff looked about the barren hotel room trying to order his thoughts, asking himself whether it might be possible for him to somehow collate the chunks of information just delivered by the physician, who with measured footfalls and flat slaps of his shoes now was descending the stairs on his way out.

"First thing we oughta do is contact his family," Jeff suggested when they a quarter of an hour later left the hotel where the dead judge still was lying, now stretched out on his back.

"He had none…He was a single," Kimble asserted, sounding as though he was panting for breath, wiping his forehead with the sleeve of his shirt.

"Anyhow, we gotta send a message to his bosses in Cheyenne an' then I go send for Petersen to get 'im removed from that room…By the way, how do you know he had no family?" Jeff couldn't help asking.

"Just know, that's all," Kimble said stubbornly, his eyes set on his wrinkled boots, caked with trail dust.

Jeff relinquished further comments and left for the funeral home, his mind full of unanswered questions. When he was back on the street, he looked up the pinnacle. The painters were not to be seen. Just young boys, actually. By now 'em boys are likely to crank out 'round town what they were watchin' when perched up there in the forenoon, Jeff thought to himself. He recognized them both by sight. To judge by appearances one of them was the half-brother of the stable groom, a kid about twenty, one considered mentally retarded in some way.

VI

Birgit Süsskind and Jeff shared household by the widow of a deceased preacher, where they each rented a room, Jeff's comparatively roomy, Birgit's somewhat more modest. When Jeff entered the kitchen at his daily lunch-break around one o'clock on the same day, he found Birgit sitting there giggling with the landlady who right then was in the middle of some narrative about one of her grandchildren down in Tennessee. On the whole the old lady appeared to have a beneficial impact on the young woman, who no longer looked that glum as she used to. As the two women both were dedicated God-believers, they also had the most important thing of life in common. The food was ready, and now they had taken a break, waiting for Jeff to show, Birgit scrunched up on the round-arm couch, and the old woman in her rocker, her favorite.

"Jeff, you come already?" the old lady chirped, her standard words of welcome. "Well, in that case we just tuck into….hope you hungry!" she twittered satisfactorily and stood up and went back to her cooking. Jeff doubted she was uninformed as to the latest news in town, and Birgit's behavior confirmed his suspicions. Still lingering on the couch, Birgit said addressing him, her head bowed, "That judge…He is found dead, isn't he?"

"Yeah, right," Jeff confessed, brows puckered-up, his eyes settled on her.

"Well, actually we heard about it at the store…in the morning…our daily regime, you know."

"Well…everyone around knows it already, I reckon," Jeff answered, his voice muffled.

After a momentary pause she went on, her head still declined, "He got killed, didn't he?"

"Yeah, I guess so."

Birgit raised her head and looked up at him and responded, her gaze strangely expectant, "In other words…you've got yourself another crime zone, right?"

"I guess we have."

She stared at him for a heartbeat then proceeded, her tone a little taut, "Do you believe this murder has anything in common with the killing of…my folks out there?"

Jeff thought for a short while, then said, "Well, frankly it ain't precluded. There's somethin' odd goin' on." He looked straight at the young woman, who now appeared hagridden, then continued saying, "The tricky thing is to find a motive."

They got interrupted by the landlady who signaled for them to join her in the kitchen.

Satisfied with the fact that the conversation at the lunch table didn't linger that long around the come about hotel killing, but more around the health problems of their landlady, Jeff half an hour later excused himself and hit the dusty and densely populated main street. The Indian summer rolled on, one day alike another, the nights almost as hot as the days, and so it had went on now for fully thirty days. The drought soon would lead to water dearth. The nearest dwells were almost dried-out, and the stable boy was forced to widen his excursions in hunting for water.

At Jeff's visit in the stable a little later the groom was in the process of lugging water pails to the horses. The appearance of the vice sheriff gave him a good occasion for a break, and a possibility to wipe his sweaty face with a soiled bandana. Jeff motioned for him to step forward so he could see his face in full. The groom got erect in the back, and as if unsure of the decision he was at making stood and looked to where Jeff stood. Eventually he put down the pail and began to lumber in Jeff's direction, his left hand squeezing the bandana, his worn grayish Rebel shirt sticking to his muscular back.

"Jeff, huh, are yo' goin' out ridin'?"

Jeff intensively looked back at the hale-looking groomer, seeing him better now.

"I ain't, not right now…Listen Paul…tell me 'bout 'em strangers comin' here recently…three cowboys at the saloon the other day."

The groom squinted, fumbling with the bandana, but since it already was soaking wet, he had to take help from the front of his shirt hence displaying a cobblestone-alike stomach.

"Strangers, eh?" the groom echoed in a high-pitched voice, shifting and frowning at the same time. Jeff gave him some time for reflection, focusing on the gray, battered and peaked-up Rebel cap, a relic from the civil war that was adorning his square bald head. The man was a mulatto, had narrowly escaped from being hanged by a drunk lynching mob down south somewhere.

"Let me think," the groom said looking dismal. He stood silent for a time then continued, "The only ones I can think of right now's three, yeah, three fellas comin' here…Pretty nice horses, tired out, but they left the same day….All I did was feed 'em horses, water 'em and give 'em some curryin'…an' couple of hours later they left town…just paid an' rode on, you know."

Jeff nodded to this then asked prompting, "Can you describe their mugs?"

"Well," he began, scratching his buxom right cheek, "they were all lookin' mean, rednecks you know. No class…yo' understand what I mean, Jeff?"

"I reckon I do. Listen, Paul. If you recollect somethin' further, then you get in touch, right."

He looked at Jeff and said with a smile, "Sure. Whatever you say, Jeff."

After a short time of small talk, they said their farewells and Jeff drifted away. He turned into the street and walked by an assembly of kids, some of which winking at him as he passed. He strolled by the smithy and the barbers' shop, the one he used to frequent. He halted and turned around in mid-step, walked his way back to the windblown door, jerked it open and stood in the door. He was immediately greeted by the busy keeper who stood brandishing a razor. He turned to Jeff by half suggesting, "Half an hour or so, Jeff…" then added cordially, "You sure can need a haircut."

Jeff swung open the door and stood, his gaze sweeping over the faces of the people that sat crouched in there, awaiting their turn. Bill Buchanan, the eternal bachelor, a rancher from out the county sat fronting the mirror, the shaving lather partially removed from his face. Jeff met his reflection in the mirror, and immediately discerned his cheerful smile.

"I heard you just got yourself a battle to fight, O'Halloran," he blurted out as their gazes met.

"I'm lucky not bein' alone," Jeff shot back, taking a step inside. He went on, facing the barber, "Might as well take a seat right now."

"Alright, yo'll have it your way, Jeff."

Two little boys waiting, supervised by their mother, watched Jeff when he joined them. One of the kids after a while in silence focused on Jeff with his nearsighted eyes, spotted the badge on his brown worn leather vest-coat, then asked precociously, "Is it interesting bein' a sheriff, sir?"

Before Jeff had time to respond, the other boy parried, "I'm gonna be a sheriff, too."

The mother, now alerted, glanced shyly in Jeff's direction, hushed the kids and said almost in a whisper, "Excuse us, sir, I'm sorry for their forwardness."

"No problem at all, ma'am."

Out on the street a wagon rolled past in a muffled clop of hooves. At the same moment the door got open again and two old-timers walked inside. Still on feet one of them chuckled toothlessly, looking at Jeff, "Look, who's here, eh." Leaning on his crutch, he moved laboriously toward the semi-circle of waiting customers, stopped dead, chuckled anew, "You have 'im at gunpoint yet, deputy?"

"Whom, Mr. Holden?" Jeff asked back, amused.

"The fella who killed that judge, whom did you have in mind?"

Jeff looked down at his recently rolled cigarette that he twirled back and forth between the fingers of his left hand. He squinted up at the old man, answered, seeing him approach slowly, We'll have 'im someday, Mr. Holden…There ain't no other way to go, I reckon."

With no word in reply the new arrivals took their seats in the small barbershop that now was filled to capacity.

"Many people on foot this afternoon" the other old-timer tried with a toothless grin addressed to Jeff. Jeff nodded acquiescence. He smoked. The two kids next to Jeff inspected them grimacing. They all sat for a short while in a mutual hush until Buchanan raised to his full length, whipped out fifty cents from his jeans pocket and dropped it in the barber's outstretched palm, smiled at him and thanked him. Still thinking he had to move the conversation along, the toothless stopped chewing on his palate and said to the rancher, who now was re-buckling his gun belt around his slender midsection, "You ain't got some rain out there, I reckon, Buchanan?"

"No, but we sure could need some. Right now we have a pretty hard time findin' us some water."

"When do you figure there'll be any?" the old man wanted to know, his mouth wide open, waiting for an answer.

"I have no inkling, I'm afraid…We just have to bide our time, that's all."

"And say our prayers," the other old man added with emphasis.

"Right." Buchanan admitted hesitating, "That we do already."

He reached for his Stetson that hung on the wall, put it on, adjusted it somewhat until it sat centered on his head, then said so long and departed.

A little less than forty-eight hours later the judge was put to rest on the graveyard next to the anonymous hanged saddle tramp. The sacred act was following the same ritual and the mortician and the minister appeared in the same attire as they wore when burying the saddle tramp. The same horse was in action, the mortician being charioteer, and the whole equipage was acting perfunctory when it trundled to stop and then didn't budge one single inch. The air was chilly and sticky at the same time, and the wind turned to west with woodsmoke in it.

The hymn singing was followed by a lengthy and windy ad lib funeral oration containing a great deal of substance and centered around the fragility and shortness of the earthly life of mankind, its weakness and vulnerability on one hand, and a reminder of the inexpressible bliss that the Almighty has in readiness for whoever believing in his beloved Son. The small troop of ten attendants, men all, offered nothing but their best participating with their deep jarring voices in the concluding singing, and after the minister had given his thanks to everybody present, and the coffin was settled at the bottom of the grave, and the ropes were withdrawn, the men put on their hats and the crowd retook its way to the gate, the conversation still kept subdued. With the promise to drop him outside the sheriff's office, Jeff was offered a ride back to town, so he therefore climbed up the hearse, where the jovial mortician sat perched. He raised his black-gloved hand to the pall-bearers, who stood assembled to fill the grave, grabbed the whip from its rack, swung it overhead and gave a low gee up. The stiff-hipped long-eared relic pricked up its ears and with a slight jerk began her retreat along the rutted trail visibly relieved by the fact that the load now was reduced, and a downhill slope was in coming. Jeff looked down at the arched neck of the old mare and easily asked right-out, "How ol's that mount?"

Petersen studied the question for a while before answering, his thin lips pursed.

"Well, I ain't quite sure, but…somewhere between twenty-five an' thirty would be a pretty good guess…from the look of her…Uh, I've had her since I overtook the firm…she was kinda part of fixtures…an' by then she was alleged to be around fifteen…but I think she was older…" Clucking to and giving the old mare a slight slap of the bridles across the razorous hams, he smiling thinly continued, "She is an ol' cantankerous lady…shameless for attention. Every time I harness her, she makes tries to get at my fingers…I've to crochet…placate her with a lump of sugar or two, you see…"

"I see…eh, have yo' ever seen her trot…" Jeff wondered, shifting awkwardly on the cranky box.

"Pardon me…?"

"I said have yo' ever seen the mare trot…?"

"I've never seen her trot, you know, I doubt she's ever done," the mortician confided with a chuckle.

"Well…I reckon she ain't ever had a reason," Jeff returned dryly and looked down at his legs, stretched out before him. The mortician gave a mad laughter in the affirmative, and soon Jeff joined into.

In the half-light of the poorly lit sheriff's office Douglas Kimble sucked the last gulp of the yesterday evening begun bottle of whiskey grimacing with the increasing feeling of being tightly cornered, contemplating the looming re-election. Seay demanded results and the rancher's latest advices still were echoing in his mind. "We're waitin' for action, Kimble! Bring it on! If you get re-elected, you'll be guaranteed retirement pension when the day comes when yo' can't work anymore! Take charge and tackle matters…cooperate more with O'Halloran!"

The raucous voice tormented like a chimera, like a feature in some *quotidien* regime, giving a stalwart substance to the wording *juremur agendo*, you shall be doomed according to your actions, done as well as undone. And here he dwelled, beginning now to question his precarious site, even his entire life, quenching his thirst. But, basically, he was not in fact quenching it. He knew he wasn't. He knew he was using the same way out as his father, who'd left behind him nothing but a half dozen of empty booze bottles, and a greasy pack of cards, five junior kids and a bitter and disregarded worn-out widow. Death became the ultimate way out of the agony, a revolver muzzle down his gorge, and his nocturnal despair immediately got brought to a termination. Now he didn't concede territory at home any longer. His ruthless bitch, his wife, the disgust in the eyes of the kids, it all got more and more obvious to him as time went by and they grew older. All these things didn't maul him now, however, no sir, it was left behind, forever. He didn't have to flinch, no demands now pawed at him. He glared at the closed door, tightened his paw muscles surrounding his flabby face, contemplating the fact that he was in desperate need of a decent alibi so as to appease his assistant, who was likely to appear any time now. Maybe the scant Süsskind file would do, at least for a while, to flip through it, to appear concerned. He was used to it, even skilled at it. He had performed it so many times before. It gave him some satisfaction. The sensation of being pummeled now had subsided somewhat. But for how long?

He abruptly got interrupted in his tedium when someone jerked the door open and his deputy entered, but not only him. His own daughter, Sally, hustled inside right behind, leaving the door wide open. The gloomy place sort of revived for some seconds.

"You're a big smokin' baby…you know that, daddy?"

"Alright, how much money are you askin' for today, sweetheart?" her father wondered, swiveling slightly in his chair.

The teenage girl stepped to the desk where her father sat. She stopped and stood straddle-legged, her little chubby hand ostentatiously outstretched as she tried not to demonstrate too much of her down-bitten nails, but since nothing seemed to happen, she went on explaining, "It's for mum, to buy eggs for, fifty cents…please."

"Yo' headed for the store?" her father asked, ignoring her gaze.

"Yeah, what do you think?" she snapped, appearing annoyed with the interrogation.

Her father produced no answer to that. Still shunning the eyes of his daughter, he sat and tapped the armrests of his chair with the forefingers of his hands, trying not to look guilt-ridden, the girl standing motionless beside him. He considered the matter for a while, then he made his decision. Grimacing and heisting his shoulder up, he fumbled about and from out the right pocket of his jeans retrieved a purse, one that he carried with him continually. He dealt it open, shook forward a coin that he dropped into the girl's raised palm. "Go help yo' mother."

"I sure will," the girl said anxiously, leaning away.

"Tell here I'll be home 'round noon, alright," her father growled, watching her go.

"How was the burial, Jeff?" he asked carefully with a wayward look at his vice sheriff as his daughter had slouched away.

"Coffee?" Jeff asked back without facing his foreman.

"No."

Jeff poured himself coffee, brought the mug with him from the stove and placed it carefully at his desk then started to pace the stale floor. "Frankly I've done a lot of thinkin' recently," he finally explained sort of incidentally.

The sheriff looked up from his file and waited, then said, "Go ahead, I'm listenin'…you think of 'em ambushed people, ain't that right?"

Jeff had come up beside him. He stood and regarded his foreman for a short interval. Sheriff Kimble straightened up a little and rubbed his eyes. Jeff continued, "Yeah…'em ambushed people, and not only them…'em killed people…Why are 'em dead? Why's the judge dead an' buried…an' the young Süsskind kid…why's he mute?"

"Is he still dumb?" Kimble wondered and released a bored yawn, slumping in the swivel.

Ignoring the question, Jeff proceeded, "What did he see…what did he hear out there?…When will he start talk…if ever? Where's that violin at?"

Neither said anything for a long while, neither budged. Kimble sat and stared into the adjoining room where the assets of the dead family were gathered. Jeff's tin stood untouched on his desk. He stepped in front of the doorway of the jail section and stood and looked into. Half turned to his boss and announced, "I see Miss Süsskind every day. I watch her thoughts an' feelins'. We must re-find our stride, sheriff. You see whatta mean?"

"I guess," Kimble half admitted, then with a peremptory gesture went on in mid voice, saying, "But…if I may give you some advice, I'll tell you to slow down a bit…well, Jeff…it wasn't a carnage."

Jeff turned to face his boss in full. "Wasn't it a carnage?!" he almost brawled in return. "What do you call it then?….A bloodletting? For Christ sake, sheriff, wake up! People got killed, ain't that serious enough? Four innocent people ambushed, shot down….Three adults, one kid, plus one kid dumb, shocked! Ain't that serious? Why are we around?" he scowled, facing his superior who seemed cornered. "What options do we have? Take off our shields, saddle up, swing up, leave an' don't look back? Haven't we an obligation to Birgit an' the kid, her brother?" Jeff continued.

"It's easy for yo' to ride off, Jeff," the sheriff said tonelessly, studying the desktop.

"I'm gonna unravel this mess…if so on my own," Jeff replied in mid-voice right out the room.

"We're gonna unravel it together," Kimble after a while replied.

Jeff didn't answer. He stood and looked out through the barred aperture of the sheriff's office just in time to watch Birgit step by. Her stride was firm but also graceful. He looked long after her, lost in thoughts. Maybe that was the reason why he didn't catch Kimble's inquiry when he said, "Do you know how it feels not bein' able to hold your urine?"

VII

With a view across the rolling cow-trodden countryside Jeff in the hard light with a red rise on his face pulled his horse to a halt on the grassy elevation, and looped the bridles onto the saddle. Feeling the weather had turned cool he drew the collar of his brown leather jacket tighter around his neck and made sure the top stud of his shirt was buttoned up. The October wind was raw and the drizzle, a result of an in-moving cold front, made both the rider and the horse shiver with cold. The long lasting drought, the almost annual scourge, had been devastating the country, and only a week ago practically all ditches and waterholes were dried-up, but now they'd started to re-fill day by day, and the hillsides were greening up.

 He slid his right boot backward out of the off stirrup then swung his leg over the pommel of the saddle and pulled off his gloves. He brought forth his makings and thoughtfully rolled him a cigarette. He hunched his shoulders forward and struck a match to the bootheel and sat fuming for a long time, drawing slowly on his cigarette. He turned in the saddle and looked out over the wind scoured changeless country. The skies were partly overcast. A cow took to bawl far off. A watercourse beyond some autumn-colored river trees barely visible in the distance. Low-flying birds. A couple of rabbits some hundred feet or a little further on had found themselves a temporary shelter under the tiny and low shrubbery that was spotting the ridge, low because the incessant winds of east Wyoming and the frigid temperature which hadn't allowed them to grow any higher. With the lit cigarette between his lips, he reached for the scabbard and grabbed the new Winchester by its burnished butt and drew it out in a quick upward motion. He cocked the trigger. He raised the gun and lined his sights on the fattest rabbit. Picking his spot right below the neck, he aimed while guiding his finger on the trigger, then stroked it and fired with the barrel coming up short and sending waves out. The bullet hit under the left eye and tore the head to pieces, and the animal thudded flush to the ground with blood sputtering from it, and after some death throes got to rest in a rapid seeping of life. With ringing eyes he opened the fuming gun's chamber and levered the spent shell out, and levered a fresh into and set it firmly in the breech, then clapped the chamber shut. He let down the hammer with his thumb and with purposefulness jammed the gun back down into the scabbard again.

He lunged and grasped the bloody quarry by its long hind legs, and with it dangling limply from his hand made it back to the tramping stallion that backed off some, shying at his coming. With the fingers of his right hand he started to unlace the straps of the saddle bag, all the while talking smoothly to the horse. Sensing the smoke sting his eyes, he spat out the butt and extinguished it with his heel, then tried a second time and let go the dead rabbit from off his hand and doubled his grip and gave the flap another try, lifted up the lid and stowed his hand deep and reached around inside, searching the compartment for his hunting knife. After sometime he dug up a good-sized hunting knife, wrapped up in newsprint.

Squatting himself on one knee, he carefully traced the knife's edge with his forefinger to examine the edge, then stretched the handsome rodent out lengthwise and went to work on it. It was a good three feet long. Bending the long hind legs sharply back with one hand, and mindful of every cut he with the knife cut the head off and throat up, and then hacked a cut into the throat, then crushed the knife into all the way to the mold and passed it from the open throat and downward along the belly, the knife dulling quickly against the thick fur. He let go of the knife and with both hands pulled and pulled as his horse where it stood right by meanwhile took to urinate a long steaming piss. He quarried and gouged away the bowels with his thumb, and a red slash got heard as the guts seeped forth and ran down the sides, and spilled upon the ground. He let them gush into a steaming and stinking heap underfoot, then convinced himself the animal was properly bled. In the musky smell of the open belly, he when the organs were all out, picked between them, then swished the knife in the grass and wiped it clean with a clean section of paper, then wiped the blood from his hands. With one hand set to the ground for support, he heavily rose and stood and looked about the windswept country. Nothing there was to see that he hadn't seen before, and no other sounds there was to hear than those he'd heard before. He bent down and retrieved the rabbit by the hind legs, and aiming for his own boot tracks with the head of the game dripping dark blood, he retraced to his horse that had swerved to crop a ways off, and slung the lax kill astride the saddle. He replaced the knife down into the saddlebag and tied shut the compartment. He put his left boot into the stirrup and mounted the horse which already was in motion, then sawed it around completing most of a circle He then prompted it forward by pricking its flanks with his spurs as far as the hill's vertex, and when they'd crested the ridge, they topped out through some rocks then went downhill with the horse trotting pole-legged with rasping hooves its way down the draw. So, without kicking up any dust, they descended the elevation, headed for the valley that now was lying fully visible underneath them, savoring meanwhile the landscape that now was resurrected from death and dissolution. Within gunshot a livestock of some hundred head, most of which lowing, froze and ceased ruminating as they carefully watched them walking by at a quick walk.

Once out on the flats he urged on the horse into a short gallop. Ahead of them, a mile distant at the most, the ranch houses now were coming in sight and gaining structure by and by beyond some slender aspens, and he pointed his horse toward it.

A while later he sat in the windy afternoon, fronting the wooden dead-looking main building, slumped in the saddle, resting his arms on the saddle's horn. It was a one-story house of rustic style, prevalent in this region. Looking for any sign of life he sat and studied it some minute or two, listening and casting about. Low-built houses. The only sound audible was the regular breath of his horse and the clang from the headstall when it bridled up. Save a number of corralled horses standing in somnolence right beyond the ranch house, there was no sign of life anywhere in the sabbatical hush. Should he be forced to retreat without having achieved anything, he asked himself. If the worst would be about, he would. He folded both his hands on the saddle and shifted weight, then leaned slightly to the side and spat. The horse stood dead still under him. Cherishing a sensation of being watched ever since he entered the property, he sat and thought, then made his decision and stood down.

No sooner had he got down and stood by the horse than a shot got discharged from somewhere, the jacket movement heard from where the cartridge dropped. He grabbed the horse by the throatlatch and held it still by a steady grip. Chewing the bit, the horse neighed silently and took a step ahead. Calling for caution Jeff held him back. He looked about then reeled around sharply. No one was anywhere to be seen. The shot ought to be hidden somewhere, either in the barn or most likely in the bunkhouse down at what looked to be a vegetable patch. Or perhaps in the thickets of the patch. He had to find out, do something in order to break the stagnation. He looked skyward. A drizzle had started in the late afternoon that soon would be changed into evening. From where he stood now, he could see the door of the bunkhouse stood partway open. He waited. Nothing occurred. Soon he realized he was the one to get in charge. Keeping watch about him he brought the horse with him by the bridles, and walking afoot started for the bunkhouse. He slowly got nearer. When almost outside the door he made a halt and out of sheer cussedness brawled into the silence. "Who are yo' in there? Just step outside yo' damn coward!!"

He listened. Nothing was heard. A cow bellowed among the browsing cattle in the distance. Suddenly a dog barked inside the bunkhouse. It soon got quiet. He ordered his horse to stand still then relinquished his hold on the throatlatch and stood with his hands visible, then with a chuckle inside him shouted to the anonymous character hiding inside, "I'm the deputy sheriff of the county. Either are yo' Buchanan or some of his wranglers! Come out yo' in there whoever yo' are, so we can get acquainted!"

There came no answer.

Tired of waiting he took yet some steps toward the partly open door. For some reason he caught himself thinking on Birgit who yesterday went for Martha's Vineyard, Massachusetts to meet with her brother.

"You in there!…Come on out!…otherwise I walk inside…or gun yo' out if that suits yo' better…yo' hear?!"

There was a long silence then a muted voice responded from within, "Vaya!"

Jeff made it the remaining few steps to the door. Carefully he ducked in and sought the room corners. Kips with bedclothes in disarray. At the foot end of one bunk a vague shape materialized with a rifle in hand, pointing at him.

"What do you think yo're doin'?" Jeff wheezed, "Goin' out huntin' mice?"

The shape shook his head no, his young narrow face pale under the tan. A Mexican vaquero.

"Vaya, senor," he iterated, his eyes full of fear.

Jeff took a brief look around. Things scattered all over the place. He looked at the youngster again. A soiled linen covered his finely barreled torso and the caved abdomen. A pair of blue stained denim, and a pair of unpolished boots made the attire complete.

"Listen...you understand English?" Jeff went on coaxing, the barrel still pointing at him.

"Vaya, senor! Pronto!"

"Look, sonny...I don't wish yo' no harm...eh, *dónde esta' el senor Buchanan...el ranchiero*?" Jeff said, his tone neutral.

The vaquero, seemingly on the verge of a nervous breakdown, in broken English laboriously tried a third time, his voice quavering slightly, "Senor...take...caballo and go away...from hacienda!"

He was sweating profusely, his eyes blank of madness, the black long greasy uncombed hair straggling. On the whole, there was an offensive smell to the place, one Jeff couldn't identify. Where were the other drovers? A big and shaggy yellowish dog, probably the same one that barked minutes ago, rose to its feet, stretched and attended with some hesitation a short walk to the door, paying Jeff no attention. It at once got topped by the sweating vaquero, who started a verbal attack in Spanish. The dog halted, half turned and looking clandestinely at Jeff retook his place under a table scattered with Mexican artifacts. Jeff looked at the vaquero. Facing the risk of getting shot down in cold blood and secretly flung in earth somewhere, Jeff decided to launch an offensive, waiting for things to happen. He doubted the other could keep his face straight so much longer, and besides some other people may show up any time.

"What's wrong with that dog?" he asked in disbelief.

For a short while the vaquero relaxed and lost tension, threw a glance in the dog's direction and right then Jeff bent down slightly, took a run, reached out for and seized the barrel of the Remington, a .25-20, and bent it aside while drawing his own gun with his right free hand. The dog started barking. "Hand me that rod!" Jeff ordered. "I'm not in the mood for this game any longer. You've spun enough time already."

Slowly the vaquero lowered his bony shoulders and obeyed. His black eyes displayed nothing but amazement and desperation as he handed the firearm over. From its bed the dog sat barking without intermission.

"Sit down on the floor!" Jeff went on imperatively, pointing to a space by the dog's bedding, paying the dog no attention.

Clearly troubled by the order, the vaquero squatted, terror on his face.

"Down on your backside an' shuck off yo' boots!"

The vaquero thought for a few seconds, then obeyed, his eyes full of humiliation and hatred.

"Throw 'em this way!...Alright come on, in this direction!"

Reluctantly he grasped the boots by the legs and pulled them off in turn, then threw them toward Jeff.

"You understand English well, eh?...How long have you been in America?"

No answer. The dog fell silent.

Jeff holstered his gun then stood to hold the Remington in booth hands. He half-cocked and opened it and took out the remaining cartridge, eyed it briefly and stuffed it into his coatpocket, then put the gun down on the nearest bunk. The Mexican, still on his butts, glared.

"Alright, muchacho. On your feet...make it slow," Jeff said and stood with his gaze fixed on him. Sometimes there was a girlish touch to the boy's face, he thought, something weak, a poor growth of beard, long eyelashes, a feminine way of moving the long delicate bony arms. All this contributed to his picture, a complex one. He shook were he sat, and his starling black eyes refused to budge as though he was afraid of being licked. Without one more word Jeff drew his gun, cocked it and aimed at him, "On yo' feet!" he ordered.

Using his long arms as fulcrums, the other one within seconds stood without moving a twitch. Jeff holstered his gun, then rapidly moved closer to him and resolutely hit him with his right fist in solar plexus. The massive blow made the thin torso bend forward and the arms helplessly hanging down. Jeff placed two very hard licks under his right eye that made him slam to the floor right beside the dog's ratty bedding. The quick fight vexed the dog that now was on its feet, watching Jeff with evil eyes snarling with raised hackles inimical, the yellow fangs ready like it were taking a mind to tuck into the intruder's left forearm. Jeff instinctively discharged a kick that landed under the coarse cheek of the beast. The dog, shocked and surprised, started to whimper, showing symptoms of dyspnea, then collapsed next to the almost unconscious vaquero, who lay sprawling in his sockfeet astride the bedding. When hovering about for a while, massaging his scarred knuckle, Jeff detected something, and he froze in mid-step. He got sight of a violin, one sitting semi-protuberant from a duffel bag, slung under one bunk. He went there and bent down and caught hold of it. With arched eyebrows he looked into. He brought up the instrument and straightened up and stood and held it in his both hands.

A dark brown smooth violin, surely very ancient, he thought, perhaps ancestral. How had it ended up here in this hovel in the wilds of Wyoming? He looked across at the dog that still lay down whimpering, catching its breath, still shocked by the lashing. What else did the bag hold? He put the violin down on the nearest bunk and once again snuggled down. Holding it in both hands, pulling it apart, he emptied the bag in one single move and studied the findings. No weapons nor armor. A pair of round golden frameless glasses. A set of keys in various dimensions. A Bible. A bow. Another violin, one bigger and more new-looking than the other. He sat down thinking. Diddled stuff hoarded there? He continued his investigation. A billfold, yet another bow, and finally a cushion…huh…two cushions. He looked at the objects in amazement. In raising his gaze somewhat, he caught sight of something sticking out right underneath the cot where he sat. It was a guitar. He reached down and pulled it to him and clutched it and took it up by the neck. He brushed away some dust from it, and holding it in his both hands he inspected it closely from this angle and that. Scrollwork. A flamenco guitar of a kind seldom seen so far up north. Broodingly he deposited it back to where he'd taken it.

On the floor the vaquero and the dog were snuggling against one another, the vaquero still oblivious, a puerile look on his face, the dog puffy with no sign of pugnacity whatsoever. Holding a violin bow in his hand Jeff got up and stood and meditated, concerned about the suffering dog underfoot. The whimpering appeared to increase like every breath was an agony. He now had got the impression that maybe some vital structures in its throat were seriously hurt, and if so, there would be no improvement. Puzzled he looked down at the beast for a short time. The dog looked back and away and with awareness of being subject to surveillance it with rasping breath shamelessly looked back at Jeff once again, baring its teeth with the long threatening canines amber of color, signaling, "Don't get closer, you son of a bitch." Seeing no other option, Jeff, as with a will other than his own, drew his gun out of the holster, drew a bead on it and let off, then stood to look down another time. Behind the dispersing gunpowder smoke he noticed that the prostrated vaquero tried to establish eye contact.

Save some ten-dollar bills the dark brown billfold didn't contain anything. No name, no notice or so. It appeared to be relatively new. Hence it didn't offer any clue as to the possessor. Looking from the vaquero to the dead dog where it lay on its side in its running blood, and to the vaquero again Jeff said with an edge to it, "Alright, on your feet. Get your boots!"

With a slack expression on his face the vaquero with some effort very slow composed his feet and started to rise, complaining about a feeling of sickness.

"Take the dog outside so we can bury it quickly!" Jeff demanded. "Where can we find a spade?"

The vaquero, now risen to full length, nodded toward the barn.

"Alright…move it!"

In tandem they left the bunkhouse and stalked outside, the vaquero dragging the dead dog by its hindlegs, Jeff ambling last in the procession, carrying in his hand the bag with the two violins and the two bows.

Not many words got swapped between the two men during the ride where they hurrying against the rain sat doubled on the back of the heavily barreled stallion, Jeff situated in the saddle, holding the bag with the appropriated violins and the bows and some of the other findings in it. Right before him the dead rabbit lay slung across the saddle, and behind him the Mexican sat handcuffed. The rain had petered out altogether, but the sky was still overcast.

Right shortly of nightfall Jeff halted the horse right outside the sheriff's office, dismounted and beckoned for the vaquero to do the same as he tied the reins loosely to the rail. The gas lamps were on, and piano music was reverberating joyously from the saloon. The night was chilly and cloudy, no stars out and practically no wind, the air humid and raw. The office was lit, the door unbolted, so Jeff pushed his companion inside. Larry Rogers, the arrest guard, was on duty, which meant trouble of some sort, perhaps a drunken brawl, perhaps something worse. He was a feisty ex-sergeant in the cavalry, checking on some inebriate cow drivers and a nigger in a cell next to.

"Where'd you find 'im?" Rogers demanded, resuming his seat behind the desk, nodding at Jeff's subdued cohort, rising and hiking his shirt around his waist. "In some pigsty, eh?"

"The place sure was a bit disarrayed," Jeff returned shortly.

Some minutes later the captive got searched and put in a cell next to the mavericks. He was offered some food and drink and got piled under some blankets, claiming to be chilled. A forlorn appearance, grimacing intermittently as though he were racked with pain. Jeff and Rogers then produced a list of the contents of the duffel bag, and signed it both of them.

"He's suspected for a felony, eh?" Rogers said.

"Right," Jeff said, heading for the outdoor. "We'll ask 'im some questions in the mornin'...You remember that coach hold-up some months back out at Rattlesnake Canyon... four people killed?"

"Sure do, Jeff. Pictures on bulletin boards an' so...You believe he's involved?"

"Maybe so...Or he knows people who are. We gotta crank it up."

"Fine, Jeff...I remain here overnight. See you in the mornin'...Good night."

Jeff returned his wish and got out. Music and men's voices were heard from the saloon, and far out in the distance a fox barked.

When back home, sleep was not to be thought of. Let aside the fact he was mauled, he felt alert, as if bang on course. Four people dead, beginning with the holdup. A couple of days afterward the hanging of the drifter, and yet some week later the judge is found suffocated in a hotel-room late in the morning, the cause of death asphyxiation, caused by a cushion or a pillow. No signs of struggle, no blood, no bruises. At the time of the medical examination rigor mortis was on decrease. Upon examining rectum, the physician had stated the fact an evacuation had taken place, as was his bladder relieved. Seated on the sagging edge of his bed he took a last deep pull at his cigarette, stubbed it out and yanked off his boots. He blew out the lamp and stretched out his body on the bed, his eyes wide open in the darkness. The deaths of these people had taken place on various occasions. Where they accidental, or was there some connection between them? Elementary questions when it comes to assassinations of such a magnitude. As for the drifter hanged, did he carry about anything of value? We can't answer either yes or no, because we simply don't know. All he left behind was his filthy worn garments, his coarse and filthy flannel shirt, though in pretty good shape, some tobacco, a minor sum in cash. Neither billfold, saddle nor horse. Motive unknown. The doctor's family on the other hand, was partially subject to "murder with robbery." According to Birgit, her parents were "stone-broke." Both parents were great music lovers, performing musicians far above amateurish, both educated at diverse academies overseas, England and Italy in their early years, as had they been pushing their three talented children in the same direction. Birgit attended classes in violin and singing in Munich at the time of the death of her parents who had ploughed down every cent of their earnings into the education of their kids, wishing the very best for them. When it comes to the judge he got choked when asleep. No blows exchanged, no altercation. Nothing from outside appeared to have preceded death. The billfold was intact. Nonetheless the body showed significant signs of a drawn-out death struggle according to the doctor's exhaustive account of facts, where also the protruded eyeballs of the victim were mentioned. Jeff felt that a meeting with Birgit's brother might be worthwhile. He decided to send her a wire message first thing in the morning ensuing, saying to come over with him. Sometime before morning he at last drifted into a dreamless daze.

Shortly after sunup the cell doors cranked open and the captives stepped out in a scuff of bootheels. One of the mavericks, a twenty-year-old big-framed and stiff-necked character, a head taller than his two compeers, named Ron Clift, moved aside and began an aggressive palaver where he violently disagreed with the alleged alcohol intoxication. He claimed to have been as sober as Sheriff Kimble at the moment of being arrested. After having collected his few belongings and comforted by Kimble, he resumed his way out, not showing signs of being the least responsive.

"Coffee?" Kimble asked in a hoarse voice, kettle in hand.

Jeff nodded affirmatively.

"Listen Jeff," Kimble said, rubbing his three days' worth of stubble. "Larry just tol' me 'bout the buck in there," he jerked out condescendingly.

Jeff waited for his foreman to go on, but he stayed focused on stirring his coffee.

"Yeah…I brought 'im here, alright," Jeff countered, waiting for the other one to proceed.

Kimble sighed and asked, "On what grounds?"

Jeff said, "I want 'im questioned by way of information…all that stuff." He took him a sip of coffee, then went on, "You see I stumbled across him in the lodgings out at Buchanan's…an' that's where the guy lives…claims he works for Buchanan."

Sheriff Kimble sat quietly for a moment, his right hand cuddling the refilled tin mug, then he said, "Alright…What did…Buchanan say?"

"He didn't say anything. He wasn't around."

"Nobody else around?" Kimble asked contemplatively.

"None but the buck."

"Funny."

"Why's that so funny?...Let's say 'em others were out on the pasture somewhere. They left the buck home to take care of things...Not much of a watchdog though."

There became an instant lull as the sheriff took to pack his pipe with long stringy shag. He gave an atishoo and lit the pipe up and puffed until he got it going, took it from out his mouth, jutted his chin at Jeff and said, "Actually thinkin' of Wayne Seay, you know. Met him at the saloon yesterday night. Do yo' wanna hear what he said?"

"Frankly, I don't care."

"Well...I got the impression I'm still a prospect at the reelection, next year," Kimble continued with a smug.

"I got another impression some days back," Jeff snipped off. "What do you suggest we do with 'im in there, the captive? Set 'im free...is that what you suggest?"

No sooner had Jeff finished his sentence, than the door flung open and Betty, one of Kimble's kids, an opulent hare-lipped girl, stumbled inside dressed in the same frayed blouse as always, leaving the door open behind her. After a couple of purposeful paces toward her father, she at once stopped and burst out, ignoring Jeff, "Mum said she wanna see you. Said it's urgent!" Her eyes downright glittered.

Without insisting on further details, her father just promised to humor her straight away.

"At last Paul got that vixen sold," Kimble said matter-of-factly when his daughter had withdrawn and slammed the door shut.

"You mean the judge's mare?"

"Yeah...heard it yesterday. Some homesteader just outside town bought her."

"Did Wayne Seay mention the judge when you talked with 'im recently at the saloon?" Jeff asked.

"You mean yesterday?"

"Yeah?"

"Well, Wayne thinks he killed 'imself...That's what he said."

"Suicide?"

"Yeah...somethin' like that...That's what he tol' me."

"So it was just a fool-around, eh?" Jeff tried, scanning his foreman's face.

The sheriff studied the inquiry for a short while then said, "I got the impression he was serious."

"Suicide, eh," Jeff mumbled, his voice barely audible. "That Seay always has a sad attitude about matters," he said, then continued, "That wasn't neither my nor your impression when we watched 'im lyin' in that hotel room, dead, right? An' furthermore, it ain't what the doc thinks either…Can a man be able to strangle himself? What do you say?"

"I doubt that," the sheriff replied, though not sounding quite convinced.

"Now…supposing that he had plans to kill himself…why?…For what reason, and why here?" Jeff said.

Weighing his words carefully Kimble sat silent for a while, then he looked at Jeff and jerked out, "Don't you know he was crippled?"

"Would that be a reason to kill oneself? Is that what you are sayin'?"

"Well…it's one reason…'mong others, I reckon."

"What 'bout 'em other reasons?…Tell me 'bout 'em…" Jeff demanded, looking fixedly at his superior, who stood and held his pipe in a steadfast grip, adjusting meanwhile his swivel at the back as if he were in the act of subsiding, then muttered, "Well…he was beyond schedule."

Jeff took place at the edge of his desk and half turned to the sheriff while unlatching his gun belt. "He ain't alone" he replied casually without a wincing.

"Yeah, I know, but he was passed over for a promotion. Hit 'im hard."

Jeff got to his feet and began to pace the floor, stopped and stood and studied his boss anew while Sheriff Kimble stiff-hipped subsided in his creaking swivel then reached out for his mug with the lukewarm coffee in it and took himself a good swig. Jeff eyed him briefly then looked away and said, "Hit 'im hard, you said, eh…What do you know 'bout that, sheriff? The judge wasn't that kinda' man that exposes 'imself…He was a mule…in my opinion. You sure didn't know 'im better than I did."

"Maybe I did."

"Well, does all this mean we drop the matter, just forget 'bout it?…Is that what Seay says?"

"He didn't say that, Jeff."

"Well, I ain't droppin' it…You know why I ain't?"

Kimble thumbed open a box with pipe tobacco and looked at it forlornly as if he didn't know what to answer. He formed his lips to say something, but withdrew before saying it. He tried again, saying, "'Cause he got killed, eh?"

"Who got killed?"

"The judge, he got killed, eh?"

"Yeah...a real good reason, ain't it...?"

"I reckon. Look Jeff, I head home for a short while. You heard the girl."

"I heard her, alright."

The sheriff bounced forward and composed his feet one beside the other to stand. Jeff walked to his scarred desk and reached across it. He seized the ashtray and slid it toward where he half stood and finally situated himself. Deep in thought he brought forth his makings and rolled himself a smoke, and when he was finished he took a long pull and sat and stared right in front of him. He felt awfully tired – and alone. As for Kimble, was he still a nominee for the sheriff's office in June next year? If the answer was yes, then why? Because of fondness for the office? Jeff hadn't asked him. Probably the man would have laughed it off. Would he face a painful decline instead? Questions, but questions too hard to just shrug off.

For obvious reasons the catching hold of the young vaquero got things unsettled and got subject to a magnitude of inquiries, none of whom being solvable, though, prima facie. For one thing he craved surveillance for twenty-four hours a day. From the moment he alighted from the horseback outside the jail the previous night, a sensation of alienation had taken its toll on him, and made him feel maudlin for one moment, and roused to a frenzy in the next. One moment he sat on his bunk with his head bowed and eyes shut, praying for strength, the next moment he just brawled out oaths. There had been suggestions on letting the doctor supervise him for a day or two to make him catch up with the daily routines and the uncertainty that lay ahead. For obvious reasons his lack of knowledge at English appeared to be another aggravating circumstance. As far as both sheriffs knew, no one in the closest proximity was Spanish spoken. Nor was anybody around to post him bail for sixty dollars. The district prosecutor didn't accept less. As for the vaquero's knowledge at English, Jeff had a serious suspicion the man was faking for some reason. When asked about his name, he on one moment claimed it to be Felipe, on the next Rodrigo. His surname he didn't submit, pretending he didn't understand the question. Kimble had made a suggestion they should contact Buchanan, his employer, but Jeff dissuaded with all the force he could obtain. Why wake up a sleeping dog, he reasoned, and Kimble had nodded in agreement. You may have a point there. We'd better wait till he contacts us, was the sheriff's suggestion yesterday. He sure will, he added.

Why haven't he already? After four days? Wouldn't that be the most logical? Jeff had asked.

The sheriff agreed cautiously.

"Then why hasn't he already?" Jeff had demanded, looking straight into Kimble's liquid eyes.

"He hides somethin'," Kimble grunted back.

"It sure looks that way…an' it's our business findin' out what," Jeff said.

The sheriff was hung-over and didn't say much, his face disclosing nothing, his heavyset body sloping in the squeaking wooden swivel chair. With an accusing eye at his deputy he from his left breast pocket rooted out a creased packet of tobacco and began circumstantially to fill his snoring meerschaum.

At the same time a small gathering of three persons was assembled in a heavily furnished Boston apartment. The youngest of them, a pale ash blond youth, Birgit Süsskind's junior brother Wolfgang, sat in a German mahogany rocker with a bottle of lemonade in his left semi-transparent hand. There was an air of listlessness about his entire person. At times he vehemently sat the chair in motion by bracing his back against the backrest, and then waited until the chair went to a stop, then repeatedly went through the entire process in a never-ending succession, back and forth, sometimes slowly, sometimes fast. The contents of the bottle were still untouched, he hadn't asked for it. He no longer did ask for anything. A psychiatrist, Doctor Stanford Williams, standing next to him, deemed his motions to be erratic and unpredictable. Mood swings occurred on a daily basis, and he was likely to strike out in anger or hostility as a defense against being hurt. He in other words did embody the picture of a disharmonic youngster, resentful and distrustful, and a lithium treatment was suggested by the doctor. It was obvious, however, according to the doctor, that the patient had an explicit sense of being the center of the others interest.

"How are you doing today, Wolfgang?" the doctor asked routinely when flipping through the case book in search for a proper page for his notations. On a massive writing table by the gigantic window an ink bottle and a quill rested, shortly ready to be used. Doctor Williams was very particular about his notes, every utterance, every comment from the capricious patient, carefully got scribbled down by the ambitious psychiatrist.

There was no immediate answer, so the doctor for a second moved his eyes from the pad and repeated his inquiry, the tone now more demanding. The patient felt the tension, aware of the fact that everybody around was watching him anticipatory.

"Stop rocking that chair for a second and answer my question!" the doctor demanded, looking straight at the boy. "Tell us how you are feeling, please!"

"Alright, I suppose," he said shortly, sitting unmoving, his voice disclosing nothing in particular, his tone totally neutral, impersonal.

"You slept well last night, didn't you, Wolfgang?"

"I suppose," he echoed, again picking up with his rocking, now more intensely.

Addressing Birgit, the doctor went forward by disclosing that her brother normally sleeps profoundly and well most of the nights, saying also that the night staff had problems waking him up in the morning every once in a while, probably in consequence of heavy medication. Birgit, now stationed behind the rocker, had finally managed to make her brother stop the rocking by grabbing hold of its back and force the chair to stop, summoning all her forces in the process. She looked weird through lack of sleep. Never had she anticipated to see her junior brother in such a miserable condition, almost beyond contacts. From her elevated position she looked down at Wolf's head top and tousled his hair gently. Scarcely had he started to than he withdrew.

"I don't believe what I see, doctor," she said in disbelief, giving the psychiatrist an aghast look.

"You have to consider what your brother has gone through, Miss Süsskind."

"But here back in our home! My brother! He's acting as if he comes here for the first time…Nothing seems familiar to him…Does he even remember being here before?"

"Just go ahead ask him, Miss Süsskind…I see no reason why you shouldn't."

"Wolf," Birgit tried gently, "can you tell us where we are now…Wolf, come on, tell us."

"Of course I can. We're at home…We're at home in our Boston residence!"

He looked up at his sister vigorously and iterated louder, "We're at home!! Do you think I am an idiot?"

Birgit parried, "Alright…that's what I wanted you to say, Wolf."

"You think I'm crazy…don't you?" he wondered fervently, looking burdened.

With a placated eye at the doctor, she directly shot back, "Don't talk like that little brother, nobody thinks you are crazy…"

She looked at the psychiatrist with a relieved smile. The atmosphere was now somewhat softened. Doctor Williams forestalled her and broke in saying that the time was come that they confronted her brother with all the horrendous things he recently had experienced, by focusing specifically on the gruesome killing of their parents and little sister. As the doctor put it: "We have to give Wolfgang access to his past so that he will be able to work himself through it mentally over and over….In other words, make him relive the miserable occasions and process them."

Looking at the doctor Birgit inquired, "What about medications? Haven't you put him on tranquilizers?"

"Yes, but beginning this week, I'll try to take them out and replace them with lithium in order to stabilize his mood. Neither likes these mood swings, Wolfgang doesn't either. And by the way, Miss Süsskind," the doctor went on, "Your brother will be in need of much attention and love in the coming future, and you are the one, who best can provide all that. I appreciate your being here for your brother's sake, you know. Best thing is you live together in your home…I'll come daily to support. Of course you are free to go outdoors. It would be beneficial to both of you, if you spend much time outside this residence, so that Wolfgang gets an opportunity to confront with other people as well. According to my experience, your brother has improved significantly since he came here. Maybe you don't see it, but I do. I have been watching him now for quite some time, so I see the difference."

"Didn't he like Martha's Vineyard?" Birgit wondered with a frown.

"I believe he did, but he likes it better here."

"You sound optimistic, doctor?"

"Well, all patients are different," the doctor said when approaching the backlogged desk, "And I'm not promising anything, Miss Süsskind, remember me saying that…I deem the case inconclusive, you understand. Your brother is dependent on those around him, and that's the way things are going to be…For how long…I don't know."

"A year maybe?" Birgit asked innocently.

"Maybe a year, maybe two...nobody knows," the doctor replied and shrugged. He searched in his doctor's case with efficient hands and came up with a cannula and a test tube and a vial with disinfectant, then started toward Wolf and told him to roll up his shirtsleeve. There was a blood test that should be taken. Doctor William's way of acting had the obvious makings of those of a man of deep concern, Birgit felt when watching him approach the rocking-chair with his forehead in a frown over bushy eyebrows.

A chilly easterly wind swept over the half-filled streets in the late foggy morning. The trade was already in full swing, the traffic heavy. The well-dressed gentleman anew raised his gloved left hand, a stick in the other and two pairs of eyes for a second met in agreement. A vacant cab, at last, after more than ten minutes wait.

The driver pulled the bridles and helloed the bony roan and all of a sudden the equipage was standing by the curb. The driver gave a nod in consent when receiving the short order from the pale chubby passenger in traditional city outfit. He acknowledged the sort, and quite frankly he had nothing but despise left for them, that is on certain days, and this day was one of them. Snobbish dandies, alcoholics and insane idiots, poor bastards that's what they were, the whole bunch, acting as superiors, but he sure had them unmasked, not just once but many times. The one now installed in the resilient coach is a twenty-five-year-old ship-broker, a Boston resident, feeling inept and deeply irritated. He cursed the coach drivers of Boston, every single one of them. Why couldn't they stop before they set the vehicle in motion and regained speed? What if his topper had blown off his head when climbing aboard? He snatched off his top hat and placed it on his right knee and put the can across his stout thighs and yawned loudly. Recently he had been keeping late hours at the office where he sat poring over endless bundles day in and day out. You look exhausted, Birgit had remarked when seeing him the other night. Well, he admitted to be exhausted, but is that the only reason why she had asked him to come, he had retorted. Why didn't she instead get down to the nitty-gritty? To tell the truth, he was tired of always having to comply with her whims, tired of being a chaperon. Who knows what is happening there out west. Maybe she has nicely adjusted to the life as a dependent lodger out there? Despite she zealously disclaimed cherishing plans to stay. Maybe some illiterate gunslinger is awaiting in the wings. Evidently her intention is to go back there. What would happen if he would stop escorting her to those everlasting concertos with the

Boston Symphonic? It's grotesque, the whole situation is nothing but absurd. She ventures her entire future if she goes back west. I'm forced to act in some way, he mumbled to himself. I'm going to make things hum, he decided grimly where he sat listening to the cage trundling its way over the cobbles of downtown Boston.

VIII

Before extinguishing the camp fire, the two riders each lit his torch with a burning twig and quickly with detonations of dry wood giving way under their feet searched through the broken camping site, making sure nothing was left behind among the mushy tracks of wild pigs and cattle on the level prairie. The chilly night was overcast, no moon, no stars to lit it up, the air damp in the morning silence. Feeling the tension in the air, the three horses already stood saddled, snorting and stamping with zest to get started, their breaths pluming whitely before their mouths. "Why didn't he chose a moonlight night instead?" a light voice asked at a certain point.

"Hush!…Speak low! We've gone it all through! Don't talk so much…I reckon this night's as good as any…Just remember: Keep your mouth shut… Don't talk! You know what to do, right…?"

"I guess," the light voice responded, now quieter.

"Alright…no talkin'…no names, remember…?"

"Yeah, I know."

He looked long at the shape of his peer and shook his head in disbelief, emptied the grounds on the ashes and waddled his tin can in the saddlebag, then tied it shut and extinguished his torch and flung it into the ashes, and ordered his companion to do the same. He leaned and spat into the fading embers, then mounted by the reins, trotting in tandem with and behind his fidgety mare, a muscular palomino with the stirrups flapping loosely down her sides. With a firm hold about the saddle's horn he executed a quick-foot dance and fit a foot into the stirrup and swung himself up into the saddle, his companion coming up by his flank, hastily gaining momentum, and out of the grove they rode shoulder at a rapid trot.

"I hanker for a beer…" the light-voiced said, slowing down, helping himself to a chew of tobacco.

"Keep you' mouth shut…We've a job to do first, no more babblin'…Within half an hour we'll be in the thick of things." He spat and grinned, then continued, "Sun raises in an hour or so. Any questions before we ride in…street straight ahead, eh?"

The other one just shook his head no.

"Alright…Let's tuck into it!"

After a moment the light-voiced glared sidelong at his boss and finally managed, "When do we light 'em torches?"

The boss glared back at the shade beside him and pulled in his horse considerably, wheezed, his bushy brows arched in stupefaction, "Right before we step inside…Our man's said to be there."

"You…care if I say somethin'?"

"Go ahead…say it."

"You promise we'll stop by for a couple of beers some place after work's done?" the light voice wondered yearning.

"We'll see later."

"Put fire on yo' torch before I kick yo' ass," the boss growled and spat, sensing mouth and tongue being bone-dry. He dismounted and stood and waited, the bridle reins clinging when the horses stood tossing their heads in terror, watching the torch in flames within short. He handed over the bridles to his companion who forthwith reached under the jaws of the horses and gripped them with his both hands and held them in a stalwart hold. He then went some lithe steps upstairs, tried the door to find it unbolted. A dog started yelping aggressively somewhere in the vicinity. Another joined up.

"Now we have to act quick before whole town's in their longjohns," the horse guard mumbled between clenched jaws, watching the palomino commence to rear. "Easy girl, easy…" he prattled, beginning to feel the pangs, pulling the reins home hand over hand then taking a firm hold with the fingers of his left hand claw-like about the cheek strap, marshaling all his strength behind. In the ensuing moment he heard a gun being discharged from within the sheriff's office, once and then twice in rapid succession. Seconds later he heard the wrought-iron gate flung open and the captive emerging from his lock-up, his liberator trailing awkwardly in his scuffed riding boots.

"Throw away that torch!…Let's get the hell out a' here!!"

The palomino mare, now intimidated by the shelling and the general melee, went on bucking and scuffling as the sun meanwhile rose in the east. The horse guard dallied with the reins, not too much effect, though. The horse spread-eagled twisted and bucked itself into a clear space as the captive snatched the reins out of his keep and swung himself up onto the saddle and put the horse forward at a gallop, his liberator pursuing horseback, kicking the horse's flanks. A brief moment later all three riders were sitting in the saddles and were rushing out of town in a frenzied agreement.

At a nearby junction the posse pulled up and halted the horses. Looking inept, leaned in the saddle, aware as he was of the looming election, Sheriff Kimble directed the men to dismount and water the horses at the all but dried-out watercourse, and give the posse men a chance to rest themselves. Pensively, he regarded the tired animal's approach and carefully lower their muzzles, one then the other and drink with loud sucking noises. "They got a right to rest after they worked hard all mornin'!" he explained and looked up the sky, seeing the clouds were moving in to rain. Jeff squatted and sat whit his chin In his hands and looked at his horse that stood nibbling some grass from the sparse growth by the creekside. He rolled a smoke and cupped his hand and lit it. He got to his feet and approached his boss who just had dismounted. On his way he got stopped by Paul, a colossus of a man, the groom and part-owner of the livery stable, who looked straight at him and snorted while jutting his chin in the general direction of Kimble. "Does he think we're gonna mope through all day on empty stomach?"

"Go ahead…ask 'im," Jeff suggested listlessly.

"If I do, you side with 'im, Jeff…I bet you do," the giant chuckled.

"Alright, go ahead build a fire so we can get us somethin' to eat," Jeff directed and looked around. A gaudy rally, having sworn the oath in a hurry, unaccustomed to hard riding, the majority already manifesting symptoms of overstrain.

"How long lead do you figure 'em have?" Paul said with address to Jeff.

"Four hours…perhaps five, headed upstate," Jeff answered, his gaze set to the ground underfoot, recently trodden by hoofed creatures.

"Are we reducin' it?" the other demanded energetically, chewing at a blade of grass, studying him with concern.

"Yeah," Jeff replied gaily, "We're reducin' on 'em even on foot, I reckon."

He finished his cigarette and flipped it and trod it out with his heel on the dry ground. The wind blew and set the little grass there was to blow. He watched his boss standing sucking his sour and snoring short-stemmed pipe, his eyes looking forlornly toward the hillsides in the distance. It was quiet for a long time. Finally he turned to Jeff and said in an effort to re-catch the situation, "Alright, we unleash 'em horses for an hour an' get ourselves some grub."

Jeff arched his brows in surprise, said it sounded alright to him.

It turned out to be a troublesome job lighting the fire. Some willow twigs, far from dry, no hardwood, was all that came handy until they finally could watch the sparks climbing up. Eggs, beans, buns and coffee disappeared quickly and the atmosphere around the camp soon improved. Seven men around a fire in a locus of a pastoral idyll away from the haunted civilization. A blurred feeling of ambivalence arouse in Jeff's mind, sort of melancholy. He'd liked it much being outdoors all his life, and he did not miss that office. He thought of a dwelling somewhere else, a ranch, a woman, a couple of kids, something to live for.

They watched the fire where it sawed about, and they spoke among each other, and when they had finished eating, Kimble suddenly rose to his feet, took Jeff aside, disconsolately asking, "Do you really figure the judge smothered?"

"Yeah…?"

The sheriff shook his head no.

A dozen or so crows were convened in an old oak tree nearby where the horses waited, swishing their tails.

"This grub sure tasted better than the usual mush you live on marshal," the stable giant bawled when bridling his groomed sorrel.

"You mean me?" Jeff shot back.

"No 'im," he answered nodding at Kimble, who didn't seem to have heard him. A hang-around who had overheard the altercation, grinned and spat and adjusted his bandana around his birdlike neck, then awkwardly moved his horse forward.

"Upcountry…'Em are headin' upcountry." Sheriff Kimble announced in surprise while looking down at the partially blown-away prints underfoot where the ground sloped abruptly. "How ol' are you figurin' 'em to be?" he continued addressing his vice sheriff.

"Five hours…six maybe…perhaps more, perhaps less…Those prints are round at the edges. We're not reducin' on 'em, that I can say for sure," Jeff answered and squatted next to the prints.

"What if 'em are lyin' in ambush somewhere up in 'em mountains…?" Kimble said.

"Then the game might be over an' it's all for nothin'," Jeff replied dryly.

Looking as if he wasn't happy with the answer, the sheriff squinted northward, then looked at Jeff again and asked, "Why are 'em headin' upcountry, yo' figure?"

"Why shouldn't they?" Jeff countered and slowly stood. He thumbed back his hat at the brim, then went on, "They wanna get out of the country. Mexico's too far off, so they pick Canada…In two, three week's ride 'em oughta be there…But there's some funny thing goin' on…I figure 'em guys are split."

The sheriff looked off toward the north where the mountains stood skylighted in a mist. He took off his hat and clawed his fingers through his light greasy hair and said, "So you mean they ain't no longer travellin'… together?"

"One has left, that's what I believe."

"But there are prints all over" Kimble objected. "How can you be so sure, Jeff…I mean, just look around," he went on and pointed at some other prints about the same age.

"I see 'em alright, an' I've seen 'em long enough to say 'em ain't belongin' to our men. These horses ain't shod."

"But it ain't quite light."

"Indian horses," Jeff elucidated, ignoring the objections of his foreman, "Two or three Arapahoe out reconnoitrin'…We've entered Indian territory…They know we're around, alright."

"You mean they are watchin' us?"

"Yeah, scouts…their chief's sent 'em out."

"You figure 'em have seen the men ahead of us?" Kimble went on his inquiring.

"You bet."

"Listen, Jeff," the sheriff continued, his voice now lower, "I've been thinkin' on one thing. Maybe we both shouldn't be away from town much longer."

Without answering Jeff rounded his horse and mounted up onto the saddle, picked up the reins and with some caution booted the horse forward, saying, "There are back-ups, ain't there, sheriff?"

"Yeah, you're right, but you know things haven't gone our way, eh."

There came laughter from the grouped men where they stood out of earshot by the horses. Jeff demanded with a nod in their direction, "What about 'em? Hopefully you bring 'em with you when you head back."

Kimble spat, looking uptight, keen on veiling it though, asked, "Does that mean you move on by yo'self?"

"It seems to me I have no choice…But look…I gotta move on…I can't afford to spend more time here, alright," Jeff replied.

"So yo' ain't even askin' 'em boys?" Kimble wondered faintly.

"No way, I ain't."

Another laughter erupted from the group. The colossus now was sitting on a rotted and twisted windfall tree trunk. He said something of "full meals." The rest Jeff wasn't able to grasp.

"Alright Jeff." Sheriff Kimble said sharply, now fully realizing that his deputy was unyielding then ordered the men to prepare themselves for retreat. The colossus, unwieldy on his feet, started rambling, then cried out his frustration, "I wish 'em redskins will scalp you, Jeff…I sure do…an' I'm serious 'bout it. Yo' know, I ain't a man to shirk duty, Jeff. I could go with yo', just me, eh," he suggested loudly with a thick forefinger pointing at his voluminous thorax. "Just me, eh?"

"It's lookin' like yo're goin' back home, big boy," Jeff said gravely and went on, "Before you leave I want to have your grubstake, eh, the stuff you can manage without…hope I ain't askin' too much."

"Uh, not at all. It's alright with me, I guess."

It was by forenoon of the fourth day. Picking with slake reins gingerly its way at a slow jog, the black stallion trudged up the elongated slope inch by inch in the twilight underneath the faultless skies that were giving the prospect of yet another beautiful and sunny day on this high altitude.

Suddenly the horse stopped abruptly and stood with ears clipping, showing the whites of its eyes. He snickered nervously and stood without budging. Nothing there was to see or hear but for a billow of thick smoke under the skyline far off to the north. Very soon Jeff heard a sound, the hissing unmistakable wheeze of a rattlesnake, and he watched it approaching its prey coiled into an ace, ready to deliver the lethal bit. On the spur of the moment, well knowing the shot might perhaps unveil him, he boosted himself up in the saddle then felt for and closed his gloved hand upon the hilt of his Colt and drew it, angled his arm out and took sight. Aiming low, he discharged and hit the snake in the head. One shot ringing out echoless. From where he sat in his saddle with the fuming gun in his hand, he watched the snake dying in a twist and immediately get still. The horse got livid and snorting started dancing. Seconds later it slackened off and stood glaring. Jeff took up his field glasses from where they hung down from his neck and glassed the country about. "Em bastards out there are smart," he mumbled to himself. They had many times exposed their entire repertoire of tricks in trying to mislead him, and once he seriously suspected he had lost them once and for all, at the ford, six, seven miles south in the bottom of a valley, where they'd been using an old trick in practice since antiquity. It took him long until he was back in trail, and for a while they'd most certainly had taken advantage of the delay and relaxed for a couple of hours. But still, upon studying the prints of the hooves, he had noticed that he most certainly was gaining ground on them, he was closer now than even before, whatever that might mean. He now was considering two options: They might ambush or attack from behind. He now made a decision to find an appropriate place to encamp. Sticking to the tracks of those he pursued, he exhorted the horse to proceed, moving faster. He had a plan in mind for the coming night.

There was every indication as to the coming night being overcast, the temperature some degrees over the freezing-point, and patches of flimsy ice underfoot where the cold winds could get at them. Up in the mountains winter often hits early, and the direction of travel was going to be northerly as the outlaws out there were targeting on the Canadian border. Within a couple of days, perhaps a week, if maintaining the same pace, they were entering Montana, and the nights would most likely grow colder. In the next town Jeff had to wire for cash so he could buy supplies and a packhorse and some clothes. He also needed an army tent or at least some means of wind shield and a map. There would not be much talk of rest until this mission was completed. From now on the decision to lay hands on those refugees was given highest priority. He hoped the reds out there weren't chalked and painted and armed for war.

The few cicadas that still were left had ceased altogether, and the first birds were already about when he woke up from his comatose state. He opened his eyes and listened. He heard the horse, tethered to a nearby willow shrubbery, start whining and tramping in anxiety, signaling some kind of danger, pricking his ears within their range of motion.

Lying on his back in the compact night darkness he remained unmoving under his blankets for some long seconds. He neither saw nor heard anything. Still had he a primitive sensation things weren't quite right. His neck turned red and he thought of his hunting knife that was lying beside him, ready to outmaneuver whoever or whatever threat that might occur. Sunup couldn't be far away. By gradual stages his eyes adjusted to the dark. Whoever the intruder, he was no Indian. With great circumspection he raised his head a little and looked out at the ill-defined dummy that rested on the ground some hundred feet away. Nothing moved. The behavior of the horse was back to normal, and it had begun to munch on the lush grass that covered the site. What should he do? Stay immobile and await twilight? He had no concept of time, but estimated it to be around four. He looked at the horse again. It went on grazing, so no immediate danger was at stake. He felt frustrated in a ghastly manner, and thought the best thing would be to pursue the matter and bring it to an end soon. Before the felons hit Canadian soil.

The coach stopped careening with a jerk outside the three-story antebellum edifice situated downtown Boston. The bony roan stood pulling the bridles in a fret with nose wrinkled when the door got open and the young gentleman in gaudy city outfit climbed his way out and banged the door shut and stood in the keening wind and looked about with sad eyes. He handed over a bill in the driver's outstretched gauntleted hand, then turned without a word and in a slow progression made for and eased into the marble stairwell with crunching steps. Nice surroundings he used to think when climbing these steps, but not so today. Time was ten forty-five, he was late, but he didn't care. These little meetings had begun to bore him stiff. He felt jittery, tired of being a replacement to some illiterate cattle driver from out west. He had to be brutal, stop backing off, and to be honest, he felt the feelings growing colder and the arguments turning nastier by each rendezvous. Dammit! He felt like killing someone with his bare hands!

He weaved away upstairs and tapped the nearest magnificent oak door. He waited then tried it. It was locked. Muted voices were heard from inside. Alright, he knew he didn't arrive at the precise hour, but forty-five minutes delay. But he had compelling reasons. No cab handy. Talking about inconsistencies, what did she call this behavior? I guess her brother is sitting glued to that rocking chair still in his nightwear, and I wouldn't be surprised to see that psychiatrist around either.

There was the play of a key then the door opened slightly, no doubt planned that way, the visitor guessed again. They had planned to grill him, make him meek, make him feel like a guest among other guests. The boy stepped aside and the visitor entered without expression.

"We are reading a letter," the boy declared softly in broken English. "Birgit is reading it to me."

"I see. Where is she?" he asked dismissively.

"In the kitchen."

He had already seen her. She half stood by the kitchen table. He stepped in her direction. The hand-off approach was still current, so they discretely exchanged their hellos, and anxious to ground the rules, he immediately asked about the letter.

"Ah, the letter…Actually, I got it yesterday…and Wolfgang insists me reading it all over again. Probably that's eh…part of his…dysfunction," she said, her voice trembling a little, but enough for him to register.

"It's probably so," the visitor agreed furtively.

"Do you want me to read it for you?" she wondered lightly.

"That really wouldn't be necessary," he replied crossly, waving a hand impatiently.

Without a word back, she started to read it in verbatim. From the living room piano music got heard, a subject with variations. He had listened to Wolfgang playing that particular piece once before, he remembered. It was "The Last Rose of Summer," Opus 15, a fantasy with variations for piano by Felix Mendelssohn, an old Irish folksong. That lad sure was no duffer, he'd thought when hearing him play. It's like a spear penetrating my soul, he'd thought. Someone who could play so beautifully, couldn't be that abhorrent, he'd thought to himself. What he didn't know was that the ill-matched siblings had devoted a great portion of the morning singing duet, rehearsing a piece out of the oratorio Paul by that same composer, Mendelssohn: "Ich danke Dir Herr, mein Gott."

In his opinion the letter didn't contend anything of particular interest until it read : "Jeff wants you to get back here as soon as you possibly can. Of course I do too. We both miss you very much and are waiting for you. Jeff mentioned something about some violins that he wants you to see."

The visitor flinched. Jeff. Talking about cognatius spiritualis. Birgit evidently had invited him here for yet another torture session, no doubt about that. She knows about my jealousy. Now she had got herself a perfect alibi, one that he could refer to. If she did not go back, then she would jeopardize the crime investigation. All he managed to say regarding the letter was, "That Penn lady, is she…"

"She's…my landlady," Birgit helpfully explained.

He thought for a moment, then he frowned and inquired in apprehension, "Are you doing good with your brother?"

"Well…he's on medication. Efficacious drugs, you know…He has become…how shall I say…effete."

"Don't put him aside. Remember what your father said: A family shall operate as a unit…always."

She let out a pained chuckle, her weary eyes betraying a tinge of lingering anger. "What shall I do?…Put him in a crate?" she asked, her voice now harsher, "Once now and then you have to drop the leash, don't you…But I know you don't understand such a reasoning…Your distinguished family doesn't need you, but you…you need them the more."

Noncommittally he clenched his white chubby fists. What could he say? Birgit realized she had got him excited almost to the point of hysteria. Neither talked for a long time. The boy, having overheard some parts of their dispute, returned to his piano, playing now by heart a meditative piece, humming while playing "Stille Betrachtung an einem Herbstabend" by another German-spoken composer, Anton Bruckner. The boyfriend, with his outer clothes still on, looked like he had nothing more on his mind. He pushed back the chair and stood and looked out the window. Low gray skies. A spitting rain. He looked into the room and at Birgit again, and left the kitchen where she sat. After a while she heard the outer door slam shut. She had barely met his eyes, she mused while inhaling the musky spice of his cologne hanging in the air. I could use a re-start, I certainly could, she mumbled to herself and picked up the letter and refolded it. "Ja, ich möchte gern einen neuen Start haben," she repeated to herself in German.

After a lengthy stretch of silence Jeff reached up and drew the coarse army blankets away. Shivering in the lonely darkness, he kicked his feet free, then gingerly rose to his feet and approached the bedding, arranged as a sleeping human. He bent down and inspected it thoroughly. The light was still dim and the heaven gray and crouching, the daybreak soon ensuing, though. The four cuts in the rolled up blanket were barely noticeable, but still deep enough. The dummy was stabbed. Fatigue and fear gripped him. He hadn't slept much that night and his nerves were frayed. But still, after all, he was alive. He was not the one who had got those vicious nicks. He quickly gathered his stuff in the semi-darkness, then gulped in one go what was left in the coffee pan, and tipped it and shook the dregs out. Sensing the first rays of sun touching his face he then saddled the horse and gave chase, and kept on riding all day.

Indians wouldn't get themselves hoisted in a petard that easily, Jeff mumbled to himself, looking hither and thither for prints. Time and again he set the horse and dismounted and scrutinized the ground in depth. As if it hid some sign which he'd missed from horseback. At least one shod horse, two at the most, had operated in the neighborhood during the past night. It was still all but windless, no rain so far. He mounted up and pursued at a brisk walk the trail that now began to turn somewhat west. After a couple of miles he came upon a crossroad with a wind-shattered aslant sign elaborately carved in florid ill-written letters saying "HENDERSON 2 MILES." He knew that town as being trafficked by Wells Fargo and hence a watering hole for travelers.

He chucked up the horse and set it to blow. He swung a leg across the pommel and slid off his gloves and shoved them down into the side pockets of his coat. Enwrapped in thoughts he from different pockets rooted out his tobacco and makings and went through the motions and deftly rolled himself a cigarette. Sensing the slight and fresh breeze fanning his scuffed face, he sat and looked out the country about, twirling in his fingers the cigarette, beguiled by the colorful scenery, a land more open, more flat-out with swathes of forest. The half-dead leaves, still clinging to the few oak trees, rattled dryly in the wind that now was blowing up. Besides the faint seething of the wind there was no perceptible sound anywhere. With his back to the wind, shielding the flame with his both hands, he set fire to the cigarette, and reflectively sat and smoked in long pulls, and kept on until he all but got his fingertips singed. He swerved and flung the butt onto the ground in a slow acceleration, and beginning to feel a chill, he buttoned the top stud of his shirt against the growing cold, then dredged up his gloves and put them on, one then the other, then set his horse at the spring.

After a little time, the town got visible in the valley the better part of a mile out. It was built on a field dotted by scrub cedars and appeared fairly new to the eye with low buildings built with raw clean timber. He slowed the horse and approached the town at a walking pace. Right outside the small town he met a wagon with a long slatted bench with a pair of mules yoked-to coming his way at a slow clumsy and wheezy trot. A young female driver was sitting in the seat in a patch of sunlight with the bridles in her left hand, her right hand shielding her eyes from the low-set evening sun that temporarily had penetrated the head of clouds. Once their eyes eventually came together, he gave a nod to her, and she nodded back, eyeing him searchingly. He was unshaven and felt hog-filthy and looking forward to a long hot bath and a drop-in-visit at a barber's shop. He rode on at a rapid trot. Another young woman, looking lost to the present, carrying a great armload of soiled clothes, looked up at him as he rode by at the very top of the street. He reined in on her, and touching the brim of his hat asked where he could get him something to eat.

"I reckon the saloon can fix you somethin', mister," she answered, raising herself up somewhat while giving him a shy look, sounding like she just had cried.

He thanked her then touched the brim of his hat another time and put his horse forward.

When at the heart of town, he among a row of black-painted wooden buildings discerned the words "LONGHORN SALOON" ornately lettered in black on a new-looking bullet-scarred shield that hung over the entrance of a two-story building with a foundation of stone. He steered his course in its general direction and stopped the horse outside it. For a while he wistfully sat and looked at it with the reins doubled in his contracted fist. An almost empty street with darkening shadows in one of which a small gathering of three people stood making small talk, and fell silent, and one by one turned to watch him.

He removed his gloves and put them into the side pockets of his coat, then stood down from the saddle and fastened the tired horse to the bar where already four other horses stood tethered. Stiff-legged he rounded the horse's posterior and drew his rifle out of the scabbard and with heavy boot tread made it the short way to the five gritty stairs and climbed them. He crossed the porch in a long-legged stride and put the batwing doors aside and with slow progress sauntered inside. The doors slowly swung shut behind him, and a wall-clock chimed seven. He stood in a funk of burning kerosene. A middle-aged man with a youthful face in a checked shirt stood in the shaft of light from outside, polishing the long bar desk with a rag. Surprise-like he looked up at him and eyed him studiously. At a table at the far wall a solitary guest in city clothes wreathed in tobacco smoke scraped his seat around to face him steadily, his eyes deeply shadowed beneath his hat brim. From another table got heard muted voices and clips of chips and counters.

"Evenin', cowboy…Yo' hungry?" the barman greeted him, his hand holding the rag froze as he regarded Jeff long and watchful-eyed with suspicion, measuring him up from top to bottom, the muscles along his jaw tightened.

With no word Jeff started toward him, the rowels of his spurs clinging and cracking load against the plank floor when he walked.

"New around, eh?" the barman said, not raising his voice, eyeing him with a fixed gaze.

"Just ridin' through…an' I'm hungry alright…Starved one might say," Jeff responded, closing into while shifting the gun from hand to hand.

"Well, then you've come to the right place, mister. We're famous for our large servings," the barman said, slapping a hand heavily upon the bartop.

Undoing with the fingers of one hand the top button of his jacket Jeff grunted, "Sounds fair enough…Then tell me what you can offer."

"We can offer buns, newly baked, still hot, uh… beans, eggs…oatmeal… some ribs, coffee… Just say…an' you'll get it… Some ham maybe, too, I figure."

"Alright…Gimme all of it…Like I said…I'm famished."

"How do you like your eggs, mister?"

"Fried on both sides."

"Alright. It won't take long."

The barman lingered for a while as if he'd gotten his mind set upon something and might be going to talk some more, but there came neither comment nor question. Instead, his eyes cut away and with an air of briskness he swung around and withdrew. Jeff knit his brows and thumbed back his hat and laid down his rifle on the desk with a muffled clang. Pots clattered in the kitchen, and after sometime a little girl peeped out from inside an inner nook.

"Hey there," she said shyly, holding his gaze expectantly for a long time in the manner of kids. She had two milk teeth in the front fallen out.

"How you doin'?" Jeff returned, crooked over the spittoon underfoot.

"Are you…a glutton, mister?" she inquired, studying him with her hands behind her rear. At the same time a lean-hipped blond young woman with sunken belly loaded with plates and sundries moved out from the shadows and motioned for the kid to get back into the kitchen. "I'm sorry, sir," she said and smiled thinly. She's so precocious," she added explanatory.

Jeff shrugged, then said loyally, "American kids usually are, ma'am…Don't regret."

She watched him, then continued as she moved slowly toward a table at the far end of the room.

"Is that really a fact, sir?"

"Accordin' to my experience, it sure is," Jeff said then asked her for the name of the town.

She said it was Henderson.

The woman with no further word put the plates down on a next-to table then began to spread a cloth onto another right by, hesitated in mid-action, asking, looking across, "Will this table be alright, sir?"

"I figure it be just fine, ma'am," Jeff said and placed one boot on the gilded foot rail.

"New around, eh?" she asked from the gloom, the sudden blush on her cheeks barely visible.

"Well, I ain't stayin' if that's what you mean, ma'am."

"That's what 'em always say," she said and managed a mysterious smile.

"Is that a fact, eh?"

She nodded and moved back into the shadows. Some minute later she brought Jeff from his reveries by reappearing, asking if he wanted his coffee served right away. He nodded yes and shoved out the chair and sat. The clock on the wall chimed half past seven. He wistfully looked at the potluck before him and began forking in, his shotgun centered upon the table within reach. In the kitchen doorway the kid stood and looked at him openly, hands behind rear, her lips cracked into a toothless winning grin.

The shadows were growing longer toward night and It was all but dusk when Jeff reappeared at the saloon shaven and refreshed after a hot bath. The middle-aged waiter in the checked shirt greeted him cordially, and without asking what he could get him poured up a whiskey. Jeff leisurely propped his spurred boot on the rail and looked across the half-full place, enlightened by kerosene lamps, burning every few paces. then looked at the barman again, asking, "How did you now I wanted a drink?"

The man's facial muscles tightened. He responded distraught, "Don't you…want a drink, mister?"

"I didn't say that," Jeff said, his voice softened somewhat. "I asked how do you know I wanted a drink…You didn't answer my question."

He looked out the half full space, his gaze followed by the barman. Stark cowboy-faces, men all, huddling engrossed in poker games, none of which having as it seemed taken attention as to their argumentation. Clicks of markers hitting the scuffed tabletop. Jeff again dropped his gaze on the barman, who held out one hand in a gesture of reconciliation. "Listen…I didn't mean to affront. You look like a guy who prefers whiskey…to me you ain't no beer man. Am I wrong, maybe?" he wondered anxiously, his eyes narrowing a little.

Jeff shrugged, then declared, "Well…If I have to…make the choice myself, I stick to the whiskey, but occasionally a beer may be alright, as well…Let's drop the subject, right?"

"Alright, sorry…I surely didn't mean to harm…the drink's on the house."

"Much obliged. Thanks a lot," Jeff mumbled. He again cast a glance in the direction of the packs of guests, cowboys mostly, their features grown more enshadowed now. He started to roll a cigarette and cast some occasional eyes at his Winchester that sat before him on the desk. The barman gave him a boring look as if considering the matter, then inquired, "You've fixed the lodging, mister?"

Jeff gave an unelaborated yes while he studied for some time the dead and cold cigar in the ashtray sitting before him. Meantime a raw-looking half-drunk hick in mud-splattered breeches, a drover by appearance, carrying a five-shot ivory-handled gun in its holster, parked next to, asserting he and his party hadn't got enough gravy with their steaks. Outside in the street two riders passed in a slow clop of hooves.

"I'll bring you some more. It won't take long…you may go back to your party in the meanwhile," the barman promised benevolently as if trying to avert a conflict.

The hick gave no answer. He looked at Jeff, pursed his lips, half turned, then seized Jeff by his arm and said in a slur, "Do you…care if I stand here, cowboy?"

Without condescending to give him a look, Jeff just answered kindly and slowly, addressing the air, "As long as you stay quiet and don't babble, you're free to stand…it's a free country."

The lean hick studied Jeff, his blood-shot eyes widened. "Listen to 'im!" he brawled to his pack over his shoulder, then faced Jeff again, "Stuck-up, that's…whatta are, eh!"

Within seconds another two other of his kind with ungraceful gaits amalgamated, one of which bearded and big-framed, his compeer almost his size, long-haired with bad complexion and hard evil eyes. "What's the problem?" they asked in one voice, boring in, their eyes shifting among them. The first of them seemed to be half drunk, as was the second, all three beginning to kick up a rumpus.

"Hey, you…You heard my buddies!" the first mongrel said, raising his voice over the noise, eager to make things hum, then went on, "They wanna know what's…the problem…"

The barman was back at the counter, a pitcher in hand. "Don't molest my guest, you hear. Here's your gravy…I follow you back to your table," he pleaded lamely.

Let alone a drunken oath from the darkness of an inner nook, silence reigned the room, everybody watching. Jeff stood silent, hunkered down a bit, resting his elbow on the polished bar desk, realizing that whatever he said would be used against him. Immobile he just stood awaiting their next move, head hanging down dejectedly. He studied the ashtray and the cigar that lay in it, as someone again seized him by the arm.

"Remove yo' hand," he ordered toward the ashtray, his voice low, not more than a half whisper. Time sort of froze. "You heard me…Take your hands off me," he repeated still in a whisper.

"What's gonna happen else…chicken boy?" a voice said, one attaching itself to a boorish-looking runt of a man with red complexion in drover's togs and sagging bags under his eyes huddling at the gaming-table. He turned around in the chair and faced Jeff with keen interest to see what he would say.

Jeff remained mute, though, said nothing in reply. Out in the kitchen someone was scraping mush from a skillet. Otherwise there was so silent one could hear a needle drop. The barman, now lined up at a distance, watching like the rest, didn't appear to have more to say.

"This gonna be huge…that's what's gonna be," one voice ultimately uttered in satisfactory from the semi-darkness, sucking his pipe alight avidly. A ripple of excitement went through the place. A match scratched and popped, and a light flared up.

"You've got it in your bloodstreams, compadres," Jeff hissed and pulled himself slightly up on his elbow.

"What do they have?" one at the gaming table demanded after a momentary pause in afterthought, one with a stark face that demonstrated no features.

"Evil," Jeff hissed with the slight making of a fake smile.

Suddenly a quick deal got struck, and a swift decision made within the trio. They looked at Jeff who raised his head and started toward his torturers, waiting for the first thud. Jibbing he divested himself of his hat and coat and slung them across the back of the nearest chair. Right then he acquired a pop from behind, a cross that hit him on the back of his left shoulder blade, not stone hard, but hard enough.

"You like…'em…odds, don't you…Three…against…one…suits you just fine, eh?" he pressed out between clenched teeth, ready with his future strategy. He spun around and took a couple of steps in their direction and hit the nearest, the bulky one with the bad complexion and wavy hair, his hat now off his head. A heavy uppercut from Jeff made him wail. Jeff's first priority now would be to keep the three in the front, not giving them any chance to get him encircled. The second antagonist came toward him, waved his arm a little and slashed away. Jeff ducked, kept low, waiting for the perfect moment. He charged at the bulky one, who quickened his pace in a counter attack. With amazing quickness Jeff with no holdback unloaded a long right cross that caught him right under his left eye, and yet another under the chin. He screamed and loaded his fist as hard as he could and landed it in Jeff's belly. Meantime Jeff got attacked from behind. He cocked his arm, bended at the waist, trying to conjure up the best of his repertoire. He charged and hit the man straight in his face. His features froze in terror, his nose broken, bleeding profusely. With a vicious strike Jeff now finished the job. His antagonist hit the floor, immobile. Jeff, just for a second having forgotten the risk of a from behind attack, turned around, seeing one of them approach him with a knife in hand, the first one, the one a while ago ordering a refill with gravy. Fatigue now was gaining on Jeff, and by mustering the last of his forces, he grabbed hold of and wrenched the weapon out of the man's hand, smelling the odor from his lean body. Specks of blood trickled from his hand as did it also from Jeff's. "We come back an' finish you…off, cowboy," he snarled gruffly, his eyes blazing with anticipation.

Jeff sensing blood oozing from his right hand made no answer. From one table was some claps of applause. Standing pat, Jeff just grimaced out of pain, and breathing hard asked his antagonist if he'd got enough, or if he wanted more.

The other, milling about as if he was drunk, didn't respond.

Meantime the barkeep loosened himself from the mute crowd and went into the kitchen and soon came back, the blond waitress following, carrying a tray with soap and water and a bandage kit in her reddened hands. She placed the tray on an empty nearby table and motioned for Jeff to get there as the place faltered into silence. She inspected the wound, then moistened a shred of gauze in whiskey and wrung it slightly. The deep cut from the palm of his hand was dripping with blood and appeared also to be relatively extended. Down on the floor a ways off, the tousled out-knocked warrior was regaining consciousness.

"First step is to make stop the bleedin'," she declared matter-of-factly while arranging a makeshift pressure bandage that she pressed into the moist wound.

"Pretty deep," Jeff grunted in a grimace, knowing what it meant. He was in great pain and the cut needed to be closed.

"Yo've done this before, eh, ma'am?" he went on, his hand kept high.

"Yeah, it happens occasionally…since we don't have a doctor in town," she replied quickly with an eye at the crowd, the bulk of which now having retaken their seats. She watched Jeff again but didn't speak, Jeff still with his hand thrust high above, pursuant to her instructions. He looked down at her gaunt profile. She looked uptight. How come she's ended up out here in the boondocks?

"How 'bout that other buck?" he inquired after some time, looking across at the lean hick, who recently had tried to stab him, now hanging by the counter.

"He is mauled but ain't that badly hurt, I figure. Just a swollen eye," she declared curtly in a hushed voice, then added, "Look, mister, my suggestion is you go to Lancing to see the doctor…a full hour horseback."

She told him to lower his arm. Without a word she in the last light of day daubed salve onto then with agile fingers started to dress the wound with sheeting while displaying an accuracy that surprised him. The salve had a cathartic and astringent effect, she imparted. It purges the vile infection. It ignited a pain one that quickly receded when she applied it on the precise placement of the wound. Searching his gaze, she said him it was important he moved his fingers once in a while to coax circulation. Jeff nodded in acquiescence, said nothing. The old clock on the wall was about to chime eight strikes, and the voices in the saloon grew more agitated. Jeff flexed his fingers and ordered himself a beer after having offered the woman one. She declined with a grave nod of her head, looking as if occupied by somber thoughts. The snub-nosed kid was back and stood and peeped smilingly at him through a slot in the kitchen door, gnawing on an apple half. Somehow Jeff had a feeling something bad was going to happen. In the livery stable stood two rested horses waiting for him. Realizing it might be dangerous to stay the night in town, and knowing a long ride was underway, he wished to have them saddled. He put on his coat and hat then went to the bar and drank his beer, then bought himself two bottles of Scotch and started out, sensing evil eyes were following him.

IX

The young doctor gingerly draw the arm nearer to the lamp for the better light there. He then put up the lamp so that the room went lighter.

"When did it happen?" he demanded, focusing his patient from behind his round gold-wired spectacles, cajoling meanwhile the bloody winding away after having taken in the full extent of the wound.

"Last night at 'bout seven, seven thirty…at a brawl at the saloon."

"I see…and how are you feeling right now?"

"I'm beginnin' to feel cold."

The doctor nodded and stood for a moment, gathering his thoughts, then snapped his attention back to the hand and announced, "The edges are dry, which means they are a potential medium for infection. First thing for me to do is to numb the hand, and then excerpt the edges in order to provide fresh bleeding."

"Alright, do it yo' way, doc," Jeff said, his eyes set upon the wall before him, lined with bottles of medicine.

After having numbed the area, the doctor said with a trustful smile as he meanwhile faced around the place, "Since you plan to stay on the road for a while, I enclose a set of bandage that will last for ten to twelve days. I recommend you to re-bandage twice a day, morning and evening. You probably will experience a low-grade pain in the hand every once in a while, but that doesn't necessarily mean the hand is infected."

"Alright," Jeff said, nodding approvingly.

Minutes went by in silence as the doctor shut the wound, working the needle from side to side. It bled very little. Eight stitches were required to close the large cut. Having swathed and tied the hand, the doctor looked up and said with a quick smile in a tone almost avuncular, "Rest much, drink a lot and…most important…no bar brawl within the next couple of weeks."

"I'll try to keep that in mind, doc," Jeff smiled back.

"Go see a doctor after eight, ten days...to get the stitches removed. You have any questions, sir?"

"Can I dab with whiskey?"

"Whiskey is the best, even better than Laudanum in my experience," the doctor responded mildly.

"What about the fever?"

"It's declining now that you've been taken care of...I don't estimate your injuries to be life-threatening...I'm more worried about your journey...It might be hazardous."

"Alright," Jeff said. He reached for his coat and asked, "How much do I owe you, doc?"

Wiping off his hands on his apron the doctor studied the question for a second, then said, "Two dollars and a half will be fine, sir."

The man behind the counter brought Jeff more coffee and poured a cup for the sheriff of Lancing, a tall beanpole of a man, now standing next to Jeff, studying on the sly Jeff's swathed hand. The sheriff had just finished eating and pulled his plate back. He withdrew his hand and pursed his mouth as if in doubt, and reached up for an inner pocket of his faded greatcoat that sat loosely wrapped about him. He absentmindedly groped for his tobacco sack, dredged it out and stood to examine it from every angle as if to verify its authenticity. Having related his story on him, Jeff shook the ash from the tip of his cigarette, then crossed his sprained foot over his right heel and grimaced. The sensation in his hand hadn't fully returned. Not moving a twitch the sheriff looked about, keeping a special attention to the card players who sat huddled as before, their faces now scantily illuminated in the lamp glow, making sure no one was eavesdropping, but there was no one to hear. He then pressed a dollar to the center of the bar as Jeff doled his coins onto the counter ready to hit the potholed street without alerting the townfolks. The sheriff touched the brim of his hat and pushed it backward on his head, then raised his coffee and sipped it, froze in mid-air cup in hand, cocked his head to the side and said silently, "Sorry I couldn't be of much help, but...we'll keep in touch. Interesting story. You said someone broke his solitary cell with a firearm? That's what you said, right?" he demanded and studied Jeff in the back bar mirror.

Plucking the cigarette from his lips Jeff grunted, "Right, that's what I said," then continued, "I figure we'll have to fix another gratin', but hardest thing to swallow's that they are still out there."

The sheriff raised an arm in greeting to a couple of passersby, swerved and spat into the cuspidor on the floor then raised up again. Jeff smoked as the sheriff sprinkled tobacco into a paper.

"You're headin' north?" the sheriff asked after a moment of silence, studying his reflection in the mirror while licking the paper shut.

"Yeah," Jeff confirmed, stubbing out his cigarette.

"Listen…you could stay overnight with my family. My wife fix a bed for you. Wouldn't it be better yo' start fresh in the mornin', yo' figure?"

Jeff, pulling himself erect and pushing his empty coffee cup away, answered immediately, "Appreciate your hospitality, sheriff…but I have to get started tonight." He freed himself from the bar desk and stood leaning to go, rifle in hand.

The sheriff shrugged and lit his smoke, was silent a while as he blew the match out and chucked it into the ashtray, then answered in a low tone that resembled resignation, "Alright, O'Halloran. Good night…an' be careful."

"Good night…I'll try to be," Jeff assured. He turned around and with slow boot crunch with a stiff-backed stride started to walk to the doors with a slight limp. He paused and looked out at the dark, then clapped the doors open and stepped outside into the star-bright night, the doors quickly flipping shut elastically behind him. He stood in a faint smell of woodsmoke. It was dark out there, as of yet just a few streetlights were on at the top of the street, burning every few steps. As far as he could see, there was nobody on the street right outside, no one saving a woman in black finery and rouged cheeks, who illumed by the light from the saloon, stood vomiting by the hitching rail. She was so full of liquor, she barely could stand straight.

Facing the northerly headwind the two shapely horses with mud-spluttered hocks in the mid- afternoon of the day following, tramped their way through the swampy mire somewhere up in north Wyoming, where the ground was so barren at places not even weeds would grow on them.

Once back on dry ground Jeff spurred the high-shouldered stallion forward, the packhorse trailing behind, snorting and sidling in the spongy ground. When they set out over the mesa he re-found the tracks of the horses he was pursuing, seeing them bearing straight northward. Below him he could discern the flatlands below, a desolated landscape, not far from the stateline of Montana. Some stray Indian horses patrolled the territory, Arapahoe, riding them not in war dress though, keeping distance. During the past hours, they had showed up from time to time, far off, but still visible, then withdrew, as if they were cautioning him away, or wanted to tell him to watch his steps, saying him we are watching your movements.

He halted the stallion, and soon the packhorse came up on his left and stood sniffing into the headwind that had taken to blow hard from north, hard enough to set the manes and the fringes of the horses into slight motion. They now had solid ground underfoot for the first time since long. And some tufts of grass as well.

He slacked the bridles and let the horses graze as he sat and listened to the singing wind and the breaths of the horses coming deeply and regular. Turning in the saddle he studied the country at large. Blow wilting flowers and pats of cattle in the ground. Far out west cattle watching mutely with breaths pluming. Otherwise nothing but the nature. He dismounted and dropped the reins and ate some parched biscuits and drank cold coffee from a keg. Thinking about a lot of things, he lit a smoke and consulted the map while the horses walked about cropping bleakly, swishing their tails.

Taking in the pain in his hand as he cupped them about the horn, he eventually levered himself up onto the saddle and put the horses forward along the rutted driveway. Overhead on the heaven dark clouds had begun to pile.

He'd gone not more than a good mile or perhaps two when he beyond a steep curve spotted what he figured was a ranch house with woods and outhouses. The main house was a one-storied unpainted wooden building with a newly chalked chimney with a thin wisp of smoke issuing from it flattened against the westerly wind, and rising above the trees a creaking windmill a little further out on the grassland with blue wilting flowers in it. Barely visible there was to perceive a long distance out, a pack of cattle, formless articulations, most of which in attitudes of repose, and beyond the windmill what appeared to be a log hog-pen, the house and fences of which beginning to tilt as though it weren't no longer in use. A little ways away from it was dimly to see another small building, one having the look of a smokehouse. He slowed down the pace and went on pursuing the multitude of prints on the ground, prints of shod horse feet. Suddenly he stood frozen when he in craning his neck caught the sight of a rider galloping in his direction a good mile out to the west. It was a female. He watched her as she rode toward him at a quick gallop initially then at a measured canter and finally stopped and stood in front of him. A robust female in a capacious almost overlarge fur-trimmed greatcoat buttoned up to the collar of sheepskin that stood so high it almost covered her ears, looked across at him. She had cowhide chaps about her tights and ankles and dun spurred boots caked with old mud, and a dun somewhat oversized Stetson sitting low and askew on her head with her grizzly hair pulled backward and twisted into a rope, clinging to her back. A firearm hung fully to view around her waist, an old-world Whitfield, stocked in rose. Her right hand was close to its hilt, dangerously close, and for a short interval it looked like she had in mind to close her hand upon it, but she didn't. Her horse, a handsome dapple-gray filly, tramped around nervously, biting the bridoon, gingivae at full display, a white foam seething between the yellow teeth. The woman's eyes watched Jeff critically and broodingly, as though she was figuring he was one looking for work, her gaze drifting from him to the packhorse and the horse he rode. Her weathered furrowed tanned face was stone-like with the firm jaw clamped shut, her cheek firm. She looked to be past her middle years. A Spencer rifle hung in a boot under the saddle. Forestalling her Jeff at length touched his brim and said politely, "Hope I'm not trespassin', ma'am...I'm a marshal out in official business."

He removed his gloves and stuffed them into the side pockets of his coat, and struggling with the studs opened his jacket at the top and flipped it aside, displaying his badge. She looked at it and nodded her head in disbelief as she slacked her hold on the bridles. "Say what's on your mind, mister," she ordered, her voice hard and vacant.

"I'm after three people...an' I lost 'em five, six miles back south...nasty folks, you see. They've used all tricks there are to make the pursuit difficult. I've just seen unshod horse prints recently. For some time it looked like they'd shaken me off, but now I've found their tracks...I estimate 'em be 'round some twenty-four hours ahead of me, ridin' north," he said and turned to her for an answer.

She nodded and studied his face, her both hands folded on the horn of the saddle hand over hand, the nostrils of her horse pluming in the cool air. She then lowered her gaze somewhat and said, "Pretty good mounts you've got there, marshal...It's a good thing to have if yo're journeyed upcountry."

He looked past her while shifting weight in the saddle, nodded toward the corral then said, pointing west, "Is it your remuda yonder, ma'am?"

"Yes, it is....I'm running the ranch...me and my son."

He nodded again and looked out across the flats, overgrown with lush vegetation. Nothing was heard save the wind where it whistled smoothly in the juicy grass where a little mist was building. A taciturn landscape. They let the horses crop, neither talking. After a while Jeff asked her if it was alright he stepped down for a little. She nodded yes.

"I figure 'em outlaws keep away from open country," he said and began to roll a smoke.

Her eyes again hastily swept over him, lingering for some long seconds on his wrapped-up hand.

"My son and our…ranch hand, actually watched three riders at some distance from our place. Yesterday mornin'."

"Headed north?" Jeff asked shifting, re-stuffing his tobacco-sack with his sound hand and flexing the other.

"Yeah, single filed in a hurry, the boys tol' me…You know, we seldom see riders out here, since it's Indian land," she shared, watching him thoughtfully.

He scrabbled about inside a pocket and fumbled a match out of the box and stroke it against the heel of his boot, then steadied himself as he said, "Looks like they're my men, alright…Then I don't have to veer."

"No, they were headed straight north 'em boys said…drifted upstream, ridin' light."

"So they were in eye-sight?"

"Yeah…for quite some time 'em were…Listen, marshal, you'll come with me home and talk with the boys for yourself…I expect 'em home for supper any time. You wanna join us?" she demanded, a trace of a smile visible on her weathered face.

"I do very much, ma'am."

They stood in the silence as he smoked, distracted by the beauty of the landscape. The crickets had begun sounding. Eventually he let go the stub and reflectively tramped it down with his heel as she caught at the bridles of her horse and seized them and tightened them. She turned the restive horse roughly and clapped spurs to its flanks and rode on at a slow trot. Jeff grabbed hold of the saddle and swung himself up and followed and eventually caught up and rode up beside her, the packhorse trailing, roped behind, and shoulder they together approached the ranch.

They reined in the horses at an old-looking stone corral and set them as the day darkened more and more. A low star was already visible beyond a parkland of yellow Douglas spruces to the west, as was there to suggest on the purple sky further on to the east a thin glow of a three-quarter moon. From somewhere about the voice of a dog got heard. In the withering alfalfa, underneath a crabapple tree, the crickets had intensified their strident autumn cheeping. Jeff remained astride his horse for a while, waiting for the woman to dismount her filly. He looked out toward the corral in which already stood dormant several horses grouped in immobility in a shimmering cloud of gnats.

Once the woman had stepped down from the saddle and was standing next to her horse, he chucked his right boot out of the offside stirrup and swung his leg across the horse's posterior and cautiously, steadying himself with his hands cupped on the saddle touched the ground and stood for a while. His wounded hand did not ache any longer. Favoring one leg, steadying himself against the moist blank withers of his horse, he tried to shake the stiffness out of his shoulders. The black stallion shifted and looking off at the penned horses in the corral, stood tossing his head, snickering softly. Having an uncertainty as of his next doings, Jeff turned to the woman and dusted himself off. The woman, as though she'd been reading his thoughts, craned her neck toward him and said it soon will be dark, and he might as well make his horses ready for the night.

"Thanks for the invitation ma'am, but to tell yo' the truth I'm beginnin' to get unaccustomed to sleep indoors," he declared, pumping his scathed hand, taking meanwhile in the modest-looking ranch building.

"I see what you mean, marshal…Head to the cantle by the campfire beneath a canopy of open sky…and all that romantic stuff, eh. I can tell I've pretty much experience from it myself."

"Yeah…I sure believe you have ma'am."

In silence they saw to the horses and brought them grain and hay and watered them. When they were done and had closed and latched the gate of the corral and had lugged the saddles and the tack inside the stables, she spied around the compound and declared explanatory, "The boys ain't home yet, but they'll be around any time…I go inside and fix us supper." After having scraped out and examined the hooves of the horses for fissures and clawfuls of mud, Jeff heard a distant clopping sound of horse feet and faraway voices of men brought there by the wind in the falling evening. The sky was still light with the forests of Montana faintly perceptible to the north underneath the starlit firmament, and the wind had abated somewhat. The sounds came nearer. Unsure as to where to wend his way, Jeff with slow tread made for the raw plank wall of the stables. In the meantime, two horsemen stayed for a little while and sat parallel looking across the distance at Jeff where he was sitting bow-backed astride a wooden bench right outside the harness room against its wall with his hat over one knee, his head bent down. A little ways from him stood an empty horse wagon with a chaff-dusted flatbed. Underneath and about it a dozen or so speckled hens and a rooster were chasing each other and then picking hungrily in the earth afterward, like nothing had happened. The rooster time and again made a stop in his activities, raised his head sharply and looked at Jeff with his round bold eyes, as if he were some malign form sitting there. Bold-looking it then stretched up, cried out and resumed. The two horsemen said something between themselves where they stood in the road rutted with wagon tracks, nothing of which he was capable to hear. The older of them was wearing an eyepatch. Soon they started their horses again, Jeff following their progress until he watched them pulling up to a halt, and then sitting astraddle their saddles looking across at him searchingly. Neither spoke. At length they simultaneously, as if commanded to, clutched the horns of the saddles and swung themselves down, and without a word between them commenced to approach Jeff afoot, swaying their shoulders, reins in hands, the horses in tandem falling into step behind sluggishly with feet clopping flatly.

"Evenin'," Jeff began, still seated, raising his head at them, putting his hat back on.

"What can we do for you, mister?" the younger, dressed in a loose-hanging sheepskin-lined jacket, muttered business-like with a reserved suspicious nod while hitching his breeches, his compeer staggering catching up behind in a slow tread of boot heels, carrying a branding iron in one hand. He was dressed in a large and disheveled brass-buttoned blue uniform capote torn at the elbows and open at the front, and underneath an uniform shirt, an old blue washed-out Yankee. In the same moment the kitchen door of the ranch building flung open and the woman stuck out her head and called out, her voice almost lost beneath the snorting and wheezing of the tired horses, "We've got a guest, boys…a marshal come here to see 'bout chasin' three outlaws…He rode by, an' I invited 'im for supper!"

The older one, a squint-eyed, pimple-faced and long-haired man with ill-spaced teeth and a graying mustache, and voluminous midsection, demanded shortly, his head a little atilt as if he had a bad hearing, "Where are yo' from, mister?" There was an unmistakable reek of booze and sour tobacco about his person.

"Name's O'Halloran…I'm from Sioux Falls," Jeff declared, squinting up at him.

"You're a marshal in Sioux Falls…uh Montana…?" the younger asked deliberately.

"Vice sheriff," Jeff said and stood. "No, I'm from down Wyomin'…I'm after three men."

"You're sure 'em are headed this way?" the older asked, almost pleading.

"I'm sure, alright."

The younger took hold of the cheekstrap of his standing horse and began to undo the headstall, hesitated in mid-action and while craning his head and seizing up the stranger with his gaze, announced matter-of-factly, "We watched three riders passin' by yesterday at full blast…mid-mornin'…"

"Yo've traced 'em so far?" the older one cut in, eyeing Jeff quizzically.

"I lost 'em…'bout five miles south…they shook me off, but now I've picked up their tracks again.

"Can't be the easiest thing roping 'em," the younger remarked, still scanning Jeff's face in some wonder, scratching his right sideburn, his co-worker flanking him, straddle-legged and hale-looking.

The woman ubiquitous watched while the three men were seated in the low-ceilinged grand kitchen in a lingering smell of home-cooked food, some kind of stew, a fresh boil which they spooned up in huge portions, eating at the rustic pine table set for three. Either she had already had her supper, or she ate alone, later on. Among them at the table, in the warm air from the stove, yet another man with a careworn face and a balding head, dressed in his long-handled underwear was sitting in a wheelchair. She looked at the fire burning in the stove and fed it with some chunks of wood that she fetched up from a zinc bucket right by, and she looked at Jeff again and out the window where the shadows were growing long toward night. She rose with astonishing litheness a couple of times and got the kettle with coffee in it from off the stove and returned to the table and offered the men a refill. Seeing Jeff watching the gimp man in the wheelchair where he sat breathing hard, crunching his palates, she explained sad-eyed that he was her husband, a former rancher in his best years, and now a gimp.

Jeff cast a furtive eye at the man's furrowed features and down at his veined gross hands, passively resting in his lap with just three fingers left on his right hand.

"Sorry 'bout that, ma'am," Jeff said, glancing casually around.

She turned her head away and put the pot back on the stove.

"In combat, you see. Shiloh, the war…I've already given him his meal," she added as though anxious to steer the conversation away into something else.

"He ain't able to eat…has no energy for it…needs help…got smallpox in the war," her son chimed in, speaking low, buttering a roll that his mother had heated up a while ago. "I figure he has little recollection of the war. He got a trauma to the skull once," he in looking clandestinely at his mother added, sounding as if he'd just given away a secret.

"Yeah…" his mother said, "Some of us life hits hard."

"Yeah…remember Shiloh. Was there myself," Jeff said.

"I was too," the older shared, inclining his tousled head. The conversation lagged, and they faltered in silence and ate as if there weren't much more to say.

The woman after a while opened the stove, and singing quietly to herself stuffed in some more firewood. She peered into at the flames, watching them wooshing up before long, take and eat their way up with hissing pops, and subside again. She held out her hands to the small warmth. She had strong-looking, rope-scarred hands, the hands of a hard worker. They went on talking about old days, and about their closest neighbors, the Roberts family. Billy spoke about Gregory, one of their three sons, a young man, age twenty-five that was all mad when he came back from the war, thinking the war ain't over. He doesn't dare to go to bed at night, because he dreads 'em Rebs, and says they will get there and pierce them with their bayonets. The others have tried to talk him out of it, but he doesn't listen, and now his ol'man can see no other way out than bring him down with a bullet to make an end to his suffering, but that he would never do, Billy said and looked at his mother. She glanced across at her husband and said that we can't escape from our destiny, and that we have not much power in ourselves, and that the little power we have comes from God, and that we can be lucky in one sense, because we can't guess out what's coming. She said that she had no reason to complain about God's mercifulness, because her prayers had been answered to hundredfold.

They'd all done eating now and by the light from the stove they sat in a hush, sipping their coffees, listening to the fire ticking. It was dark outside. Eventually Mrs. Acuff rose to go and slammed the door of the stove and withdrew into another room. Looking at his guest and leaning toward him the younger man inquired while spooning sugar into his coffee, "Em thugs out there...what sentence do you figure 'em gonna' carry...Prison?"

Having his gaze on his swathed fist, Jeff tightened it and slowly raised his head and said they are under sentence of death, and will get their necks stretched in the gallows.

Coming back to the table, leaning in low and hearing this, the woman flinched, visibly mired in a funk.

"But before that...there's gonna be a trial, ain't that right?" the other one added, sounding as if inspired by the frankness of the response, packing his pipe with long strings of Richmond tobacco.

"Well, there ain't much to say about it, I guess...but a trial there's gonna be," Jeff confirmed, his gaze shifted back to his hand.

When this was said they didn't talk much more among each other in a long time. A couple of times the woman rose to check the stove to ensure herself the fire wasn't gone cold. Jeff inquired them about the harvest and about the winters up there. The older man said they could be hell. He had arthritis as a consequence of the hard winters, and areas of his vision were blurred, the doc in town said. He could do nothing for him. It went in the family. Still he gave off an impression of power. They also talked some about their distant neighbors, living three good miles away, and Jeff told them about his brother who fell in battle at Gettysburg. By the time he told them this, there was a creaking and the man in the wheelchair jerked forward and gripped the armrests and started to cough, almost choking, his lips cyanotic all of a sudden, a vein in his head pulsing darkly. He muttered something which cracked in his voice then shrank backwards slump-shouldered, his blue hands limp and passive in his lap, his high forehead blank as though it were waxed. The top phalanx of his left thumb was missing. The disabled man again mumbled something, and they waited for him to speak, but he didn't say anything more where he sat with a hunted expression on his face, his colorless eyes bleary and lips fluttering.

"Phlegm the doctor says," the woman explained stolidly between coughs with a knowing wink in the general direction of her guest. "Keeps 'im under surveillance…Every third month we bring 'im to town for a check-up. He's on medication, you know…The doctor is a pulmonary specialist. Well, we do think that the reason why 'em Indians don't bother us, has to do with him…They've seen 'im, know he's unable and sort of a saint or something, you know," she went on with something cracking in her voice while looking at her husband searchingly with raised eyebrows.

"Yeah, harming you would mean serious trouble to them," Jeff agreed. "They are superstitious, and assaulting a cripple would bring a curse on the entire tribe."

Putting down his coffee cup, the older man said earnestly, "No, as long as we keep our stock away from their pastureland, 'em reds won't bother us…But if we don't…"

They all nodded to this, the fire ticking in the stove. The woman poured more coffee into their cups and pulled out a chair and sat down. She talked for a while about people who had lived on this ranch in the long ago, about how they'd lived, and how they'd died. Suddenly she interrupted herself and peered out the window. It was all black out there, so black she did not see anything but her mirror image. Turning to her guest she said after a while, "You see mister O'Halloran, we use to finish every day with a reading from the Scripture. Right now we are studying Ezekiel's book in the Old Testament, and S:t Marc's gospel in the New, and we do study one or two chapters each evenin' after sunset, and after we've done, we close up by reading from a book of sermons…Hope you…don't mind."

"Not at all…I sure can need it, ma'am…Frankly…you haven't mentioned your own names."

"Oh…I'm so sorry…I am Mary Acuff."

"An' I'm Billy Acuff," her son shared, clutching the top of his fair head with one hand, and motioning for the employee to introduce himself.

"My name's Brendan Acuff…John's brother," the older one said. He made a sign at the disabled man in the wheelchair, sitting half sleeping, eyelids slightly fluttering. Mrs. Acuff twirled her reading glasses and looked at Jeff and forced a smile. A much-thumbed black Bible with a black ribbon decorated with small roses in different colors across one page sat in front of her at the table. She opened it with great wariness, and by the soft light of a chandelier she started to read in a distinct and clear voice with a slight mountain twang one chapter, and another. Struggling the man in the wheelchair, as if an emotion had come over him, braced his feet once and once again in a try to free himself, his left hand shaking in paroxysms as he squeezed the armrests, the tongue quivering in his half-open mouth.

"Try to straighten him up, someone," his wife ordered. "He's tired…it's always like this every evenin'," she added, addressing Jeff, who at once made a quick visual check of John Acuff to see him being considerably slumped back in his seat, fighting to keep his eyes open.

"You see Mr. O'Halloran in the past he was always hemmed in his feelings, but nowadays he shows 'em," Mrs. Acuff said. "Frankly I don't know which is best," she went on tiredly, looking straight at Jeff and at her husband where he sat with his lips in motion, seemingly unable to express his words.

Alerted by the sudden attention, the handicapped man made some futile efforts to brace his feet against the footrest of the wheelchair, but brother Brendan came to his deliverance, and within short John sat in straight attention, almost martially. Gathered there the little group went on with the worshipping for a good while. Brendan sang two songs out of "The first book of consort lessons" by John Dowland, accompanying himself on the lute. He had a beautiful, full-toned and distinct voice, somewhere between base and baritone. At the very latest, before they withdrew, his sister-in-law fervently said a prayer, and closed the Bible, and blew the flames of the candles away.

Jeff got asked if he could imagine share rooms with Brendan down at the bunkhouse on a bed with a ticking of husks. "Maybe I could fix us a nightcap." Brendan hinted, helping himself to a chew of tobacco then rubbing his square hands together, Mrs. Acuff out of earshot. "It's gonna be you an' me an' the dog," he announced, making a charitable gesture toward his home, the bunkhouse with its small porch, where he had lived since the fall of 1865, when he escorted his benumb brother back home from the war.

At gray daybreak, right before full light, a jangling note of a triangle sounded. Jeff awoke early, had already been up for half an hour after a good night's sleep, and had shaved and scoured himself with cold water that he'd taken from the washtrough right outside the door of the bunkroom. He'd also checked on and swathed his hand and combed back his wet hair. For a moment he hesitated, then tore off the bandage and moved his fingers back and forth, floating the idea of letting the cut stay un-dressed. There was no cavity left and the edges were come together just nicely, the stitches still there. Brendan had already left him, preparing for the weekly trip to town. The place of the dog was empty as well. He stepped outside. The crickets had stopped and the air was smoky and cold. At the barn Brendan and Billy were in the process of yoking together and bridling two big and short-legged mongrel wagon horses.

"Just go inside an' get some breakfast in you…We come in when we are finished!" Billy greeted him jovially, checking the cinches.

"Your husband ain't up yet? Jeff remarked, entering the kitchen after having wished his hostess a good morning.

"He's resting for a while…He looks pretty drowsy today. Sometimes you have to coax 'im…a ticklish procedure, you see. Has to do with his brain lesion, the doctor says." She flicked a glance at him then continued, "Go ahead, help yourself…the boys will be in any time…I go down feed 'em hens."

From a bench in a corner, she without a further word took a hamper and went outside.

It was well after daylight and the sun had long since topped the mountains in the east when they ultimately said their farewells and Jeff struck out in the morning wetness, leaving the aloof ranch behind, headed for the mountains upcountry. His objective was to cross the stateline of Montana the same evening, given the weather held.

Time dragged on and soon enough he left the prairie behind and met the hills, following an old Indian trail much overgrown, but still wide enough to let the horses walk side by side. Northbound they heavy-footed plodded up the hill, picking their way, uncovering in their progress small stones that appeared frozen at patches where the sun hadn't as of yet warmed the ground entirely on this altitude. Judging by the sun time was past nine, and there would be several hours of daylight left still.

He'd now been traveling the rest of the day and entered in the late afternoon Montana. There was no sign of a human being anywhere, except for a cart a bit further out, slowly pulled by a chunky squirrel-headed bay coat with sagging back and breath venting from its nose in the very clear air. It disappeared behind a knoll and reappeared a while later from behind the same knoll, still rolling as slowly as before. Jeff made a halt and stood and watched it under the white clouds that were moving eastward. He smoked for a short while, dismounted and distinguished the stub, checking the ground for prints of hooves, and sensing the wind gusting up, he flapped up the collar about his ears and pulled on his gloves, then mounted and moved the horses forward.

The man on the cart appeared in the bright temporary sunlight to be a half-blood Indian, a very old man by the looks of him. He had a face hardened by sun and wind and great protruding ears, and a forehead set in a perpetual frown. He was in ill-fit clothes and slouch hat, glaring wildly at the sight of Jeff. He pulled in the horse and the cart piled with stove wood stopped. Granit-faced he studied the rider with long contemplation, his sullen eyes showing no expression at all. Seeing him showing no inclination to say a word, Jeff addressed him politely, "Howdy."

The old man didn't respond, just went on keeping his gaze fixed upon the strange rider. Without taking his gaze off him, he charged and pinched his nose with two fingers, and then dispatched a yellowish slimy gout.

"You live up here in 'em mountains, sir?" Jeff began, looking askance at the load and the horse's harness that was so worn and old one could see the wood through the leather.

The man looked at Jeff in incomprehension for a long moment. "You live where you reside," he bad-temperedly replied eventually, his voice a thunder.

The black stallion kicked back and shifted awkwardly, then stood about uneasily. Jeff, who barely had heard what the old man had said, chucked it up and sawed it about a little, answering, "What does that mean, sir?"

"It means what it says," the old man answered shrewdly, the last word all but carried away by the wind.

The bay tossed his head, the bridle bit clinking. The old man slacked the bridles and kept watching Jeff with a suspicious look.

"Listen…can I ask you a couple of questions, sir?" Jeff demanded politely.

The man bared his few half-rot teeth, winced, still wordless, though. He squinted at Jeff.

"I'm followin' three riders movin' straight north…ruffians…Yo've seen 'em?"

The old man nodded, wiping his nose with his sleeve, contemplating the quest, his black eyes still glaring at Jeff, who now had closed into and was standing right by his side. He removed a rolled cigarette from out his breast pocket and offered it to the man standing on the cart, who licking his chops reached out and without comment greedily took it in his crooked fingers, displaying no sign of gratefulness. Concealing the match as much as possible against the wind Jeff helped him light it up, and then took one cigarette for himself. The man sucked, his gaunt cheeks ballooning, and for the first time his gaze left Jeff. He looked out the hillsides to the north, then again stared boldly at the stranger. He claimed to have seen three horsemen by sunup this morning, evil-looking folks. He avidly sucked at the cigarette, then shifted his gaze back to Jeff.

"Did yo' talk with 'em...?" Jeff asked.

The man brushed away some ash from off his poncho that he wore over his thin shoulders, then panned out, the cigarette hanging stiffly between his thin lips, "They asked me 'bout the quarry up in 'em mountains."

"An' what did you say to 'em?"

"What?"

"I said what did you say 'em...?" Jeff repeated, his voice raised.

The old man renewed his grip on the bridles while he quietly contemplated the question before responding. "Here ain't nothing 'but scavengers...that's what I said to 'em."

Jeff spat out a flake of tobacco, shifted in the saddle and hiked his shoulders a little. He eyed the man long, then demanded, "Alright...did 'em ask yo' somethin' else?"

The old gaffer remained quiet for a short time as if trying to remember, then grunted sulkily, "No....Nothin'." He took a long pull on the cigarette and discharged a mighty cloud of smoke.

"In which direction did 'em ride on?"

With a trembling finger he motioned north.

"Alright sir, I better get on...Thank you," Jeff mumbled, searching his eyes.

Tugging at the bridles, without a word of farewell, the man turned and gave a cluck to the horse then slapped the reins and sat the cart in motion, passed by and wheeled on, the cigarette that now wasn't much more than a butt, dangling from the corner of his mouth. Jeff looked long after him. After some minute the old-timer turned around and raised his hand to Jeff, who shook his head in disbelief, then raised his boots and kicked them into the horse's flanks, and set out at a slow canter.

X

"What has happened to my brother?" Birgit lamented miserably, looking at Doctor Williams, her eyes almost flowing. Before them Wolf was sitting practicing at the grand piano, a Bösendorfer from 1805, his practices beyond brutal. Quite recently he'd limbered up, playing Toccata, E minor, BWV 912 by JS Bach and before that he had gone through an ad lib session, and a Sonata by Domenico Scarlatti. On any given day, he could start performing, the psychiatrist announced in amazement, listening with mouth half-open.

"He is still on medication, as you know, Miss Süsskind, but the dosage is adjusted down. What I don't like, though, is his, well, to put it frankly…his lack of social competency. Basically it might have to do with the medication, but…just to a certain extent. What we lack is sufficient experience from those drugs, but I'm going keep him under surveillance, as long as you need me. Best thing is not be too hot to trot."

Birgit didn't answer, just paused in mid-thought long enough to dry away a tear from her moist eyes.

"Wouldn't it be beneficial for him if he didn't put on more weight?" she wondered eventually and brushed away an unruly wisp of hair from her eye.

"Well…I have put in some tonic that will stimulate him eat more," the doctor explained evasively. "Has he gushed lately?"

"Well, as you know, he isn't that glib. He must have the right to show feelings…like everybody else, mustn't he? Do you believe he has insight in his, how shall I put it…does he consider himself different?"

The doctor said nothing for a while, then answered deep in thought, "Well, as you know, Miss Süsskind…as you know, there is a history of mental illness in your family. All we can do is wait. Occasionally he complains of headache…and nausea, right. That's a side-effect of the anti-depressant, as is his hearing voices. We have to keep in mind what he has experienced. He's just a kid, he should talk about all the gruesome things he had gone through, and above all…he ought to pick up school soon…as soon as we have obtained the proper dosage of lithium."

Much talk about drugs and adjustments back and forth, less of talking directly to my brother, Birgit mused. This did not mean she had much been thinking on weeding the doctor out, as did she scarcely dare to think of the ultimate bill. Regarding Birgit, she of course wanted to see her junior brother restored to health. He was all she had in life, now that the rest of the family was gone and the contact with their kinfolks in Europe, the old world, was sporadic. "The old world" was a metaphor their father always used, when referring to their roots.

She got stirred in her thoughts, hearing a loud jingle among the hangers when the doctor took his greatcoat and left. Birgit and her brother were on their own, and now free to use their own language, German.

The letters from Mrs. Penn back in Sioux Falls never ended to elicit questions. The news about Jeff were always so tenuous. But how could it be otherwise? Still there was no sign from him. That's always what the old lady keeps saying: No sign of Jeff. Neither did she, Birgit, dare to ask too many questions about him. What she knew was, however, that he "is not out carousing" and "he goes after those refugees and get them adjudicated, he's doing his job" and such, and "when do we see you around?"

It was not quite fall and not quite winter. The days were dark mostly. He sensed it had grown colder by and by, and the country had taken on other colors, and campsites were numerous in the wilderness.

He packed away his telescopic spyglasses and buckled shut the saddlebag where he stored all equipment he needed, then looked up again and peered steadily ahead from under his hat brim, his eyes wet with the whispering constant headwind. In the unmoving light not far from the horse-path, that stretched on as far as he could overlook, a shape was lying in full view with a plenty of cranberry shining red all about him with his hat over his face, his broken kidskin boots crossed at the ankles. Reaching down his hand he caught at the bridles where they sat slung across his knee and re-started the horses, prompting the feisty stallion ahead with his shanks, driving up in his coming small birds from their refuge in the low wind-tattered shrubbery. Horse manure on the road, not fresh-looking, but not old-looking either. One day old, perhaps two at the most. An abandoned campsite. Yellowed newsprint crumpled in the mud. Birds bursting skyward on clipping wings. Stools of humans in the hard all but iced ground, and more shreds of soaked newsprint. He kept on drawing nearer at a steady pace. Sometime later he halted the horse under him, the leashed-up pack horse filing in short-gaited, twisting, its breath rising whitely from its mouth. He dropped the bridles of the packhorse and drew the rifle from the scabbard, cocked it and sat and held it across the saddle. He boosted himself upright and looked about. The stallion shied and stepped. As if it was frightened by the strange place. He one-handed reined it about a little in the cauterized terrain, prodding the fractious animal with the spurs. He couldn't at that distance make out the features of the shape up there. All he saw was a long scraggly disheveled beard, and a lifeless body in a set of bloody tattered togs in different stages of disintegration. Sensing his stomach getting tight, he put the gun at half-cock, fitted it to the scabbard and drew it back into, then stood down of the saddle, and bracing his feet he afoot in a shuffling gait turned off into the overgrown path with its dying partially tramped-down vegetation, the horses filing in behind, short-gaited with edgy tread and feet sucking slightly at the ground, following him at either his arms up the quagmire as if they were curious and barely able to control themselves at the immediacy of water, stirring and driving forth in their coming a grass snake that momentarily uncurled and soundlessly glided down in a hole under a roadside boulder.

Treading heavy-footedly his way up the slippery path, stopping time and again to examine the ground, uncovering tracks of shod horses and indentions of boots in the partially frozen dirt, he with his features going from anticipation to disgust stopped when within fifty feet of the lying corpse. His eyes traced their way upward as far as the peak then back to the lying man again. He called and looked about him, listening for any sound at all, but there wasn't any. By craning his neck skyward, he could spot two hawks circling slowly far up, eyeing him mutely with icy eyes. Saving only for this, nothing of consequence there was to perceive or hear in the vast wilderness. Not even a crow cawed. All there was to the place, was just a melancholy peace of a dying nature, preparing itself for winter.

He went up to and broodingly bent to examine the shape lying there underfoot with a muddy crushed-down hat covering half of his face, his pants slipped down to his ankles. With the tip of his boot, not knowing what he was about to witness, he with circumspection nudged the hat to the side and straightened up and retreated a step. He saw a shapeless thin face most of which indistinguishable and full-bearded, and a residue of coalesced blood below, blood that hadn't as of yet entirely sunk down into the dank and partially flooded earth. He lowered his head yet a little the better to see. The eyes of the man were half-shut with the thin lips drawn tight over the moldy teeth, his coarse, stained shirt torn to pieces, the hairy abdomen fully exposed in the sparse afternoon light, and the pants torn down the thighs almost to knee-level. All that once had hung between his legs was detached. Partly seeped away funnels of feces were detectable on his thighs. A crimson pool underneath his crutch. He craned his neck some more and stepped forward the better to see. The wind blew down from the north, cooling his face. He went down into a squat, his eyes uneasy. He could observe it all better now. He once again scrolled his eyes upward. Faint tracks of night-hunting coyotes underfoot, partly trampled out. His eyes sought the corpse again, and he reached out his hand across the little space there was between them. There was no way he could detect any sign of life in him, thus he relinquished to palpate his carotid artery. The body was gone cold, as cold as the air about him. He had been dead for five, six hours, perhaps more. He was scalped. A bullet hole had penetrated the belly. He pushed himself up and stood for some time in a quandary. He went to and seized the stallion by the cheek strap, Colt in his right hand and thumb hooked over the hammer, for what reason he didn't know. He looked about uneasily, re-holstered the firearm and faced the body once again, regarding it long and closely. It was one of the tramps from the saloon in Sioux Falls. Yeah. Although he didn't look himself, manhandled as he was. Same hard lines about the mandible and mouth, same outfit. With his breath easing he stood in the cooling air contemplating his next move, seeing two options. Either he should clear a piece of ground and inter the mutilated remains, or leave them to coyotes and hawks, the latter, five in number as of yet, circling the skies overhead, having their awry necks already torn in their direction general as though prepared to strike. In essential he'd neither the time nor the tools to bury him. Time was his enemy. Having ultimately dismissed the idea of just riding on, he took the canteen from off the saddle, twisted the cap and drank then stood and cast about, the keg pointed halfway to his mouth, his other hand hidden in his coat's pocket. Save for the dead man and the horses he was alone. He listened for sounds other than those he'd heard before, but there weren't any. The days are drawing in now, soon dark will be over us, he deliberated and thumbed back his Stetson. The site where he stood wasn't much more than a cattle path with tracks from them visible all around it. He pressed the stopper back with the thick of his thumb and restored the empty keg onto the saddle, then dawdling stalked his way to where the packhorse stood cropping bleakly with its long tail swishing. He went around it and with fingers numb from the cold untied and pulled the spade from the packsaddle and looked upcountry, but there was no form of life there that he could detect. The place seemed devoid of life.

    Nothing but the dull clang of the spade was heard when he kicked it hard into the hard-packed dirt and started to dig acting purposefully, his cheeks growing tight. Resting briefly but a couple of occasions, he dug frantically, widening the hole while the horses went about nibbling bleakly at the dying grass at the way side. A myriad of questions rushed through his head. The half-blood on the cart, and the bay with the broad hind. Where did he reside? For a brief moment he just stood and looked off toward the pass in the north. Along the path to the east, there was a water hole that spilled over some water not more than a trickle in their direction, leaving were it run down a section of perpetually fresh growth. He slipped off his gloves and pitched them into the soil beneath him, then fetched up from different pockets his smoking things and rolled himself a smoke in the half dark. Smoking thoughtfully, he stood and studied the tomb that soon would be ready and deep enough to prevent the coyotes from dredging the corpse up. And he studied the scalped man in the grass underfoot. Who were those out there, the men ahead of him, those he was chasing? Who had done the killing, the assassination?

    It was late afternoon and all but dark when he chucked the spade into the mud. He pulled off his gloves and brought forth his smoking things and with his back to the wind popped a match to the heel of his boot twice till it caught fire. Protecting the flame with his cupped hands he set fire to the cigarette and turned back. Feeling a temptation to just run away he looked off toward the browsing horses. Where should he head? Back home? Why? To save his life? Would that be the only purpose? No way. He had to move on. He was forced to, he'd a work to do. He took a last draw on the cigarette and dropped the butt and tramped it out with the sole of his boot. The stallion now was almost out of sight, and the packhorse was tagging along in a heavy lift of foot in the same direction. He sought his way out to where the stallion stood cropping. He grabbed hold of the headstall and led the horse back to where the dead body lay. The horse flattened his ears and shied when approaching upon it, as the sharp yapping from a jackal wolf told them they were not far off. He took the empty canteen from off the saddle horn and made it for the water hole up in the quagmire where he squatting dunked it and filled it up, listening for sounds other than those from the snuffling and cropping horses, but there was nothing but quietude, just the sounds of the nature itself. He closed the filled-up water keg and brought it back and attached it to the saddle from where he'd taken it, and with his boots heavy with mud went back to and bent down over the corpse where it lay in its blooded shabbiness. He strained his muscles and forcibly lifted the now stiffened burden up with a groan, and bellowing from exhaustion he made his way slowly tracking the ruts, sliding the dead man behind him with his toes up and head aloll, mouth half agape. He closed in and dropped the stout body in the hole to wither, then erected his back, his heart surging and his chest heaving vehemently. He felt crestfallen like somebody groping about, barren of feelings, longing for some revelry. He went in search for and gathered some sections of withered limbs and stones and placed them over the body for protection against the wild animals. He quoted some Scripture from memory and said a prayer before refilling the grave. Once he'd done he stepped on the fresh-turned earth to set it firmly until it looked much the same as it had before. He then bent down and fetched his hat, then got erect again and run his fingers through his hair and donned it and squared it low. In stamping the mud off his feet, he noted it now was all dark about him. One thing he knew for sure: The killing of this stranger wasn't performed by Indians. Somebody out there wished to intimidate him.

It was going toward night, and up the firmament the stars had come out, shining bright. Suddenly an owl's hoot broke the serene setting. He went back to the packhorse where it stood inert head-down as if it had dropped asleep. He patted its neck and re-hung the spade to the saddle then reached into and by the throat took the bottle of whiskey up from the saddle's compartment. It now was so dark he could but see half of what was in front of him. He held the bottle up to the oasis of starlight so as to check the level, then unscrewed the cap. He straightened in the back just enough to funnel a long drink down his throat so as to take the worst chill off his body, then lowered his arm, and looking about screwed the cap back. He bent his fingers to test them. The hand felt much the same as it did before that saloon brawl. A small cold wind blew down from the mountains. Any day winter cold would set in. He wrestled within himself as to whether he should create a fire and roast the last shreds of veal enough to sustain him for a week that Mrs. Acuff had bestowed on him.

He relished its rich nourishment. Should he risk a fire? At the end he resolved against it.

He fetched the horses and walked them higher up and into the trees and into a wood so dark he couldn't see the path but had to feel his way forward. He kept on walking until he eventually was out of the wood and down a long slope until he finally found himself standing in the bottom of a ravine in a compact darkness.

Bedded down in his bedroll he awoke in the twilight with a start, the echoing of a ricocheting bullet still ringing in his ears. He raised one hand to the eastern sky to shade his eyes against the rising sun, shotgun in the other, listening for sounds in the tranquil morning. Looking downstream he knelt and sat listening. Unsure of what to do he got to his feet and crouched, gun in hand, made a circling motion headed for better shield behind a gigantic stone block, when another slug, one discharged from another direction hit somewhere behind, no more than thirty feet away. He chanced a rapid glance at the horses to watch their reaction. They hadn't panicked either of them, but stood and tossed their heads in the dark of an old oak tree with severed roots about which they were tethered. Yet another bullet whistled past his head. For a short second he watched a raven black mop evince behind a cliff up the draws, and withdraw, no hat on.

"Raise your hands and step forward!"

A female voice. Then silence. "You hear...Raise your hands and step forward...in my direction!!" the same voice admonished after a while.

Having no intention to succumb to the order, Jeff remained still. They are at least two, he guessed. Maybe more, but not less. His fingers squeezed the hilt of his firearm as he listened, alert to any disturbance.

A quiet settled, then a voice called out, "We know you hear us...an' we ain't sayin' it no more! Come forward...keep your hands up so we can have us some fun!"

It was the same voice, although the tone more ominous. Then again he recognized the familiar silhouette and the black mop. It moved lithely, scanning the surroundings, then withdrew.

"I'm gonna shin up you son of a bitch..." Jeff hissed between his lips. "I see to it yo're gonna get yo' a ball..."

He made an on-rush and zigzagged to make of the sniper a target for a time long enough to hit him, well knowing, that if he didn't take action quickly enough, he might risk getting hit in the back, convinced that the other one, a female, judging from her voice, was in the process of surrounding him and bring him down. Most of all were they looking forward to torture him and then kill him, which meant they weren't willing to risk their own well-being too much. Since the sniper was positioned to his right, Jeff therefore had in mind to run the risk of rushing to the left and discharge his firearm in the same moment. He might be successful in the enterprise, provided his antagonists weren't too experienced in terms of close combat.

A lengthy silence ensued until the same light voice called out another time, "You'd better come forward…you hear!…Drop yo' firearm an' raise both hands!"

It might be worthwhile running the risk, that is if the black-haired in fact was the freed vaquero. As for the companion, Jeff had no inkling as of his or her identity. He knew one thing, though: Whoever it was, he or she was anxious to get him within an appropriate angle of fire. They sure could have chosen a better ambush. But on the other hand, there weren't so many of them in these surroundings.

Jeff gritted his teeth and spat, now ready to try the second part of his plan. Keep goin', stay in constant motion, constant motion sideways, zigzagging. With some luck, I might blow 'im down from that ledge next time he exposes himself, he meditated.

At the top of his voice Jeff bellowed back, "Hey vaquero! You up there?…Yo' hear me?"

For an instant there was a dead silence as if the two up there were parleying, calculating odds.

"Yo' are comin'?" a voice eventually shouted out, quizzically.

"Yo' told me raise my hands an 'move forward, an' that's what I'm doin'!" Jeff yelled back.

Another quiet settled, neither budging. Jeff's heart skipped some beats. Would there still be anybody up there? Were they looking for another and better place to attack him from? Maybe they had already found it and were watching him right now. In that case they would have him trapped and were free to shoot him down whenever they wanted, just to make a short work of him. There was no way he could recede, not now, he reasoned, still in motion, looking up the ledge, the pipe of his rifle pointed up there in as steady a grip as he could obtain. He knelt for a second and cast about, then pushed himself up and advanced slightly forward thus trying to improve his shot angle somewhat, the tension almost making him scant of breath.

"You are coming…deputy?" someone asked from up the ledge, the voice now more tense. The voice in some way sounded younger than before, or had he for a second forgotten to disguise it as a consequence of anxiety? Suddenly Jeff observed the right arm and the outer part of a man's right shoulder up on the ledge. Primed for that to happen, Jeff didn't hesitate to fire three shots in rapid sequence, the angle oblique. The figure flinched and watched his firearm fall down with a dull metallic clatter. Jeff dashed forward, gun pointing up, but there was no one left, so he held his fire. He bent down and quickly appropriated the rifle by the stock, whipped around and running crouched zigzagged his way back to the camp site. Once there he grinned humorlessly, gun in hand. He looked down at it again uncertain as to what he should do with it. He made a quarter turn to the hill side and made his decision, thinking the best thing to be was to crush it. He sensed a void inwardly, knowing his adversaries still being there, one of whom wounded, perhaps seriously, but nonetheless.

He made a quick decision to abandon the place with all the speed he could obtain. Shielded, as he hoped, from view, standing in the stone ravine, he saddled up, scooped up his bedding and rolled it up, then tied the bedroll to the saddle and sat off, the packhorse trotting behind by the rope halter. Making concessions to the driving wind, having no source of cover, he followed the creek north all the while keeping a strict watch in all directions. There were no fresh hoof prints ahead, no sign of followers behind. By and by the ride way widened and the scenery got more open, just occasional downpours slowing his progress.

In the seething headwind the horses plodded their way along the mud cattle track until they the best part of an hour later came in view of a hill ranch with longhorn cattle spread all over the treeless luxuriant valley. He dismounted awkwardly and walking afoot with the horses behind him mounted an inclination in the nearest vicinity so as to reach an elevated site from which he would be able to supervise the landscape in all directions.

Minutes later he found himself standing on a site in the wilderness, flat as a parlor floor with withering wildflowers, and some small aspen trees about which to tie the horses. There were also rocks enough to keep him protected, and some blowsy grass for the horses, still comparatively green, all but knee-high at places. There was not much wood to build a fire with, yet he found enough fuel to make coffee. He watched the country back with slow movements of his eyes, then cut some slices out of his last loaf and cut himself some dried deer and brought up two eggs from one of his saddlebags and consumed them raw. When he'd done eaten he sat stiff and erect, looking about with his lower arms on his knees. Barely a mile down beneath the draws to the east he spotted some ranch buildings. Smoke was issuing from one chimney, and a small number of horses stood grouped in a holding pen, running their heads along each other's necks, and from one of the outhouses a shape got out walking in a list while hauling up his pants, and with slow progression made it into another house. A chilly northeasterly wind sang on the hilltop, and up the skies some clouds were running southward at a rapid pace. Time dragged on and he was beginning to feel cold. Looking down the decline he waited, not knowing what he exactly was waiting for. No change ever seemed to take place. He began feeling giddy being alone so much. What had his boss, Sheriff Douglas Kimble, made to make an end to this long stretch of silence? Had he sent out sketches to the sheriff's offices of the northwest parts of the country? That's the last thing he had told him to do, before they split a week back. "Scatter 'em sketches about the whole country, boss!"

"Sure, Jeff, first thing," the sheriff promised. Would there be any particular reason for his indecision? Did he in reality possess of more information than he was willing to admit? Why was he so elusive? Did he protect someone?

It was early afternoon. Seated horseback he checked behind him to see if he was followed then let the horses wade out into the water of the ford to drink their fill-in. To the south the country lay open and deserted, offering a good lookout.

He turned the horses and slowly rode ashore and dismounted. Tugging them slowly over his swollen feet he shuffled off his boots, stripped off his stockings and clothes and stark nude waded out and took a long swim in the chilly water. He soaped his entire body and shaved, changed wear and washed his soiled clothing. After an hour he returned up the ridge with filled canteens, refreshed, the filthy sensation gone.

When back on the peak, he shielded by some rocks stood in the stirrups and peered down the valley southward. All there was to see was packs of longhorns, cows, calves and bold-looking steers, keeping watch over the outliers. Otherwise nothing moved out there. Everything was quiet and still, just the wind murmuring about the cliffs, setting the few remaining dry leaves of an nearby oak tree in slight motion. He collected some sections of withered twigs and lit a fire. He ate and waited, listening to the horses cropping. One or two more days by this encampment and he would be in serious need of provisions. He consulted the map to see nearest town was some hours ride northeast. Hopefully his laundry would be ready before the day was out. Right before dusk came on, he went to where the horses stood tied. He unbuckled the girths and pulled the saddles and the blankets from off their backs. Running his hand along their necks he talked friendly to them then left them neck-reined.

By sunup he woke up with a jerk and reached for his gun where he'd placed it underneath the saddle. He took it up and cocked the trigger and carefully raised his head and looked about for anything moving there. The horses stood pricking their ears, shifting weight as though in some way alerted. He didn't know what had awakened him, nor did he know why the horses were looking alarmed. He got out of his bedroll and half stood and remained so for some minute while adapting and tightening the gun holster around his waist, then pulled himself erect so as to re-adjust it. He gingerly peered downhill, but from where he stood he was incapable of seeing anything of certain relevance. He bent down and took hold of the saddle by the horn, shifted it from his right hand to the left, then reached down for the saddle blanket and took it up. He then jerked upright and lumbered away to the stallion and saddled up in a haste. He mounted and stood in the stirrups, his forehead creased in concentration, listening, looking off down to the south. He reached for the rifle and drew it from out the scabbard and cocked it. He sat down in the saddle again and gingerly booted the horse forward so as to afford a better outlook. He let the horse walk until he called a halt. He craned his neck and looked down the valley and out the flatlands. He now was able to distinguish a rider on an appaloosa perhaps a mile down the hill, gradually enlarging. He snapped open his saddlebag and fumbled out his glasses and put them to his eyes. He made some adjustments of the wheel until the object was in focus. A bareheaded horseman came toward him with a broad-brimmed sombrero hat hanging to his back by a strap, black hair, young, his right arm hanging down to the side while he held the reins at belly-level in his left hand. And yet another, riding at his side, was as far as Jeff could establish, a male. They rode alongside the sheer cliffs of the hill, not hurrying, trotting steadily as if they were in the process of tracking someone down. At a certain point the companion reined in his mount and said something to the vaquero. They booth sawed their horses around and quartering about investigated some tracks underfoot. Before neither of them had got time to look aloft, Jeff's decision already was made. "Bring it on, ol' boy!" he half whispered to the stallion. He drew his gun out of the holster and pressed the flanks of the horse and galloped it down the slope while discharging the gun in the jump. The first bullet hit the brachium of the nearest rider. He pointed anew and fired. The vaquero let go the grip of the reins and began squeezing his left forearm with his right gloved hand, his beardy face contorted in pain. His companion instinctively reached for his gun then lifted his arm as if in farewell, his look bewildered. Holding them at gunpoint Jeff advanced on them, seeing that neither of the riders even seemed to consider taking to flight.

"Alright, hold it there! Unbuckle your belts an' drop 'em!" Jeff ordered while coming along, slowing and bringing his horse to a final halt.

The vaquero didn't budge. His companion, sitting a bit separated from the vaquero, reluctantly halted, slumped in the saddle. Jeff motioned for him to move into, then gave a curt nod to him and said, "Unscabbard that gun! Pronto!"

Jeff watched him. For a lengthy moment he just sat and glared nastily at the unexpectedly descended rider on the black stallion. A thin gray mustache covered his over lip. Gray sideburns and gray hair, gray breeches, gray winter jacket with gray lapels. He appeared to be gray all over, save for the shineless battered boots. Like a conscript in the Confederacy. Jeff didn't remember ever having seen him before. He regarded him long and quizzically. Suddenly the man seemed to see things in a different way, realizing he was captured. Very slowly he reached out for and grabbed the rifle by the stock and slid it from out the scabbard, his movements elaborated, almost defiant. He then sat for an instant and weighed it in his hand.

"Drop it to the ground, you hear," Jeff exhorted, voice icy.

"You oughta be glad, deputy," the other one said, his tone mild.

Jeff eyed him long then eventually said, shifting, "Deputy? Do we know each other?"

"In a way, we do, perhaps."

Jeff eyed the gray man sharply, then asked, "Glad...what for?"

"I stumbled an' fell down…at the pass, yesterday mornin', sprained my ankle…otherwise you'd been dead by now, deputy. I had you…at gunpoint…just the way you've me right now."

"I said, throw down that gun," Jeff said again, his voice icy.

A hollow clatter got heard when the rifle clashed to the ground. From somewhere out the flats a party of longhorns cried out in chorus.

"Get off 'em horses," Jeff ordered harshly, "If you try somethin', I'll kill you."

Without moving the vaquero glared bleakly at Jeff, his dark eyes unblinking. He modeled his lips like he were about to say something, but no word came forth.

Jeff said, his tone impetuous, "Climb down from that horse, else I blow you down."

The Mexican continued staring brokenly. His both hands trembled as though being void of stability. "Both my arms are tattered," he replied carelessly with a foreign accent to it.

"I don't care if you pitch, we are waitin' for you to come down, but we don't have all day," Jeff snarled. "An' that goes for you, too," he went on with a short nod to the gray-haired.

Almost simultaneously the two waylaid riders slung the loop of the reins over the saddles and then almost simultaneously slid down to solid ground, their horses shifting weight from one hind foot to the other. The gray-haired half turned to Jeff, squinted saying, "I'm regretful I didn't squeeze off that bullet yesterday, deputy."

Jeff answered with an implying gesture and dismounted. He took a couple of steps away from the stallion and halted when in front of the men. He said them to pull off their boots and leave them on the ground. The gray-haired immediately formed his grim lips into a protest.

Jeff snapped with a scowl, "Get down on your butts an' take 'em off!"

A sweeping from Jeff's gun made the two men crouch low and soon they were sitting. Very circumstantially the gray-haired began to yank his boots off, and within soon a foul smell got carried along the air. Jeff instinctively retreated a couple of steps and looked down at the vaquero sitting ahead of him. He watched the young Mexican try and try again, his desperation growing by each attempt. Eventually he looked up at Jeff, as though he couldn't feel any surge of hope elsewhere. He levered his both arms until they were fully stretched in a gesture of capitulation. His face was writhing in pain.

"Yo' don't manage jemmy 'em loose, eh?" Jeff confronted while edging closer.

The vaquero raised one leg to try again, then lowered his arms and nodded helplessly, then snapped his face up and looked at Jeff. Jeff hesitated for an instant before deciding to let him keep his heels on. He turned around and stuffed the rifle back into the saddle scabbard.

"Hey, deputy!" the gray-haired one howled in his characteristic voice, "You gotta swathe our wounds...you see he can't even yank 'em boots off...else his legs might give..."

"Alright. Get to your feet!" Jeff commanded brusquely, his gaze settled upon them both. The vaquero tried twice to rise, but stumbled back, startled.

"Get up," Jeff grumbled. He reached out and grabbed him by his coat and forced him up, seeing his cheeks growing paler in consequence of the strain. The gray-haired already was standing up, his hale face clouded over, the self-satisfied smile all vanished. He looked like a man besieged by self-doubt. The bedraggled sleeve of his gray coat was dark red, penetrated, soaked through. Jeff ransacked the pockets of their clothes, finding nothing of significance. Doing the same with their saddle bags, he from the bag of the vaquero picked up one new-looking Smith & Wesson waistgun. He inspected it from every angle then broke it open to see it was loaded, then stuck it inside his belt. As for the bags of the other bum it contained two boxes of ammunition, one intact and one broken, and a dagger, one bearing evidence of heavy use in the past. Jeff deliberately searched the gazes of the men in turn, exhibited the objects to see they both stood squirming. He then stuffed the findings into one of his own saddle bags, and leaving the cases unsnapped told them to strip off their clothes.

"All of it?" the vaquero whimpered defensively, turning to his tormentor, his frail hands shaking.

"Just coat an' shirt...so I can see yo' wounds," Jeff replied as he took a closer look at the gray-haired felon, who now stood in his shirtsleeves, bareheaded, his thick hair receded at the temples, a man of indeterminate age. He sensed Jeff's intensive gaze, searched it and demanded in a neutral tone, "You just seized our stuff, deputy...we'll have it back later, eh, all of it?"

"You mean 'em hardware?"

"Right."

"I doubt you guys are gonna need 'em anymore…Take off your shirt."

The man looked away and left-handed with trembling fingers began to unbutton his sweat-stained shirt. Circumstantially he then undraped himself all the while noticing his left sleeve being partially stuck to his brachium. He turned to face Jeff, who now was standing at his side.

"The blood's clogged, eh…" His eyes bored into Jeff with realization.

"Looks like the bullet's still in the muscle," Jeff said, his eyes set to the wound. "We gotta get movin'. I'll fix yo' a makeshift dressing." He paused a second then went forth, "It will be one or two hours by horseback to the nearest town…"

The captive rejected raising his hand in a stopping motion, "There's no way I…"

"That's the way it's gonna be. Just shut up an' do as I say you!" Jeff snapped. "Get back on your horses and ride in front of me up that slope. I've some stuff to get up there before we move on. Then the marshal of Liberty's waitin' on you."

Up on the camp Jeff drained the last of his coffee, ate some bread and two eggs, leftovers since the previous night. He extricated from his saddlebag two clean stockings and tore them into rags and bandaged the wounds of the captives. Afterward he recharged his guns and fed his ammunition belt, saddled the packhorse and broke camp. A while later they descended the slope and set out headed straight west, pursuing a trail cut by livestock.

XI

Right before the crossing place the vaquero halted. The big appaloosa with caution lowered its head and drank, Jeff and the other captive sitting watching on their horses right behind. Everything was quiet about them. When the appaloosa had finished drinking and raised its head out of the sliding water, Jeff told the vaquero to put it into. The young Mexican didn't obey, just stood.

"Alright, move it on," Jeff ordered harshly. "We have no time for a long ride 'round."

Reluctantly the vaquero booted his horse forward and down into the current. He stopped midstream where the water touched the abdomen of the animal that bucked and stepped out of agitation, sensing deficit of stamina in the reins. Jeff drew and cocked his gun and pointed at him. "Move it forward. Don't try me no more, you hear!"

"If I fall into the water…I can't swim," the vaquero lamented bitterly.

"I can't either," his companion added, grinning from obliquely in front of Jeff.

"Just bring 'em horses over an' don't try to escape!!" Jeff ordered, standing behind them, pointing at them with the gun in his left hand, holding the packhorse by the halter strap in the other. Out of horror the young rider cautiously pressed the speckled giant mount forward. The horse walked on with black mud swishing at its feet, its rider's beardy face grimacing in pain and sheer frustration. He went on almost in trance. At some distance out the bottom grew sheer and the horse's legs seemed to give way and fold under it, but the intimidated animal raised itself by the strength of its knees then again went down while the bottom in a flickery instant plumb went without depth of it. Right after that had happened, the horse started to hesitate, almost seized with panic. "Press his flanks!" Jeff brawled, "Press hard forward, else he'll stroke with the current!…He'll start swimmin'!"

The young rider gingerly with lips livid futilely nudged the swimming gelding ahead with his both frail arms slung around the horse's neck hence providing an illusion of movement. The horse must have been swimming though, breaking for the shore, for some minutes later he rode it ashore on the opposite bank with his breath soaring, his face burning out of excitement. Once standing on the bank he turned in the saddle and snapped his head and flung Jeff a scornful look, seeing he was still pointing at him with his gun.

Hard glances got exchanged and nothing was spoken when Jeff some moments later handcuffed the two captives to one another. Just in case, so you not drift apart, he told them matter-of-factly. The vaquero did not display any reaction whatsoever, whereas his companion went on glaring at their tormentor with a grim smug under the gray mustache. During the ride they both grew paler, something that Jeff had foreseen ever since he got them disabled. Once in a while they were even hanging down in the saddles, and more and more often they reached for their canteens, so Jeff therefore considered it best to re-examine their wounds. He reined in his horse and set it and motioned for them to join in. The Mexican took off his sombrero and wiped his forehead with the back of his shirtsleeve. He sweated profusely as though he had fever. Jeff removed the manacles and settled him on the rutted ground, his companion still remaining horseback, glaring out the windswept reaches, his hands folded together on the saddle's horn. His pockmarked features were grimacing in pain. Jeff looked clandestinely at him speculatively, thinking the man might as well be faking and punch out any time. He told him to dismount. With some clean rags he then re-bound their wounds and offered them each a drink of water. He then rolled himself a smoke while taking in the country.

The shapes of the mountains they had quit stood behind and a blueish formation of some variety materialized in the horizon further out west. He frowned and watched.

"We wait an' see what's comin' up," he told the others.

The gray-haired stood leaning against the withers of his horse, holding a cloth-bundled arm aloft, looking back at Jeff, who stood watching the formation out there, as of yet seemingly motionless to his eyes in the bright sunlight.

"Horsemen…a cavalry detail," he eventually grunted and exhaled a cloud of smoke. He dropped the butt and tramped it out with the heel of his boot, distinguishing meanwhile the steady tramp of approaching horse hooves, and a cavalry flag snapping and heeling in the wind. The clops of the hooves grew harder as they got nearer. They waited. An instant later a squadron of cavalrymen all in similar dress came up to them at a short trot with puffs of dust rising from the horse's hocks. The young light-hued blue uniformed soldier riding point raised his right arm and pulled up his big sorrel, that approached wild-eyed, stamping, and a minute later it all got silent, and all there was to hear was but the sounds from the horses.

"Howdy!" he greeted in a resonant voice in a pomp of West Point, and was quiet for a moment as he chucked up the horse, then turned to watch Jeff. "I'm Lieutenant Jury, patrol-leader of this squadron. We're out on a routine mission, garrisoned some fifteen miles west," he announced, his words coming clipped and evenly spaced in a military manner. He sat erect on his horse, waiting for Jeff to answer, his gauntleted hands resting on the saddle's horn, one propped upon the other.

Jeff looked off to the north, then aloft at the young officer, looking where he sat scarce grown in his dusty gold-encrusted blue Yankee uniform.

"Are 'em Indians on the warpath, lieutenant?" Jeff inquired, standing a pace away.

"You guys seen any recently?" the blond officer forthwith asked back and bent slightly forward in the army saddle, then picked up the reins and reined his horse about a little.

"Well, not recently, 'bout a week ago I rode upon a bunch of Arapahoe pretty far off south."

"Arapahoe?…No sir. I'm talking about Crows…Where are you headed, sir?"

"Liberty."

"Liberty, eh," the lieutenant repeated and swallowed. He was quiet for a short time as if processing this, then continued dolefully, "Town got attacked by Crows a couple of days back. The sheriff got killed…hit by an arrow, a couple of buildings got burnt down."

Jeff shifted and looked up at him with great earnestness, uncertain as to how he should formulate his answer. After a while the lieutenant broke the abrupt silence, asking cautiously without looking down, "You figure on staying in Liberty, sir?"

"I'm not. I figure on deliverin' those thugs to the law back there," Jeff declared nodding toward the captives.

"Outlaws?" the lieutenant asked with a subdued smile nodding in their general direction, seeing their inadequate dressings.

"Yeah."

The lieutenant boosted himself up a little bit in the saddle till he sat ramrod straight then said dryly, "I sure can see you were forced to...negotiate with a position of strength, sir."

"Yeah...well they are more easy to handle like that, you see...but right now they are at the end of the tether," Jeff replied.

The officer turned and looked at them, and then turned back to Jeff, holding the reins in one hand, the other braced leisurely upon his thigh. "See what you mean, sir...You're a lawman, sir...?"

"I am," Jeff confirmed taking in the country, then continued, "Frankly, I'm a bit worried 'bout what you said 'bout the sheriff bein' killed by 'em Crows."

The lieutenant looked past Jeff and sat silent for a short interval as if he was valuing what he just had heard, his white gloved hands squared on the horn hand over hand.

"Well, some other guy's replaced him...quite young individual. Seems alright...not easy to scare," the lieutenant shared in his clipped high voice. Suddenly his expression lightened a bit and a playful glint got visible in his light blue eyes. Jeff followed his gaze, certifying the officer was looking in the direction of the captives. The gray-haired tried to get to his feet, didn't succeed and fell back, now again trying to get up leaning against his right arm, creeping on all fours. He again failed to come on feet and fell back, then remained lying. The lieutenant approached him slowly, still on horseback, Jeff following afoot. They stopped beside him and stood and studied him for a moment, the cavalrymen still on their horses watching in bewilderment at a distance.

"Either he's drunk or unconscious." Lieutenant Jury suggested dryly without taking his eyes from him. Jeff took a step forward and knelt. He clapped the beardy cheek. It remained motionless and totally void of sentiment, neutral, all but sepulchral.

"Unconscious," Jeff murmured out into the air. With his gaze aloft he went on, "Poor bastard's lost a lotta blood."

"Sheriff, what do you figure's gonna happen to the poor bastard...if he gets over it?" the lieutenant asked hotly.

"I reckon he's gonna get hanged," Jeff replied shortly.

The lieutenant made no answer. He looked out the country then back at Jeff.

"Town's not so far off," he explained after a while, his voice businesslike. "I order two of my men to ride in and get a wagon. They ought to be back in an hour or so."

Jeff stood up. "Sounds fair enough…I appreciate your cooperation, lieutenant."

The officer sawed his horse around and rode back and delivered the order to two of his men, expectantly seated in their saddles. Within a minute they detached themselves and rode away in a constant falling, the rest of them told to dismount. They got down and stretched, looking about while stumbling around on stiff legs, throwing regular regards in the general direction of the two captives. The vaquero now was sitting, his eyes semi-closed, his gaunt beardy face turned in the opposite direction, his narrow back turned to them, sort of demonstratively.

The gray-haired dumpy wretch at once got placed on a single cell wooden bunk. Half an hour later Jeff was greeted by a jailer, the same one that beforehand had forewarned the doctor. Jeff was told that the captive now was examined and in fully conscious, but it was imperative to look after him regularly, the doctor explained after having removed a bullet from the vaquero, who was laid in the opposite cell.

"I advise you against taking them away before they are stable. I come back in the morning by eight," the doctor promised before leaving. The sheriff was out of town and due to be back around six, according to the same jailer who had taken care of them and brought them some food from the hotel. The mugs of the captives were placed on different places around the small town, the guard declared with satisfaction, an open-faced mongrel with pitch black hair, a talkative in his mid-forties. Upon seeing Jeff's frown, he just laconically responded, "Routine around here, sheriff's order, when we face this sort."

"Watch your rear when you go back home, deputy," he said repeatedly to Jeff. "Those Crows were 'bout to burn down all town…you've heard about it, right…"

Jeff just sipped his coffee and nodded shortly. The jailer jerked his head nervously around trying to be cooperative, a giveaway, one not the least elusive.

"Same thing was 'bout to happen back in Sioux Falls some months ago," Jeff informed with a slight burp.

"Crows?"

"Arapahoe," Jeff said listening to the painful moans from one of the lockups. "Just let 'em have 'em buffs an' 'em will stick to 'emselves."

"Is that so, deputy?"

"Sure. They need food like everybody else, yo' know."

He stopped abruptly as the door got open and a young man entered, a straight-backed tenacious-looking character with a firm handshake and a badge pinned to his vest.

"So yo' mean we're gonna detain 'em right away, O'Halloran?" he inquired businesslike, having heard Jeff's narrative.

Jeff nodded yes.

"I wire the DA first thing in the mornin'. Then we arrange a convoy to get 'em back the same way they've come. When the doc says it's alright to take 'em away, then we let 'em head home for a trial." He looked at Jeff as if to see how he would reply.

"Practical proceedings are to take place before that, sheriff. Just a formality," Jeff rebuked.

"Yeah, yeah," the young sheriff snapped with a short frown, standing outside the cell of the gray- haired, uptight.

"He appears dazed," he went on, roaming around, glancing at Jeff.

"That'll make 'im easy to handle, right?" Jeff countered, folding his hands behind his neck. "Don't worry, he'll survive. Pursuant to the doc's instructions, he's gonna stay with you for a couple of more days. That goes for 'em both."

He scraped the chair back and stood. He began digging in the breast pocket of his coat. Turning to the sheriff he said, "I've got a warrant for yo'. Just sign it before I leave."

"When are yo' leavin', O'Halloran…?" the sheriff asked.

"I leave tonight. I need some supplies from the store, my horses need a re-shoeing. Then I go back. Yo' have a blacksmith in town, else I fix it myself."

"The blacksmith is at the saloon right now. He ain't sober, yo' know. Yo' fix it yo'self, deputy?" the sheriff said, signing the warrant.

"Yeah, I've got the stuff in the boot of my packhorse."

Inside the lockups the two detainees talked to each other in hushed tones, the vaquero gnashing his teeth in fever. Jeff placed the signed warrant back in his bib pocket, looking meanwhile at the sheriff, who appeared to be very intrigued by their conversation. Jeff held him briefly in a steady gaze before saying, his tone a bit somber, "Alright sheriff. I'm finished with this case. It's now all your responsibility."

"Don't worry, O'Halloran…we take care of it," the other one shot back in a haughty tone with a chopping motion with the heel of a hand.

Jeff slowly walked past him. "I bet you do," he murmured, "So long, Presley." He nodded to the jailer and said, "Thank yo' so much."

He got an encouraging eye and an askew smile in return.

Liberty was, as it seemed, used to strangers and conmen of different kinds. A magnitude of hagglers and peddlers in a medley of different smells, trappers in particular, were loitering offering their items of merchandise in the coming of the night, some of them circling around, others standing by their boards demonstrating and appraising their goods. The townsfolk didn't, however, pay them much mind. Gaudy attires, hides, boots, saddles and tackles were hanging from hooks, scabbards and holsters, skins, pottery, dainties and suchlike, and candies for the kids, the presumptive costumers gawking with hard gazes while dawdling around the packsaddles, everybody joining a big party.

From a hawker Jeff purchased tobacco and matches, dried meat, cornbread and ten cans of beans and five bottles of beer. He stuffed the things into one of the saddlebags of the packhorse.

He thumbed forth the brim of his Stetson against the low red sun and rode out of town at a brisk walk. At regular intervals he turned in the saddle and looked back. "Watch your rear!" the turnkey had advised with his neck awry. He gave the clean-brushed sides of the newly-shod stallion a slight kick with the spurs making his eyes roll wildly, urgent as it was to pick up momentum. He felt a sensation of void inside. The feeling of satisfaction didn't occur, neither pride nor relief, no, nothing he sensed but emptiness. Fundamentally he wanted to laugh, for some odd reason, but then he considered it best he fought it all off, and instead asked himself what plans had he for the future. He turned in the saddle and looked back at the darkening town, then slacked the grip on the reins, the packhorse trotting after with a springy gait, anxious to keep pace. He rode on two miles or perhaps some more then pulled up and set the horses close to a willow growth on a mesa dotted with cedars, looked back and dropped the reins on the saddle. He consulted the roadmap that the jailer had given him then boosted himself up and chucked his boot backward out of the stirrup and threw his leg over the horn. He brought forth his makings and slowly and methodically rolled him a cigarette and lit it and sat and smoked, feeling the coolness on his back. He flipped the collar of his coat around his ears. Why did he head back south? Why not head north instead, looking for another place? Why not Canada? The bridle bit clinked when the big stallion tossed his head up and down, wrinkling its nose as though in agony. He had smelled a wild cat, not far away, and himself he had watched it leaping up a steep rise up in the headlands just recently, but it was like he didn't mind. Was he really started home? Your home is where you reside. Is it so? So simple? Everything changes. Yearning is nothing but imagination, something fluent. Was that the meaning of the forming of that old half-Indian up in the mountains? "Your home is where you reside." Yeah, Jeff said into the crisp air, he's right. Perhaps is it as simple as that.

Eleven granite-faced Indians, none of whom having any likeness with the other, wrapped in buffalo robes and black about the eyes, sat on the gravel beach astraddle their speckled horses, glaring mutely at Jeff bathing in the chilly water that was running down from the frost-exposed high country to the north. He had washed his clothes and hung them in an oak tree to dry in the afternoon sun. The air was clear with small clouds moving in at a rapid pace, and a chilly wind blew from north and stroked the water. The Indians studied him in amusement, mute and unmoving, as if he were beset by some evil and portentous force. Eleven young men with owl feathers about their soot black heads, well-fed looking all in skin leggings and arrows sticking out from their quivers, hunting utensils that were expected to reach at least fifty yards. One of them, a huge-headed sitting in the forefront, straight as a ramrod with his arms crossed over his chest, turned his head sideways then held out a blue swollen hand. Shivering Jeff followed his gaze to see it was set on his two horses leisurely cropping the sparse vegetation all the while swishing their long tails. He said something, nodded at the horses, then at Jeff's grinning face, then again at the cropping horses, his sinewy pony placed under him, immobile and statuesque, fringe and mane whirling in the wind. Eventually he moved his eyes to Jeff's newly laundered wear and then down to his own saddle blanket and then back to Jeff where they finally stayed. His look was glassy. One of them, a chunky square-cheeked, by all appearance the one in charge, said some words in Indian and pointed at the low fire and the empty frypan. Jeff ignored them. He made some diving in an effort to appear casual, resurfaced and shook his head, snapped some air and then dived again. When he re-appeared for the fifth time, the Indian in charge throw up a hand in dismissal as though warning of some danger, looking all the while at the bathing man, who had, at least in the chief's opinion, made a fool out of himself and even proofed himself as a maniac by diving. The chief let out a word of command and quickly, as if in struck by horror, they sawed their mounts around sharply, and riding slowly two by two left him and set out at a slow walk. A man washing clothes and disappearing in water! They'd seen enough.

Come morning he in the early sun nudged the horses south and rode all day across the fields of a wayless country. A fine sleet fell upon him when he at a certain time in the early evening doubled the reins in his left fist and untwisted the cork of the whiskey bottle with the other. Rolling the liquor between his teeth, he drank some while he studied the spire of smoke in the distance. On a place where the whole countryside lay open, he set the horses. He put a hand to his eyes to break the glare of light and looked out in all directions. Autumn drifting into winter. He shucked his boot out of the stirrup and flung his loosely hanging leg over the saddle's horn and brought forth from a pocket a yellow cornhusk paper and wet it with his tongue. Methodically with slightly quivering fingers he cupped and sprinkled shag onto, then took to roll himself a cigarette. Thinking hard, sensing a pressure coming up inside him, he folded and licked shut the paper. He fumbled out a match and drew it alight against the saddle, looked at the match how it flamed fretfully, then set fire to the cigarette and thoughtfully sat and smoked. Visible far out along the creek is a vacant falling-down settlement with windows broken and roof caved-in. A door rattled as the wind passed on. His horses were tired and he thought he'd lost his bearing. The place where he sat wasn't mapped up.

Next day he halted the horses at a stack of firewood a bit away from the veranda of the unpainted main house of a homestead built entirely out of lumber, a kind of house one usually sees up here in this part of the country. It was situated beneath the mountain and shadowed by an ancient pin-oak on a twig of which a sparrow sat roosting uncertainly. He studied the country about. Further out, where the watercourse made a sharp bend, a solitary black horse stood in solitude in a holding pen, stranded-looking. A couple of puppies were playing outside the one-stored house and a five or six-year-old girl with a short light spiked hair was running about back and forth, her feet swinging faster at the appearance of the strange rider. She turned around, stopped abruptly and looked the stranger over for a second with serious eyes, then turned again, lost footing on the packed ground, fell heavily straight down and began to whine unhappily. The wind rustled the top of the all but naked hollow oak making the bird take off and flow away, and some red leaves let themselves go and slantwise came floating down. The girl sat ruddy-faced by herself, sneaking across at the rider and the two horses, watching them, her tongue lolling out, her gaze not quite astute.

"Hey," Jeff commenced affably in try to address her.

The kid stiffened a little and pensively regarded the horseman. He looked out the compound then back at the girl then continued riding.

"Hi there. What's your name?" he tried again, his voice a little tightened.

The girl remained quiet. All there was to hear from her was a still release of breath. As if intending to rise she dug her heels into the ground then got still and raised her face and peered squarely up at Jeff, looking like she might start crying, her mouth opening and closing. He stood the horses, shifted in the saddle and bent forward a bit so that the girl might hear better.

"You live here, missy?"

A muffled sob, no answer.

"Where are your ma an' pa, girl?...They home?"

The kid didn't react when spoken to.

"They in labor?" he again tried.

There was no response, just a hurt look. It was as if words failed her where she sat with her chin dropped to her chest petulant. In the ensuing moment she turned and smiled at Jeff. She lashed out an arm and pointed at a coop just by the barn where some chicken were cooing. Six spotted puppies come forward swishing their tails, taking corrections in the air, looking off at the intruder with small wrinkled faces. Whoever lives here sure doesn't live in superfluity, Jeff reflected while casting about. The place seemed old, perhaps from the turn of the last century. He now was beginning to feel intrusive. Involuntarily he once again scanned the compound. The girl, still sitting in the loamy clay, all of a sudden let out a laugh. He turned to study her anew. The horse shifted and snickered under him while the kid floundered on the ground, prattled something to herself, looking again as if she might take to cry.

After what seemed to be an eternity the front door of the main house got open and a finely featured young woman went out, leading a little boy by her right hand. When outside she let go the grip of the kid and stood with her feet widely apart, looking at him and the horses directly, her arms folded across her chest like somebody who needs to protect oneself. The shape of her breast and tummy pulled discretely against the cloth of her blue inexpensive thin and high-necked rural ancient summer vintage dress of ankle-length, one making her look like somebody from an older age.

"What do you think you are doin' on my property, mister?" she asked in a draw nasal twang not common that far north. Without giving Jeff time to answer she went forth, her tone now harsher, all but belligerent, "I advise you to ride on before my husband gets back."

Jeff touched the brim of his dust-colored hat. "Name's O'Halloran, Jeff O'Halloran…Well, I didn't come here to bicker…just passin' by. Yo' know, I was just doin' some thinkin'…"

She relaxed a bit and stepped into an inch or two, still keeping a comfortable distance. She halted and shifted, her gaze now without malice. She placed her palms in the small of her back. "Tell me 'bout your thinkin', mister."

He flashed an eye at the groaning girl sitting underfoot then asked, "Well, ma'am…forgive me for askin' it, that girl yonder, is she deaf?" Had he touched her on the raw? Soon enough he was to find out.

"Yeah, she's deaf an' that's why she hasn't got any mental competency. Birth injury," she declared almost friendly. She cast a quick glance in the kid's direction then looked up at Jeff again where he sat on his horse forward-bent with his lower arm pressed upon the saddle. Putting a hand over her eyes she went on, "Her name's Gloria but we mostly say Glory…Here's Martin," she said, pointing at the boy.

Jeff turned his head to the side and let his gaze drift over to the kid in question, now standing in half profile, one hand patting the half sleeping packhorse.

"Alright," he answered and continued, "He seems to have a nimble intellect, hasn't he?"

"I reckon he has."

He again looked out to where the girl sat. He reached to push back his hat then again looked back at the woman. "You latch on to the idea I stretch out my legs, ma'am?"

"Go ahead, do," she returned, her tone a little reserved.

He straightened himself up and shifted his weight of body to his left side and stood down from the horse and stood with the reins in his hand. They both stood in silence for a while as if they were absorbing the implications of what was said, neither looking at the other. He led the horse afoot a few steps in her direction. They exchanged glances. "You sure have a sense for quality, mister," she said while studying the prancing stallion, her eyes melancholy.

"Thanks, ma'am." He half smiled at her as he reached out and run his hand alongside the horse's muscular neck. He continued, "You sure have an eye for horses yo'self, ma'am."

"Yeah…Well, I'm supposed to, I guess…bein' a Kentuckian…raised among 'em…"

Jeff froze in mid-motion and looked the woman into her narrow severe face.

"I guess you have ma'am," he admitted sounding as though he was calculating likelihoods. The kids had imperceptibly drifted away and were dancing around the naked flagpole that stood rooted in the center of the compound a ways out. He looked out the country, his eyes narrowing somewhat, "You heard the shelling out there, ma'am…barely an hour ago?"

"Shelling…an hour ago? No, I didn't," she responded her blue eyes sort of rebelling. "Why?"

"Happened out there by the high gap…I came upon a flocka longhorns, you know. A party of Arapahoe Indians drove 'em…Well, 'em were in a stampede 'bout to tramp me down. I had to shoot me out…"

"I'm sorry," she responded on a weary breath, shifting her weight. "That's our stock, well that is the half of it. My husband rounded 'em up for 'em Indians, one-hundred an' fifty head for the winter, so we don't get trouble with 'em when it's getting' cold an' the snow's comin'. There ain't buffalos enough for 'em around an' that's why we cut this deal with 'em. 'Em cattle are part of their staples. Don't it sound fair to you, mister?"

"Well…it's your stock, not mine…Do you make it with the one-hundred-fifty head you got left"? Jeff said shifting, hooking his thumbs in his belt.

"I guess…we ain't', anyways…It's worth a lot not bein' bothered later on, like my husband says, we partner with 'em, one might say."

She got quiet and stood cagey to watch her tawny heels for a spell, as if admiring their intricacy, then looked up again and said that their farm had three thousand acres playground, and that they get along.

"How do you know you don't get bothered in the future?" Jeff asked.

She shifted and pressed her hands into her sides and glanced over her shoulder at the playing kids, intrigued by their song: "Got to save one more for Jesus." She then craned her head back and regarded Jeff for some long seconds, looking as if she prepared her response. "Last winter went on just smoothly. We didn't even see 'em around."

"What does the cavalry say 'bout you goin' whacks?" Jeff inquired still, his gaze again settled on the kids.

"Well, my husband's told 'em…so they know 'bout it. Says it's alright with 'em, you, see. It's our chattels. Cavalry's lookin' after us regularly."

"So that means you feel safe, ma'am?"

"Yeah, we do, I guess."

The girl again was sitting on the ground in a moan, her face impassive. Jeff slowly turned around and stepped past the head of the stallion and made for the packhorse. He tried and stretched the cinches of the packsaddle then re-caught the grip of the packhorse's halter rope and arranged the reins of the stallion with his other hand and went clear of the packhorse and stepped up into the saddle. He shifted his weight from one butt to the other while looking down at the woman and the girl, who sat peering near-sightedly at him now. The woman looked up at him with one hand shading her eyes, the other set to her slender hip. She looked as though she were concerned about him.

"I'd better get started, I reckon…I've a long ride ahead," he said, seizing the reins.

She looked up at him and quietly nodded as her son approached her from behind. "Where you goin' at?" she demanded and their eyes got connected for a lengthy moment.

"Wyomin'…Sioux Falls…small town yon'."

"Yo've eaten recently?" she wondered, her forehead wrinkled in apprehension.

"Yeah, I have, ma'am. Thanks for askin.'"

He told her he figured he'd come astray and asked her about the way to the nearest town. Pointing south she announced that the nearest town was Clearwater, two miles southwest.

"You figure we are in cahoots with 'em Indians, don't you, mister?" she said, fighting futilely to keep the boykid, still standing at her side.

Sensing the horse shifting from foot to foot he thoughtfully looked out across the compound, then back at her.

"They are livin' creatures, they gotta eat," he said then went forth, "You don't have to levy war, well…that's the way look at it."

She studied him solemnly, her gaze melancholy and strangely expectant. The lines on her face were relaxed.

"Yeah, that's 'bout how we look at 'em too, mister. Why did you come here…I mean to Montana?"

"Well, I'm here…on duty," Jeff responded, his tone a little guarded. "I've tracked down some people, you know."

"You're a price hunter, mister?"

"I'm not, ma'am."

"Yo're a lawman?" she asked reflectively.

"Yeah, I am, ma'am, a deputy sheriff."

"Well, then I figure that crowbite has to show his meddles, ain't that right?" she said, studying the stallion.

"Right, he has many times. A good horse…Both horses are good," he confirmed and purposively pulled up the head of the stallion with a firm grip of the reins. She looked up at him and said with a shrug of familiarity, "Thanks for comin' by Sheriff O'Halloran…Jeff."

"You're welcome Mrs…I didn't get your name, I'm afraid…"

"Mary…Eleanor Swift," she said dropping her gaze to some place between the front hooves of the stallion, absentmindedly placing one hand on the her son's headtop.

"So long Eleanor…Swift."

"Mary Eleanor…"

"Yes. Mary Eleanor."

He touched the brim of his hat and with care put the horse forward some steps, then stopped it. He looked at her long then again touched the brim to leave then sawed the horse around, the packhorse trailing with reluctance. When away from the compound the halter rope slackened considerably as the muscular roan eventually picked up pace and soon came up trailing a few paces behind. Before out of view from the modest settlement he turned in the saddle and raised his arm in farewell. All three on the compound had their arms lifted. When he was almost out of their sight, he reached under the flap of the saddlebag and jerked free the cord and retrieved his whiskey bottle with just the heeltap left. Urging his horse on he set his mouth to and uncorked it with his teeth. He spat the cork out and lifted the bottle up to the light to check the level in the bottom then tilted it to his lips and took him a good swallow. Feeling a warm sensation coming up his body, he chuckled slightly. Above the distant mountains to the west the sun had sunk lower. Sometimes there is a special sensation of loss at the moment of parting, and grinning humorlessly at the very thought, he shook his head in disbelief.

XII

"Do you remember Jeff, Wolfgang?" Birgit asked when they were walking the snowy streets of Boston.

She craned her head sideways, waiting for an answer, but there wasn't any. He could visualize him clearly, but that he didn't tell.

Uncertain of whether or not her brother had heard her, Birgit made a quick decision to try anew, her voice somewhat raised, "Wolf...did you hear what I asked? Do you remember Jeff....from Sioux Falls?"

"Yes, I remember him, not so well, but..."

"He wants us to get there next week. We leave on Monday and..." Birgit cut off in an energetic tone.

"Yes, you told me that yesterday. I am not going there," he declared grimly, shaking his curly head. Birgit didn't respond. Her mind reeled in the words of Doctor Williams, her brother's psychiatrist.

"I estimate your brother's condition hasn't worsened. I agree to the trip." And now, when asking her brother, his reaction was quite opposite to that of the doctor. She felt the frustration emerge with difficulties in thinking rationally. His condition hasn't worsened. That's what the doctor said while sinking deeper into the red plush chair. Today is Friday, she thought, her walk a bit hesitant, her eyes searching.

"Why do we slow down?" Wolf asked with a fierce intensity.

"Wolf, listen to me. Do you know what you are?" Birgit said, trying a valid point. Maybe was there still a possibility to coax him into it? "You are a quitter," she said nonchalantly, feeling a bitter taste in her mouth, uncertain of whether it was a wise word to use in this situation. But, on the other hand, she was no psychiatrist, nor had it been her intention to besiege the feelings of her junior brother. She just tried to be as outspoken as was craved from the current conditions, she reasoned.

"Whom do I let down?...You?" her brother snapped unyielding.

Being now at the outdoor of their residence, she resolutely pulled the door open, stamped the snow off her heavy boots and said before entering, "You let us all down, me, mum and dad, Hannelore, the coach driver, Jeff…everyone," she rumbled indignantly. "I'm not dressing you down, but occasionally I think you are giving yourself up too much. The loss is grievous also for me."

Wolf stood. He was too astound to respond. Was he really that hateable? he wondered while contemplating the rambling monologue, his puffy face immobile. He went upstairs in silence, his senior sister following behind.

After the door was bolted and chained nothing was said for a long time. Birgit knew from experience what might happen after her brother had gone berserk, and she was tired of sitting amid debris. From the living room she could hear him start playing the first piece out of "Acht Novelletten" by Robert Schumann who wrote them all very inspired in the year of 1826, the same year he married his beloved Clara Wiek.

Sitting atilt in the chair Reuben Lindsay shifted his weight, watching meanwhile his boss rambling the sheriff's office.

"Run the story O'Halloran!" he ordered loudly. "Come on, tell us, sonny!…Go ahead!"

Lindsay, his foreman, though, remained expressionless, sitting quiet in melancholy, his lean muscular barrel on the slope in the wooden seat. Sheriff Kimble's desk was empty. The sheriff was out, alleged being at home. Seay paced, stopped occasionally commenting on specifics while putting pressure on either leg, and then again some pacing, hanging all the while on every word of Jeff's narrative. He wasn't quite sober. He seldom was nowadays, his foreman, though, almost a teetotaler. Unused as he was to be the man in the center, Jeff selected the heights by delivering an extraction of his movements, without going into details. Lindsay just nodded and hummed at times, his eyes expressing nothing. He had neither wife nor children, his past certainly not flew-free, but he had a good hand with horses and cow drivers, and he was the best broncobuster in the territory, according to the expert knowledge. He now sat there deep in his chair.

"He just led 'em away in shackles, you hear that, Reuben?" Seay chuckled at a certain point and shifted his weight to the right leg and folded his gargantuan arms across his stocky chest, his gun belt surrounding his solid midsection. Turning at and regarding the deputy, he went forth, "That's what

I always have said…here we've got our man, haven't we, Reuben? He has wind of office, yo're runnin' for it, O'Halloran…say you are!"

Jeff could think of no response. In his opinion it would be ludicrous to confess that these events would imply obligations.

"Tell us you're runnin' for office next April, Jeff!" the rancher repeated, pacing.

"I ain't runnin' Wayne," Jeff answered. "Thanks for offerin' me, but I'm serious sayin' that."

Seay halted and glared at him pointedly.

"Well," he went on, "we have to get a grip over things around." He peeked out the filthy high-barred side window. Noncommittal Jeff bent forward in his swivel and placed his head in his hand and glared down at the scratched desktop. Lindsay studied him on the sly, looking as if being in slumbers.

The legal proceedings were set to take place at 10.00 hours a.m. in the courthouse of Casper some two hours ride away from Sioux Falls. Jeff, Birgit and Wolf had left at dawn in a buggy rocking them toward their destination at a good pace. At the rear seat Wolf sat tacit in sulkiness pouting, a flat straw hat on top of his frizzy flow that flowed well below the collar of his blue suit of dittos. Birgit sat placed on the driver's seat next to Jeff with her left hand on the armrest in a fast hold.

"The rain will come over us soon, don't you think?" she said in a squeak, looking sidelong at Jeff.

"Well, then we lower the top…this jalopy has a top, remember, don't forget you ride nice today…I told you this buggy is bran' new. You like it?"

"Well…it's lithe, isn't it?…It's like bumping in a boat," she answered with amusement.

"Yeah, the springs are a bit elastic, I guess…We'll be there in half an hour or so."

Sensing the sweat breath venting from the bay filly trotting ahead of them, they sat in silence for a long time. At a certain point Birgit looked overhead and said into the direction of the driver's place, wondering in expectation, giving Jeff an enigmatical smile. "By the way…this top…couldn't it serve as an awning as well…I mean, when it's sunny?"

"Yeah, right," he confirmed, repaying her smile.

A motley scud of clouds lay across the sky when Jeff reined in before the courthouse, a two-story wooden from the turn of the century. Taking the bridles with him in his one hand, casting about for some appropriate place to make fast, he climbed down from the seat, the others following suit. Taking two steps sideways, he loosely tethered the horse to the hitchrail next to yet two another equipages. He stood for a while looking about, seeing the area being crowded with a variety of folks, expectant and curious, many of which women with wicker hampers in hand out running their lines. Wondering what went Birgit eventually stepped to his side, her gaze very intense, as though she had difficulties understanding the place. Finding it best to face the subject head on, Jeff leaned into and told her to enter the building and hand over the application to one of the officials.

He stood and studied her when she with difficulty threaded her way through the crowd, waiving the document in one hand, followed by her frowning brother, their impromptu show–up being subject to a lot of speculations. Thump of hooves and rumble of wagons out the street. People talking and watching. When he saw they were inside he released and took the filly by the throatlatch and walked her to the nearby stable, fighting his way in the heavy traffic with crowds of people surging up and down the streets.

Once inside the courthouse Birgit glanced over her shoulder and smiled nervously at six men in city clothes standing in front of her, lined up outside a door with no sign on it. One of them, a tall and curly-haired, who claimed to be a reporter, frowned at her uncomprehendingly until she spoke. When she asked for the official's room, he servile maneuvered her through a maze of doors and stopped before a door that just flung open and she found herself looking into the grumpy face of Patrick McCrea, the judge and chairman of the proceedings, dressed in a black gown, a stocky man between fifty and sixty with a protuberant belly. He had already gone through one heart attack and looked as though he was due to another, his square beef-like face flushed. He studied her impatiently, asked where the hell she was going. She informed him that she was the daughter of the plaintiff, and asked whether he could take care of the document. Keeping his features stark, he showed her inside the room out of which he just had made his exit, and told her to close the door behind her.

"This is confidential stuff…I certainly hope they ain't transcripts," he grunted, intrigued though.

"Not…as…far…as I know…" Birgit stuttered, taking a backward step, fighting to control her nerves.

The judge put on his reading glasses and spread the paperwork over the solid mahogany desk of the vast chamber that was having a certain musky air to it. He heavily sat down and flipped the papers through in silence. Some minutes later he leaned back, shifted his legs at the knees, looked at Birgit, bent forward, organizing the paperwork and gave it back to her. He took off his glasses and placed them on the table.

"Sorry, Miss Süsskind…you can't be too suspicious these days. Everything seems to be in the best order. Sorry if I got you upset," he said truthfully.

Pausing for an instant he studied her. He then declared himself being on his way to a conference room and offered her escort to the chamber were the proceedings were due to be held.

"There is still some time to strike dead," he grunted, looking at his clock. 09.40.

"Have you come here all alone, Miss Süsskind?" he demanded sternly as they shouldered walked their way through the maze in the opposite direction.

"No, sir. My brother Wolfgang is here with me," she announced in an expressionless voice, her face pale and set.

"I see…well, see you around soon, Miss Süsskind."

He nodded farewell, and smiling to himself he opened the door to the conference room, stepped inside and banged the door to behind him.

A half-drunk usher pointed at a small table in the front row of the cramped chamber, where a young man, one not much older than she herself, dressed in a new-looking shiny black suit poised on the edge of a wooden chair, rummaging through a brown briefcase. His tapping came to an abrupt end when Birgit defensively addressed him, "The janitor just brought me here…I am Birgit Süsskind. I am supposed to meet with Mr. Thomas Benson."

Without a word in response, he dropped the bulky briefcase on the floor, his fingers quivering a little.

"Yes…that's me…well, actually I've been waiting for you, Miss Süsskind. Nice to meet you," he said and stood. He hastily thrust forward his right hand and they met in a warm handshake. Birgit laboriously sat down. She fought off a panic, feeling the thick tension in the room. Eventually the lawyer turned to her and whispered matter-of-factly, "You see…I received the preliminary investigation late last week, but I have been studying it thoroughly during the weekend, which means I'm prepared…well, I really think I've got a handle on things…"

His client nodded in comprehension and rubbed her right ankle. She remembered having signed a warrant, but she hadn't picked the attorney. Federal authorities had, according to Jeff. Maybe this young man was a genius. He looks staunch, she reflected. She ogled at him. Right then he buried his head in the paperwork, his left manicured hand fiddling with his red bow tie, his sandy licked hair parted in the middle. Here she sat next to a freshman fighting with herself not to disclosure herself. Maybe she should ask him when he graduated? Or would that perhaps be too much? She forgot about it and tried to relax. Maybe she was too strict with the young counselor. She instead bowed her head and folded her cold hands and said a prayer.

In an adjacent modest look-up, the gray-haired captive lay flat on a rickety bunk, mumbling rapidly to himself in some soliloquy. He was transferred there in a convoy by four handpicked and reliable cavalrymen. In a corner of the same den, partitioned off by a thin wall, the vaquero, brought there by the same jail coach and arrived there just after lights-out the evening before, stood ready to within short enter the cramped courtroom. Both were dragged there from a small custody in the basement, half-dressed early in the morning, shaven and washed, their scant belongings catalogued, and a clean set of prison garb dropped on a rickety wooden table before them, placed in the center of the room.

Convinced there still might be a flicker of hope, the gray-haired laboriously got to his feet when hearing the keys rattle from outside. It was almost midnight when they arrived at Casper, and during the long transfer he had had a lot of time pondering on the forming saying you are not guilty until the opposite is proofed. He had heard those words many times, latest this very morning from his attorney at their brief encounter. They have nothing substantial to refer to. That was about all he said during their two-minute-long session in the bunk downstairs. Nothing substantial. In other words: Still some hope, maybe not much, but nonetheless! To the vaquero, however, everything had gone awry. "Son of a bitch." That was his only contribution to the conversation when they crossed the flatlands. "Son of a bitch." Again and again. His eyes had been aglow with hatred, his teeth gritted. Who had he been alluding to? None knew-- but himself.

The courtroom was filled up when two late arrivals inched forward and crawled into the back row before an usher pressed the door shut and bolted it. The door from the next-to chamber opened and the gray-haired entered the courtroom, edging his way in shackles, followed a few paces behind by the handcuffed vaquero, the black eyes of whom glowing with intensity at the assembled jurors. At the sight of them the cramped room almost started to rock. As of yet the chairman's seat was empty. The vaquero visibly was trying his best to ignore the onlookers and the jurors, his pale face contorted in panic, his shoulders sagged, realizing that whoever they were, they could lay his life in ruins. With heart pumping violently and the hardware clattering with every move, he turned to the jailer and reported himself in dire need of water to fight back the upcoming nausea. The jailer, though, didn't even seem to reflect the desire. He just shook his head gravely at the prisoner's predicament. Against regulations was all he said dryly, and the vaquero cursed to himself bitterly in Spanish. Yet another request declined, he thought to himself and let out a scornful laughter. The jailer escorted him slowly down the aisle and pressed him down next to his waiting counselor, a middle-aged stocky man with an arrogant scowl.

An abrupt silence expatiated upon the room as the black-robed chairman a minute later made his entrance. All raised and stood until he took the chair and ensconced himself behind the heavy refurbished desk, his eyes lingering on the two felons before banging his mallet and delivering a quick going-over.

"As first witness I call forward Mr. Jeffrey O'Halloran. Will you please approach the bench," he said, his words coming strong.

Jeff rose and approached from the rear and stopped when standing before the bench where a Bible was placed. The judge dipped his quill in the inkpot and wrote something in his paperwork in a swift efficient hand in a neat lettering, then shifted in his chair, looked at the Bible then at Jeff and then again at the Bible and said dryly, "Lay your hand at the Book and say after me, please." He cleared his throat and swiftly consulted his paperwork another time, then proceeded, reading from it, eyes fixed steadily, "I Jeffrey O'Halloran, swear to tell the truth, the whole truth and nothing but the truth, so help me God."

From the witness stand Jeff then was told to produce a brief introduction as to his identity. The judge got silent for a short while when scribbling something down in a legal pad then laid the quill down. Then he looked up, took off his glasses and leaned back, and nodding at Jeff went on asking him to take his seat.

"Mr. O'Halloran…will you tell exactly where this stagecoach hold-up took place," he said in a kind, slow voice.

"It took place at the flatlands…at a rise where the prairie meets the woodlands, some ten miles northeast of Sioux Falls, Your Honor," Jeff announced, his voice steady.

The judge gave a cock of his head. "So there wasn't just all flat about…?" he asked grimacing, not raising his voice, his brows arced.

"There's a canyon between the woods, Your Honor."

"In other words, Mr. O'Halloran…this canyon is the scene of crime, is that correct?"

"That's correct, Your Honor."

"Thank you for now, Mr. O'Halloran. No further questions," the judge declared with a look at the lawyers.

Mr. Benson had squirmed for a while, and now he stood and began pacing the place with his hands folded together in front of him. He stopped short, turned to Jeff.

"Would you please tell us your profession, sir," he demanded pale and earnest. He had a childish innocence to him, something unbroken.

"I am a vice sheriff…of Sioux Falls, sir."

"Since when, Mr. O'Halloran?"

"Since two an' a half years, sir."

"And you have been operating no place else…as a deputy?"

"I haven't sir."

"I see…thank you. No further questions right now, Your Honor," he said and withdrew and plunked himself down next to Birgit. The vaquero's lawyer thereafter asked permission to speak and pushed himself onto his feet and slowly started toward the stand.

"Mr. O'Halloran…may I ask, how do you like being a vice sheriff?" he said in a loud nasal twang. Jeff detected a malevolent gleam in his eyes and was about to respond when the district attorney snapped, "Objection, Your Honor…the question's irrelevant!"

"Objection overruled! Answer the question, Mr. O'Halloran!" the judge rumbled.

"Well…it's a job…I try to be professional. That's about all I can say about it, I guess," Jeff replied tartly and smiled at him.

"You just stick around, that's what you say, Mr. O'Halloran?" the lawyer tried to allege, looking down at his wrinkled garb.

Feeling Sheriff Kimble's gaze set at him, Jeff replied, "I'm not jaded, though."

"You mean, you are not blasé…Being a vice sheriff was not exactly what you dreamed of when preparing yourself for entry into adulthood," the counselor said trying to specify, looking long at him, smiling unctuously.

"Yeah, I reckon that's about the way it is," Jeff committed, his voice thickening a little.

"Thank you…No further question for the moment, Your Honor."

Where did he ferret out that? But again…that's part of his job, Jeff thought coolly. He again felt the eyes of Sheriff Kimble. For a very brief moment their eyes met. Hastily the sheriff looked away, though.

Leaned back in his chair the judge then inspected all participants, looking at each of them, asking whether any of them wished to take part in the altercation, but received but some spread deprecating headshakes in return.

Now the time had come for the district attorney to make his entry. Reading from a legal pad he produced a lengthy and thorough description on facts, providing the assembly with all the necessary details. His statement was accurate and to the point in every aspect, and presented in an efficacious way. Time of the day, distance, meteorological situation, the damages of the dead people. Nothing was added. Nothing was omitted. Jeff listened intently, focusing on every detail, even intonation. He had himself produced the report. Nothing in the narrative appeared unfamiliar.

"Have you anything to say in addition to this, Mr. O'Halloran?" the judge wondered, studying him expectantly. "Did the narrative stick to facts…or would there be anything to change in retrospective, anything omitted, anything to add or withdraw?"

"No, Your Honor…it all did stick to facts," Jeff responded in satisfaction.

"Alright, Mr. O'Halloran. You can step down. Thank you," the judge said dryly.

The district attorney asked for Wolfgang Süsskind to testify. Evidently his name wasn't written on the judge's list. Süsskind's lawyer had requested it beforehand, but the judge seemed to have forgotten.

"How old is the young man in question?" the judge asked incredulously.

"Sixteen." Benson reported, having scrutinized all details.

"Sixteen...? To me he looks too rambling for a man his age?" the judge blurted out then bit his lip as if he'd said too much. He turned at Birgit, demanded, giving her brother a glimpse, "Do we have your claimant, Miss Süsskind, your brother relives this nightmare-crowded event?"

"Of course, Your Honor," she answered guilelessly. The judge nodded and held her gaze for a moment. He didn't doubt for an instant the young woman was serious. He told her brother to approach the bar and swear in, and sat and watched him push his way through the crowds, everyone following his movements. No sooner had the youngster taken place on the stand, than the district attorney had conjured forth a violin that now was sitting on the desk right before him.

"You may proceed, Mr. Wariner," the judge said and poured himself a glass of water while raising his left hand as if to signal he could get started.

"Thank you, Your Honor." Mr. Wariner coughed discretely and rose. Under the stern gaze of the chairman, he crossed to the witness stand, carrying the violin in hand. He made a stop when right before the witness.

"Can you please tell the jury what you see here in my hand, Wolfgang?" he quizzed, trying to sound sufficiently awed when exhibiting the object.

The witness reacted as having been looked upon as an egregious fool. "I see a violin," he replied curtly, his face glum.

The district attorney exhaled slowly and leaned in a bit, "Alright, young man...you see the same thing I and the jury see. Then my next question is: Have you seen this instrument before? You may hold it if you like."

Without a word he handed over the violin and the boy grabbed it. He scrutinized it and finally placed it under his chin.

"Do you need to see the bow?...Well, that can easily be arranged, if you need to?" Mr. Wariner suggested keenly.

"I know this is my father's violin," the boy said, looking furtively. "I don't need to see the bow."

The district attorney didn't respond. Wolf's eyes followed him on his way back to his desk. Within an instant he again was standing in front of him, holding the bow that he solemnly gave to him. Wolf took it and reset the instrument to his chin and played a long cadenza. Everybody in the room sat watching in admiration. All of a sudden he made an abrupt stop, put the bow aside and began to pitch the instrument. The district attorney squirmed. A deep-set unease had begun to form across his face as though he was uncertain of how to handle the up-come occasion. Spread snickers were soon heard and within short the entire assembly was united into nice laughter, the audience, the jurors, the janitors, the ushers, almost everyone, save the doctor, the district attorney, Jeff, Birgit, Wolf, Sheriff Kimble and the judge. As for Birgit she looked annoyed with the situation, cursing the unmanageable behavior of her brother. Her people assassinated at a set attack, and now this! It was precisely at that point that the judge reached for his mallet and stroke a half dozen blows and hollered them back to order, his voice raised quavering. Birgit looked up. She searched her brother's eyes. What she now was watching, though, was the district attorney standing facing her brother saying something to him of which she was able to distinguish only fragments. It was, however, obvious to her that he was trying to wave the whole thing off in order to get Wolf in a better mood. Eventually all the laughing and talking stopped, and the district attorney commenced harping, louder now, "Wolfgang…do you still claim this is your father's violin?"

"It's my father's…I'm absolutely sure, sir," he assured, his eyes taking a steeliness. "It's a Storioni, built in Italy in the late 1700s," he specified and extended his hand, gripped it cautiously by its neck and held it before him. Birgit lowered her head and studied her hands that rested lightly in her lap, her eyes large. Wolf had admitted to being fidgety before the trial alright, but that he would behave like this, that she hadn't foreseen. She lifted her head a little and gawked in his direction. There was no way she could believe what she heard and saw. Her brother had matured, grown up, had so far done a great job. She was abruptly taken out of her reveries when she watched her lawyer stand up and participate in an argumentation of some kind. The first word coming from him had been "fortune" aiming at the Storioni. That association had been obvious to her ever since her early childhood, even since the day it came into her father's possession back in the mid-forties, when it was left to him from his father in Austria, who passed away in 1846, five years after she was born. To her father the precious item had never been solely an artifact, a museum specimen, but a musical instrument that he loved to play each and every day. Back in Boston her father had been a violinist at the Boston Symphony Orchestra. Like the rest of the instrumentalists he had to try out before an audition and then prevailed receiving "Magna cum laude approbatur." She had once seen the opinion and had read it verbatim. Her mother had once showed it to her. Her father though, never addressed the subject. He was to a great extent an autodidact, her mother told her. Her thoughts now began swirling together and she felt as though awakening from some surrealistic dream. She raised her eyes and continued moving her gaze in the general direction of the chairman's seat to watch his lips move and hear him say, his drawn face turned to where she sat, "Do you know the exact value of this instrument, Mr. Benson?"

"No...I'm afraid I don't, Your Honor," her legal advisor answered straightforwardly. There was a short silence during which the lawyer retook his seat, discretely leaned into her and shared in a whisper, "To this day I didn't assume it to be so extremely valuable...did you?"

"I did...but not how much it's worth," she hissed in return.

The judge plowed on, grunting tentatively, "Well, I don't think that would be that important."

The majority of the jurors nodded in agreement, as did nobody else in the room seem to agonize over that statement. The judge paused for a minute as he scribbled in his legal pad, then asked, his eyes set on the district attorney and the lawyers, "Is there anything else you guys want to ask young Mr. Süsskind about...otherwise I excuse him from the stand."

He looked out at them waiting for a lifted hand, but they all shook their heads. Judge McCrea smiled amiably at the young witness and said him to retake his seat.

The next witness to step forward was Birgit Süsskind, stone-faced, although a little bleary-eyed, boots on feet, dressed in a frilly white silk blouse indicating the milky color of her breasts beneath. On her ears sat small round clip-ons, green to match her green eyes and light curly hair composed in a knot behind her neck, her heavy eyelids reinforcing her tired look, a look that got rosy with excitement from the moment she was called to the stand which she took with a straight posture. She swore in and was at once asked about her implication in the pretrial investigation.

"Well...I haven't read it, Your Honor, if that's what you are alluding to," she replied curtly, her face stark and unsmiling. "Mr. Benson, my attorney has though. He is well prepared, but that she did not confess to the jury.

"Mr. Bertrand, you commence the interrogation, please," the judge ordered and peered out at a man in his mid-fifties, flanking the vaquero. Before rising

Mr. Bertrand whispered a short message to his client, who still was gnashing his teeth. The counselor then addressed the chairman asking for a brief recess, asserting his client being worn to a frazzle, claiming he hadn't got a wink of sleep in a week, and also claiming his man being innocent, ignorant of the reason of being here and such. The judge though, didn't consider it, but literally shrugged the notion away, ordering them both not to step out of the bounds another time. He also announced to have little understanding for counselors who take liberties using delaying tactics and as for the innocence of the client that will be up to jurisprudence. The vaquero looked far beyond frustration, as did his counselor, who just managed a lame, "I'm sorry, Your Honor. I didn't mean to act improperly."

As though the altercation with the chairman never had taken place, the counselor now riveted his eyes on Birgit recognizing he had a client to protect, a pro bona client to defend and that was the reason for him being there. After having received a nod from the chairman, he slid back his chair and teetering somewhat began to advance toward the stand with quick, nervous strides, addressing her, his body still in motion as he moved across the open space between them, "Miss Süsskind, you are still alleging you have not read the preliminary investigation…is that correct?"

"It is, sir," Birgit returned shortly, noticing a reek of booze and stale tobacco in the air.

"Miss Süsskind…don't you think this is a bit remarkable?" the lawyer demanded suavely while arching his eyebrows.

"Objection, Your Honor!" Mr. Benson called out high-voiced. "It is not important what my client has read or not read. The important thing is that I have read it, being her legal advisor. It may rather be an advantage she has not."

"Objection sustained!" the judge trumpeted, rapping the mallet. He then asked the lawyer if he had any further inquiries. He answered yes and plowed forward by questioning Birgit if she had any theory as to why her family got extinguished. The question hit her hard. She got stiff and looked straight ahead and venomously said a short no. Her lower lip started to tremble. Her folks, her beloved folks, they weren't just abducted, they were dead and not only so, they were murdered, killed, someone else had taken them away forever. She now first of all had to face that fact. She couldn't wriggle away any longer.

That lawyer had slapped her hard, a blush suffused her face, and she felt ashamed and nauseous.

"Are you alright, Miss Süsskind?"

The judge's question sounded like a whisper and slowly put her back to reality. For a short while she was imagining having her folks sitting in this very chamber. She tried to get up her courage, looked at the judge's stern face and gave a delighted laugh.

"I am sorry, Your Honor, I didn't catch your words," she said, her face turned solemn.

The judge studied her with an expression of warning that she should know better than to burst out into laughter when in court of law.

"Are you feeling well, Miss Süsskind?…Otherwise I suggest we take a short break," the judge said politely.

"I'm alright, Your Honor, I guess…just continue," she replied ruddy-faced and shifted her gaze to the vaquero and gave him an outraged eye. The lawyer, still on feet, went closer to her stand and made a stop when right in front of her. He stood for some seconds as if in search for words with both hands hidden behind his rear. Finally he looked into Birgit's eyes asking, "Miss Süsskind…did you think your father to be…how shall I say…invulnerable? I mean, did you consider him a protection against the world, the evil of life?"

No objection ensued so she couldn't forbear to respond.

"He was a loving father," she explained still, her gaze dropped to her lap. She felt like being in a daze. Yet she formed her lips like she had more to share, the lawyer, though, forestalling her suggesting, eyeing her attentively, "A patriarch?"

"Objection, Your Honor! The question's undue!" the district attorney cried out from his recumbent position.

"Objection overruled!" the judge rumbled. "Please give your answer…a straight answer wouldn't tarnish your father's posthumous reputation, Miss Süsskind…"

"I understand, Your Honor," Birgit said, her voice slightly hardening. She looked up at the lawyer, her tone almost reverential when addressing him, "I beg your pardon, sir. Can I hear your question once again?"

Some spread giggles went through the hall, then a short moment of silence.

Fighting hard to maintain his courtly manner, the lawyer lowered his head and studied his footwear for a short while, then reminded in a lower voice, "It's about your father, eh…what was he like? Describe him, please."

She sat quiet for a moment, gathering her strength then said, "Yes…my father…well, he had a strong devotion for his family. I assume that answer comprises all there is to say."

"Alright. And you, the family, were the acquiescent ones?" the lawyer tried and raised himself up on his heels as if to get added weight to what he alleged.

"Well, there was a great acquiescence in most items, sir…We were getting along alright."

"You were harmonious?"

"Yes, very much so," Birgit said, her voice scratchy.

The counselor seemed to weigh the facts for a short while, then turned and started toward his desk, asking, a sudden animation detectable in his voice, "Miss Süsskind, do you think your father was in any way acquainted with any of those indicted seated in these premises…right now?"

There was a pregnant silence as she contemplated her reply. "I doubt that very much, sir," she said after a long time, barely perceptibly, lowering her head slightly.

"Thanks, Your Honor," he lawyer said. "That will be all for now."

The quiet in the chamber got interrupted by an incoherent murmur from Birgit's estranged brother. Some spread snickers soon joined in. Judging by the chairman's body language he had heard and seen, but washed out so far. He didn't appear too enchanted, though. The sun, still half hidden, threw its light into the filled unventilated court room. The judge cocked his head to his right-hand juror and whispered some words, then rapped his mallet and suggested they convene in a re-gathering in half an hour.

Two ushers walked about the premises extremely particular about having them emptied for the recess. No lingering was tolerated and virtually everybody was told to leave and within a couple of minutes they all found themselves standing outside the door that got slammed shut behind them and bolted from the inside by two conscientious glum-looking elderly men in dark uniforms.

Birgit's first concern was to spot her erratic brother, who under the hearings had captured everybody's attention by his odd behavior. She marveled at seeing him so soon reciprocating in the semi-dark hall, Jeff standing by the main entrance watching him. They were alone. Jeff at once noticed her coming, her brother evidently not, his glum face just looking distraught. Birgit approached her brother and grabbed him by his left hand and the boy, not prepared, reeled a little and came to a halt and brother and sister swung their intertwined hands back and forth in a moment of mutual harmony.

"What do you say, deputy?" she asked between chuckles while looking across at Jeff, shushing her brother who now was applying a waist hold on her the way one boy might when wrestling with another. Now he was het-up due to frustration and powerlessness. He wished to be somewhere else, Boston maybe, any place, but here. His shy eyes showed an abysmal of melancholy and distress.

"Take it easy, Wolf! Don't be that rough, please!" Birgit pleaded.

Her brother stood, saliva dripping from his half open mouth. A short moment of quiet took over the place. She looked across at Jeff.

"I'm glad you endorse me, Jeff," she panted, her smiling face still pale. She appeared to have lost a lot of weight recently, he thought and smiled back.

"You are welcome…that's the least thing I can do. Well, I mean what's done is done…an' I ain't the one to undo it, I reckon," Jeff said eagerly.

"Are you suffering doubts?" she asked, looking in exasperation again at her brother, ordering him to behave like a grown-up man. He was making faces at her.

"Have YOU any doubts 'bout how this is gonna end?" Jeff jested.

"Yes, I have really."

"Well, I figure we can't do nothin' but stick to the truth."

Suddenly Wolf embraced her sister who immediately wriggled herself free, though. "It's enough now, Wolfgang!" Jeff rebuked. "Show your sister some respect, you hear! Neither of us likes your behavior."

Wolf froze for a little while, then lop-eared started to walk toward the door.

"We'd better watch him carefully," Birgit said, addressing Jeff. "What I need the least now is seeing him abscond."

Walking toward her, Jeff stopped and stood dead still.

"You mean…he's gonna traipse away?"

She gave a short nod and looked in the direction of her brother who stood with his back against them, facing the outer door. Jeff turned to Birgit and said with relish, "He ain't goin' nowhere, just try to relax."

With a mischievous glint in his eyes, he then turned and began to walk to where the boy stood. In the same moment Thomas Benson appeared at the door just in time to prevent Wolf from opening it. There was a curious look in the lawyer's true-hearted face when watching Jeff catch the boy and throw his arms around him and playfully toss him into the air. He failed though, the young man being too heavy and now gasping with horror. Birgit, as usual feeling an overwhelming pity for her junior brother, took him in her arms sensing no resistance from him. He rather appeared comfortable with it. It didn't take long, however, until he freed himself and settled on a bench and rested his head in his hands.

XIII

Having declined Mr. Benson's offer to join him for lunch at some eating house two blocks away, Birgit and Wolf went with Jeff to a nearby haberdashery where he purchased himself and Wolf a new Stetson hat each. Thereafter they quenched their hunger from the lunch-boxes which they brought with them from Sioux Falls, cold leftovers that they ate hastily at the buggy.

"Who do you think they will call forward this afternoon?" Birgit asked between chews, addressing Jeff.

"Both 'em indicted, I reckon," he answered and took a puff from his newly rolled cigarette. "There will be two, maybe three hours left," he added, blowing smoke through his nostrils.

"So you don't believe they will need one more day?" she asked hopefully.

"I doubt they will...One day with that lunch-box's more than I can take," Jeff said firmly.

"I agree...it was unsavory, barely edible!" Wolf broke in loudly, perched on the driver's seat. Birgit's fork froze in midair, her eyes darting around in frustration.

"It hasn't occurred to you guys that you might be spoiled...and I'm disappointed especially at you, Jeff. You already must have forgotten the war, right?"

Jeff inched backward a couple of steps and resumed his position on the bed of the surrey and sat with his legs hanging down the side, contemplating the severity of the scolding. He let out a sigh while glancing Birgit's way and announced in an effort to smooth things over, "No way I've forgotten the war, and I doubt I ever will...but it's just so that I rather have warm grub, that's all. I suggest we finish off this discussion...we've a trial ahead of us."

Re-packing the leftovers Birgit just gave a short nod to that, her faint smile shrunk. He waited until she was finished, then he bounced to the ground and grunted, "Let's get movin.'"

"Wait for me!" Wolf yelled from up the seat, gesturing with his fork.

Jeff didn't reply. His face was concentrated. The day was going fast now, he thought, and started to advance in the general direction of the square court house, Wolf following and his sister tagging along, her face wrinkled in apprehension. If it starts raining, then we lower the top when going back, she mused, trying to catch up with the two men ahead of her.

The courtroom, cramped to capacity, at once fell silent when Chairman Patrick McCrea entered and settled in the midst of the assembled jury. The afternoon session, the last part and the epilogue lay ahead and the audience, the half of which being out-of-towners, were waiting to witness something dramatic.

Jeff immediately got his statements corroborated when the district attorney was called forward to present his claims that within short turned out to be a quick cut to the bone. Not many in the courtroom got the least surprised hearing him crisply report he bring charges against Manuel Jimenez and Daniel Freeman "for first degree murder of several people at a stagecoach hold up on August 15. 1868 at Rattlesnake Canyon. Rightfully these two individuals shall be put to death, the sooner the better. That was what he insisted on. "The state must face realities and put an end to their criminal career. They are full of shit, demonstrating no mercy whatsoever, and they are guilty beyond doubt. Neither of these gentlemen has ever showed an interest in beginning anew. Freeman, a man of forty-four, has never had a regular job. He is an itinerant in the agri business, as he says himself, but nonetheless: He hasn't ever fulfilled any of these seasonal jobs that he was offered. He hasn't harvested any single one of those crops he claims to have sowed. After having received his first payment, he just left. Always the same story. In other words: Mr. Freeman is simply unable to keep a regular employment," the district attorney announced loudly with a malicious glee until he almost climaxed, his massif torso twisted in the direction of the glum-faced jury. He paused for a second when the man's lawyer finally jumped to his feet in an objection.

"The prosecutor is insulting my man!" he yelled, making the most of the occasion, expansively gesturing with a hand in the air. The chairman's reaction showed nothing but a dismissive gesture, no doubt adding a chilling effect to the wording of the prosecutor. The gaunt face of the vaquero revealed him getting his beak wet as well. What was that prosecutor likely to spew forth now when it comes to MY whereabouts? The vaquero hung on every word that was uttered in the cramped court room. For the first time he now looked involved in the proceedings. He stared straight ahead, focusing no one in particular, all the while taking in the whispers now louder and more excited, his common aggressive appearance now exceedingly diminished. In essence he just waited for the blowout to come. A whipping-boy, that was all he was. As for Freeman, he didn't know the man that well. They had spent some time together, alright. But still, that bad-guy-look, did it possibly conceal anything goodhearted, or was he simply just that good-for-nothing creature, that featureless individual, feisty and grim? Perhaps that district attorney was right when he now was doodling the picture of the goon. He is a little off in the head, but for me the best thing was to grin and bear it. So he had reasoned. Just go through the motions for my own benefit. That was also what the lawyer had advised when they met for the first time early this morning. Yes, as long as I am in this dangerous territory, I stick to it. Basically I don't expect him to make a grab for me, no, just get me out of it, profess me to be innocent. That's what he's paid for. Why put it on? Innocent, always say you are, then I handle the rest of things, the counselor repeatedly had said to him while looking down at his ratty appearance, shackled, the hardware clinging by every movement. Remember they just have flimsy evidence against the two of you guys, he repeated, nothing substantial, nothing whatsoever. And now in this courtroom, where a crowd was gathered around him, retirees, out-of-towners, city people, Americans all of them, waiting until he had given them a full confession so they could see him hang, him a worthless dago from Sonora, Mexico. Now they sure had him at gunpoint. The shortcomings, all the mistakes and sins grew. One of the small windows was still open. Yet he was sweating. Why hadn't they just gunned him down, that deputy when uphill? True is we couldn't, he didn't offer us a chance. He was too smart, too fast, moved too fast. And now they were both charged with robbery and manslaughter and attempt of murder, anchored, submitted to justice. The vaquero lowered his thin shoulders and grimaced helplessly and swallowed hard. He looked cautiously among the faces. The deputy was looking straight at him. The vaquero quickly withdrew his gaze and tried to recall what his lawyer had said to him right after the lunch break. "Just keep a defensive line. Duck all questions and hand them over to me, alright. Just comport yourself." In pursuance of their agreement, they were going to make a big deal out of his limited skills at English. Yeah, best thing probably is to just play along.

The counselor, now sitting beside him, abruptly waked him up purring into his left ear with a breath reeking of stale whiskey, "Listen…there's a certain blur in your speaking. Is it alright with you if…I inform the judge about that?"

The vaquero didn't understand much. What he did understand, however, was that he wasn't in the position to haggle. He had nothing to lose anyway.

"Inform!" he responded tersely. For the first time ever, he had made a decision, his own one at that. He was well aware of the metamorphosis he had gone through during the last hours. He could imagine his restless and skittish eyes after so many hours of scrutiny among all these incisive voices and stoned features, not to speak of the stilted language. Occasionally he didn't grasp one single word of it. He lowered his head and glared morosely at his moist hands and made a try to wipe out the sweat on his gray too short prison garb. He was all prison garb, as was his fellow accused, who just had been so brutally wacked by their powerful assailant.

The vaquero relentlessly was taken out of his reverie another time when being aware of a resolute movement some place to his left. Daniel Freeman let out a guttural grumble as he laboriously rounded the table and lumbered forward. A subdued chatter arose from the audience. The judge immediately established eye contact and the clamor abruptly came to an end, and instead a profound silence took charge everybody understanding the hint and everybody now was staring at the convict with disapproval. The district attorney already stood waiting, his penetrating eyes following every toilsome step. His ambition now was to make this man glib. He knew he was well prepared, and he wouldn't concede this game. A quizzical look from him told every single individual present that he was anticipating applause, not boos. The judge bent forward his buxom frame and in a sharp tone reminded the vigilant defender that his client now was answering under oath. From his place at the stand, Freeman now was crouching down so the vaquero barely could see him. Soon enough he himself was the one to be put through the wringer, he thought, already in a funk. The judge immediately pounced upon, "Straighten up and speak loud!" he ordered and motioned for the gray-haired man to erect his back. The man reluctantly took along the instruction as the crowd sat watching in muted fascination. For the first time since entering the stand he looked straight at the chairman, his brows arched in a frown.

"Tell the jury your complete name and place of residence!" the judge ordered icily, studying the prisoner over his gold-framed round spectacles, his voice expressionless, his forehead sheened with sweat.

"Daniel..." his voice failed him, "Daniel...Heathcliff Freeman..." He made an elaborate pantomime of innocence and looked straight ahead as though he hadn't heard the whole question. The judge dipped his quill in the inkpot and scribbled something in his legal pad, then looked up at the man.

"Alright...And where do you live. Mr. Freeman?"

A hush ensued during which all eyes almost entranced were watching the crouching man in the stand. Eventually the judge questioningly looked up from his pad and demanded solemnly, quill in hand, bug-eyed, "Did you apprehend my question, Mr. Freeman? The jury expects you to tell your address. Come on...sock it to them, Mr. Freeman!" he went on with a morose smile.

"I don't have any...Your Honor," he answered, no emotion in his voice, nor in his face. The judge gave no answer. He dipped his quill in the inkpot yet another time and scribbled something in his pad then looked pleadingly at the prosecutor.

"Alright Mr. Wariner...you may commence asking your questions."

"Thank you, Your Honor." The prosecutor squinted hard at the penned goon and began walking toward him, holding a sheet of paper in both hands. He stopped in front of the stand and stood hobbling contemptuously, still studying the paper. Freeman felt a fear one he hadn't acknowledged since being a child, now for the first time realizing the significance of all the forces that were arrayed against him. He bowed his head and looked down at his shackled legs, waiting for the lethal blow. The prosecutor discretely cleared his throat then fell silent for a while.

"Where were you born, Mr. Freeman?" he wondered quietly.

One of the lawyers exploded into action. "Objection, Your Honor! The question's undue!"

"Objection not sustained!" the judge brawled.

The prosecutor braced his feet against the floor.

"The defendant is obliged to answer the question. Please do, Mr. Freeman!" the judge admonished and motioned to the man in the stand, who now appeared flummoxed. The prosecutor's cunning eyes studied him intensely. "Go ahead...tell the jury," he nudged, his voice almost avuncular.

"I was born...." His voice trailed off... "I was as born in Corpus Christi...Texas," he finally managed with a drawl of the South.

"When Mr. Freeman...when were you born?" the judge asked hard-voiced, musing on him.

"1824...tenth of Mars," he explained in a subdued voice, his face grave, his eyes having a ragged character to them. The prosecutor nodded then spoke to him directly, saying suavely as he scratched his aquiline nose, his body no longer in motion, "Mr. Freeman...how have you earned your living so far?" He kept on scratching and started to walk, then turned right-about, stopped short and stood waiting as the defendant thought hard, his body now showing an alertness. The prosecutor took a step closer toward him and said, "Tell the jury, Mr. Freeman...What do you live at? That's something that puzzles the jurors?"

The man in the stand didn't budge. After a lengthy silence the judge broke in, determined to dig as deep as possible, "Mr. Freeman...do you comprehend the inquiry? Please, answer yes or no." His temper was almost boiling now. The defendant breathed deeply and took off, "I understand, sir...Well, I've been workin' as a cook." He turned to the judge and looked him directly in the face.

"Alright...You are a cook by trade...Is that what you are doing currently?" the judge tried.

"Yes, sir."

There was heard some titters from the audience. Freeman realized there was no chance for him to recoil. The prosecutor took a steadying breath then took over, asking matter-of-factly, "Where do you work, Mr. Freeman?"

The gray-haired defendant felt a shock of fear and searched the eyes of his attorney who was studying him intensely like one taken back to a relentless reality. After a brief interval of hesitation, he motioned for his client to answer.

"I work as a ranch cook," he explained curtly. The ragged quality in the man's eyes were more evident now, and he looked around as if he was searching support, knowing his employer was around, but there was no way he could spot him from where he sat in the stand. He began having obvious trouble sitting still.

"Ranch cook, eh?...What ranch do you work at, Mr. Freeman?" the judge demanded, shifted and gawked, removed his glasses and swayed a little.

"It's named T Bar Crossing. A horse ranch." Freeman cringed when he said it. Obviously most of the folks in the room had heard him. The prosecutor backtracked somewhat, then he hung in mid-thought for a long moment. The judge opened his mouth as if to say something, but the prosecutor forestalled him, "T Bar Crossing…a horse ranch, eh?" he said and started to walk a little, then he swung right-about and said, his voice suddenly sharper, "Where is that ranch, Mr. Freeman?"

The defendant ogled at his counselor in hope for advice, but all he got in return was an expectant eye.

"Down at Sioux Falls, eh…in that region," he finally answered.

All got still and nothing was heard in the cramped court room but the creak of the prosecutor's footwear. All of a sudden it got dead silent, and they heard him ask, "What's the name of your employer, Mr. Freeman?"

"His name's Buchanan, sir," he said, his voice muffled.

The district attorney started lounging the floor with his arms folded behind him.

"Bill Buchanan…you work for him?" he inquired for clarification.

"Well, right now I don't." Freeman countered grudgingly as if to weep, looking askance toward Judge McCrea, who was swapping some words with his right-hand juror. He then shifted his attention to the dark-clad man fronting him and whose watery eyes now were flashing.

"You don't, but you did when you hit the road up north, right? You were in fact headed for Canada…isn't that correct?…You are not the first guy Buchanan jacked outta the sewer, Mr. Freeman. Tell us what kinda food Mr. Buchanan did provide! Not much of nosh-ups, eh? Egg, ham, bacon, beans…the usual ranch stuff…"

"Mr. Wariner…Mr. Wariner!!" the judge roared, banging his mallet vehemently.

"Please…Your Honor…I was only trying to…"

"Stick to facts, Mr. Wariner…I will not accept any further…excesses!! Is that clear?!" the chairman thundered, his angry eyes turned to saucers. The prosecutor stumbled backward a step as the judge paused to glance out toward the others. He gathered some papers and then bored his eyes into the defendant and again took a run, shouting, "You were in fact headed for Canada?…Isn't that correct, Mr. Wariner…uh, sorry, Mr. Freeman?"

Freeman shifted awkwardly while giving a hawk. His voice felt constricted. Nevertheless he answered, ogling at his frowning attorney, "Yeah...yes, sir, I was."

Right now it was all a blur to him. He could hardly believe it had in fact happened, but still it had. He sensed the vaquero sat glaring at him. His black eyes were showing no mercy, his face motionless, expressionless. He was no friend of his, and he never would be. What was he contemplating? His misdeeds? Did he feel sorry for them, or was he instead alarmed for times to come – the future, if there was any ahead of him. What about his zest of life? Was there any left?

A short quiet had occupied the packed courtroom that now was more stuffed than ever. The judge swung his mallet and coughed discretely. A short break was suggested.

XIV

Outside the courthouse, the air was chilly, and a light drizzle had made the rutty streets damp, and every once in a while the skies got enlightened by flashes of lightning. There were heard some occasional thunder in the distance and a gust swept through the plain boulevard that went past the court house whirling up debris of diverse origin that temporarily were lying underfoot among the multitude of horse fecals that lay scattered along the streets, it all giving an outlandish touch to the setting, a significant whiff of the exotic world. A dwarf in a clown garment sat in the clay not far from the front door of the court building, giving his clump foot some massage, grimacing, watched by a horde of young people that were making a mockery out of the non-athletic and squared little gimp, incessantly repeating his clamors in a try to appear facetious. Repeatedly he thudded his small fists in the clay. A Negro jackal of some variety, stood hovering over him, making his best to pep him up a notch or two, something which made the kids niggle the poor disabled yet more, and everybody launched into a laughter, one that never ever appeared to come to an end. Apparently, a happening was about to take place in town, beginning this night, or early afternoon. The town was already partially festooned, and out of an intersection downtown a brass orchestra came marching and advanced in their direction in perfect time, their steps kept back and restrained. Wolf Süsskind looked impressed by the artistic temperament of the little man where he sat floundering in the middle of the street cracking his endless jokes, some of which plain witticisms, though. It soon got apparent to him one thing: To some of the people around the clamor was looked upon as a source of frustration, to others as something beneficial, a means of relaxation, an innocent thing. To all appearances Wolf loved it, whereas the judge was growing alarmed to the verge of an outburst, and was making motions to the colored batman to get the hell out. The dwarf, now at last aware of things, turned his head and looked askance at the hard-faced stocky man in black gown. He raised his arm and pointed at him and burst out into laughter, a prolonged, contagious one.

"Where do you think they come from, Jeff?" Wolf said interrogatively, looking sidelong at him.

"Well, I heard 'em speak in Spanish…Mexico, I figure," he replied. He was knowing this to be a post-bellum phenomenon. He had already seen a lot of these vaudeville theatres during the war down in the South when serving in the army. He could note that Wolf's face was looking less drowsy, and that his cheeks had a brighter luster. Birgit also had noticed the same, and she turned at him and wistfully half whispered, her brows puckered up, "What if things always could be like this, Deputy O'Halloran."

There was something in her way of saying this that almost prodded him on, and for an instant he felt a strong temptation to squeeze her shoulder. For a short moment he repressed the impulse, then he got repentant for not having fulfilled his first intention. The thunderbolts had come right above their heads, but got drowned by an usher calling them inside as the brass orchestra, now far off, shifted into another tune: "The Italian Woman in Algiers" by Gioachino Rossini, the overture.

By their entering the courtroom the chairman already had placed himself behind his desk. He ordered the parties to quickly retake their places and declared the sessions to be reopened by giving the top of the table a resolute bang with his mallet. He put on his glasses and turned pages in his record, raised his head and coughed discretely then glared out at the parties.

"Is there anything you guys want to rectify with respect to what we've ploughed through already?" he asked loudly, adjusting his trim.

Sensing the lingering gaze of the judge, Daniel Freeman tried his best not to show his disquiet. It was, after all, nothing but a pro-forma question asked by the judge, all ephemeral, and he didn't manage to hear any discernible trace of empathy in his voice when asking. Irrespective of this, he felt as though he had fallen prey to vultures. He furtively looked across at the judge who flipped pages in a pad, his face as rugged as always, then looked across to where the Mexican sat huddling, eyes downcast, despondent-looking.

"I ask Mr. Manuel Jimenez to step forward," the chairman exploded peremptorily, anxious to get started.

The vaquero, cuffed at the ankles, flinched then laboriously rose to his feet and dragged himself forward, the rattling hardware following, his entourage watching every step from their seats. He made a stop when at the bench. The judge raised his head and glared at him over golden glasses with estranged eyes. All eyes now were watching them with a certain respect to the bodily reactions of the two men, the judge now acting like he was analyzing the situation in detail. He looked out into the ocean of eyes then removed his glasses and turned his attention to the defendant's counselor and faced him squarely.

"You are still asserting your client being innocent, counselor?"

The lawyer nodded confirming.

The judge wet a finger and leafed through some pages in his legal pad, read for a moment then raised his head and addressed the prosecutor, "You still press charges?"

"I certainly do, Your Honor."

The judge put back his glasses and gave a nod at the defendant and told him to place his hand on the Bible. He did and swore in.

"You may take your seat," the judge grunted.

Seeing there were no immediate reactions from the vaquero, the judge repeated his command a bit harsher. The vaquero was slow to sit down, his eyes dropped, but eventually he got himself settled, his breath short.

Judge McCrea for a short instant looked at the man almost pleadingly, then demanded shortly, "Inform us of your name, please."

Not one single syllable came forth. Some long seconds went by during which the defendant sat studying his lap.

"Manuel Jimenez," he eventually answered, disrupting the quiet. He was repeatedly considering the specific advice of his attorney, thinking he was probably right. Best thing is to let him handle the talk. The prosecutor's gonna try impish tricks on you, and he is said to have a special bias against Mexicans. This was what the lawyer had told him, and also, "They haven't come up with anything substantive…"

The judge studied the vaquero's bad hairdo, and inquired as though that should be unimpeachable, "You are Manuel…Jimenez, right?"

"Si, Your Honor." His mouth was dry.

The judge motioned for the district attorney to take over. He slumped somewhat and took off his glasses and began chewing at a stem, absorbed by what he saw before him. The prosecutor already stood fronting the vaquero. He paused some seconds for better effect all the while scanning the spectators then stepped a bit nearer to the defendant and launched into and began, his head dipped, "Incidentally…Mr…Jimenez…where were you in the night between…14th and 15th of last August?"

A hush settled as the vaquero deliberative sat contemplating his coming response for a short moment before announcing, looking up, glum-faced, "Home…asleep." His heart was pounding.

"Speak up so we all can hear you, Mr. Jimenez!" the prosecutor trumpeted, wedging on his heels.

"I was at home…sleeping," he said petulantly. He swallowed hard and declined his gaze.

The prosecutor began to pace the room while looking down at his squeaky footwear, his jaw twitching. Suddenly he swung right about and strolled in front of the stand, asking, "Do you know why you are arraigned, Mr. Jimenez?"

The vaquero slowly levered his gaze and looked sideways at his lawyer as if in search for aid. Upon capturing the gaze of his irresolute client, the lawyer just produced some short nods. Then he declined his head and went back to study his hands. Uncertain as to how he should interpret his lawyer's body language, the vaquero repeated, his apparition even more woolgathering, "I was asleep."

"Remember that you are under oath, Mr. Jimenez! Do I have to ramp up my warnings?" the judge wondered in a rising voice.

The judge's voice echoed in his head, and he marveled still at him being participating in this trial. He cleared his throat and swallowed. Why did his voice quaver when he spoke? He felt a shock of fear where he was sitting with his hands entwined before him on the table, thinking this could only be trouble. Slowly he'd started to recognize that he had in fact no cover, no camouflage, no back up anywhere. He sensed his courage now being on the brink of erasing, and he could hear the gnashing of teeth around him, and he could watch all wrinkled foreheads and glum expressions on their faces. Yet the benevolent advice of the lawyer still resounded, "Let me take care of the talk, and behave like you don't understand!"

"So you…were at home asleep…is that correct, Mr. Jimenez?" the prosecutor resumed.

"Si…yes…sir," he replied defensively.

"Where do you live?"

The vaquero jerked his shoulders a little, then said, sensing his cheeks flush, "T Bar Crossing."

"Buchanan's ranch, eh?"

"Si…yes, sir."

"What a coincidence! Same employer as your chum beside you!" the prosecutor interjected matter-of-factly.

The vaquero made no comment upon that remark, thinking that wasn't necessary.

"Listen Mr…Jimenez! You are obliged to answer every question and not disregard any of them! You are charged with robbery and manslaughter, and we are gathered here for one reason: dissect facts! From now on you answer every ensuing question!" the judge hammered, forgetting his dignified mask, sounding as though he was losing his temper.

In response to this the vaquero's counselor squinted hard and hopped to his feet.

"Please listen Mr. Chairman! There's an explanation to my client's sparing of words…his lack of knowledge at English!"

The judge lent back and leisurely removed his gold-framed spectacles and rubbed his eyes, leniently asking, "Does it mean your man will relinquish his right to speak for himself? And besides…I haven't got the impression there should be any serious slouches when it comes to his knowledge at English."

The lawyer looked at his client as he slowly sank down beside him, seeing his pallor had turned grayish, his dark eyes studying the hardware strapped to his pipe-thin shanks. A lengthy palaver on the vaquero's future verbal participation followed, where the lawyer with gross magnificence, with no hurry, taking a good time about everything, referred to the post-crime investigation, signed by Sheriff Douglas Kimble. The judge as well as the prosecutor both agreed on that investigation being scant – practically worthless. Off the record it got apparent that the prosecutor had a certain interest in calling Kimble as a witness, an idea that the judge approved of prima facie, thinking this would imply indictment and conviction would take place in one day. It also would imply the prosecutor would be given free hands, and no counselors would lash out at him! He glared at the lop-eared lawyer now in a gloom, and bent slowly forward in his cushy chair, smiled satisfactorily and asked everybody involved if they had any objections, or anything to say in addition. He waited for a short moment as he in a broad gesture reached out for his mallet. No, that did not seem to be the case. Hence he clutched the mallet and slammed it once. Perhaps everyone now had begun to understand with increasing clarity, that something extraordinary was to come up in the near future.

Sheriff Kimble didn't only dislike the venue, he didn't like the way things had turned out either. He had assumed him being called to the stand ex officio, but of the two other witnesses to emerge, he did know nothing at all. Up to this moment he had tried his best to appear invisible and not get daunted, and he realized that he one way or another had to find a way out of this distress. What was this all about? Did they consider him a would-be accomplice? Or were there some other explanations to his alleged barren record? And when it came to his deputy, would he make intercessions for his boss? No way. It wasn't likely. Not many people would, no one at all. No one he could think of, anyway.

Deep in thought the judge stroke back his gray hair and closed his eyes for a brief moment, then opened them, by all appearances provided new stamina, then announced, "By rights I consider it appropriate to call forward Sheriff Douglas Kimble as a witness. According to my list Mr. Kimble is due to be present."

Douglas Kimble, a rural sheriff from out the sticks, now it was time for him to make his appearance. He took a deep breath as the jitters hit, he who seldom lost his control in the heat of battle. All memories came roaring back when he composed his feet and raised himself up, and tottering approached the bar to swear in. He knew they would come about. He made his best to appear stable, though, his movements slow, both his legs sleeping. Easy now, he said to himself, this ain't the crack of doom. I ain't bookish, I ain't feelin' cushy when it comes to express myself, I've no glib tongue, can no fancy words and such. Don't let nobody patronize yo'…yo' hear…? He felt his chest heaving. He cast about. Doctor Bernstein's eyes followed him vigilantly and with great amusement, asking himself whether this display would be career-ending for his sheriff. Had he drifted away too far this time? Was there any substance behind all allegations? Or was it just plain and simple trash-talk?

He looked across at the old rustic grandfather's clock where it stood in the right corner of the sheriff's office with its golden pendulum slowly revolving. It had just chimed, telling a time of three thirty. Twenty-five-year-old Russell O'Connor sat tilted to one side behind the desk of Sheriff Kimble, his face obscured in shadow and his shiny boots nonchalantly resting one atop the other on the scratched surface. He glanced down at and shucked the pillar of ash from off the tip of his cigarette and sucked again on it and exhaled, watching the smoke how it drifted away and gradually thinned overhead. He tilted his head back again and studied his footwear in depth and rearranged them then moved his gaze from his boots and respectfully, like a man recently entrusted with the keeping of a devise which he hardly knew the use of, took to regard the primed double-barreled carbine resting before him on the desk, "a thing of great value," according to his boss, Douglas Kimble. He was in no way prepared for it, but nonetheless. Late yesterday night Kimble had paid him a visit and asked him if he was willing to make himself available as a deputy for a shorter period of time, "ten to twelve hours or so, at the most." He, Kimble, had nobody else in mind, at least "no one as fitted." That's what he had said, anyhow. He, Russell O'Connor hadn't answered for a minute but then one word gave birth to another and within a couple of months there will be an election, and without consulting his mother, a destitute and overworked widow, Russell had accepted, though not without a certain amount of reluctance. Kimble on the other hand, had enticed the irresolute youth by holding out the prospect of "a favor in return in the near future," whatever that was supposed to mean. Russell wasn't quite sure about it, and he'd not strained the meaning of the sheriff's wording by asking him further questions. And after all, five bucks for ten to twelve hours starting at seven in the morning doing nothing in particular, just "hang around," well, that was not that easy to decline. "That shield you got there suits you, Russell," that's what his mother had said to him when he left home early this morning. He smiled to himself and repeated his mother's words over and over again to himself. Mom has always been a good adviser, always around when I purchase something in the way of clothes, a couple of shirts, pair of denim or whatever from the local dealer. He touched his red downy boyish face with his left stalwart hand and tilted the squeaking chair. Sheriff for one day in an out-of-the-way-spot like Sioux Falls, Wyoming, that's what I am, me Russell O'Connor, he kept contemplating. The carbine lay resting and mute on the scratched desk some inches off. The firework now was in his keeping. Kimble hat put it there and he, Russell, the sheriff of the day, was to be paid to keep it there, whatever might occur. So far not much had happened to it, nor to him, though. Two of Kimble's kids had been in to say hidi to their old man, both evidently being ignorant of him being out of town.

The girl, pretty titivated on a weekday like today, and one of the boys, that bulky thug who uses to practice target-shooting with Jeff just gawked and shrugged when Russell asked him if they could go out shooting someday – just for fun. One of his own, Russell's chums had been in as well–– Fritz Nelson had been in for a while.

"Heard yo' here…yo' ma' tol' me…Look Russell, this place sure could need a real clean-up!"

"Sure Fritz. See what yo' mean…"

"Look at this!" he exclaimed and regarded with disgust his right forefinger after having touched the writing desk.

"Table over there's Jeff's," Russell said nodding at it.

"I bet it ain't that goddam' dust-laden…no way…"

Fritz went there and subjected it to the same testing. He was right. It wasn't that goddam' dusty. Fritz chuckled contended and grinned an affable grin. He took place in Jeff's chair and tilted. Russell extolled him as his best friend, fatherless like himself. Actually, both their fathers got killed in the latest Indian attack, both found dead, scalped, right outside the livery, both arrowed in their midsections. Now the next generation was making its best to stay afloat. And here they were.

"Listen, Fritz…we're in the same boat…yo' an' me, right," Russell announced gravely, thrusting his arms upward and clasping his hands overhead. "The same fix, one might say!"

"Hell we ain't! Yo're the sheriff…I ain't…" He paused for a moment, then craned his muscled neck and went on saying, "You sure start it up brilliantly, but…suppose there's gonna be some operational actions…" He shunned the gaze of his mate, he deliberately kept away from it. Russell, though, ignored the question, pretended a yawning, stretched and jumped up.

"Yo' like some coffee…I'm havin' some myself…else I wouldn't ask…"

"No…I reckon yo' wouldn't…but no thanks, anyways…Like 'em use to say – some other time maybe," the other said, shrugging his shoulders.

"Yeah…see what yo' mean, I guess…See what yo' mean…" his chum repeated sullenly.

Basically Russell disliked being alone in the sheriff's office making his best not giving the game away, being ambivalent as well, proud in some way. After all he was entrusted with something, yeah, basically he was. The sheriff had confided in him, relied on him, had handpicked him, otherwise he had chosen somebody else, one of those Mac Allister's big tough boys, or Kennedy's even tougher or whoever. Feelings are transitory, most often they don't mean nothin'.

"You ain't got much edibles in this rat hole." Fritz half insinuated and pushed back his hat and rose.

"Don't know…haven't looked around so much…couple of bean cans, couple of gravy cans. That's all, plus some coffee in the bean."

"No grinder…?"

"Haven't seen none anyways…must be hid somewhere, I've frankly no idea."

"Next time you bring a hamper, you hear!" Fritz suggested cajoling, and started to walk for the door. "I gotta' walk…have a couple of horses to shoe…the undertaker's ol' jade, yo' know an'…"

"Couple of ol' jades," Russell corrected, "COUPLE of ol' jades," he said again. "I bet you shoe nothin' but ol' jades, right?"

"Some young jades every once in a while, too, I reckon," the buddy replied grave-looking, almost whispering. Fritz was trading in the steps of his deceased old man, who'd been a blacksmith and farrier.

Russell sat with his hands between his knees to warm them. Upon his mate noticing this, his features grew yet more troubled.

"Light a fire for Christ's sake! Yo' do have a fireplace, right?"

"Sure…a stove right there, but no fuel. Burned the last logs in the mornin', and now the bin's empty. But I ain't squeamish…Yo' whinin' like an ol' hag, that's what yo' do."

"Just go ahead…band words…just like your ol'man…You're a replica of your ol'man. But…if that's the way you want it…You forfeit your health…yo' hear?" Fritz complained, his gaze wandering over the huddled-up deputy.

Russell raised up. "Why don't you walk out an' gather some firewood…instead of complainin'?" he demanded in irritation. "I tell yo' what…Yo' are annoyed with things, 'cause I was the one Kimble picked, not you. That's the reason."

Fritz, right in front of the door, neither turned nor answered. He just opened the door slowly and walked outside and viciously rattled it shut behind him, his jaw muscles taut.

XV

Sheriff Kimble was chewing the cud, trying his best to duck out of the questions asked by the glib and diligent prosecutor. Consequently, he took every little chance there was to shoot his way out, to make his getaway into a secure location, but soon enough he learned there wasn't any. The prosecutor had indeed a mastermind. All contingencies appeared to be foreseen and planned against, and now Kimble's reaction was one of impatience and anger. Douglas Kimble had started to show irritation, like he acknowledged himself beaten, his entire body language, all he said, all he withheld, it all pointed in the same direction, i.e. this man is in serious trouble, he somehow hides something. All jurors noticed it and frowned on it, as did the judge. Using from time to time some occasional trick is one thing, doing it all the time, thus triggering one's misfortune is another and more serious one. As for the prosecutor, he had gained his reputation over the years by his accurate and careful planning, and they were all having great confidence in him. He was in their opinion a skilled lawyer, a chevalier of law, and the judge, looking from time to time as if he'd dropped asleep, hung on every word that came from him. Occasionally he opened his eyes and sternly glared at the stone-faced man in the witness stand, his cool eyes saying, "Don't fool authority…no way it pays off." As for the judge, the word was put out that there wasn't much on this earth that he despised as much as untrustworthy maintainers of law. He enjoyed seeing them crestfallen, and consequently he didn't do much as to pouring oil on troubled waters. At a certain point in the hearing, he had interfered, producing a serious warning by saying in verbatim, "Stick to the truth, Mr. Kimble! Remember, you are under oath. One more misstatement and I'll have you stand trial in a court of law," Kimble knew the meaning behind the warning. He knew very well that the sentence for perjury would be one. He would be put to death.

The prosecutor paced the floor something that was a source of irritation to Kimble, one that grew over time. Instantly he turned to him and arched his thick eyebrows with streaks of gray in them, asking comradely, "Douglas Kimble, do you, being the sheriff of Sioux Falls, assert that you have performed your utmost to bring order in this stagecoach assault…this…foray? Have you done whatever necessary…Sheriff Kimble?"

A good question, one that hit hard. For a long time now he had awakened early, dreading the coming day, hating the dawning of a new. He had his family, alright. He made his best to be loyal to it, and he had tried not to make fatal mistakes. In some way he was pleased with how he had conducted his life so far. He also had tried not to be foolhardy. He drank a lot, gambled a lot, facts the prosecutor already knew of. And now the prosecutor appeared to have reached the point when he began to impeach every word from the witness. The trial was sort of transformed to a proper dissection, a veritable, fine grind. And nobody did even try to make intercession for him, the sheriff.

Jeff leaned forward a bit and studied the prosecutor's manly impassive face, a carnivorous face of a master of law chasing facts, pressing, at times almost besought, his features still as expressionless as before, seeming to have many things to ponder. He had been cunning and farsighted, even brutal when necessary, vagaries weren't unusual. After all a dreadful crime was committed, followed by a series of other grisly crimes, and the deeper he dug into them, the more incomprehensible he found it that the sheriff had showed so little interest in solving them. Instead, his features by degrees grew into the truculent look of somebody about to commit strong-arm.

Sheriff Kimble's expectations on a near dismissal from the witness stand got thwarted when the prosecutor asked directly while observing him shrewdly, "Where did YOU spend the night of the stage coach assault taking place, Sheriff Kimble?"

Kimble's attitude at once got woeful and he was near asking, "What the hell kind of a question is that?" Well, that little bastard couldn't backtrack the whole way, he said to himself. Soon the judge would stop him by pecking that mallet. The blunt inquiry, however, alerted some people in the room and a gabble broke out in a short time, Kimble now leadenly watching the mallet of the judge when it hit the desk in a series of loud bangs, and the judge had to go at it with all the forces he could summon to make his voice heard in the increasing noise. "Silence, please!! *BANG! BANG! BANG! BANG!*…Silence in court!!" the judge roared and slammed the mallet another time.

In all the whirling pandemonium Douglas Kimble watched his entire life pass by, starting in his early childhood and plodding on until it eventually subsided. The prosecutor's voice echoed demandingly, "Where did you spend the night, Sheriff Kimble…?"

No reply.

"You alright, sheriff?…Where were you?" the prosecutor repeated with bloodthirsty enthusiasm, rubbing his hands.

He looked up sharply and said, his voice hardened, "At home…I guess…" He got silent for a moment as if vetting the inquiry, then proceeded, "What makes you ask that question, sir?" He sternly looked around the room, his eyes squirreling about until his gaze finally found a resort on Judge McCrea.

"Just answer…Sheriff Kimble!" the judge admonished dryly with a fanning motion of his right hand.

Kimble could hardly suppress a grin, shot back, "I did, Your Honor, when I said I was at home."

The prosecutor pursed his thin lips and weighed the words, studying the answer for a long second then asked, "So you weren't journeyed anywhere…sheriff?"

"No, sir."

The weather had lifted and the drizzle had almost petered out altogether when the young deputy looked out through the filthy glazed and barred rectangle of the office door. The air outside was smooth with a smell of stove wood in it, and the temperature more pleasant outdoors than indoors. A wagon with a long bed stood outside the front door of the grocer's shop, a pair of horses with blinders standing hitched before it, their heads down, hind feet put to rest, croups aslant. Nat, one of the grocer's sons, crossed the street, hunched-up, heavily loaded, and eventually turned into the hotel. Other than these, there was no other living creature about. Russell gave a wrench at the filthy knob and the clattery door went open with a squeak. He stepped outside, sucked in the air and looked up the sky as he rolled the stiffness out of his massive shoulders. He stood for a while and looked out the almost empty street in both directions. There was no sign of commerce, at least not yet. A long minute passed then he heard a cat whining somewhere and the slamming of a door. Uncertain what to do next he yawned and turned around, walked inside in contemplation, wondering whether his foreman might be bound homeward or not. When back inside, he glanced at the grandfather's ticking clock. It told time to be 4.15. He scooped some lukewarm water from the pail and took a long drink. He wiped his nose with a sleeve when hearing somebody open the door and the clinking of spurs on the plank floor. His eyebrows went up and he looked back at the door, at the figures there. What he saw got him startled, the former drowsiness now subordinated. Right inside the shut door two men had materialized, standing side by side, one svelte, the other being his contrast. The svelte one looked around the place, the other one stood nervously shifting from foot to foot. Neither gave evidence of being in a hurry. The svelte one took a few steps as though in contemplation. He moved slothfully, his spurs clinking.

"Hay there, Russell…You play truant today?" the svelte figure spat out in a cringing tone and smiled grimly.

A brief uneasy silence descended until Russell finally managed a reply to that insinuation. He turned and looked at the man. "I finished school long since, Mr. Buchanan."

"Yo' alone, Russell?" the rancher went on, still studying the filthy hovel, tarnished with decay. Russell felt the warmth of blush move off his downy roundish cheeks. "Yeah," he managed.

The rancher turned, refocusing, saying in a toneless voice, "An' now you 're havin' a bash at this business?"

"Huh, yes, sir."

The rancher stood glancing at the floor as if in search for vindication. He could see that the boy was shaken, although he tried the best he could not to show it. In a way he felt bad about that. He looked at the boy again.

"Listen Russell…I need to be headin' home soon," he announced and tucked his thumbs in under his gunbelt, letting the anticipation build. For the first time since their appearance Russell looked straight into the tumescent babyish face of Buchanan's escort. A pair of icy black eyes glared back, the eyes of the groom and part-proprietor of the livery, the stooge of Sioux Falls, the subordinate partner, the mortified part. He had quit walking when entering. The rancher continued talking, "Incidentally…Russell…Your ol' man was one of those buildin' this office back in the forties…right? I remember he was, an' you remember, too, Paul?"

"I sure do, Bill…I'll never forget it," the groom promised, his voice silky.

"It ain't much mortar left on 'em walls…just look at 'em!" Buchanan bantered and succumbed to hoarse laughter, his escort joining with yet more hoarseness, his laughter being a lot louder. The entire man kind of bounced in paroxysms all the way from his voluminous bosom and all way down his midsection, his sweat-stained shirt undone almost until on a level with the navel, the whole fur visible. He wasn't quite sober, whereas Buchanan was regarded upon as an abstainer, at least as far as Russell knew. When frequenting the saloon, he ordered black coffee.

There was no word from the groom. Ever since they appeared, he hadn't taken his eyes from the boy. Russell looked past the groom and studied the door, sensing his heart laboring. Buchanan following his gaze, asked, "What are you thinkin' at, son?"

"Nothin'."

They exchanged some hush words between them, then turned to leave when there was a short knock at the door that got open, and Russell watched his mother step inside accompanied by a lady friend of hers, Ellen Raw, who was carrying a hamper with a coffee pot in it and a plate covered with a cloth. Holding a baking-tin in her both hands Russell's mother took a couple of steps in the general direction of her son, giving the two men a bewildered look when passing them, her lady-friend partially hid right behind.

"Howdy, ma'am..." Buchanan managed, touching the brim of his hat. Mrs. Raw did pay the men no attention as she passed them by, whereas Buchanan made a lifting motion with his hand and said in a modulated voice, "So long Russell...we just went by to see you're doin' alright."

They said their farewells and bowed outside and walked the short way to the saloon.

He rinsed the plate and the other utensils he'd used for cooking in the creek, and coercing a little packed it away in the saddlebag and redid the two fasteners, then stood for a while in the waning moonlight, looking down into the cool purling water. He unbuttoned and divested him off his riding coat and dropped it in the ground, then took a few steps nearer, squatted on his heels and cupped his hands and held them against the fast-running drift for a while, then sank to his knees and filled them, and lifted them dripping and dabbed his face. Shivering he re-cupped his hands and dabbed another time, enjoying the refreshing sensation provided by the life-giving water. Since it hadn't rained much since the latest drought, the water level was low and the chilly temperature by night with a sting of approaching snow cooled it off and offered the water a fresh taste, filtrated on its way down the mountains in its passing through the fertile flatlands up alongside the plateau with cattle everywhere raising up and setting off in seeing wayfarers coming. He rose and walked up to the waiting roan where it stood tied under a roof of swinging treetops. He unfastened and snaffled it and looked a last time toward the tidied camping site to check the fire that it hadn't caught again. He'd stamped it out and water-drenched it a while ago, and the last thin smoke from it long since had vanished overhead, but the earth underneath was warm with invisible waves of warmth still issuing from off it. It was cold in the mountains now, and not much warmer here in the ravine. Clad in a dark blue cotton shirt, Wentworth Hayden stood for a while and dusted the seat of his denim, then adjusted the shirt that hung out in the back. Finally, he went back to the creek and took up and draped himself in his long riding coat, did all the studs then got in the saddle and resumed his ride.

He had been en route for more than forty-eight hours now, most of the time deliberately following long-ago abandoned trails with scorched places where fires had burned, in these days used only by stray Indians and outlaws, people who travel light, and antelopes, puma, lynx, deer and moose displaying footprints, and a multitude of hoof tracks from mustangs as well. He had also discerned prints from grizzly up in the highlands some hours earlier. His horse had scented it and got alerted and began to cry with fear, rolling his eyes, ears laid back, and in the bluish sunless light of dawn he in the north-facing slope of the low hills had heard sounds of boughs being cracked in the clear stillness, and a spooky figure moving among the roadside trees and a jackal wolf standing in the narrow trail right before him, its fur white with rime. Testing the air and sorting the varied scents it watched him with its black eyes, neck slightly awry, hackles reared and one forefoot raised to the chest as if it would charge or withdraw. He watched it back astraddle his standing uneasy horse until it eventually turned around and set off due south at a heavy gallop. Up in the mountains there would be snow any time. One could smell it already. The first blizzards often hit without previous warning.

He had reached the outskirts of town and pulled up the horse along the passageway and stood. They look very much alike, he thought. He had seen a lot of them already, and this one was just yet another in the row. Sioux Falls. A distant flock of speckled hens poked in the horse manure that lay dotted along the thoroughfare. Two church towers rising and two or three blurred silhouettes of humans walking the street stood out against the purple skyline in the west, and the clouds were decreasing to the north. A presage of a cool night.

Given free reins the nice roan carried the rider the last stage along the street at a brisk walking pace. On its way to the very center, the heart point of town with all its important facilities, the equipage was followed by curious eyes. A stranger in town, a long-haired and light-blond-whiskered, mustached, inclined to thinness, vigilant, watching blue eyes, black Stetson tilted forward, making a sunshade against the setting sun. He sat like poured in the saddle with the reins sitting loosely in one hand, the other braced upon his thigh, a horseman from head to feet, an abundance of verve, a bask in power, appearing rapt in thought, his head slightly tilted up and eyes flickering left and right, not missing much, though. Some onlookers winced when watching him ride by the rank of buildings and broke eye contact, abashed and disconcerted. Even the faded saloon beauties lowered their lecherous eyes at the sight of this extraordinary appearance. The rider smiled at them encouragingly, doing his best to escape their innuendos. He rode in front of the sheriff's office where he stopped the horse, got off the saddle right away and hit the ground in an agile bounce. He gave the outstretched horse neck an affectionate clap while giving the ramshackle building a quick squint and slung nonchalantly the reins over the bar and tied them loosely to it. With both hands now free, he routinely touched the gun holster that sat around his waist as a foursome of saloon beauties with shawls about them stood watching every movement from the saloon's balcony while talking drunkenly between them.

The door wasn't quite shut so he walked in and stood for a short moment just inside the fading threshold. The office was ghostly still. Three people were gathered around one of the desks, one of which being a young man, who immediately greeted him with an upraised hand, then pushed a plate aside and rose. Hayden noticed the badge on his chest glimmering in the semidarkness. The young man frowned, one of the ladies slouched about, disinterestedly looking at nothing in particular. The other lady, though, seemed genuinely interested, taking in the stranger with every sense. The young man swallowed and licked his chops studying the leaning man in the doorway.

"Evenin.'" he commenced and made a motion with his hand toward the brim before continuing, "Hope I ain't disturbin' you guys."

"It's alright, mister…what can I do for you?" the youth responded, staggered and stood with his arms hanging down to the sides, his massive shoulders risen. He thereafter began spewing out a vile stream of explanations as for him being a deputy, a back-up for Sheriff Kimble, who was spending the whole day in court. The visitor shook his head gravely, anxious to pick up details and let the young man babble on without interfering with him.

"Alright…so Kimble badgered you before he went?"

The deputy nodded ardently as he shifted and explained proudly, "Well…yes…he put it here on the desk…and I fixed it to my waistcoat."

At that moment Mrs. O'Connor turned directly to the stranger and remarked straightforwardly, "I have seen your face before…not only once…I just cannot place you…"

Her lady friend nodded in agreement, still silent, regarding him speculatively. A deep sense of melancholy hit him.

"Yeah…you may be right 'bout that, ma'am. I remember your son since he was little." He nodded at the deputy, who stood frozen behind the swivel with a stalwart grip on the back of it, his knuckles whitened.

Obvious sounds of an out-broken pandemonium all of a sudden brought the chat in the sheriff's office to a prompt stop. Hayden turned around and made for the exit and pushed up the half-open door and crossed the doorstep. Russell grabbed his Stetson from off the back of his chair, donned it in a hurry then took the rifle up from the desk where it sat charged and followed right behind with surprising speed. They rushed out and past the horrified roan that stood tossing its head, eyes rolled upward. Staring ahead focused on two men right outside the bank, both in the process of pulling themselves up onto the backs of their tramping horses, they set off toward them at a clumsy run in their riding boots. A sudden realization then hit their minds when also watching an elderly woman following afoot in a vain effort to advance upon them where they set off in a crash of hooves, bellowing out of frustration when realizing she wouldn't make it. Eventually she stopped short watching them ride away until they dropped from sight a little way more. On hearing Hayden and the deputy winded coming up behind her, she swung around to face them.

"Don't just stay there!!" she yelled at them. "Go after 'em!! They just robbed the bank…you understand?!!" she cried out and flung out her arms in a helpless motion.

Hayden reeled around to face Russell, who eased in behind and flanked him, short-breathed.

"Get into the bank an' figure out what's happened!"

"Buckle down to it!! Go out there an' get 'em bastards...!!" the woman protested loudly.

"Alright, Miss McCarthy!" Russell nodded, ignoring her yelling, "Where do you reckon they're headed!?" he went on, turning to, refocusing the man beside him.

"North...up the mountains, I go after 'em," Hayden replied, looking up the street.

"Be careful...It will take some time before I can send away a posse!" Russell said.

In the interim a handful of men of various ages had gathered on the rutty street and stood talking among themselves in agitated voices. Russell looked among the faces. The men were all rustics, one of them uttering immodestly with a harshness in his tone, the wind blowing his hair, "If you are lookin' after volunteers, then you've seen 'em..."

Looking again at him, the young deputy blurted, making his voice as peremptory as possible, "Yeah...go saddle up your horses, but don't ride out 'till I'm back, you hear!"

The men shrugged and gave a short nod.

The charlady was back inside the bank, stooped down, engaged in losing the catch rope that was attached to the bank clerk's wooden swivel. Russell helped the old man up.

"Yo' alright, Jimmy?"

The clerk, choleric, wailed for a while and massaged his sinewy wrists, his jaws clenched into a grimace.

"If...I...Just could...go out there...an' rehash..." he muttered with a harsh and quivering old voice.

"Yo' alright?" Russell snapped again.

"Yeah...I'm alright...Feel loggy, but it ain't serious...must have crashed out!" His peaked cap sat askew, and his eyes rolled.

"How much money did 'em get yo' figure, Jimmy?" Russell asked, looking about.

"I got a punch that landed flush on!!" the old man whined, his breath slowly coming back.

"Jimmy...listen!! How much did 'em get in cash?" Russell asked another time.

"No idea…They forced me to open the vault…'Em bastards were trigger-nervous…filled a sack an' then just chased away…Listen, I've seen 'em marauders in town before…in the saloon, you know." He pointed with his crooked forefinger out the street.

"They weren't masked?" Russell demanded from the doorway on his way out.

"No, they were not," he confirmed and gestured vaguely in the air with one hand. The charlady half turned and glanced at Russell questioningly. After a moment she re-shifted her attention to the stove to chunk more wood into.

Less than ten minutes later Russell O'Connor swung his petulant piebald horse onto the street and set out, taking the lead. Four men horseback filed in behind, gaining momentum. Within short, at the far end of the street, they had overtaken the leader.

Hesitating over one track leading west, and another going north Hayden paused in his pursuit and sat crouched in the saddle, studying the mushy fresh horse prints underfoot. It was evident to him that the two men he was following were riding abreast, headed northwest into the mountains, and he accounted for their reappearance on the prairie a couple of miles north. The tracks were giving evidence of the men having quickened their pace recently. Left-handed he pushed his hat brim backward on his head the better to see and with his shanks nudged his roan ahead. The black sides of the mountains were standing in front of him, far off and clearly visible now. He twisted his frame to capacity and looked back to discern five riders silhouetted over the plains following the wagon road in his direction. The wind had abated significantly, and no onslaught was perceptible anymore. A cattle flock of longhorns stood studying him as if they were wondering what was in his mind. At times some of them gave a call so as to ask when watching him pass along the rutted wagon trail, and some partridges got heard clucking from the tussocks of grass at the roadside. He pressed the flanks of the horse following the hoof prints up the crest. The horse snorted and moved his muscled neck up and down, trudging uphill.

From up the bluff he now was capable of overlooking the flatlands beneath. There he could spot them about a mile and a half out, riding their horses at a tempered trot. He reached for his rifle sheathed in the scabbard of his saddle and pulled it out, slacked the reins and clapping the flanks of his horse pushed on and set off at an accelerating gallop. Initially he quickly caught up on them, but within short he heard one of them cry out in despair when acknowledging the unannounced approaching of the mortal danger behind. In his estimating likelihoods, realizing they should be given no opportunity to ambush, one of the men ahead of him very brutally pulled in his horse until almost on the point of tumbling over, then pulled it up shortly and sawed it around and stood waiting for the pursuer to advance on him. Hayden slowed down his pace and set the rifle to his shoulder, concentrating on the other rider who was trying to disappear by forcing his horse forward at a brutal gallop toward a giant boulder a half mile out. He aimed and fired away twice and bummed. He tried to lever his point of impact and charged away toward the crouched rider that now was storming forward, now faster. He pressed the trigger and squeezed off. The report rang out and the rider fell down in an embrace of the horse's neck and hung until his lifeless body by and by slumped to the right side and finally slammed to the ground. At the distance from which he regarded it, he could see a bulging sack sitting tied to the empty saddle.

Alarmed by the shelling the posse advanced on them as Hayden let the roan jink its way sideways and reined it around with one hand, all the while holding the smoking gun in the other. The other bank robber had set his venting gelding quarter-wise and sat in the saddle with his shotgun pointing at him. His smile was almost rueful, his thin lips slightly parted. There was a patch of dried blood between his deep-seated, narrowly set eyes, now settled on his pursuer. He straightened up in the saddle and motioned him forward toward him with his gun and said, "Let's do it real quick, eh…like you did with him out there…What do you say…?" A tic on his cheek quivered.

Hayden sat in silence, pretending to give the question some thought then said, "Tell me what's on your mind."

"I'm thinkin' it over," the other answered somberly and pushed back the greasy brim of his Stetson with his free hand. "Lucky for yo' our horses bein' worn-out…Too much ridin' these days," he added gravely and eyed his pursuer long as if to see what he would answer. A calf bellowed not far away. The clay-dotted gelding turned its head to it and glared at it, as if the sound had evoked in him some anger. The man's narrow-set eyes hardened and he nodded knowingly at his pursuer and raised a gob and leaned to the side and spat, then straightened up and said, his voice harsh and menacing, "Less I don't kill you…you do me. That's the way it is…We'd better get this over with.

Hayden didn't respond, just kept his statuesque frame upright in the saddle, his horse shifting under him. "Scabbard that gun an' keep your hands before yo' on the saddle so I can see 'em," the man ordered mildly in a voice lowered to a grumble.

Realizing he hadn't much of a choice, Hayden obeyed though with gross reluctance.

There was an impenetrable somberness in the man's eyes now moving over him. "You ain't the sheriff of town?" he said and shifted.

"No, I'm not," Hayden confessed and looked down at his hands crossed before him on the saddles' horn.

"Ain't much of a talker either, eh…shot 'im in the back, eh…" He made a gesture with his head toward his comrade. The horse was walking about a quarter of a mile away on the open country, grazing. He quickly turned to face Hayden and concluded with a menacing grin, "But, after all…nobody's flawless." He grinned, displaying two or three moth-eaten tusks in the front and went on, "A crazy son of a bitch, that's what he was, an' thanks to yo' I don't have to share the loot with nobody."

He spat anew and grinned, his loquaciousness sort of making him distraught. The posse, having made an outflanking movement with the intention to take the looter from behind, was advancing on them, the hoof clattering barely hearable. Unsuspecting the looter took off his Stetson and with a sleeve sleeked back his blackish hair, holding the shotgun in his right hand, squared up. Hayden eyed him furtively with his both hands still squared on the saddle. The looter's horse wore a chrome-trimmed Mexican saddle and stood inert with its head bent down with hanging under lip and ears startled and twitching. He watched the spotty gelding raise his head to let out a whinnying, taking in the scent of strange horses coming up behind. By and by they went closer in a tramping of hooves, their steps and snorts increasingly manifest. The looter remained still, sitting upright with his gun aiming at Hayden. He now appeared to have registered that something extraordinary was in making behind his rear. With a controlled motion he extended his right arm and levered it until it stood horizontal. There it stopped, slightly trembling. Facing Hayden squarely he hissed with rancor, "If you move, I blow you out."

Hayden tried to look past the muzzle of his gun, his gaze searching the man's winced face. He didn't manage to see it in full. What he saw was his diaphragm sucking in and out with the motion of each breath. Hayden felt cold inside and his mouth was bone-dry. There was a moment of deathly silence. The horsemen got nearer to where they stood until Hayden was in eye contact with Russell, the deputy, now a man of stature. To Hayden it now was evident that something exceptional was in making. "Drop your gun, mister!" Russell's voice was almost thunderous and full of authority. Hayden watched the muzzle in terror, sensing like his heart was pounding its way out of his chest. He was still unable to see the looter's face. Instead he looked beyond the muzzle to cast a last sweeping eye at the four horsemen that stood grouped, defining a semi-circle around their fresh commander. In the same moment he observed Russell clapping spurs to his piebald and advance upon the looter and halt when right behind him. "You heard me. Do as I told you. I count to three."

The looter's gun was still pointing at Hayden.

"What if I don't?" he grinned. "What if I…squeeze off instead?" he wheezed, his arm extended, using steadily increasing force.

"Then you will be sentenced to death, mister. I tell you in the name of law."

The looter's over lip had started to tremble as had his right arm, the thin mustache pulled up to the nostrils, his eyes full of contempt. His jaws were clenched when he suddenly lowered his right arm and let it hang down to his side, gun still in hand. Hayden exhaled, his hands forgotten on the horn of his saddle. "Drop the firearm!" Russell commanded peremptorily.

Flooded with frustration or whatever reason he had, the looter squeezed the trigger of his gun and emptied the magazine, five shots in rapid sequence. He then sat and glared down at the crater with his arm hanging loosely, fuming gun in hand, as the horses, suddenly gotten snapped to attention, buckled and tramped while tossing their heads in a pervading cloud of ascending gun smoke. "Congratulations," he said after a spell, slowly looking up, "You guys just beguiled me of a fortune," he hissed sweetly.

Hayden shifted in the saddle and studied the man intently before answering, "Happiness is real only when shared…do as the sheriff told you, mister."

A subdued clatter ensued as the firearm hit the ground. Russell swung his leg over the horse's ham and jumped down. Over-bent he made for and picked it up, un-breeched it and breeched it shut. He stopped short and looked up at the rider in the Mexican saddle now sitting crouched in it, looking across the tranquil idyll with no great curiosity as if this idyll was calling back for him to re-approach it, but there was no way he could, not now, not any more. Some distance off his comrade lay glaring at him. His extinguished eyes displayed nothing, though. There was to perceive in them no compunction, no sympathy, nothing.

XVI

The majority of the lawyers and participants involved in the ongoing proceedings had begun to relinquish the whole idea of a one-day-settlement. Consequently the gray-haired captive and the vaquero were hauled back to their underground custody, their defenders still asserting with determination their clients being innocent and arrested under false pretenses.

"My first priority is to elicit facts, gentlemen," the judge announced coldly, laying a certain emphasis on the word "gentlemen" when giving them a long look one they dodged seconds later. Furthermore the judge had demanded that the prisoners should be kept parted, the order immediately met with approval from the jailers. The judge thereafter had engulfed himself in his legal pad. In the meantime some spread whispers got heard in the crowded and stuffy premises, whispers seeming in accordance with their own view of things. The judge then turned to the jurors, and after some palavering back and forth he declared the sessions of the day to be closed. There were, however, some names out-crossed in his legal pad, names of individuals of special interest with whom he was anxious to meet in privacy before their dismissal. He explicitly named Sheriff Douglas Kimble and wrathfully he said, searching his gaze, "Sheriff Kimble, you are prohibited from leaving the premises. From now on you will also be kept under constant surveillance."

"I hope you know what you are doin', Your Honor," the sheriff exclaimed, giving a goofy grin, then gazed at the judge for a few seconds, then continued, "I ain't gonna say one word without a legal adviser."

Judge McCrea ignored the man completely, though. Grim-faced he looked out the crowded aisles and then down at his paperwork. He looked up again and his eyes searched for Jeff. Their eyes met briefly.

"Vice Sheriff Jeffrey O'Halloran…I want you to reappear here by 2.00 p.m. tomorrow." He then went on, turned to Birgit, his features a little more relaxed, "Miss Süsskind…you don't have to appear…and that goes for Mister Süsskind junior as well," he added almost laconically and started to assemble his paperwork. "Any further questions?" he inquired casually with no emotion, neither in face, nor voice. He removed his glasses and looked out the sea of faces. Finding no evidence of glibness, he closed the sessions, saying they draw back till 10 a.m. on the next day.

Outside the court building the streets were teemed. Time was 5.15 and Jeff had recently been witnessing his boss being ushered away, two jailers flanking him, both of which having an innocent grin planted in their smug faces. Birgit looked at Jeff and said thoughtfully, her face twisted up in discomfort, "Listen, Jeff…do you really believe he's guilty in some respect?"

Her brother was standing a little apart from them, distracted by a little gentlemanly dressed doctor from Iowa, bringing with him certain "precautionary items" just in case anyone needed the best cure available for diarrhea. He had it right there with him, on his cart. The boy looked relaxed in the red twilight, and his eyes sort of twinkled, and often as not he laughed outright. A fine rain had just fallen and a light bed of rainwater lay over his high forehead. As for Jeff, he was surprised at hearing his name called. He therefore didn't answer immediately. His eyes wandered up the red mountains to the west all the while pondering the question, simultaneously noticing that she intercepted him, fixing him with her searching somber eyes. He stood aside to let some walkers pass, a smoldering cigarette in his fingers. "You doin' alright?" he said and pushed back his new Stetson hat somewhat.

She eyed him back, cocked her head and drew a nervous breath, "I guess so, thank you…Well…you didn't answer my question…"

"You mean Kimble, right?"

"Yes…I mean, can you imagine why they took him into custody?" she wondered again with a faint smile.

"He's hidin' somethin'…that's what they think. An' they put him behind the coulisses for some time for his best as well, you know. But that doesn't mean he's involved in the shelling. Frankly I don't know for sure what they might be up to," he declared in a high whisper.

Birgit didn't respond. A smattering of applause caught her attention not far off. A blue-clad juggler had been in constant motion ever since they hit the street, and now he stood bowing, taking in the ovations. His pale ice blue-colored face expressed no sentiment worth mentioning. Beside him a female assistant of some variety sat cross-legged, smiling, right below a wagon, parked alongside the broad boulevard. The juggler kept on bowing at the crew, expressing his gratefulness in a slight accent that she thought might be Mexican. Birgit was struck by the boyishness of his figure, slight and frail, one bringing about an image inside her of something subnormal, something alien.

Jeff studied her light hair flaming in the early evening with a faint starlight coming from overhead. They walked slowly back their way to the livery stable, Wolf tracking far behind, sallying forth among merchants of all kinds, mesmerized, his head craned in all directions, austere and bewildered at the same time. It wasn't until Jeff had got the filly between the shafts of the buggy when the boy eventually showed up at the enclosure. Birgit motioned him up and the little filly set out for the flatlands at a quick trot. Birgit clenched her brother to her chest and they huddled together on the box, Wolf in the middle, his curly hair tousled by the up-blowing wind coming from northwest all the way from the endless Canadian prairies. Fatigue hit them quickly, the sounds from the town now significantly muffled and soon it all got out of sight. In an hour the sun would be quite gone. A cur barked somewhere in the far distance. Laying ahead of them were now but unfenced grasslands.

The barman dried the whiskey glass and slung the towel over his shoulder. He inclined his head and looked into the back mirror. He studied the reflection and froze for an instant. He slowly turned around to face the man. He somehow looked familiar to him, and immediately his features with three days' worth of bristle grew troubled. Slowly he raised a hand in greeting. "Hayden…Wentworth…Hayden?" he stuttered, his jowls shivering a little.

"Yeah, that's me alright," Hayden admitted, stepping forward a bit as his eyes searched the almost depopulate premises. Four young cowboys in silence engaged in a poker game huddled in the background, none of which paying him any attention. "You run this place nowadays…?"

The barman gave a pensive nod, his forehead creased in thought.

"You've…grown to manhood, eh?" he said.

"Well…time goes by."

"Yep, it sure does…an' you seem to be in pretty good shape, eh?"

"Never been in better," Hayden answered with a teasing smile. The barman smiled back at him.

"Alright…ham an' eggs…an' a beer," Hayden ordered earnestly. Too much talk wouldn't avail much, he reasoned, and besides he already knew what there was to know about the town and its inhabitants. Just let 'em stick to their humdrum. He thumbed his Stetson back on his head and looked straight into the mirror. The barman hastily withdrew.

"Best thing would be to let the man dangle!" the barman said almost jovially after a moment in quiet, jolting Hayden out of his trance, his commentary setting the four cowboys at the gaming-table to laughing. Hayden had begun to eat. He cut a section from the bacon and forked it up, awaiting. One of them at the card table went on to say there will be no need of a trial. That bastard was guilty.

"No way you can get more guilty," another voice broke in, the harsh voice of a weather-beaten rancher in a windbreak thicket. Hayden showed no inclination to speak. The barman already had shoed back into the rear.

"He has got busted, remember, an' if you're gonna lynch 'im…we're in for it," the same man went on. "He'll soon be in the dock," he added, his mouth crumpling.

"Why not behead the bastard?" another member of the four-leaf clover suggested, one appearing to be the youngest, a twenty-year-old some with a bulky midriff and garish shirt. The barman, now back behind the counter, evidently impressed by their philosophizing, reappeared and stood in enchantment listening and watching Hayden who ate in silence, his features impassive. After a time he freed himself from his place behind the desk and moved toward him. Big talkers, nothing more, Hayden thought to himself, having encountered the sort many times before. There were after all other people around who he considered more dangerous. He eventually pushed away the plate and looked squarely at the barman, who stood close to him, drying his hands on his gingham apron. Drumming his fingers on the table Hayden declared himself ready for coffee.

Russell kicked off his boots and stretched out on the bunk. Minutes later he'd slowly drifted off into a well-earned slumber. From the lockup the detainee went on snoring, the proof against him irrefutable. In the bank the old clerk extinguished the light after having counted the bills restored. Not a single dime was missing.

It didn't take long, however, before the young deputy relentlessly got taken out of his slumber when hearing somebody bang at the wooden door with great deliberation. He swallowed hard and listened as a throng of evil thoughts and suspicions run through his head.

"Russell!!" came a voice from outside the door.

Still in a semi-conscious state Russell pushed back the blanket and slowly got out of bed and stood and looked toward the door barred shut. He was draped in a ragged blanket, slung over his regular garb for the purpose of maintaining warmth. He took it off in a hurry and tossed it onto the bunk and in his sockfeet tottered away to the door. He removed the bar and pushed open the door and stood back, watching it screech open. It was past midnight. Jeff reflected an instant before stepping inside, nodded into the rear, his coat draped on one shoulder. Russell stood aside and motioned him in. They crossed the floor and stopped when at one of the desks.

"I reckon yo' ain't alone," Jeff said.

"I ain't," Russell admitted and propped his butts onto the edge of the desk and crossed his arms across his chest. "Somebody robbed the bank yesterday afternoon."

"Yeah, I know 'bout it," Jeff answered and shifted.

"Has been a havoc before he went to sleep. Wasn't much left in the pantry…stewed beans was all there was."

Jeff regarded him gravely and asked out of awe, "You took 'im without nobody's helping…that's so…?"

Russell studied the boots of the other as if contemplating how to answer. He looked up. "Some people helped me…some stranger."

"Stranger, eh? Somebody adrift?"

"Yeah…I figure…" Russell replied, his eyelids grown heavier. "Listen, Jeff…how 'bout the two of us takin' turns watchin'?"

"You know who he is?"

"Didn't tell…Look inside…I reckon he's asleep."

Jeff stepped to the jail-section and looked inside to study the detainee, then went away again.

"I can't see his face…his hat's jammed to it…You go home an' get some sleep."

"You take over?…What 'bout…Kimble?"

"They kept 'im…he ain't likely to be back tonight…I tell you more in the mornin'."

"Alright, Jeff. See you in the mornin'," Russell said, his tired eyes for a short while coming to life. "Good night."

"Good night."

XVII

In the scantily decorated second-floor hotel room Hayden dressed himself in a hurry in the moon-ridden darkness. He leaned and looked out the window, watching the sun beginning its ascent to the sky. The room looked out over the main street that turned off and led into a thin road that led inland through the hills in the northeast. Down the side of the building a spotty cat walked its way along the empty street. Watching something indifferently, it stopped short for a spell when in the middle of a sunbeam, laid down and rolled and set about cleaning itself, rolled and sprawled and sprawled again, then stretched hugely, having as it seemed a good time in its solitude, having found itself a suitable sojourn as there was no one else about. The air stood still and a smell of smoke held the odor of firewood, indicating the town was awakening to face yet another workday. He combed his light hair backward on his skull and went to the plush armchair of dark red and picked from off its backrest across which he'd slung it, his gunbelt with the gun sitting in it. He fitted it to and adjusted it to his waist and buckled the belt shut, then tied the straps and let go his hands, then grabbed up from the same armchair his long coat and draped himself in it and did the buttons. He next stepped to the diminutive mirror that barely framed his face. He looked sourly at himself, thinking his outfit be too ostentatious, but again, he wasn't that particular. And besides, he was sent here on duty. He turned to face the rickety table with a box of cigars on it. He went there and selected one and lit it and soon the room grew embedded by its fragrance. Finally he picked up his Stetson from where he'd placed it on the table and donned it then stepped into position before the mirror two steps sideways and curled his lips into an awry smile, then did his getaway.

    The morning sun was surprisingly warm on his face. He paused and stood for a short while on the depopulated street, uncertain as to which way to take. He skirted a puddle and followed the street past the bank and the general store until he was on a level with the saloon. He went in front of the door and tried it. It was bolted. He let go then went closer into and raised his hands to break the glare on the glass, and looked inside. A one-armed square-hipped young woman with a flat bust rose laboriously from a table and advanced on the door motioning for him to wait until she had got it open. She was a small woman so small she seemed to weigh almost nothing, her thin face shining with serenity. Hayden backtracked a bit and stood and held his hat in one hand, his right arm sort of raised in benediction, whereas the woman meantime stood and looked at the door's lock like she wasn't competent in her ability to deal with it. Eventually she turned the key and wrenched the doorknob and stepped away while gazing up at him intently. Her face was blank, her eyes remote and bleak. She had the apparition of somebody who involuntarily had slipped into another world. "Hello, Molly," he said casually.

Still standing within reach of him, she looked longest at him as if to remember him, her features displaying no sentiment whatsoever. "You remember me?" he asked pleadingly.

She asked his name. She had rests of food that stained the lower seams of her thin face.

"Wentworth Hayden…I'm Wentworth Hayden, ma'…sorry, Molly."

"Is that so, eh?" she answered tonelessly, licking her lips.

"Yes…it is."

The little woman all of a sudden seemed to think many things. She slowly formed her lips and pronounced his first name, "Wentworth."

Hayden nodded encouragingly and looked inside at the varnished wainscot until an annoyed brawl was heard from inside the curtained rear. Suddenly the barman stood in the doorway chewing, a flour-dusted apron tied about his burly midsection, his jaws ballooned. His features shifted at the sight of Hayden and he smiled and kept chewing slowly.

"She has a blur in her speech," he said with a casual nod at the woman.

"Didn't mean to interrupt breakfast," Hayden replied, moving his eyes from the gaunt woman to the barman, who was making his way back to the kitchen, probably to finish his last bite. To Hayden's surprise he soon reappeared, looking as though he was having things on his mind.

"We'll make you some breakfast…uh…a heapin' rounda pancakes and maple syrup…sapid stuff I tell you."

A big dog appeared from the rear, its tail swishing.

"I'm finishin'…just anything's fine with me," Hayden responded and looked in the direction general of Molly, who now was pretending he didn't exist. Basically, he didn't have to ask why. It was evident to anybody, that the barman's sister still demonstrated insults of her confinement in that Indian camp. He would never forget her fervent eyes in the early morning five years ago when he and some other cavalry men dragged her out of that chief's tent. Now she appeared devoid of sentiment. Who would take the rap? Why that resignation? Hayden asked himself as he walked a half circle around the dog and made it for a nearby table and sat down.

The conversation during the breakfast was held to a minimum.

"She has been hoverin' between life an' death," the barman explained at a certain point, following Hayden's gaze. "The doctor was forced to amputate her arm," he went on matter-of-factly. "Some infection, an' we feared we would lose her," he specified and shrugged as his sister burst out laughing, glancing at the guest over her shoulder.

"We're in your debt, Hayden," the barman declared, ignoring her, his voice having a dull permanence about it.

Hayden slouched back in the chair and looked straight at him. "Well, I wasn't alone."

The barman looked at him a moment, then looked back at where Molly had stood before retreating into the curtained rear. He quickly glanced about quizzically and returned to his guest, announcing in a lower voice, "An' now we have to…patch up what's left…"

Hayden gave no reply. He watched the reflections of two riders setting their horses at the rail outside the saloon. Pensively he reached for the coffee mug and drained it in one long gulp. He set it back onto the table before him and pushed the empty plate away as the barman retook his usual place behind the desk.

Out on the street the horsemen tied their horses to the bar. When done they stepped inside and stood and looked toward the place where the barman was standing.

"Mornin' gentlemen," he greeted them deferentially and coughed quietly, his eyes betraying nothing.

Wayne Seay seemed not to hear. He slid stiff-legged toward the counter, his lean foreman trailing, both with rifle in hand and gun sitting in holster around midsection. They made a halt when at the counter. Meanwhile Molly reappeared from the rear and limped her way to the place where Hayden was sitting. Without a word, shunning his gaze, she reached across the table and studiously collected the fork and the knife with the help of her hand, placed them on the plate and started her way back to the solitary of the kitchen. For some reason she never touched the coffee mug, recently drunk dry. To Hayden's knowledge not much of substance so far had been said among the three men at the counter, distracted as he was by the appearance of the handicapped woman. The rancher looked around the room, then turned back to the barman, announcing in mid-voice, "We've been ridin' all mornin'."

Reuben Lindsay, now fiddling with his cigarette makings, gave a quick nod in the affirmative while hearing his boss rumble on addressing the barman, who stood looking toward the batwing doors as though waiting for some other to appear.

Turning at the barman, Lindsay said, "Your sister gets thinner by each day…she's almost emaciated. Don't you give her enough to eat, eh?"

The barman morosely regarded the foreman who with dexterity had started to roll himself a smoke. "She eats alright…actually moren I do," he announced morosely. He took a deep breath, then another and even deeper then said, "Would you guys like somethin' to drink?"

Seay half turned to his foreman who was standing with his both hands cupped, lighting his cigarette.

"Beer." Lindsay announced curtly and took a deep draw.

"Alright, you heard him," the rancher said to the barman an octave lower. "Make it two…like I said…we've been horseback all mornin'."

"Yes, sir…Maybe we could fix you somethin' edible?"

Seay studied the inquiry for a short while, looked questioningly to the side at Lindsay who shook his head from side to side then said, "We've done eaten already…Listen, yo're yo' sister's custodian nowadays, ain't you?"

The barman nodded and put the beer before the rancher. Hayden slowly rose from his chair. He reached into his shirt pocket and removed a bundle of bills while meeting the searching eyes of Reuben Lindsay in the mirror. The foreman stood fuming mutely, keeping him in his sights with a show of great concentration, his head kept still, his look fixed, face austere. The barman, now on his way back into the bowels, stopped in mid-step and stood for some seconds as though he was calculating a number. He took a step forward and made a dismissive gesture with his hand and said, looking square at Hayden who shaped himself to go. "Yo're welcome…it's on the house."

Hayden repacked the money and looked like he might be ready to leave, and after a careful deliberation he nodded and thanked. From outside came the claps of horsefeet and trundle of wheels, announcing the outbreak of yet another day of labor. He looked back into the mirror just in time to meet with the red-swollen eyes of Wayne Seay, trying his very best to offer the half-drunken rancher a look of indulgence. Seay sank a hand to the ashtray where it sat on the desktop and said something to his foreman. Hayden picked his hat from off the table and put it on and pushed back the chair. On his way out he nearly stumbled over the ancient dog that now was laying on the newly swept floor with its head resting between its paws. When stepping by, he heard the voice vociferate, "Hay…you cadger…I've seen that flaxen hair of yours some time before…but…I can't place it. It must be long ago, I reckon." He gazed vigilantly over his massive shoulder toward the exit, where Hayden stood frozen. You might be right 'bout that, you ol' drunk, Hayden thought to himself.

"We've met before, alright. Five years back… name's Hayden… Wentworth Hayden," he said, still frozen.

The rancher hid his weathered face in his giant hands and cursed himself for being so forgetful.

"The cavalry, eh?"

"Yeah," Hayden admitted.

"That's what you said, Reuben, right?" Seay grunted to his foreman without looking at him.

"In that case yo' know my name…don't you son?" he continued brawling toward the exit. He shifted and turned around, his liquid eyes almost lachrymose, increasing Hayden's sense of discomfort and awkwardness.

"Yes, sir. It ain't that easy to avoid. Despite the passage of time…I haven't forgotten you, sir," he grinned.

The answer evidently raised the rancher's spirits. "You heard 'im Reuben…you heard what he said, right?" he asked his foreman, waving a hand in a hoarse laughter.

"I heard, alright," the foreman mumbled half asleep.

"An' now yo're back in town?" the rancher bullied on, addressing Hayden.

Hayden nodded his approval, said nothing. He bent down and patted the dog that had risen and started circling him as Seay stood with the bear stoup close to his mouth waiting for Hayden to answer his assertion, but there wasn't any. Molly stood in the door of the kitchen in her ill-fitting robe, holding a long-handled broomstick. Pumping her only hand around it, she said polite and monotonously, "Don't pat the dog, sir. She might bite you…she…did me…the other day…an' Warren forbade me to…touch her for all time," she added hesitantly, looking pleadingly at her brother, who still stood grim-faced behind the counter.

Seay was standing right before the huge mirror that covered the wall in front of him.

"I asked you a question, Hayden," he reminded harshly, looking into the mirror, his back stiffened, determined to take up where he left off before being interrupted. Looking steadily into the mirror Hayden inched backward toward a table and stood with his fingers lightly drumming on the table's polished top. He looked back at the rancher and catching his eyes said, his voice rising, "That's none of your concerns…that's the answer."

Seay drained the stoup in one go then slammed it down and ordered another. He smacked his lips, his scanning eyes bored into the mirror. His foreman sent a puff of smoke toward the ceiling then craned his neck and looked out the spacious local. He gave his boss a quick glance in the mirror before extinguishing the butt, saying in mid-voice, "Listen, Wayne…there's no way you can force the man to tell…unless you get yo' a festered situation. Is that what you're after?" he asked, his features somewhat softened.

This tickled the old rancher who was in rage, but the foreman had saved him from many perils and was dear to him as an adviser. Maybe he was right, sure the aftermath would be too risky. Seay straightened his back, his eyes glued to the mirror. Quite frankly he felt himself being in a dangerous dilemma. He took a gulp from the stoup, asking himself how he might get that dude strong-armed some day, some other place. He kept studying into the mirror and saw nothing but the image of himself and that of his foreman flanking him. He turned right about and saw nothing but the dog sitting in the doorway, sorrowfully exhorting whimpers. The bastard had already exited. The rancher's face set and he rubbed his chin, sensing his hand being steadier now. Molly withdrew from her place behind the curtain, her hollow eyes abstracted after having added up everything in her mind. She renewed her grip around the broomstick, anxious to get started finishing her scant breakfast.

"Didn't expect you back so soon," Jeff mumbled and stretched. "You're still working in the army?" he continued and stood with his legs in a straddle, holding the smutty coffeepot in one hand and a barely cleaned mug in the other, studying the man sitting slumped in front of him. He had slept bad and tried to shake off the fatigue.

"I am…all day," Hayden admitted and managed a sly smile. "Special post, one might say, including investigation."

Jeff sat down and choked a yawning, tilted heavily back in the swivel and caught himself squirming. He tried to relax making his best to ignore the sharp pain that was knifing through his stomach.

"Soon?…You said soon. Five years's a long time, it ain't soon!" Hayden remarked almost brusquely. A rush of wind sounded from outside.

"Yeah, sometimes it is," Jeff admitted and smiled questioningly, and continued, "Listen…I've an impression you know quite a lot, 'bout things unknown to me, right?"

Hayden shifted his weight from one side of the chair to the other and sat for a while and drummed on the desktop with his fingers, contemplating the remark. "Well, first of all I gonna ask you somethin'," he said, looking across at Jeff.

"Go ahead, do."

"When can you have those gallows ready? You figure tomorrow mornin' would be too soon?…Or tomorrow night…what do you say?"

Jeff brought the mug to his lips and took a long sip. He put the mug back on the desk and placed his hands on the arms of the swivel as if he might be going to rise, but he didn't. Eyeing Hayden squarely he said, "You figure there's gonna be some hangin'?" He leaned down and pulled out the bottom drawer of his desk and propped his right boot upon it.

"Sure. Some people's gonna hang. Soon enough they're gonna' hang in shoals," Hayden said and jerked his head to the right at the lookups.

Jeff scratched his head and looked at the man sitting across from him. Sensing Hayden's gaze on him he reached for the tobacco pouch in the pocket of his denim. Hayden's eyes met his, and Jeff said, "Appease my curiosity…You've anyone particular in mind?"

"Why not begin with that drifter in there?" Hayden said and again jerked his head in the general direction of the gloomily lighted lookup section.

"So we're not gonna court 'im before? Is that what you're sayin'?" Jeff said and tossed the compressed sack onto the table before him as Hayden, now all but mendicant, for a second contemplated the question, realizing that he perhaps had gone too far and now was trying to find a way out. He said smoothly, "Look, sheriff, a bum taken in action, robbing a bank, and now captured. What more evidence do we need? It would be foolproof."

"I would rather say foolhardy," Jeff objected and squirmed uncomfortably.

Hayden cursed himself for bringing it up. He looked across the desk at Jeff as his mouth broke into a faint smile. "Alright…I just wanted to study your reaction," he announced apologetically. He shrugged and asked, "What are we jawin' about?"

Jeff sat smoking. Suddenly the two men sitting in the office got a reason to finish their meditation as the door got open and Russell went inside, carrying a gun in his left arm.

"Mornin' Russell," Jeff grunted. He reached forward a wee bit and shook some ash from his cigarette all the while holding the gaze of the young deputy.

"Listen, he hasn't shown the slightest hints of thawin'…has been screamin' most of the night, almost delirious," Jeff shared, deep in thought.

Russell was standing in the center of the room, his eyes looking somewhere in the distance.

"He's crazy," he replied and went on, "I guess he can do whatever he's a mind to."

Neither said anything in response. Jeff took another draw on his cigarette, then continued, addressing the deputy, "Yo' go over to the saloon an' get 'im some leftovers, alright."

"Alright," the deputy said and took a few steps backward. Jeff inquired, looking up at him, "Where did you get his accomplice?"

"You mean that crooked bum?" Russell wondered, keeping walking.

"Yeah?"

"In the coppice."

"Alright. We get 'im buried first thing tomorrow."

"What 'bout him in there?" Hayden broke in and turned to Jeff.

"I'll send a message to the judge in Casper an' ask 'im," Jeff said, drawing on his cigarette.

Hayden eyed him interestedly. Within short he broke eye contact, though.

XVIII

"Can't you hear? This old piano sure needs a pitching!...It sounds terrible!" Wolf interjected, his fingers searching the keyboard while addressing his landlady, who for a short while was situated in her old rocker, glasses pushed to her forehead. Birgit was standing right behind her. One of the two windows stood open and from outside came occasional crunch of horsefeet and spread sound of voices. A pair of oxen harnessed to a heavily loaded cart leisurely labored its way out of town. The boy made a stop and withdrew his chubby white hands from the keyboard and sat for a moment giving them some massage. The two women regarded him solemnly, waiting for him to continue. Within short they watched his fingers commence their dancing on the keyboard performing the final movement of Fantasy in D minor by W A Mozart. He played by heart, the score being far off, at home in the Boston apartment. The old woman rocked gently, her prudence for once forgotten, her veined hands folded together before her, passively resting on her lap, thinking the youth was dispatched to where he belonged - the world of music - an irrepressible existence. There was always a dread that it all would explode, though. It didn't take that much for that to occur. To a certain extent, however, the young man at the piano had undergone a complete transformation of character, she thought, musing on him. There were tears in her eyes, deeply set in her gaunt, pale face, framed by a gray, thin hair, combed back and pinned to the neck. She had a great affection for her three roomers, and she had the sense of that affection being requited. She loved to see them gathered in her living room, the core of her home, the principal asset of the well-groomed house, the sanctuary with its varnished furniture, and the sanctum with the altar and the crucifix hanging over it. Mrs. Penn's vice always had been charity.

Eventually she got up to go. When reverting to the kitchen routines she clapped her hands in raptures. Noticing there were tears in the old woman's eyes, Birgit got up and followed her landlady, unused as she was to her rare shows of emotion. Nothing was said for a long time, both women attending to their courses, neither bothered by the silence, the work allowing lapses while thoughts were gathered. Finally their eyes met in a smile tinged with sadness. Abstracted Birgit clasped the old woman's hand with both of hers.

"Listen, dear…you defer to me…but…well…what I appreciate the most is you being around. I'm very thankful to God that you are. Can you understand that? Maybe you can't. Maybe you are too young."

She looked directly into Birgit's mild eyes, and the young woman pretended to give the question some contemplation. She didn't respond, though. The old woman trigged memories inside her, stirred her subconscious. It was like seeing her own mother standing before her, the white porous skin so warm she could imagine the blood flow underneath, her small beautiful hands, her well-shaped face, her alert intelligent squeamish eyes.

"You see, dear, you need a man, a good homely man," the old woman went on, her voice now somewhat relaxed.

Birgit was suddenly deep in thought. In the parlor Wolf had commenced playing again: "Humoresque in B flat major" by Robert Schumann, a virtuoso piece from the year of 1838.

"You consider me being in need of refuge?" she asked, taking a step backward.

"Like every woman you are," Mrs. Penn said, looking at her over her glasses.

The both ladies were standing on either side of the table in the kitchen that was overlooking the main street. Birgit said, "I have a brother to take care of. An unripe young man, but he's still my brother, and he's all I got left, and I love him…and I believe he needs me."

"Sure, dear, I know what you are getting at. Just give him some more time."

Birgit frowned, uncertainly asking, "Mrs. Penn, what do you say…do you think that I…overindulge him?"

"Overindulge? No, I think every young man in that age has a certain quest for the truth. You are doing alright, dear."

"I'm doing alright," Birgit repeated. She suddenly remembered their father saying that a family shall operate as an unit, always as a unit. For some reason she now felt uplifted.

Frank Driscoll stood in front of the huge mirror in the giant bedroom of his Boston apartment, inspecting himself. Clothes were strayed all over the floor. He was naked, studying in the predawn light as if for the first time his stocky body with its tumescent belly. He liked roaming around naked. An unblinking star and pallid sleep-swelled face met him in the mirror, boyish and undestroyed, yes, undestroyed if it hadn't been for the patch of skin that had flaked off from his chin when he toppled down from that crazy horse. He was stocky, alright, yet he didn't look strong. When standing there, he thought of Birgit. Had she even had the slightest spark of sexual interest in him? As far as he could recall, she hadn't. None whatsoever. In school many of his mates mistook him for a girl. The smooth, ruddy complexion, the rounded cherubic features, his way of motion and his habit of wearing a purple tutu, no doubt emphasized the chaos within them, or rather, the chaos within himself. That tutu would do no harm, his mother had told him. In summer it would not. He stood entranced with his own image. Right now, in this very moment, he would sacrifice his own life if he could make that undone, but there was no way he could, and as for his current life, it could fairly be called a life. In essence he was crippled, his eyelids gummed shut, the cornea opaque, all void of life. In practice had he never begun to live. A dwelling among prostitutes, what else did it provide but undermine his emotions, his emotional life as such? And Birgit? Always off-putting, every once in a while even railing against him, for no reason at all. He kept looking into the mirror, focusing his face, seeing there was an almost angelic touch to it. Or might it be the light that played tricks? Or might it have to do with his brief and troubled sleep last night? Things turned even more arduous, every simple task! Should he arbitrarily succumb to his female identity? Would that make him happier? What should he do? There was an ambiguity in everything, the book collection, the pictures, all beautiful drawings and oil paintings decorating the walls of his fancy residence where he was living all by himself. Not to speak of the jewelries. Not many in town knew about all these secrets, which, if spread out among the people, would cause rioting, which wouldn't make things better for him. He was fortunate that he was able to sleep at all. Not many in town knew where he came from, or how he could be the proprietor of such a fancy three-story-high edifice downtown Boston. Not even a handful of people knew. He was beginning to be disinclined to fight. But, on the other hand, he couldn't make friends to his flaws, either. A tingling sensation made his way to his heart, a nauseous sensation.

In dropping his head a little, he got aware of the discrete knock at the door. He clenched his jaws and listened. He stepped closer to the door, naked, patiently listening. Another knock from someone outside, now harder. Somehow Driscoll felt blindsided. Who wished to contact him at home so early in the morning?

"Who's there?" he asked in a hushed tone, closing in, gazing into the door.

"I'm supposed to deliver a message to Frank Driscoll," somebody wheezed from outside.

"I'm Frank Driscoll," he said to the door, standing hands on hips. "Ease it inside through the slot under the door."

A silence as if due to resistance followed, then an envelope emerged underfoot. He waited some seconds then he bent down and picked it up. He whipped off some specks of dust and studied it, his face frowning upward. He walked through the spacious bedroom and made a quick stop when at the even spacious window, shadowed by a thick row of heavy-branched maple trees. He parted the draperies somewhat and opened the window a little so that the balmy air could get inside. The dawn was newly born and the daylight fell into the room in a triangle, and there he stood in the midst of it. He tore open the message with shaky fingers and read still frowning, his hands trembling and heart racing, partly as a result of anticipation, partly out of reluctance, reminded of a whirl from old times. He experienced a tickling sensation all across his palate when reading the lines that said, I GOT SOME REAL BAD NEWS STOP K. IS TAKEN INTO CUSTODY. B.

He expired slowly and read the short message one more time. The stationary didn't say anything about who might be the sender, but he knew who it was. The note had made its way from the sender and all the way to this bucolic part of Boston. Frank Driscoll acknowledged the true vocation of the sender, his brain now processing the information. He looked at the letter, his face in tension, pale as ivory. This meant trouble, he thought. He made for and dropped the letter on the seemingly antique wooden writing-desk, and bent down to collect his clothes and slipped them on. If K was taken into custody that would mean K had drawn attention to his person, and how did that happen? He was specifically ordered to maintain a low profile, wasn't he? Weren't the precautions enough elaborate? There was no doubting that the orders given to him had been straight enough, but evidently someone had out-smartened him. He sat down on the edge of the unmade bed for a final moment of solitude as a maze of different thoughts zigzagged his head. He was still young and could make a new life, flee the scene and start over fresh somewhere else. He rose to go into the kitchen. Oddly enough he felt hungry – and thirsty. Maybe somebody in the office could vouch for him.

"We're ridin' NOW?" the looter repeated wonderingly, sitting on the bunk with a mug of hot coffee in his hand, looking up into Jeff's face.

"Yeah, put on your boots an' drink that coffee an' let us scram outta here."

"What for?"

"How much money have you got?" Jeff asked ignoring the question.

"I ain't goin' nowheres, you hear?" the rough-hewn appearance on the bunk protested lamely.

Jeff tightened his gun holster around his midsection and looked out the small grating. The street outside was empty except for two stripe cats enjoying the warmth of the rising sun, and two women carrying a hamper with laundry between them. He stood for a while, listening to the prisoner's grumbling to himself from inside the squalid arrest.

"Alright, on your feet! Let's go!" he ordered curtly.

The man crouched cowering, the mug standing on the floor beside the light brown boots. "You ain't mad at me…are you, sheriff?" he wondered plaintively.

Beginning to struggle with his inner feelings, well knowing there was no time to analyze what moved inside his head, Jeff without a word drew his gun and took aim at the sitting accused and said, his tone decisive, "Try me! Get on your feet! I count to five. Haven't you got yo' ass off that bunk before I come to five, you'll be dead, I swear you will…One…two…"

"Alright sheriff, I give up. Sock it to 'em, right!"

On three his derrière was lifted. He looked into Jeff's stern face. For a short instant he felt ashamed. He studied a fly that lazily circled the cell until it made a halt on the ceiling overhead and sat moving its tentacles up and down. He lowered his gaze and offered Jeff an asinine eye. Pretending oblivious, Jeff re-holstered his Colt and gestured with his chin at the door.

Sitting slumped in the saddle Jeff looked out over the limitless pasturelands toward the mountains in the west. A gale without intermission blew from north and made the air cool, the sun from time to time penetrating the cloudy skies overhead. "Looks to me like we are gonna limberin' up 'em horses," Jeff wheezed between clenched lips.

The looter looked away from him, then back chewing the quid, his masticate muscles covered with several days' worth of gray-yellow beard, framing his hollowed eyes, most of the time arch-looking, now suddenly apprehensive. "Crowinjins, eh? We are in for it…ain't we, sheriff?" he said, following them with his eyes, watching them approach.

Jeff drank a second time from his keg then sat and held it by its neck. "All we can do is to stave 'em off," he said silently.

"Are 'em dangerous, sheriff, yo' figure?"

"No, those there ain't."

From out the slough seven black-haired Indians came riding upon them at a rapid trot, their small unshod ponies moving almost soundlessly.

"Can't we rout 'em, sheriff?" the other one demanded and spat, his eyes sweeping over them.

From out the quagmire the little caravan drew nearer, led by a flaccid-looking, middle-aged shape wrapped in a blanket. All seven Indians were carrying quivers filled with arrows and deerskin boots kicking the flanks of the horses.

"There's still a chance we can rout 'em, sheriff," the looter suggested almost enthusiastically, his voice now louder, refocusing on the coal black eyes of the Indian's main man.

Instead of answering Jeff discretely moved his black horse some inches closer to the captive and took the rope that sat belayed to his saddle and loosed it from the saddlehorn. He disconnected it and uncoiled it a little and raised it into the air to a level right above his own head and swung it over the looter's head, the rope landing on his shoulders. He'd gotten the loop on him and twisted it closer to his neck. The man swore and spat while looking about gasping. Jeff closed into and seized the rope and tied it around the man's neck. With looks expressionless the Indians in the meantime watched every movement from their horsebacks, although nothing was said between them. Gathering up the lasso Jeff backed off walking his horse along the rope then with his both hands drew the rope to him hand over hand and tied it to the horn of his saddle as the Indian chief curbed his paint and sat it before them, the rest of the party filing in behind, one then the other. They didn't stop until they had circled the white men. By then the chief raised his hand in salutation and sat and looked across at them with serious ardent eyes.

"Keep your hands still, you hear," Jeff admonished between clenched lips, addressing the roped man to his left while pondering meanwhile what other more steps he could take to prevent future tragedy. Keeping his face impassive he waited in the absolute stillness. The chief's face shone with complete serenity, his hands placed before him on the blanket. A roundish face, thoughtful eyes, ill-spaced teeth, short in stature and fatty with flaccid flesh as though he'd been raised on cream and sweet milk. Stray men put to rout by their own tribe, taking inventory of everything about them, now hiding by the wayside, Jeff meditated. He had encountered the sort during the war. The young Indian deployed next to the chief, was his opposite. He sat with the reins in one hand and the other on his thigh, having the appearance of somebody who any time might be indulging to a whim, swift to anger, loath to take reason. Here they sat in glaring contrast to one another on their horses, shouldered side by side, neither of whom speaking English.

Suddenly the captive's horse jerked out. One of the Indians standing at their rear had put his horse forward and stood patting the prisoner on his shoulder. The rest of his brethren set to laugh in chorus save for the old chief and the young one fronting him. Their faces showed nothing, but evidently they weren't appraising the situation. They exchanged quick glances and swapped a few words in their own tongue. In the next moment the old chief straightened up and with an agility that belied his age slid to the ground, and with a scowl started to walk and stopped right in front of the brother responsible for the action and said some words with his voice at a high pitch. Jeff didn't budge. It was not to his interest for the war to be bloody. He felt the stallion shift under him, pricking his ears. The young Indian went on watching them while the old chief made for Jeff and resolutely with both hands pulled his rifle from the saddle scabbard, un-breeched it and looked inside and shook his head, and with fumbling movements of his both hands circumstantially breeched it shut. He then looked up at Jeff and motioned for him to tender him his gun holster and stood waiting impatiently with his arm outstretched, Jeff deliberately seeming genuinely astonished, just for the hell of it, then obeyed. He could see the old man's eyes darting up and down when he lustfully strutted back to his pony after having collected the firearm. Meantime the young Indian sat staring levelly at Jeff with cold calculating eyes. The chief put the gun in a pocket about his saddle blanket then retrieved to Jeff and stopped gingerly close to him and handed over the empty gun belt, keeping the Remington rifle for himself. He then lumbered back to his horse where he paused and looked up at Jeff and grabbed the reins and swung his buxom body back onto the horseback and sat waiting, looking like he was concerned with important things. Jeff now had a hunch as to what was going to happen. The chief delivered a few words of command to his waiting devotees, and the encircling wall of pinto horses and Indians began to dissolve under surveillance of the chief and the young man beside him. Jeff still didn't budge, nor did the prisoner, so the two men in charge both motioned for them to file in behind. The prisoner discretely turned to Jeff and asked meekly where they were heading, his voice choked with emotion, his face showing despair. Jeff didn't reply. He only shrugged, still keeping the struggle hold around the man's neck while asking himself what might have happened if he had opened fire when first stumbling upon this fraternity. There is a small possibility that he might have had them torn apart by a hail of bullets, but the likelihood of themselves being shot to death with arrows, would have been overwhelming. The prisoner, being unarmed, didn't exactly improve their situation. From time to time giggles were heard from the company in front of them, as some of them hooted derisively while making remarks on the lasso where it sat around the neck of the paleface.

Riding two by two at an easy pace they crossed the flatlands in silence, passing in the fertile country a wilderness with close-grown shrubs and thorn thickets among which got visible a long-abandoned all but overgrown dilapidated habitation with gaping windows and curtains yellow by age rattling in the breeze, and with chimney and walls partly collapsed with bricks fallen from the sashes, grown with dense moss. Underneath were the ruins of a horse carriage, atilt, wrecked but for the wheels and the shafts that appeared intact. Underneath it a sawhorse and pieces of tack, and in solitude a skull and bones that perhaps had been a dog's, or perhaps a coyote's, withered and brittle, and miscellany kitchen utensils, and stove wood strewn about.

Following with labor by ones and twos in the dusty light a trampled mile-long causepath, flooded and potholed as a result of recent rains they in a cloud of clapping particles of stone made their way up through the raw hills with birds and autumn rabbits flying off of the shrubs at their advent, and into the mountains in the west. They eventually crossed a ford of standing water that deep it came but to the horse's knees, and rode up and put the horses forward on a flat country with cattle standing mute and still, all of whom watching them, and they kept on riding, all the while hearing the water sucking and sloshing at the hooves of the horses as they moved their feet with great circumspection and lifted knees.

A while later, out on the broad plain ahead of them, a dozen or more teepees materialized in the south-facing valley. A handful of women and children in buckskin dresses sat cross-legged on blankets of buffalo hides outside the tents cooking in the diminishing light, some of them with home-made blankets over their shoulders. Hides and flayed meat was hanging on dry in the weak sun. A small bunch of kids with blankets over their shoulders and two grown boys sat cross-legged before a low fire holding before them some kind of meat suspended on sticks. All of a sudden, they got aware of the strange riders presence and said something to one another. They jiggled and then turned back to the fire again. Two blackish mutts with long peaked noses moved out of the shadows, thereafter another two of the same kind got visible in the mid-day sunshine and started their barking and advanced sluggishly upon the riders with their hackles reared alongside the emaciate spines. Angular heads, baleful eyes, unknown extraction, inbreed most likely. The beasts halted a few yards ahead of them behind a broken section of limb, their slant eyes watching them, their hair bristled up when taking corrections in the breathwarm air, tails hanging down to their haunches motionless. The women, saying hardly a word, proceeded stirring the caldron, seemingly paying the riders none attention whatsoever.

The Indian village had the look of an old ore mine of some variety, now fallen into ruins in this country before them open and rolling. A wide riverflat. A ramshackle cottage partly caved in, and shingles blown off the roof, as were there the remains of a stable with scraped-out and staked-out hides hanging to dry outside it with flies swarming among them lazily. A four-some young girls there were, perhaps ten or so years old with maudlin grimy faces, whispering something to one another. A cart lay tilted over, two kids climbing on it, half-hid behind the frame while keeping a vigil over the two palefaces horseback, everything adding to the impression of decay, all about them poor and primitive. Stray people in reticence, harried like livestock, strangers wherever they settled down. A toothless kiddy mouth grinned at them from one of the out-dotted tents, the black eyes squinting in the declining sun.

No sooner had the palefaces set their horses than a matron-like pregnant woman of indeterminate age looked in their direction general as did the other women and the kids as well. They swapped some words between them. Some of them slunk away from the others and stood, their faces in toothless laughter.

"We're cuttin' a dash! They are makin' a fool outta me, 'cause a 'you… don't you see 'em bastards are laughin' at me?" the looter whimpered almost lachrymose and with both his hands clawed took a firm hold of the lasso that firmly sat around his neck. Jeff slackened it and let it go, thus allowing his prisoner to pull it overhead to release himself from it.

"Gimme' the hemp!" Jeff ordered brusquely when seeing him sitting holding it in his gloved hands.

Without giving a word in return, the looter collected the rope and put his horse closer to Jeff and gave it over to him. Jeff reached out and snatched it out of his keep and coiled it, advising sarcastically the man to not getting crosswise of law, knowing that the future of the two might now be in peril. He draw home then re-hitched the lasso about the saddle, his horse standing browsing under him. The bank robber sat looking doubtful before him, his facial skin shining waxy in a blank beardy face. Like Jeff he awaited further instructions, knowing better than dismount before the chief said so, no doubt knowing that the Crow Indians were having strict rules. In the interim Jeff took in the entire view, the compound, the pitched tents, the women and the kids, all of whom in home-made rawhide dresses, the dogs, a handful of speckled ponies, the abandoned ore mine with its dilapidated facilities. Seemingly his captive also was taking an interest in it all, whereas it frightened him as well, his lips in constant motion as though he was reasoning with himself, corroborating to himself in words what he actually was witnessing. On observing this, the young Indian in the front set about to cackle with glee and rode past his brethren and reined in beside the palefaces and looked them full in the face, his entire body quivering with revulsion. It was no longer any doubt him being the chief's right-hand man. Jeff tried to read the speculation in his eyes, but he found none. What he saw was but the Indian's eyes roll wildly when he spat out his order in English, "Get down! Move!" His dark baritone echoed over the compound that now was dead still save for the seething of a cold wind coming down from the mountains in the north. Suddenly Jeff watched the looter grab the pommel of his saddle and moaning sink to the gravel underfoot and stand on stiff legs, reach for the bridles and sling them over the horse's head. When he was in the doing of this, the young Indian, now being at arm's length from Jeff, motioned for him to dismount and grabbed the bridle reins from the offside of Jeff's horse and waited for him to climb down. Jeff patted the neck of his horse and tapped the rim of his badge. Whom was there to apply to now? For a brief moment he saw Birgit and remembered her saying once: "Apply to the Lord and trust your life into His care. But for Him there is none to apply to."

XIX

Thinking about a lot of things the young deputy sat behind the badly knocked-about writing desk, the only place in the office where the sun ever managed to penetrate in form of a long patch of sunlight, finding its way through the small iron-barred rectangular window for only two good hours of the afternoon. An hour or so back, that person in authority, Hayden, had forewarned him alleging there might be something brewing, some mischief of some sort. Before leaving the office, he had specifically told the deputy to keep his mouth sealed up, no matter whoever was standing before him, and right now Bill Buchanan stood looking down at him with an ingratiating smile on his pretty-pretty face.

"I reckon Jeff has rode out. I couldn't see his horse anywhere…neither in the corral, nor in the stables. When did he ride out?" the rancher asked casually watching the boy intently, his face wrinkled with apprehension.

"I can't say exactly, sir."

"Yo' weren't around?"

Russell hesitated, centered his eyes on the rancher, now standing over him, then replied miserably, "Sorry, I can't tell you, but…he'll come back."

"He has seen things out there, right?" Buchanan went on softly, watching him with wide eyes.

Russell looked away from him and then back. "I guess," he said.

"So now YOU are holdin' the fort?" the rancher demanded, his voice having a brittle quality.

"Yeah…that's right, sir," Russell admitted, his face contorted with thought. "May I ask, sir…is there anythin' in particular that you want?"

The rancher thought for a moment, studying the desktop. Eventually his eyes searched Russell's face. "Listen, son, if somebody tangles with you, then tell me, alright. Then I'm gonna take a sock at 'im…you understand, son?" he said craftily and moved toward the door. "An' I don't give a damn' whoever it is, you hear?"

"Sure," Russell responded and shifted in his seat, and without reflecting upon the consequences, having his question ready, asked interestedly, trying to keep his voice neutral, "What are you gonna do with him or…them…well, if 'em tangle?"

"Kill 'em outright," the rancher answered, smiling archly, making a gesture as if he was groping for his waist gun. In an effort to bridle a little he turned around, asking hastily, "It's your job to watch over that stuff, right?"

"What stuff?" Russell wondered, trying to keep his face impassive.

"Stuff from that coach hold-up." Buchanan snapped, stalling for time. He looked down at the gun that hung dangling from his belt, pulled it and aimed at the boy. Russell crimsoned, then instantly went pale. The rancher was in rage.

"Get to your feet an' gimme' your gun belt, you hear," he wheezed, his pretty-pretty face now contorted. "Hurry up, move it!"

Russell haplessly looked at the shut door, realizing there was little hope someone would come to assist him. The man was batty and the best thing for him was to obey, so Russell decided to do what he was told, although reluctant to it, the warnings from Hayden now forgotten, knowing it was said around town that Buchanan was hard to argue with, and when the talk shifted to the stuff stored in the custody, he began to understand that serious things might appear. But now he, Russell O'Connor, wasn't the man in charge. In a flash he was stripped of his gun, and in the next moment he had his senses knocked out of him. His legs gave way under him and he floundered, and then it was all dark about him.

The two captives sat without speaking in the mine stable looking at each other. Their hands were tied behind them. Still in slumbers Jeff slowly opened his eyes and looked across at the man that was sitting opposite to him against a wall below some bits of tack, hesitant as to whether he had heard him address him or not. His lips moved, so evidently he had.

"Hey, you…sheriff, whatever your name is…you see that rat underfoot…that fat shaggy bastard. You see 'im, sheriff? Whom do you think he's gonna bite first?"

"I've no way to know if he's gonna bite or no," Jeff growled and attempted to bend his arms a little at the elbows in an effort to straighten his upper body somewhat. It was all in vain though. He tried anew and crouched down. He felt thirsty, made his best not to think of it, though. His tongue seemed actually to have swelled. The sweat on the forehead of the man opposite to him shone in the spare light. Supposedly was he suffering as well, but if so, he gave no evidence whatsoever. He looked intently at Jeff for a long moment.

"You know what, sheriff…Now you an' me be much in the same position, right? We're gonna die by sun-up. Em heathen savages are gonna maim us, right, torture us, eh. I've seen a lotta what those devils are capable of doin'…'em are gonna feed us with rats before they torture us…I know 'em are…sheriff…all injins are the same."

Jeff didn't respond. He only tried to disengage his ears, breathing in and out quietly, his head resting on his chest. After a while the man started to laugh the laughter of a mad human, a maniac. Finally Jeff raised his head and looked at him, dozing.

"We are in much the same fix. I tell you I'm sorry, sheriff, it's gonna end up like this…'cause I know a lot," he shared grinning.

Jeff pondered this for an instant, and then he began digesting the gravity of it, but got interrupted, slightly mollified when watching a woman on soundless feet coming into the stable hall. Jeff tried to raise up on his elbow, his face contorted with pain and stiffness. He looked up at the woman, a squaw. At a glance she could have been twenty or twenty-five, big-boned, broad-shouldered and heavy-breasted, very strong-looking hands. She had a full womanly figure with peasant muscularity. Jeff peered up at her, but she wasn't looking down at him. Eventually he sensed the woman's eyes being hardly fixed upon him, and in that moment he only wanted one thing: He must quench his thirst, he was in prompt need of a drink. He raised his gaze a wee bit more and took to regard the woman in depth. As for her eyes they reminded him of those of a chased animal. Her bum protruded under the rawhide dress as did her belly. She was far from displeasing to the eye. From his languid attitude he could see yet another human stepping inside, a young boy, lean and trashy even by the standards of this clientele, well-formed features of face, though, friendly looking, arms and legs thin and wiry. He was carrying a pot of some sort. At the sight of the two incomers, the other paleface tried to move with his leg shackles. He didn't succeed and started to brawl in frustration.

"Gimme' a bucket of water, you hear! A whole goddamn' bucket…you hear that you savage bastards!"

The man went on calling all the forces that were arrayed against him, and braced his feet against the half-rotten flooring. He willed himself to get up on his elbows, but had to give it up at the end with a dire sigh. The two Indians didn't pay him much attention. They had spotted him for a maniac, an individual possessed by a devil and condemned to death.

The young Indian squatted behind Jeff's back and started to untie the fastening around his wrists while the squaw stood beside and watched every movement. Eventually the squaw made a gesture with her hand toward the pot with a wooden spoon standing in it placed on the floor beside him. Jeff grabbed the spoon by the hilt and greedily helped himself to the contents, meats simmered to shreds in a soup of wild vegetables, bracken and other varieties of wild herbs. The hunting grounds around had a lot to offer, deer, moose, rabbit, hare, capercailzie, grouse, wild boar. He ate well, whereas the protests of his companion in misfortune in the interim grew more vehement.

"Listen, sheriff…leave the leftovers to me, you hear!"

Jeff raised his head and looked up at the squaw and the boy and smiled helplessly, then turned earnest again. He couldn't rid himself of the impression that the boy's eyes hid a little bit of mirthfulness. As for the woman, there was none.

When Jeff had done eating, he said his thanks and descended with a pleased smile on his lips. This irritated his brother in misfortune, who went on delivering endless taunts.

"Why don't 'em bastards just let us leave out?" he demanded when the Indians were ready to walk out.

"Ask 'im," Jeff suggested and made a motion of his hand toward the boy, who just had got up to follow the woman and stood hesitating looking around his shoulder down on the big talker.

"You reckon 'em holdin' a grudge, sheriff?" he exclaimed, his gaze resettled on Jeff, who, fed up with the bickering, forced himself to hold back his tongue.

"What do you think, she…?"

"Just wait an' see!" Jeff cut off. "If the boy walks out without feedin' you, it means yo' ain't well-liked, and then you will be dead soon."

"You mean…'em bastards just let me starve to death?"

"Yeah."

"An'…what 'bout you, sheriff?" the looter asked somewhat melted.

"Well…I ain't quite sure, but now I figure 'em havin'…other plans with me," Jeff grunted, watching the boy beginning his exit, holding the empty bowl firmly in his both wiry hands.

The Indians had left him without retying his hands.

The soup had helped him regain a little of his stamina, as had it sedated him somewhat and forced him to suffer in silence for a while. He didn't know for sure how long he had been half-sitting awake in the fading dark with just a narrow ray of daylight flickering in from outside through a slot in the dingy windowpane, listening to the looter giving utterance to his fears. After all they both had been taken against their will to an Indian camp. Denuded of horses and saddles and firearm they were locked up in a ramshackle stable, vulnerable to the predators of nighttime.

He drew in a long breath and rose to his feet, his eyes all but growing dim, then limped over to the prostrated man. He knelt alongside him and watched him where he sat slouched against the wall with his boots crossed before him in a thin strap of light from the window. A jaundiced face, dimmed with streaks of tobacco juice in the beard. A tic shivered on his cheek. It was still dark of night and it wouldn't grow darker, Jeff thought, having no idea as to what time it was. No one could claim the ruffian slept blissfully, but at least he slept, Jeff concluded, listening. He spread his palm across his breast. He was breathing hard. A puddle of evaporated urine was to see underneath him, and the studs of his shirt were unbuttoned to reveal a hairy brisket and a brushy ridge of fuzz extending from his pubic hair and upward to his navel. Deep in thought he buttoned up the man's shirt while reasoning with himself in the act. No, there was no way he could make himself escape without bringing the poor bastard with him, no, there was no way he could. He looked down at the unformed beardy face. What if he was disinclined to escape? What if he preferred to stay rather than subjecting himself to justice? What if he was incapable of riding? Jeff felt the tightness of the moment swelling. He carefully grabbed the man by the shoulder and squeezed hard. There was neither movement nor resistance. Suddenly he opened his eyes and met Jeff's gaze. He was awake.

"Uh…you're tied up, sheriff?" he growled incredulously, focusing Jeff languidly.

"We're checkin' out," Jeff grunted and began to loosen the man's shackles, the stink from him almost engulfing him. The man sat still with his eyes closed sallow-faced and his tongue in motion in a try to moisten his cracked lips. Jeff felt nauseate, sensing the cloying smell emanating from the mouth of his protégé.

"Alright, get up!"

"Have yo' removed the fastening, sheriff?"

"Yeah, just get up!" Jeff commanded, raising himself up.

"What for? They track us down anyways," the other one whimpered miserably, running his swelled tongue between his lips.

Being on his way out, Jeff gave no answer. He set the flat of his hand to and yanked the rickety door open. He looked out to see how the weather would be. The moonlight outside was barely sufficient enough to help them establish their position relative to the Indian huts. The skies were flawless. No rain in the air.

"We are lucky they didn't put out guards," Jeff mumbled, addressing the shady hunched-up character trailing saggy-trousered but a couple of inches behind him, the raw-sawn half-rotten plank floors sagging under his feet. He stunk incredulously. He'd pissed himself, his breeches soaking wet. The night was still, and all there was to hear within the close proximity was the faint intermittent chirr of the locusts in the shrub growth. Stiff-arming Jeff the looter droned peevishly, "What are you waitin' for? Why don't you…move on?"

The man appeared dazed and disoriented. Jeff hushed and muttered, "There ain't a beacon around…we gotta go the whole hog an' find 'em horses. Just keep your mouth shut…stay here until I tell you to follow, right?" he ordered and looked into the man's eyes until he had to look away and stand still, watching his benefactor from behind the gable of the discarded stable. In this moment he would gladly have sacrificed his right arm for a drink. He felt the night growing colder and his moist garment cooled him down, making him shiver. He sat down to wait with his back to the wall of the stable, his brows knitted.

He flinched when hearing Jeff hiss from behind the stable, beckoning for him to advance on him. He parleyed with himself as to whether he was strong enough to rise, then gave a dry heave and braced his feet against the ground and rolled over until he stood on all fours. Tremulous he braced his hands against the wall of the stable, passing them from one level to the next. A dog barked excitedly. On the spur of the moment the particulars of his life stood right before him. Is this the way it's gonna end up? Ill-joined among an entourage of Crowinjns? He was about to start walking when he watched Jeff reappearing, leading the horses by hand by the headstalls side by side. To his surprise he could see they were saddled and bridled.

"Get up on the horse! Hurry up!" Jeff commanded. "We've to make it without firearm! Come on!"

Feeling his heart beating violently inside his chest the captive almost knelt over the dirty mud until his left foot eventually found the stirrup, the horse still in motion. With a steadfast grip of his both hands around the pommel, he swung himself onto the saddle of the fractious animal. Bent down over its neck, he almost at once managed to capture the reins, sensing the tussle had enforced his nausea. He looked over his shoulder. Three or four Indians were advancing toward him at a run, slowly gaining momentum. In the same moment the sun rose above the horizon in the east, thus providing the silhouettes of the rider ahead of him a brighter character with colors and nuances more outlined for every minute, until the entire setting was basking in the reddish morning.

Jeff curbed his poorly rested stallion, turned it around and flailed his right arm. He thumbed down his hat a bit to shade eyesight and stood waiting for the looter to catch up. He reached out for and took the canteen from off the saddlehorn, screwed the cap off it and took a mouthful of the tasteless water. Catching the scent, the horse flung his head a couple of times while pricking his ears within their arcs of motion. He screwed back the cap and hung back the all but empty keg and sat slumped for a while thinking and waiting with his elbow propped on the saddle. There was dead still, no sign of life, a most ominous sign. Thinking about this he then raised himself up and felt for and caught up the reins with both hands, and pursuing his own traces started back in the self-same direction as he'd come. He hadn't gone far until he caught the sight of the looter's horse standing with empty saddle a little way east of the Indian camp, and five spotty ponies standing circled around it. Two of the Indians had already slid off their horses. Their brethren horseback appeared to have acknowledged Jeff, who now was coming their way. They exchanged words between them. The other Indians, assembled around their prostrated fugitive, shaded their eyes despite they didn't have the sun in their eyes, and looked off toward Jeff who nudged his horse ahead then slowed it and stood in contemplation in the sun that now was some minutes high. Had it really been the Indian's intention to rack them in the first place? He put his horse forward.

The Indians had again focused themselves on the prostrated looter. Why hadn't they already given the paleface a short shrift? In their opinion he was considered mad, anyway. Or was he already dead – or seriously hurt with an arrow? All five Indians out there were young bucks, and neither of their chiefs was around. Were they about to deliver a message of some kind, or were they just acting out of malice? After what appeared to have been a thorough deliberation, two of the Indians nodded their heads and motioned for Jeff to join them. Either they were about to blindside him, or were they serious, anxious to dress wounds or whatever. Either was the man in the dirt alive, or was he not. Jeff put his black stallion forward toward the party.

The young Indians, wrapped in their home-maid clothing, reverentially stepped aside to make way for the big stallion where it came skittering their way with slobber seething in a and out of its frothy mouth, jerking its head until it finally halted forward of the assembly. Jeff sat for a while and sawed the horse about with one hand, all the while looking down at the center of attention, estimating the outward condition of the captive as his horse flattened his ears and wildly rolled his eyes neighing silently. He reflected a moment and hauled the horse about until it was manageable and stable enough, the Indians watching in bewilderment. Eventually he set the horse and got off the saddle and started walking toward them, his eyes moving over the body lying face-down in the dry grass underfoot. It was all windless with no other sound about save the gurgling breathing from the looter. One of the Indians, the youngest, or maybe second youngest, a walleyed youth with shoulder-length black hair and a lean build, knelt and looked down at the man and then back at Jeff, as if witnessing something dramatic. Jeff looked past him and stepped closer. When at the looter's head he sank to one knee and bent over him and said semi-loudly into his ear, "Hey, you...they sure haven't give you the cut...not yet, anyways."

The kneeling Indian instantly rose and joined the party. Jeff seized the man's right arm and began to roll him over on his back. The man tried in vain to formulate his lips into a sentence, his half-open eyes flashing up at him. He shivered. He appeared to be in a daze. His breathing was almost imperceptible, and from his nose oozed some blood. The young Indians stood watching in muted fascination, their demeanor somewhat less harsh. Jeff carefully removed the lid of the man's right eye and looked into it. It didn't take long to see a trudge was lying ahead. Jeff levered his head and cast about, taking in the surroundings. He was about to speak, relinquished, though, having nobody around who understood. He bent over the man a second time and whispered into his ear, "You hear me?"

There was no reply. Either was he unable to speak, or was he loath. Jeff repeated his question starker, "Hey… do you hear me?"

The man's languid yellowish eyes looked straight into Jeff's, his lips framing the word "thirsty." Jeff got to his feet and went back to his horse and got the canteen from the saddle. Unscrewing the cap, he walked back to the man and squatted on his heels when beside him and offered him a drink. Meanwhile he looked around the place for anything moving. Apart from pasture, there was nothing about, saving some windbreak thickets.

Despite alleged thirst the looter didn't drink much, not more than a good mouthful. Keg in hand Jeff went back to where he had set his horse and mounted up and hung the keg back to the saddle. A ways out to the northwest there was a creek, a sheltered place where he could water the horse and fill up the water kegs. He brought the horse there and stood and watched it drink. Why jettison the idea before having given it a fair try? Deep in thoughts with his lips in doubt he untied the leather straps of his saddlebag and plucked out the butcher's knife. This was his only option, and there was just one way to find out whether it would end up fine. Another issue of high priority was reclaiming his firearms. Standing with his knife in hand, he looked across toward the Indian party to see they stood vigilant looking his way, wondering what he was up to.

XX

"You're figuring there is an odds-on chance of filin' suit against 'em...is that what you say?" the barman demanded rapt in thought, his double chins quivering, dishcloth frozen in action. Standing opposite to her brother his sister flashed a quick smirk and looked steadily at Hayden, her eyes as imperious as ever before. Whatever she's trying to say, she sure ain't wooing, Hayden thought and looked away from her.

"Gettin' the knack of it, that's what's all about, right?" Hayden confirmed, buttoning his jacket.

"I guess. Livin' in suspense ain't much of a livin', my ol'man often used to say," the barman confessed and went on trimming the desk with great deliberation.

"No, you're right 'bout that, I guess," Hayden admitted thoughtfully and continued, "Well...talkin' 'bout folks...that shapely Süsskind lady, she's of German descent, ain't that right?"

"German?" the barman repeated, his lips pursed. "No, sir, she ain't German. Jewish...from Boston somewheres...back east," he said defiantly, tipping his head aside, not removing the cloth from the desk. "Why you askin'?"

"Nothin', just thinkin'. Nice girl, eh?"

Molly discharged a discordant eye in Hayden's direction.

"Yeah," the barman agreed, "But, frankly, I haven't even talked with her...just seen her at a distance...Tellin' you the truth, we don't blend with such folks...not our social circles," he added with an edge to his voice.

"Alright, see what you mean. Just curious, that's all. Don't get upset!" Hayden said, anxious to smooth down.

The barman shrugged, then shot back, cloth in hand, "Well...I'm just goin' about my business...an' that's the way I gonna stay 'till I'm a centenarian, yo' see."

"Yeah, yeah, don't get upset."

"I stick to my own, else I might run outta business," the barman mumbled. He shifted uncomfortably and glared gloomily at his sister as for support, didn't get any, though.

"Yeah," Hayden answered again without looking at him. To him it grew more apparent that this man for some reason disliked him, Wentworth Hayden, an army scout and marksman, who had left town at an early age, whereas this bulky redneck behind the counter got rejected by the army.

He swaggered out along the street in the clear and quiet mid-morning. The rain had petered out and growing cumuli with slowness sought their way inland bound. He skirted some big puddles of water while glancing up the potholed street. He looked off to the sheriff's office, shouldering his way past a bunch of reluctantly yielding female pedestrians in their cheap finery out on a shopping tour. He pushed his hat back on his head and quickened his pace a little. The better part of a minute later he ascended the gritty and footworn stairway of the sheriff's office. He yanked open the door and stepped inside the stuffy den. Squall emerged from the lock-up section, a female voice in affection. "Where do you think 'em are headed?"

"Anywhere…it ain't easy to say," another voice responded resignedly. A subdued and fainted voice. Hayden recognized it. He stepped inside and made the squeaking door to. Russell O'Connor, the deputy sheriff, was sitting on the jail floor, his mother standing over him. Mrs. O'Connor peered near-sightedly at the doorway where Hayden stood.

"Gagged…Russell was gagged when I came an' found 'im in here. I just loosed 'im!" she yelled miserably. She glanced to her left and to her right in despair, and excited went on, "What a godforsaken place is this, Mr. Hayden?" Her twitchy eyes darted at Hayden, who in that moment experienced a strong sensation of affection, one he didn't think him being capable of anymore. The woman now was standing square to him, her brownish eyes burning when looking up at him. She extended a hand toward him to exhibit three strips of cloth, the same color as Russell's torn shirt. Hayden moved his gaze downward to the youngster, who now was making tries to come up from the clay floor. "You have any idea how long you've been impounded?" he said to him.

Russell tried anew to rise. He sloughed and sank back, his hands still in handcuffs, the iron clinging when hitting the floorboards.

"Coupla hours," he said and managed a sardonic smile. He seemed embarrassed, and shunning Hayden's eyes he continued, his tone significantly harsher, "The bastard hit me square in the face…that's all I remember. I reckon he almost cracked my skull as well." He tried to reach his head with his hands, but failed. He looked down at the hardware, and then up at Hayden and said, as if excusing himself, "That sonnabitch brought the key with 'im. Mom's been lookin' for it…it ain't here," he shared unhappily, tears not far off.

"Alright, son…but there's a blacksmith in town, remember? Do you know who hit you?" Hayden asked and studied him.

"I sure do, an' you ain't gonna believe it," he whined. Mrs. O'Connor heaved a profound sigh and nodded meaning.

"That Buchanan lick-boot sonnabitch. That's 'im who did it, alright," Russell whimpered miserably.

Hayden nodded, his gaze remaining intently on the young man on the floor.

"Buchanan, eh? Well…I can't say I'm surprised," he said.

"I can't believe it, anyways," Mrs. O'Connor inflicted helplessly, studying her brown lace-ups.

Hayden stepped away a bit, stopped and again looked down at Russell with a puzzled expression while asking interrogatively, "You have any idea why?"

"Why…he hit me, an' tie…?"

"Yeah?"

"He's after their stuff. It's stored in there," Russell explained and motioned with his chin toward a cluttered cell, now transformed into a repository. He looked up at Hayden, his young downy face sort of transfigured.

"Help me off with 'em damn' manacles," he lamented pleadingly and tried to reach his nose with his hands, but there was no way he came flush. Hayden for a short moment stood chewing his lip, then he without a word approached the door of the custody. He tried it and set his foot to and kicked it open, and it flung up on squeaking hinges. He froze in mid-action and looked down at the young man on the floor, who sat and peeved at the shackles slapped around his wrists, alleging they were driving him crazy if not removed off the bat.

"Can I have a quick look inside before I take you to the blacksmith? It won't take long," Hayden said pleadingly into the makeshift repository, his voice subdued. "I'm goin' with you, son, just take my word for it," he went on, his voice now having a husky tone to it, due to heavy layers of dust and clay in there.

"What are you lookin' after?" Russell asked.

"Same as Buchanan was lookin' after, I reckon," Hayden replied, focusing on the items. He heard Russell change some words with his mother, but there was no way he could make out what they were talking about.

"It ain't in there, you hear!" Russell suddenly yelled from outside. "Jeff has taken care of it, right after the trial he did!"

Hayden threw back the battered doctor's case into a cascade of dust, and straightened his back, slowly turned around and stepped out of the cell, snapping air. "What is it…Jeff has…taken care of?"

"That fiddle, that doctor's."

"You sure?" Hayden responded, his voice now almost cracking. "Has he…got any place…to keep it?" he asked and blinked.

"I don't know nothin' 'bout it…that's just what he tol' me, that's all."

Hayden took hold of the doorpost and gripped it for support. Neither said anything until Mrs. O'Connor cleared her throat and said, "Mr. Hayden, you gotta goad things around here…you see the place ain't what it used to be. The halcyon days are history, take my word for it. Sheriff in charge, Douglas Kimble's in an unscrupulous gambler, a hack, always was, always gonna be. He is venal. You know it, Mr. Hayden, everybody in town knows. Things are warped around an' somebody's gotta raise his hand against it." The woman's demeanor turned more and more belligerent and now she stood wide-eyed with her mouth half-open, her breathing labored, her face taut with fear and anger.

"You see, Mrs. O'Connor," Hayden explained, his tone almost deferential. "I've come here because of a certain man…"

She glanced backward to where Russell sat then craned her head back and watched Hayden with interest, her eyes darting at him. From the small pocket of her robe, she retrieved a white cotton hanky and began to dab at her eyes in a twitchy manner, her little white hand almost transparent- looking.

"So…you're a do-gooder, Mr. Hayden, I mean you ain't come here on official business," she wondered, eying him half doubtfully, taking a step closer but yet keeping her distance, tinkering with the little black bow-tie, that prissily sat tied under her chin.

"Well, things are set in motion, ma'am," Hayden mumbled, having gobbled up every word, while trying to ignore the defiance in her voice. He looked down at Russell with a glint in his eyes and continued, "It ain't easy to say what's comin' up…but there's gonna be some brandishin', that's what I believe." Without waiting for a reply, he walked behind Russell, stooped and bent at the knees and locked his arms about his trunk and pulled him up from off the floor.

Jeff rode another quarter of a mile and set the horse where the creek ran down and unbridled it to graze. Holding the butcher's knife in his hand he stood for a while and looked at the clumps of willows giving thought how to put the scanty sticks together, simultaneously pushing himself to get it done with. He went to fetch the catch rope from where it hung by the saddle as two of the Indians appeared riding side by side. They reined up their ponies at either side of his horse, the older of them regarding him levelly, his black eyes flashing. Jeff queried them in English as to their business. He could watch the calculation in their heads until the older one blurted out into a guttural harangue in their tongue, which didn't say him so much, but the expression in their faces told him the more. The older Indian pointed several times in the general direction of the sick man where he lay among the wild daises, as though he were bringing a message. Either had the poor bastard gotten worse, or had he passed away. Nonetheless needed he some means of transportation. Jeff re-shifted his attention to the lasso, cut it into three, the older Indian watching him inquiringly with his bloodshot eyes.

When Jeff eventually had cut off and trimmed off the branches and twined together the six long twigs, the litter was ready. He flashed a brilliant smile toward the Indians. The solid cheeks of the older of them cracked as if he was thinking of something to say, but there was nothing said. He just squinted, his weathered, austere features bearing the scars of a life on the prairieland as an exile in his own country. And yet he wasn't so old.

He seized the litter, that didn't weigh much, with his right hand and made his way away from the grating of the willow shrubs. He laid it down in the blowsy grass and re-bridled his horse and filled up the canteens and with the litter astride of the saddle, he put the horse forward at a quick walk.

The man lay stilly outstretched in the soft grass, seemingly dead. Four Indians hovered near, their horses cropping some feet away. They had kept watch for more than an hour, watching the spot where the man was lying, resting or dead. He curbed the horse and dismounted and unhooked the canteen from the saddle's horn. The Indians glowered mutely when watching him take the canteen by its strap and carry it to where the man was lying, where he squatted and studied him. One of them uttered something in mid-voice, but there was no way to tell what he said, nor what he was thinking. He palpated the man's pulse to feel his heart was in strenuous labor. He was sweating profusely due to high fever, and he doubted the man was conscious of him being there, his eye reflexes showing no significant reactions.

He undid the third section of the cord from the saddle, knelt and fitted it to the litter, as did he the same with the end sections to the cinch, one to each side. Meanwhile the Indians stood looking forlornly across the fields, showing no inclination to assist. When he was about to rock the litter in place, the stallion shied and flattened his ears and started to trample about, having the sensation of something unusual being in progress. Jeff went to its head and grabbed it by the headstall and spoke friendly to it, looking meanwhile into its rolling eyes. The horse ducked its head and whinnied, and the mare answered back in agony. The Indians nodded solemnly at each other and within a brief moment things changed quickly. A frenzy followed, as was more than Jeff had bargained for, and in the next moment the man was lying on the litter. Seeing the stallion didn't panic, Jeff slackened his steady grip of the headstall and walked back to the litter where he knelt, and with the remaining section of the catch rope fastened the man to it for several hours to come, knowing he was making him subject to reckless conditions. Once he was done, he folded away his knife and grinned delightedly toward his mute hard-faced spectators, who had been standing in silence in a semicircle from the moment he began preparing his casual retreat, their features showing no sentiments of any kind. He turned and walked to where the man's mare stood grazing and grabbed her by the throatlatch and walked her back to where his black stallion stood grazing. He heaved himself up into the saddle and sawed the stallion about while gently booting it forward, dragging the mare with him, the stirrups of the empty saddle dangling at her sides. He twisted his torso a quarter to see the litter coming trailing just fine.

"Gotta pack 'im off to a doctor!!" he shouted out in the general direction of the Indians where they stood gawking at him, shapeless in their blankets. For a short moment their eyes grew calculating, thus giving him the impression that they perhaps understood, at least to a certain extent. The Indian ponies shied and stepped about a little when the litter went by, as though uncomfortable with the scraping sound, but he kept the stallion in motion by kicking his sides with his bootheels. He went on riding past them at a quick walk, and didn't look back until he had disappeared out of their sight behind some riverside willows.

XXI

Backtracking his way downcountry, Jeff pulled the two-horse caravan across the untilled flatlands at a steady pace, keeping watch behind him all the while. He'd crossed the upper reaches of the creek by noon with the captive jacked up on the litter, collecting the mid-day sun in his jaundiced and sweaty face. The sunbeams didn't seem to bother him Jeff could see when he checked on him by regular intervals. Once he had made a halt and offered him some water from a canteen, but he had declined with pain in his eyes, turning his head to the side, not speaking. When he had risen to withdraw from his side, he heard him whisper a name, as though he spoke about somebody, but he couldn't figure out of whom he'd spoken. He had reached about for a short while, and then he had put his arms to rest across his chest, and that was all that was to it.

It was late afternoon when Jeff looked around the plain to see three horsemen coming riding in a long sweep some half mile off. They set their horses to blow, but didn't pay him much attention at first, but after a second or third look, their curiosity took over and made them close into the stranger where he came their way with the litter in tow. Within earshot of them the riders set their wired ranch horses, and a wiry man with chaps of cowskin, the elder-most, one dressed in the common clothes of a cattleman, put his horse forward while he studied them from under brushy eyebrows, his muscular bay stamping and ducking its blazed head, the two other riders sitting grouped right behind watching, shoulder to shoulder. As of yet no word was coming from either of them.

Jeff pulled up the stallion and sat waiting for either of them to take the initiative. The rider at the head, the elder-most, after a while booted his mount some steps closer to where Jeff stood and let it walk until it eventually stopped spontaneously and stood slinging its head in a fret. He studied them methodically in turns, Jeff and the horse he rode, the looter on the litter, and the looter's mare and Jeff yet again, as he reached in his inner pocket for his tobacco. Jeff's stallion shifted uncomfortably and pricked up his ears when hearing the elderly horseman commence talking with authority in a sonorous voice, his weathered face unmoving in austerity, "You're in trouble, son?" Waiting for a reply he fished about in his pocket.

Sensing pressure coming up inside him, Jeff looked back at the one who'd talked, weighing meanwhile the inquiry for a short moment.

"Well, that depends, sir," he finally said.

"Depends on what?" the other one said and hawked and swerved in the saddle and spit out a quid.

Jeff looked across at them each separately, then studied the elder-most rider anew and replied, "On how you look at it, I reckon."

The man's gaze drifted over to the man on the litter where he lay impassive like he'd dropped asleep with sweat quivering on his forehead and the scrapes on its understructure that the rocks had jagged, then back to Jeff.

"To me it looks like you havin' your nose to the grindstone, anyways. Is he alive?" His ocean blue, beady eyes interestedly kept on studying the man on the litter, his left arm frozen in an angle, his hand cuddling the leather tobacco sac.

Jeff followed his gaze, then blurted out with a boyish grin, "I've rocked 'im to sleep."

Neither of the men showed any reaction. Nor did they speak. Jeff regarded them each separately. They were all armed. Eventually one of them extracted himself and came along from behind and made a halt when standing abreast of the oldest one. He put his hat back on his head and managed a sardonic smile and put his hand inside the chest pocket of his checked coat and commenced fishing about for his cigarette makings. He looked very much alike the oldest man, sitting on his right flank, twenty, twenty-five years younger, same build, same melancholy eyes, mustache and sideburns, same kind of coat, the collar of which turned up against the wind. He commenced to dab tobacco into a paper. The index finger of his right hand was missing. Jeff pressed his feet against the stirrups and shifted his weight, easing his seat, while watching the two men light up their cigarettes. The older-most twirled the sooty match between his fingers, flipped it away and smoked pensively as he earnestly regarded Jeff in a squint. He raised his head up and looked overhead at some buzzards sailing over them with wings locked. He plucked the cigarette from his lips and nodded up at them and said as if to himself with smoke blowing out of his nostrils, his words coming slack, "'Em up there have been feedin' on that dead steer, yonder." He gestured with his head northward.

Every head bent sharply up the air.

"Yeah, 'em sure have," the younger rider admitted silently, his razor-thin lips curled in a wry smile. He lowered his head for a moment to look down at his cigarette where it was hanging loosely in his hand, then lifted his head again to study the birds, circling over them slowly with wings stiff as in a state of lethargy.

"Nice stud you've got there, son," the oldest cowboy proceeded, grunting with pleasure, looking at Jeff again, grinning yellow-toothed under his mustache, slumping a bit in the saddle as if to get a better view.

"Yeah…he's a good horse, the best I've had," Jeff said and patted the sleek and muscular neck. With no word in response the older man took a final drag and extinguished his cigarette toward the heel of his boot. He flung away the butt and glanced about, leaned forward slightly, asking, "Listen…ridin' out here drives your appetite up. Have you done eaten, son?"

"I'm afraid we haven't so much to eat, sir."

"Not much of firearm, either, right?"

"No…'em Crowindians took…"

"You couldn't hol' 'em off, eh?" the other one cut off.

"No, sir."

The older-most rider seemed to consider this as the younger rider to his side, looking as though he was thinking about other things, chimed in, "Where are you headed?"

"Casper. Haul 'im away to justice," Jeff replied, slumped in the saddle, studying a spot between his stallion's ears.

"What are they figurin' on doin' with 'im?" the same man inquired after a while.

"Coop 'im up, I reckon."

The old man chuckled and the two others followed behind in a giggle, glancing sideways at Jeff hence making an impression of innocence. The older-most rider glanced over his shoulder, bent forward a bit to grab the reins, straightened them and turned the gelding around and let it walk back the same way as they'd come, the others turning their horses so that they followed, one and the other. For a brief while Jeff sat listening to the swishing of the horse's tails and the clopping of their hooves until the older rider raised an arm and motioned for him to turn his horse and fall into step with them.

The horses snorting trudged their way single-filed, pursuing a dappled mare rode by a rider who looked to be in early middle age in cowboy outfit and wide capacious chaps of uncured leather, who at regular intervals glanced over his shoulder as if to make sure Jeff was trailing along.

The ride didn't take long. When they'd reached the crown of a ridge barely a mile out, they could see the buildings in the canyon, the one-stored tile-roofed ranch house with its four-paned windows and a stack of firewood right by, and customary outbuildings. A good dozen of hens were scampering and pricking in front of the barn. Jeff's eyes narrowed when he looked down at the place, regretful to having accepted the old man's invitation. The young cowboy slowed down the pace and almost stood waiting for Jeff to catch up with his mare, and announced, professional in tone when they sat juxtaposed, "This is where we live, yo' know." He looked over at Jeff, his gaze very intensive. Jeff cocked his head a little toward him while giving a short nod, indicating that he had heard. He looked across at the bunk house where a man was standing in the door, leisurely tugging on what appeared to be a blade, both hands stuck inside his belt, watching the caravan with stupefaction, as if he'd never seen anything like it. Jeff heard the two riders in front of him start talking between themselves and they didn't cease their conversation until they eventually pulled up their horses right outside the barn and stood them, one then the other. The old cowboy got down of the saddle and motioned forward the lean man in the doorway to tell him there would gonna' be two more guests at the dinner, but immediately corrected himself asserting there would only be one. Jeff propped his hands on the saddle's horn hand over hand and sat and studied the place in contemplation as the old one walked up beside his horse, leaned forward in a crouch. With the capacious chaps flapping about his legs, he stepped past the black stallion that nibbled after him with ears pivoting about. He made a halt when standing beside the looter on the litter. Now he could hear the looter breathing loudly. He looked away and then back at the old rancher who quietly stood and regarded the sick man, his leathered square hands clasped together in front of him, hat pushed back.

"He already has one foot in the grave," he said, his voice rasping hollowly. He didn't say it loudly, but loudly enough for the others to hear, because in the next moment they all three stood fanned, hovering over the litter. Jeff put his bodyweight in the left stirrup and swung his right leg over the horse's ham and got down and joined them. He squatted beside the captive and leaned into the better to hear. He listened for a while to the sound he dreaded, the labored breathing, now even more labored. He looked down at him for a lengthy while to see his entire body was constricted with the effort, eyes half open. Mucus was oozing from the corners of his mouth and down his chin, and there was a reek of excrements about him.

Jeff slowly raised his head and let his gaze follow a lonely leaf drifting down from a nearby oak tree, almost bare of leaves. Masses of clouds had wandered in from northwest and put the buildings in shadow, and the onset of the wind had begun to set the grass of the flatlands in motion. He kept looking at the leaf that flung hither and thither in the increasing wind. The cowboy who looked most alike the old rancher, followed Jeff's gaze for a lengthy instant until he eventually accosted him and almost reproachful in tone shared that the man was soaked through. Jeff nodded agreement and rose slowly to his feet and deep in thought stood and looked at the ranch house, a plain-looking building, flat to the ground with a flat tile roof. And at an open field a ways out beyond it that recently had been harvested of wheat.

"We might at least wipe the crust from off his eye corners," the old rancher suggested lamely. "That's the least we can do for 'im," he added as if concerned about him.

Jeff stooped over the litter and put out his hand. In the same moment the looter opened his eyes widely and shook his head from side to side. For what reason, he didn't say. Either he did not submit, or was there something that he wished to tell them. Jeff sensed himself being taken back some years into his past, back to the battlefields and the civil war, and the dying Southerner in the front rank, badly wounded in a surprise attack.

"Huh, yo' Yank...do you believe Jesus's gonna...accept...me?" he asked uncertainly, rubbing his transparent tummy with his gunpowder-stained fingers, rolling his eyes up at Jeff for reassurance while smiling gaily, his breath coming in brief sporadic spurts.

"I sure reckon he will...I sure reckon he will," Jeff answered reassuringly and brushed some tangled hair out of his eyes. "I'm quite sure he does," he repeated, sensing himself His presence.

"I see 'im...already...He...approaches nearer..." the soldier gasped out with a Southern accent to it, blood spreading on his uniform, his green tired eyes growing initially large and deep, then fainting and inward-bound, fixed on Jeff.

"I sure reckon he will," Jeff mumbled after a short while, now to himself.

The kid didn't hear him now, because he was no more. His transition was over.

Jeff abruptly got hauled back to reality, feeling that the old rancher stood looking at him questioningly, legs slightly parted. For some reason Jeff instantly got the impression that some debating had taken place, him mentally being far away, because when Jeff was about to raise himself up, one of the men, the youngest one, emerged from the ranch house under the watchful eyes of the others. He approached upon them, carrying a bundle of clothes, lumped together to his hip. Something serious evidently was in the making, Jeff thought when he eventually met the pleading gaze of the boy and watched the old rancher charge from the crowd and suggest they strip off the man's ratty clothing and put on the one the boy just brought. At the side, a bit away from the bunk house, a water basin was situated. Wouldn't that be fair enough they bring him there and swab him off? The old rancher demanded, his eyes alive with adventure.

"The creek yonder suits better," Jeff almost rebuked, peering through the dense growth and back at the man on the litter, now being in greater agony. To Jeff this country was unexplored, but he could see there was a byway or a mudpath, making its way through the vegetation. It led down to a slow-running water, the same river from which Jeff had taken the twigs to build the litter from. The old rancher hesitated, his judgment from all appearances different from that of Jeff, but so he made a bold gesture with his hand and said in a husky voice, "Alright, we give it a try. We pull 'im down on the litter…but I figure there's gonna be some coaxin'. I doubt he'll make it, an'…what if that stud kicks up a fuss," he added with a chuckle.

"You mean it would be fatal for 'im?" Jeff wondered, contemplating the figure before him.

"Well, you know…" one of the men, the second oldest, who until now had overheard the conversation, charged in, "What my ol'man's sayin' is that the man might get thrown off that litter…in case the horse panics in the mud. It has come a great deal of rain the past weeks, an' there's a pretty thick shrubbery to penetrate with the litter, you know."

Jeff looked for an instant at the old rancher, almost waiting for a reversal, but there came none. Instead he continued to stare at the shrubbery and at Jeff alternately. Jeff just nodded to show that he understood. In that moment the old man looked quickly at him and explained with relish, "This is my son Frank," and nodding at the youngest he introduced him as Milton, his grandson. "Both nice fellas," he chuckled meaningfully and rubbed his sideburn with a solid knuckle. He unbuttoned his waistcoat and buttoned it again, as if offering Jeff some time to introduce himself.

"I'm Jeff O'Halloran, deputy sheriff of Sioux Falls," Jeff said.

"Food's ready…you may come any time!!" a husky voice announced from the bunkhouse.

"The cook…name of Skinny," the old rancher told Jeff and cupped his hands about his mouth and called back that they were coming right away.

Some half an hour later they almost reluctantly stood up from the table and slowly strolled outside. On their way out, Milton cast about, checking to see if the others were out of earshot, then sidled near and told Jeff that his grandpa was a widower and that they, from that day on, are having their meals in the bunkhouse.

"So there ain't no woman around?" Jeff asked, glancing sidelong the other's way.

"No, sir. A bunch of Crowindians killed 'em. During the war, you know…my ma an' grandma…an' our two ranch hands. I an' grandpa an' the cook, uh, we were the only ones who escaped 'em. Pa was away fightin' in the war." He slowed his pace somewhat as he again glanced off in the direction of his folks to see they now had taken to unbuckle the girths of their saddles.

Their short walk was over and Jeff got the impression the boy was sorry for it. He also got the impression that the boy's father might have overheard his son's words on the subject of them having been hard hit by life. He had looked so long at his son where he was standing very straight in the shoulders, hugging the horse's harness.

The captive lay in trance, swathed in his coarse and stinking army blanket. A subdued moaning came forth when Jeff tried to swab out his eyes, now clogged with even more mucus. The entire assembly stood re-gathered to watch in disbelief, as if trying to figure out how to entice the poor man to utter some word. One word would be enough to wear off the trance. One single word, just to make sure he wasn't dead, but the man seemed unimpressed with the unisex gathering, gawking overhead. "He's awake, alright," somebody said in a whisper.

Jeff quickly seized the moment and got the canteen from the saddle by the expediency of offering him a drink. He twisted off the stopper and bent down, and as easy as humanly possible, he sat the bottle to the man's dry lips, the entire assembly still watching the half dead man in the center.

"Sorry 'em Indians took my last whiskey bottle…we're gonna try…this stuff instead," Jeff said and tried to keep his hand steady so that no water was lost, the whole procedure now also followed from a distance by the swarthy cook. The watering took forever. The man didn't stop lapping up until the canteen was all but drained and only the heeltap remained.

"At first I got the impression he's lying much the same as when we left 'im," Frank whispered loudly and tried to squeeze between. He stepped around the cook and asked him discretely to go and get a bottle of booze. The old rancher, though, didn't seem to know what to say. In the meantime, Jeff offered the dying man more water, which he declined. Jeff then adjusted his head, so he could breathe freely. At length the looter slowly raised his right grimy hand, probably signaling he was doing alright. For a short while he looked up and his eyes met with Jeff's. Shortly thereafter his eyes quailed and his lids got together and he went into a slumber. In Jeff's opinion the man's cyanotic lips had no nice color, and he waited for them to shift, but they didn't, and when the whiskey bottle finally arrived, he was no longer awake.

XXII

"Don't you think it would be wiser to wait one or two more days, until we go after 'im?" the newly in-sworn deputy asked modestly while watching Hayden, who sat resting deep in the swivel behind the wooden desk in the somber quietness of the sheriff's office, his both legs comfortably placed on the desk, the tips of the newly pitched riding boots pointing straight up onto the gloomy ceiling.

There was a short quiet time then Hayden clasped his hands together across his abdomen and said without looking at the deputy, "Why would that be wiser? Jeff could be anywhere by now. He might even be dead, right? As far as we know, he hasn't yet appeared in Casper…an 'we have no idea why. Seventy-two hours, an' nobody can spot 'im. As far as I'm concerned, it's time for action…we can't wait no longer. Either you stick to it, or you're out."

The deputy straightened up then put away the emptied bean can. Ho rose to his feet and leaned both his palms on the desktop and shifted legs, his brown eyes like embers.

"Whole town's paralyzed with fright…even that ticklish Seay ol 'man's quiverin' like a leaf, you know," the deputy complained and lashed out both hands in a helpless gesture.

Hayden hopped to his feet and stood without having shoved the swivel backward. He started to pace the floor, the rowels of his spurs jangling. Suddenly he stopped and reeled about, and faced the deputy uncomprehendingly.

"I know that man…I know 'im moren most folks in town. He's got what he begged for. Remember that it was 'im who elected Kimble in the first place!!" he exclaimed, putting an angry finger in the air. "He think he's the Almighty an' I don't care what he says."

The deputy looked at him in disbelief, his round baby-like cheeks reddened. He broke off a match and started to pick his yellowish teeth, but in the next moment he relinquished and threw the pin in the ashtray on the desk before him. Hayden stepped closer to him and repeated, "Either yo' are in, or out. If yo're out, we ain't gonna need you, an' in that case, you might walk away right now," Hayden's face looked tight and his words echoed for a long while inside the mind of the deputy.

"Alright…somethin's gotta be done," the deputy at last admitted sulkily. "You ain't sayin' all this in meanness Hayden, I know yo' ain't." He scratched his beard then turned back at Hayden, who now stood and peered out the small barred window that faced the street. A couple of women pedestrians walked past, involved in what appeared to be a serious conversation.

"I'm in…you hear me Hayden…I'm in, it's not a question 'bout it, but…"

"Fine," Hayden interrupted instantly, "Fine…The picture with Buchanan's mug is already under distribution, you know, an' within the next forty-eight hours every sheriff's office in the northwest part of the country's gonna have it on its desk!" he exclaimed triumphantly and pointed at a stack of papers, nicely resting on Jeff's writing desk.

"What if Jeff's never comin' back?" the deputy said meekly and staggered a little when he let go of the support of the desk. "What if he ain't alive?"

"Sure he's alive. We have no reason to believe he ain't," Hayden squelched and flashed an irritated eye in the direction of the deputy. He went back to the desk, picked a picture and took a seat in the swivel and sat, one leg crossed over the other, looking at Buchanan's sneer mug. He slightly bent forward and picked the last cookie from the plate and crammed it into his mouth. The deputy studied his trimmed mustache when it moved up and down as time dragged on, listening meanwhile to the old office clock thudding in a never ending succession. Within short it was time to walk out from this office, the deputy thought. For the first time in his thirty-six-year-long life, he had a feeling that his exit this time might be going to be his very last.

Making slow progress among dense thickets of wild rose they had worked the litter well halfway into the shrubbery when Milton unexpectedly called out, "Hold it!! He's awake!! I reckon there's somethin' he wants to say!! I saw his lips movin', an' he said somethin', sheriff!!" he cried excitedly by way of explanation and raised a hand, ordering to silence. He was standing right behind the litter, scratching his neck and cursing the multitude of whirring mosquitoes. Jeff had been walking heavily, holding the stamping horse by the headstall in a steady grip so it wouldn't jerk at the reins and break into a run. There was a short silence around the man until Jeff loosened his grip on the headstall and stepped toward him and closed into, Frank trailing behind, holding a bundle of clothes, looking like he had something appropriate on his mind.

The man on the litter was not dormant any longer. The terrain was boggy and he had sunk deeper on the litter, and his limp feet were trailing in the mud, and his boot heels were partially dirtied with horse dung. His face was warped and sickly-looking, and his lips were more cyanotic than before. He slowly licked his lips, his tongue moving clockwise. His look was haggard, he neither blinked nor looked away. He looked like he was in a state of preparation, like someone who is about to tell a narrative of some sort. His proximity to death no longer was illusory but obvious. Jeff turned and walked back the few paces to the horse and reached out for the canteen by the saddle. He went back to the litter and uncapped it, the men's eyes interestedly following him. He knelt and held the bottle before the looter's face and tilted it and carefully put the pipe to his lips. The looter just kept staring, unmoved. Jeff doubted he saw it. The mosquitoes grew more intrusive, and the stallion sidled and took a couple of quick steps forward, stopped and steadied himself. Jeff now realized he was the one to make things hum. There was something perishable to the moment, so he hastily got up from his haunches, holding the keg in his hand when hearing the man talking. He lowered his head and looked down at him, then slowly squatted. "Hey, did yo' say somethin'?"

The man seemed bewildered at his sudden re-approach. He tried to speak, his jaws were in motion. Jeff bent to hear what he was about to say, but the only sound audible was that of some cattle calling out from out the flatlands. Jeff studied the man on the litter, who in this moment appeared to have much to contemplate. The wind had died altogether, and but for the whirr of the insects, it was all quiet about them.

"I don't...reckon...you...have to... rope me...one more...time...she... sheriff," the looter wheezed in a low and flat voice and smiled a pained smile to reveal a set of teeth black with rot.

Jeff nodded and waited for him to continue. "It turned...out badly...to no avail," he whispered, his chest rising and falling, wheezing with each breath. "An'...now...it's too late," he went on, gargling blood, his gaze bent inward, looking like he was studying the days behind.

"Yeah, that's life in the raw," Jeff responded and tilted slightly his head, waiting, his hands low. He shifted, favoring one leg, his boots making a sloshing sound as the men flanking him looked questioningly down at the dying captive.

"I'm just…one in that bunch," he went on, gasping for breath. His right hand strayed to his forehead that shone with sweat.

"Alright…" Jeff nudged, his forehead creased in concentration. "Go ahead, tell the story." He reached down and took hold of the man's left arm. It felt limp. He placed it back across his midsection. The man's hands closed into fists and he glanced at the men overhead.

"Tell us the story," Jeff insisted and motioned the two men nearer to listen to the man who now was about to unload his sins.

"A human…life…ain't worth…much in that pack," he wheezed.

"What happened?" Jeff said quietly, anxious to get him started.

A cow bellowed from long away, and a pair of thrush nightingales made a noise in a nearby shrubbery, else silence was total. A minute or so passed. The man on the litter had now sweated his shirt through and gasped for breath. A faint hint of thawing appeared after the lengthy pause when he finally blurted, "Sheriff…I…shot the doctor…an'…his little…daughter…she with the dog, I did…killed 'em outright…" There was a substantial gap between the two or three last words. Milton and Frank had now closed in and squatted bedside.

"Who killed the doctor's wife?" Jeff prompted.

"Buch…anan did," the captive said in a much lower voice, his watered eyes raised to the heaven. He gasped for air, and his both hands twitched spasmodically.

"You remember all men participatin' in the action?" Jeff said.

"I remem…ber…'em…very well…alright."

"Come on…tell, please," Jeff insisted, his voice raucous.

Gasping he didn't answer for a long time. He had his both arms folded across his heaving chest, both hands closed into fists. His lips fluttered and finally he managed, speaking more to himself than to Jeff, "We…were…we were…tellin' raunchy jokes…right after…when leavin'…"

Slowly he rolled his eyes upward. His breathing was temporary, and his eyes were begging for vindication.

Jeff didn't reply, just nodded comprehension. He thought for a brief while, then took a brief look around the place, then leaned into and said, "Alright…what about the names?"

"Kimble was…there…an'…" He interrupted himself and with difficulty raised his head some and spied into open space as though he'd seen something, a wrinkle formed between his eyes, then he put his head down again.

"Sheriff Kimble? Is that…what yo' say?" Jeff said, watching him intently.

"Yeah…that's 'im…alright…and a saddle tramp…from somewheres… A Reb, I don't recollect…his name…A haggard… sonofabitch…beardy…mean…rode with hackamore."

"What befell him?"

"What…?"

"What happened to the saddle tramp…?"

"We strung 'im up. He betrayed us, the sonofabitch…"

"A gray-coated…chubby…with a girlish, high voice, Buchanan's cook…a Southerner from Texas?" Jeff prodded on.

"Yeah…he was there…too."

"A young Mex…?"

There was a short pause while he gasped for air, then managed, voice lowered, "No…there…was no Mexican."

"Yo' sure?"

"Yeah."

"Who bumped off…uh…gutshot the coachman? Was it yo'…?"

Another pause ensued during which the man contemplated this. After a lengthy while he said, his voice now much weaker, "I don't…know…I didn't watch…'im bein' shot…"

"Alright…Who was in charge?"

The man's right hand clawed about a little as though having a desire to rip open the ratty shirt. Suddenly the thick-boned fingers got still. Speaking now with as much economy as possible, he went forth in a labored whisper, his breath now more raspy, "Buchanan…but…there was…another…an Easterner…Driscoll…Frank Driscoll…of Bost…on. He could barely ride, the son…ofabitch…" A light glinted from his eyes.

Milton started to say something, but Jeff made a motion with his hand to stop him, and looked again down at the man.

"You sure 'bout all this?" Jeff asked.

"I am," he whispered then gave a satisfying gasp, his voice even weaker now, his dirty face streaked with tears.

There was a sticky odor from his stained clothes. Jeff felt mauled, his stomach churning. He got to his feet and stood for a while motionless and glared at nothing, digesting the news. There was chaos inside him for a long moment. Without a word he began shouldering his way past the cowhands. He stopped short and looked over his shoulder and said while turning around, "I had as much figured…but still I can't believe it. It sounds crazy…but that' the way it is…I reckon."

Neither of the cowboys, now partially detached from the man, gave any response. From a distance could be heard a moo from cattle, otherwise nothing. Inadequate looking, Milton stepped back a couple of paces to let Jeff precede him.

"To be honest, I didn't understand so much of it…I reckon, but I understood a lot…not all of it, though," he almost stuttered, wide-eyed, his voice lowered.

He looked away from Jeff, then back at him, his thumbs stuck in his belt. A half darkness had come into the valley and the sun hung low over the hills in the west. Milton, standing next to his father, stamped his dirty boots and shot an eye at the lifeless man underfoot. "I think he's done alright, that's what I think," he said, still stamping. "Don't be too hard on 'im," he added with an urgent voice.

Jeff made no reply. He just slowly drew his gaze away from him and stood and studied the dying man on the litter, realizing it would take a special hand to work it all the remaining way down to the river. He reverted to him to see his head now was turned sideways toward him. His breathing was quieter, his eyes moving slowly and convulsively behind half-shut lids, his mouth formed as though he wished to speak. He'd just pissed himself. Jeff stood to listen, watching him make an attempt to lever his hand in a weak motion. Jeff seriously doubted he could see any more. He squatted beside him and looked at the man's hand, which again made a lifting motion.

"Do you wanna say sometin'?" he wondered tonelessly, studying his profile.

"A man's…gotta…harness…his…fear…" he managed at last, his eyes weeping.

"Yeah…I guess you're right. We are all fallible," Jeff answered lowly and rose. He felt utterly lone and stood forlorn for a moment. He thought of one last question, but decided to relinquish. What about the man's accomplice at the bank robbery? Had he also taken part in the coach hold-up? It didn't matter any longer. He was dead and within short this man would be gone, as well. His cheek had begun working strenuously, and a string of blood slowly trickled from the corner of his mouth. He didn't speak anymore, and he tried to swallow but he couldn't, and moments later he commenced to shake violently and his hands went lax, and within a minute he was gone.

"Do you believe him bein' spiteful?" Milton asked shifting, the bundle stuck to his hips.

Jeff didn't answer for a long while. His attention was still focused on the dead looter, his last words still playing in his mind. Without looking up, he slowly replied, "To be honest…I don't know. We never got acquainted. What I know is that he was a murderer, a victim to stupid dreams…a friendless and pitiable creature."

Milton squared his shoulders and nodded silently. There was a spell, one that lasted only for some brief moments, until Milton spoke again, his gaze drawn back to the corpse on the litter where it lay with urine trickling down its side.

"How ol' was he…I mean…when he…passed away?" he demanded and studied his scuffed brown boots, his face solemn.

Jeff weighed the question while performing a cursory examination of the man's nondescript features, then said, "He was ol' enough to overcome himself, I reckon. That's all I can tell 'bout how ol' he was."

Milton shifted and teetered a little when standing aside for his father to pass.

"What do you think we are gonna do with the throwaways?" Milton drawled in the direction of Jeff, who had began to painstakingly adjust the litter for the final amble.

"You mean we're gonna freshen 'im up for the burial?" Jeff asked defensively.

"Yeah…that's what I mean!" Milton responded, though not with much conviction.

A thick pain hammered deep in Jeff's stomach. He shrugged, then replied, "We're gonna burn 'em."

XXIII

"In a way it's all unbelievable, in another not," Hayden said after having listened to Jeff's narrative with interest.

"Yeah…" Jeff replied and reclined in his squeaky swivel chair. It was early morning and yet another two men were present in the stale sheriff's office of Sioux Falls. Russell O'Connor, the young deputy, stood in the jail section and peered through the metal gratings. Inside the custody the belongings of the assassinated family lay scattered in the same manner as Buchanan had left them some days back. Russell had overheard the story that Jeff had just unveiled and slowly he let go the grip of his hands around the bar that he had squeezed so hard that his knuckles were whitened. He seemed rested, he had put on a clean shirt, and the peach fuss was scraped from his face. He had had time to give things some afterthought. His mother and a couple of her lady friends, were alleging he had matured a lot, that there was an air of purpose about him, and that he had grown more manly during the last weeks. At first he had taken it for an adulation, but after having given it some reflection, he was willing to agree, but that he would never admit. For a short while he remained outside the lockup and stood and looked down at his immaculately shining boots. Eventually he half turned and slithered back into the office while rolling the stiffness out of his shoulders. No one spoke when he entered, instead they were contemplating in silence.

"You've been listenin' to Jeff?" Hayden inquired after a while, looking squarely at Russell. He had placed his rear on Sheriff Kimble's desk, his right leg swinging, his arms folded across his chest.

"I heard, alright, every single word of it," Russell replied slowly, emphasizing every syllable. He went on, "I've been thinkin' of one thing."

"Alright, tell," Jeff insisted.

"What 'bout the clay-dotted gelding?"

"You mean…Foley's gelding? That's his name, right?" he asked addressing Hayden.

"Yeah...William Foley...or Bill Foley," Hayden informed confirming.

"Well, I let im stay on the ranch. A gift, you know, shapely saddle. Nice people. They helped me bury 'im, an' all that. Showed great hospitality. That horse wasn't worth so much, you know...how come you askin'?"

Russell shrugged and looked as if he was struggling for an answer, but there wasn't any.

Jeff leaned forward with his elbows on the table and stared into the stove inside which a fire was crackling with a soft light among some red glows of coal. He pushed back his chair and rose heavily and poured some coffee into his mug. In the meantime, the old clock chimed. Eight strikes. He got his makings and sat down again and started to roll himself a smoke, sensing meanwhile a knot of disconsolation in his stomach.

"Do you figure 'em ranchers will appear as witnesses in court?" Meyron Clarke, the newly in-swore deputy intervened after a long stretch of silence. He had been studying Buchanan's mug from a drawing with great interest, had said little and sat opposite to Jeff with his feet crossed at the ankles before him.

"Sure they do, they proffered to," Jeff assured.

"Both of 'em?"

"They consider it an honor...that's what Milton...well, the boy, said anyways," Jeff replied, blowing smoke up the ceiling. "Foley's confession made a great impression on 'im..." he went forth.

"What we're gonna do right now is go out an' fetch Buchanan an' that Boston sonofabitch," Hayden interposed silently.

The deputy shifted his stout upper body and Jeff nodded, belching quietly. Hayden stood abruptly. The three other men exchanged quick looks. "By the way...that Driscoll, what did you say his first name was?" Hayden asked, addressing Jeff, without looking at him.

Jeff hesitated, then replied his name was Frank.

"Yeah, right. Frank," Hayden confirmed and went on, "Before we break up, I tell you this: Now I walk straight over to the bank an' send a wire to the officials in Boston, just to inform them. Then it will be up to them to locate the man. There are a lotta scavengers, you know, fraternizing with that sorta people." He stretched and went on saying, addressing Jeff, "Then I'm gonna check on 'em periodically 'bout sketches...reward an' on an' on...They are dutiful an' do a great job of watchin' people. Most of 'em blend with anybody, yo' know an' handle the issues expertly."

"An' in the meantime, we are ridin' out into the thickets, huntin' up Buchanan," Jeff suggested calmly and swiveled a little in his chair.

"That's right," Hayden answered almost enthusiastically, then went on, "I believe it's best I stay around an' you three go after 'im…What do you say to that? If you have any objections, then say it."

He again sat down on the desk and inspected his constricting faded jeans. Jeff returned to his coffee without a word, well knowing he had not much of another choice.

"It's alright…with me…I go…out there…" Russell said almost at once with a mouthful of cookies, glancing furtively at Jeff.

An awkward silence ensued with no conversation whatsoever. The newly in-sworn deputy had waited for this moment to occur. The last he waited was to be regarded as someone breaching faith, some sanctimonious character. Without lavishing words on the matter, he just grunted with a look toward Jeff, "I go out there too."

The giant baby-faced stablekeep looked long after the three riders when they left town, headed westward across the cow-trodden scrubland. He stood until he couldn't see them any longer, three black dots on their way into the skyline, where they slowly faded and ultimately got dissolved as if they'd never been. He looked furtively about him and raised a chubby hand in greeting to a buggy passing by, spat on the potholed ground and turned back into the obscure interior of the stables.

Not much was said between the three horsemen during the ride through the dense woodland, each of them immersed in his own speculations. Was there any deeper connection between that groom and Bill Buchanan? What about the visit at the sheriff's office the other day? Was it just coincidental? The vibrations in the air, was it all fancy, or was there anything behind, anything sinister? In truth, looking at the matter in retrospective, Russell didn't feel comfortable being alone with those characters. Not that Jeff had ever had any issue with the stable man. Everybody around knew that the stableman and Buchanan had a close relationship, but upon meeting with him in the stable before riding out, there had been something inscrutable in the man's eyes, Jeff noted.

Back on the flat prairie, they rode on shouldered and didn't halt until noon time when Jeff set his stallion and sawed it around to afford himself a view of the surroundings. He reached for the canteen and tipped it and took a long drink. Water ran from his lips. He wiped it off with the sleeve of his jacket and re-set the plug and restored the canteen to its place on the saddle.

"See 'em cattle out there?" he demanded, nodding north.

Russell shaded his eyes with one hand, following Jeff's gaze. "Yeah sure," he said.

Jeff rolled a smoke, lit it and swung his right leg over the pommel. He spat out a flake of tobacco and squinted at the deputies and asked them how many head they figured there were out there.

Meyron Clarke, the other deputy, pulled up his holster somewhat and half stood in the stirrups and craned his neck, his eyes wandering about. "Five…six-hundred…head…pretty hard…to say…Buchanan's, ain't it…?"

"This ain't Buchanan's land," Jeff said and looked out the herd from under the brim of his Stetson. "It's Woodward's land, a ranch eight…ten miles west."

"Yeah, yo're right," the deputy confessed, holding his reins loosely in his left hand. "One of 'em kids drowned last spring when throwin' rocks in the creek, right?" He looked at Jeff then twisted his head away.

"Yeah," Jeff nodded and took a mighty draw on his cigarette, "She drifted downstream during 'em torrents. She was never found…not as far as I know, anyways."

A bitter wind had risen when they resumed their ride, going slowly along a river course heading northeast. With the wind in their faces, following the swampy shore they rode on slowly until they reached a crossing place. They slid the rifles from the scabbards and held them aloft to protect them from getting wet, then prodded the horses into and climbed the ground of the opposite side in a few minutes with water dripping from the horse's tails and bellies. At a quick walk they went on across the flat country riding single-filed uphill on a narrowing path until they topped out and could see all the way down the valley. Once there Jeff pulled up his blowing horse and gave the deputies order to ride up beside him and hold it, which they did, one, then the other.

"There yo' can see the windmill an' 'em houses," Jeff said with a slight edge to his voice as the two deputies rode up beside him and they stood shouldered, the horses hopping and tossing their heads in a fret. Without giving the deputies space to answer, he dropped the reins and reached for his rifle and drew it from out the water-blacked scabbard and got down, holding the firearm in his right hand, the other arched about the horn. He seized the firearm in his both hands and broke open the gate and peeped into then breeched shut, the clap loud in the silence. He looked up the pale sky where the shelving early-afternoon clouds, coming in from west and drifting eastward, diverged and slowly dissipated. For a moment the sun broke through and then was gone. They'd been on their way for some two hours, during which the temperature steadily had sunk. All the while keeping the ranch within his eyesight, Jeff made for and stood his rifle against an outcrop of a cliff then groped about in an inner pocket of his coat for his cigarette paper and tobacco, getting at it with his fingers until he reached it then brought it up and started to roll himself a smoke. He wet the paper with his tongue and rolled it shut then set the cigarette between his lips, and tied back the leather thong to the mouth of the tobacco sack and put it back in the pocket, and out of another pocket plucked a match from out the box, and drew it alight against the sole of his boot, once and once again until it took, and with his back to the wind hunch-backed lit it. While smoking he held a throughout going-through of the strategy in which the carrying idea would be to assault the ranch house from three different spots, from the bunkhouse, from the rear and from the barn. From a saddlebag he brought forth and unfolded a map of the ranch, where the buildings where carefully marked out, and asked his deputies to memorize it and compare it to reality, saying they would startle them whoever they were, or how many they were, and if they had anything to ask, they do it now.

Neither of the deputies gave any answer, just somberly nodded comprehension.

Thinking things over Jeff slowly folded up the map and packed it away then stood looking from one to the other while holding his gaze a little longer on Meyron, who sat in his saddle and stared down at the ranch, holding the shotgun in one hand and shading his eyes with the other. Eventually he glanced back to where Jeff and Russell stood.

"Nobody seems to be about down there…how long do you reckon we're gonna stay on this height?" he groaned out with failing enthusiasm, and looked back at the buildings as if to verify nothing had moved while he looked away. Advancing a step in his direction Jeff answered, "Frankly, I have no idea. There are horses in that pen, that's all we know so far."

One long minute went by in silence. And another.

"I thought I heard a dog bark," Russell declared matter-of-factly, looking like he was in no way sure. In a casual manner he un-breeched his handgun and checked the gate to see that it was loaded, one eye in a squint.

"When do we get started?" he finally asked and breeched the gun shut again and re-holstered it.

Jeff ignored the question and turned to Meyron where he was sitting in the saddle holding his rifle across his lap, looking as if he wasn't at odds as to what to do with it, his mouth pursed in doubt. "Yo' alright?" Jeff demanded, squinting up at him.

"I don't know, I guess so," the deputy said, looking off, his chubby jaws clenched, his eyes focused on the surroundings, as if he had taken part in many such raids.

"Attack…don't recede…but don't be foolhardy," Jeff warned, his eyes for a moment meeting Meyron's.

Neither spoke for a long moment. Jeff slowly made it to where his horse stood some steps behind him, cropping the short, dry grass. He walked around it and leaned against its side and closed his eyes. All of a sudden he got a sensation of being devoid of everything. In the next instant an image came forth on his retina, that of a light-haired woman. She smiled at him encouragingly. He had a reason, the best one. He knew it, he was sure about it, as sure as one humanly can be. He let go his hand from off the saddle and squinted up at the shapes of the two riders, already waiting in their saddles. A cool wind was blowing from the blue darkening mountains in the west and swept over the fertile flatlands, a land fertile enough to sustain many horses, a lot more than those already being around. He stood for a while then he went back to the cliff where he'd stood his rifle, retrieved it by its middle and made it the short way back to his horse and mounted up. He got out his field glasses and trained them on the ranch and its surroundings, and the countryside about as far as the distant wheat field in the east. Seeing no hint of life anywhere, he collapsed them and put them back in the saddlebag.

The three riders descended the rise at a slow trot. Having watched the place for a good hour, they now had concluded the ranch to be abandoned. It was a horse ranch, breeding first-rate mounts, spread out in various locations up in the mountain land. In consequence of this, Bill Buchanan and his wranglers spent several hours per day horseback, and overnight encamps were not rare.

They rode on toward the ranch at a rapid trot, Jeff riding point. Having closed a little more than half the distance, Jeff slowed to let the others catch up, and then beckoned for them to halt. They stood abreast for a while, listening for sounds, as the cloud of dust from the horse's hooves slowly settled around them. A clank emerged from one of the houses, indicating human activity of some kind. Now, in full view of the houses, they caught sight of a yellowish little dog that was advancing on them, hesitant to begin with, then trotting closer with its little tongue lolling. It suddenly stopped and gazed about, then went on toward the riders, finally raised its head and stopped when under the horses and stood sniffing in the air. The horsemen exchanged glances in disbelief.

"Not much of a watchdog, eh." Meyron said with a gruff quality to it.

Jeff nodded in reply and raised a hand for quiet, then very carefully, so he wouldn't put the little dog to flight, swung his leg over the fork of the saddle and slid to the ground. He slowly went down in a heap, his face grown tight with thought. Gingerly, keeping watch about him constantly, he stretched out a hand. The puppy raised its tail and wagged it awaiting, went closer and commenced to lick his fingers tentatively. Jeff patted the little head and spoke to the dog in a low steady voice so it wouldn't commence yapping, the two deputies sitting side by side, watching in amusement. Contemplating facts he sat like this for a little while, squatted to his heels, ruffling the dog's ears, listening meanwhile to the piercing sound how it proceeded. It sounded like iron hitting iron, and it emanated from the barn. Eventually he stood up and beckoning for the others to get along gripped the reins and walked the stallion toward the buildings ahead of them, the others tagging along horseback, casting about for anything moving. Midway he paused and looked back and motioned for Meyron to take his position at the rear of the main building according to the agreement that was made among them, then turned to his young deputy and in a hushed voice said for him to go straight for the barn.

He then mounted up and at a slow trot set off toward the bunkhouse and curbed his horse when right outside it. He lithely got to the ground and with constancy of purpose closed the short distance there was between him and the door. He yanked the door open and went in, Colt in hand as the clangs from the barn continued without intermission. Six bunks stood against one wall, all empty, the air rank with sweat and tobacco. Insects wheeling about. In the center of the den, a rectangular table stood dominating, surrounded by an assortment of wooden chairs. No sound was heard in there but for the whirr of a fly somewhere in the air. A greasy pack of cards lay resting on the table next to two empty drink glasses and a filled ashtray. He listened. The clinging sound from the barn had ceased. He turned and deep in concentration headed for the door, the firearm still in his right hand kept at the low. He stepped outside and in a springy gait started toward the barn, glanced around and stopped to listen. Muted voices shot through from the tranquility of the high-ceilinged barn, although individual words were impossible to determine. It was obvious Russell wasn't alone in there. The double doors were open and Jeff went closer with long strides. Now he could discern the foreign voice better. It was an old man's voice squabbling. An old wagon, partially loaded with grain sacks, stood in front of the doors. He went past it and quickly slunk inside, gun in hand. Russell stood before two shapes, one of which an old gaffer, angrily turning on Jeff, worried-looking when seeing him sneak inside. Initially the old man stiffened his body, then looked away from Jeff and returned his attention to Russell who was standing before him with his gun pointed at him. The old man wore an ancient bowler that sat awry on top of his wild hair. Two young horses stood tied up in their stables, twisting and tramping out of anxiety. Almost right behind the horses sat a wooden stand to which a vary assortment of farrier tools in a wide range of sizes were attached. A half-dozen horseshoe nails lay scattered on the rough plank flooring together with a worn wooden club and a chisel. An anvil rested on the floor, not far from the other utensils. Just a few feet away from it stood a sandy-haired young man tall and athletic-looking, fighting to maintain a tough composure. Neither him, nor the old man wore a gun belt.

"Go ahead!" the old man began yelling. "Just finish us off, make it quick, you hear!!" he continued in a chattering voice. His face was red with anger and eyes glowing. He raised a gob then leaned and spat in disgust. He had a small flesh wound on his left cheek, his dark full beard slightly red-colored with blood trickling down from it in a slow rivulet. Glaring at the sheriffs narrowly he screamed some half a dozen or more obscenities, until his young buddy ordered him to hold on.

"'Em men are sheriffs…for Christ's sake," the young one growled between clenched lips.

By then the old man appeared to concede that they were overmatched, and his shoulders dropped. Jeff did remember having seen the gaffer a couple of times before in Sioux Falls, and he knew he was considered mentally defected, but back then he had no idea of where he was living. As for the youngster, he couldn't recall having encountered him ever. For some reason, Buchanan always stuck to outsiders and didn't hire his folks from around.

"Alright, let's talk, gentlemen," Jeff began, looking levelly at the men, then at Russell, who was standing nearest to the youngster, keeping a watchful eye on him. "I am Jeff O'Halloran, deputized sheriff of Sioux Falls...an' this is my deputy Russell O'Connor. We would like to have a word with your boss, Mr. Buchanan. We're gonna ask 'im some questions."

For a second the old man stopped his chomping and became brutal again.

"It ain't likely you gonna find 'im around for some time!" he thundered and turned his face to the mountains in the west, barely perceptible far away. "He rode up 'em mountains yesterday mornin'. Watched 'em ride up 'em crests!"

He ballooned his jaws and returned his gaze to his young compeer and stood with his knees slightly bent and shoulders slanting. The young man beside him shifted and put his hands into the side pockets of his breeches. In a cubicle a horse sidled nervously and neighed pitifully. Jeff looked around for a long moment. He then motioned the two men closer to the wall to lean their palms against it, legs spread. The old man protested vehemently yelling in all directions, whereas the young man just obeyed lop-eared, his eyes looking somewhere in the distance, anxious as it seemed to never establish eye contact. In their pockets, nothing of substantial interest was found.

"I reckon we've got us a big problem," Jeff said and turned to his deputy.

"Yeah?"

"We haven't got much cord, not enough to truss 'em up, anyways."

"Confound you!" the old-timer ranted scornfully, his jaw protruding.

"I was broodin' over the same thing," Russell replied, his voice hardening, looking long at the old man. "Best thing would be findin' us some place to lock 'em up," he went on and looked back at Jeff.

"No, that takes the biscuit!!" the old-timer protested.

Jeff approached him and kneeled until eye-level with him. The old man cringed without a word, a yellow quasi-smile on his lips, barely visible in the grizzled beard. Jeff eventually shifted his gaze to the less verbose youth, who flicked a quick eye over him and then angrily stared ahead. Jeff glanced back at the doors, turned to Russell and said, "I bet 'em have some shackle around so we could lump 'em together. Let's step outside an' have us a look."

He beckoned with his chin toward the doors and with gross reluctance the two men started their exodus, their features solemn and movements infinite.

"The guy here's a broncbuster!" the old-timer shared when outside. "Tames two...three mustangs each day...he's crazy," he chuckled and spat.

"But you sure are the craziest bastard!" the youngster responded, his voice having a fervid touch to it.

"The shithouse!" the old-timer suggested angrily, making an expansive gesture. Advancing at a snail's pace he seemed headed for that building and the sheriffs let them keep going until they approached a small shack, standing not far from what looked to be the privy. Jeff ordered them to hold in front of it. The door already stood flung open and Jeff stepped inside. It was a semidarkness in there.

"That's the chicken coop!" the broncobuster declared, almost whining. "I'll never step inside, you hear!" he lamented and looked at Jeff as if he was very unhappy. Without answering Jeff checked the door to make sure the reel couldn't get opened from inside. Meanwhile the old-timer wandered back and forth and spoke to himself in a guttural grumble.

"Alright, step inside!" Jeff snapped.

Jeff's order hung like a knife in the air. The old man started to say something, didn't, though. Instead, he heaved a deep sigh all the while looking in the precise direction of his brother in misfortune, who shook his light head and went inside without breaking step. They both looked riled, though, riled and hoaxed at the same time.

"What are we gonna do now, boss?" Russell demanded, looking out across the clearing.

Following his gaze, Jeff answered, "Well, it's approaching dark...ain't much else to do but wait, I figure." He latched the door and reached in his pocket for his tobacco. A boisterous discussion had already taken place inside the shanty, some fragments of which penetrating the thin wooden door. The sheriffs looked at each other, shaking their heads in disbelief. Jeff called out Meyron's name. Russell got down to the ground and placed his rifle beside him and sat tailor-wise to inspect one of his boots as though there was something wrong with it. Jeff smoked and watched Meyron coming upon them, leading his horse at the elbow by the reins, cradling his rifle upright in his left hand, the yellowish puppy trotting beside.

"Everything alright, Meyron?" Jeff asked, watching the walking deputy.

Meyron didn't answer at first, but questioningly looked down at Russell, who now was sitting with his hands on his knees. Looking at Jeff he said that he'd searched through the ranch house, but there was nobody inside it. His voice was a bit taut. He stood the horse and stood looking at Jeff as if he wanted to know why he had called him there.

"Alright, let's slide the saddles off 'em horses, an' then we get ourselves something' to eat," Jeff said and tossed the butt onto the ground and tramped on it. He turned around and walked back to the shack and halted when right outside the door and brawled into it, "You in there, you hungry?!"

"You bet we are!! We could eat you raw an' spit you out afterward, Sheriff O'Halloran!!" an old voice brawled.

Russell had already risen, headed for the horses, tightly followed by Meyron. Jeff eventually tagged along. No sound there was to hear about the place save the slight rustle of the wind, and the snorts and the clopping from the hooves of Meyron's bay coat stallion.

"Jeff!" Meyron suddenly said over his shoulder, eyeing him morosely.

"Yeah?"

"An' then we just gonna stay 'round, right?"

"Right."

"Where do you think we're gonna fix that supper?" Meyron wondered and looked back again.

Jeff didn't respond, though. He hadn't heard him ask, because he had dropped to one knee and was caressing the little dog that had circled around his legs so long, wagging its tail.

XXIV

Come evening, the three sheriffs sat in the small kitchen of the bunkhouse, staring into the panting fire dying in the stove. The kitchen was almost dark, and outside the narrow single window the shadows had grown longer yet, and the sun was in the process of finishing its descent in the west, and autumn clouds were boring in. When the last ember had faded into ash, Meyron nervously put back his chair to rise, peering at Jeff with severity. He hadn't eaten much, just one slice of bacon and some cornbread soaked in coffee. He nodded at the lantern that hung from the ceiling, swiftly tightened his gun belt around his massive waist, and looked at Jeff anew.

"You figure it'll be too big a risk to light up that thing?" he demanded, his voice a little thick, his hazel eyes drifting over to Russell, then hastily back to Jeff.

Jeff sat up slightly and shifted his weight. "Well, that might cause us some trouble…'em might be here any time. We've to watch out."

Meyron produced no answer. Instead, he rose and stretched, then started to stroll across the clay flooring as if sensing something being askew. He muttered something, but neither could make it out.

"But you don't know, do you?" he objected after a while, a wrinkled strain formed between his eyes.

Jeff pushed back his Stetson and looked up the greasy ceiling. He turned his face to Russell and in a low voice said to him, "Alright, you take the first turn…outside."

Russell nodded and stretched on the chair. He then reached across the table, gripped the sooty kettle with coffee in it to get himself a refill. He looked back at Jeff, who sat and sprinkled shag into a paper, looking as if he had some more to say, but Russell forestalled him, saying, "Three hours, eh?"

"Yeah, that's what we said…" Jeff droned, licking shut the paper. "We pick a place with an overlook in all directions, remember," he continued without looking up, fishing for matches.

"Yeah, sure," Russell said.

Dredging the matchbox up Jeff said, his voice somewhat amplified, "Cause I don't wanna see nothing' bad happen to either of you, guys."

The two deputies just nodded in agreement at that. Jeff lit up his cigarette. He took a deep draw and looked earnestly from one to the other.

"An' don't turn in, yo' hear," he continued as he shook off the tip of the cigarette onto the ashtray.

There came a hint of an awkward smile on Meyron's lips. Jeff shot him an inquiring glance and demanded on a weary breath, feeling the irritation, "Listen Meyron…you ain't sorry for comin' here, are you?"

"I just don't like to sit idle, that's all," he replied curtly, looking like somebody called to account.

Russell and Jeff exchanged glances. Russell uncertainly looked up at Meyron and back at Jeff.

"Alright, let 'im take the first watch. He already's gotten to his feet, anyways," Russell mumbled, balancing on the chair, his hands sunk under the table. Without a word Meyron walked out of the kitchen and into the pale starlight, gun in hand.

Time dragged on and it was not until the early afternoon of the day to follow, that the three sheriffs, ensconced on the back porch of the ranch house, got aware of the dust cloud in the west, slowly advancing nearer. The little puppy, spreadeagled by their feet, raised its head and hesitantly detached itself and stood listening and sniffing in the air. A while later it beat a hasty retreat and eventually sat down in the shadow of the men. Out there the dust stood like a mobile statue-building, a perishable relief to the bluish mountains far out in the west.

"They are havin' the sun in the eyes," Jeff said and straightened up. He cocked his shotgun and laid it across his lap then felt for his Colt where it sat around his midsection to assure it was in easy reach.

"How far out do you reckon 'em to be, boss?" Russell replied, sitting with his back to the wall of the ranch building.

"A mile, maybe a little more," Jeff said, his watching eyes darting around. He ogled to his left where Meyron sat nestled in his brown leather jacket. He looked like he was giving thought how to handle things, his faze puzzled, a lump of tobacco moving in his cheek. Trying to keep as still as he could, Jeff next turned his face toward Russell, seated to his right with his upper body slightly bent forward in an embodied image of studied casualness. There was no sound anywhere. Some neighs from the dust statue made the four deer on the flatlands stop their cropping and lift their muzzles and with their weak eyes focusing it, then run away, keeping out of peril or evil hasty death at the worse. By every step the dust cloud grew concreter. Out of the quivering cloud three mustangs materialized and gained structure, trotting at the head of it, snorting and tossing their heads, their long manes flapping in the light afternoon breeze. In their catching sight of the ranch buildings, the mustangs began jibbing as a result of their picture of life being incomplete, pack-animals as they were, by the Almighty programmed to escape. By every step, getting closer to the ranch, the unsteadiness of the untamed animals increased, the scent of the anonymous men on the porch magnifying their sensation of alienation. The magnificent white-headed bay at the head at a certain point started to shy, showing inclination to flight. The two mustangs filing behind, watched every move, ready to pursue. The men horseback right behind them, were aware of all this, and had plenty to do keeping the mustangs in one body.

"You reckon 'em have seen us, boss?" Russell asked at one point, turning his head in neither direction.

"'Em horses know we're here, alright. 'Em do ever since they topped the hill," Jeff answered, his voice much lower.

"How 'bout 'em riders?" Meyron wondered uneasily in an undertone, peering about uncertainly, raising his gun a little.

"There's no way to know…any time they'll know, alright," Jeff grunted in return.

Feeling this was a land they never had trod, the mustangs out there changed gaits. The two horsemen riding behind them immediately rode up to their flanks, making a try to trot them down by the ranch and head for the waiting holding pen. One of the riders loosened a lasso from the saddle, collected it and uncoiled it and swung it diligently around the head of the leader mustang and pulled the lasso together around the horse's neck, and then took to draw it home hand over hand. The horse kicked and hopped for a good while as the dust whirled up toward the sky, but got dissolved before coming that far.

The three riders out there discovered the men on the porch with an accurate simultaneousness, and were now looking directly at them, their curses reaching a high degree of intensity. Buchanan shaped his mouth to say something all the while sawing his horse, homebound. He glared at the three guns that were pointed at his chest. His eyes were narrowed in a grimace and he groped for his gun with his free hand.

"Buchanan, don't!!" Jeff cried out.

In the same second the report sounded echoless. Buchanan's torso fell down and his face for a short moment rested in the mane of the excited horse, then slowly slid down until it lay composed among the dancing hooves. The animal, now scared of its wits, trampled about, trying its best to avoid crush him. Another two reports sounded across the flatlands as the bullets leaped off with echoless sprays, and another two bodies dropped to the ground and lay in a twist at the feet of the tramping and whinnying horses. Six loose mustangs were scattered and void of leader, trotting in different directions winded with the running with a faint snorting coming from off them. Apart from this, nothing was heard of.

The gun smoke lingered long on the porch. At length the dog raised its ears and rose with a miserable whimper and trotted out toward the lying bodies. For some reason it halted partway and looked back at the men on the porch as though asking them for advice. Tired of waiting, the little fellow after a brief while trotted back the same way by which it had come and sank down next to Russell, who extended his hand to pat its yellow head.

Nothing was said for a long while. Jeff un-cocked his gun and sat and weighed it in his hand. The deputies stared right in front of them, deep in concentration, like they waited for the bundles out there to start moving, maybe rise and walk away. Eventually Russell got to his feet and stood and bent over the wooden railing. His eyes kept wandering over the landscape ahead of him, his checkered shirt out of his jeans in back. The horses had lowered their heads and walked about cropping the lush grass thick with humming cicadas. The nice bay coat stallion from time to time stopped short and stood with his head raised and his sleek muscles flexed, nervously moving his ears. He studied it long and got the impression that literally every muscle of the impressive mustang was quivering. It approached one of the mares and set about to sniff at her, and soon enough both of them were edging around and snorting in kicking position, examining each other with great curiosity, shrieking with delight.

Meyron was sunken lower into the wooden chair and sat with his arms crossed on his chest. He had stood his rifle against the railing ahead of him, its pipe pointed onto the sky overhead, where a couple of buzzards circled on an updraft, dropped a bit and ascended, awaiting their time to come. Jeff reached in his pocket for his tobacco, his legs crossed before him, rifle still on lap.

"Alright, who shot 'im?" he asked in a gloomy voice, ransacking his pocket.

The deputies, sensitive to the sounds, continued to study the plains before them.

"I did." Meyron said firmly after a time, smiling in triumph, his chubby face turned to the landscape ahead of them. "What's the problem, he was nothing' but scum, anyways," he went on, his voice sharper.

"Said nothin' of no problem, just askin', that's all," Jeff shot back, twisting the ends of the tobacco sac in his fingers.

A quiet settled on the trio, one long enough to allow Jeff to roll him a cigarette and lick it shut, his eyes moving and watching.

"Why did he grope for the gun, yo' figure…Buchanan I mean?" Russell asked after some time, looking out.

Jeff crossed his legs at the ankles. He draw a match alight on the rifle's butt and lit up his cigarette and took a deep draw on it and said, one eye squinting through the smoke, "Frankly, I have no clue. Sometimes a man ain't reasonable." He took a glance to his side for a partial look at Meyron and demanded, "Why do you figure he groped for his gun?"

The deputy shrugged and looked up at the old oak-tree, his eyes fixed upon a couple of dead leaves quivering in the breeze.

"He was chasin' somethin'," he said after a while, "somethin' that he never got, I guess, an' now he come to the conclusion the game was over."

Jeff nodded and stroked his left sideburn at the same time. He rubbed the stubble along his jaw, and watching the shadows growing longer, he sat and smoked until he'd finished his cigarette and had stubbed it out and tramped the butt down. He bent down a little to see the dog sprawled in the shadow of his legs. He took its little yellow head between his hands and cuddled it for a long while. For a few minutes he went on, then he stood and looked around in all directions, thinking deeply of something appropriate to say, but he couldn't figure out what that would be. Far out on the plain six buzzards now were gathered, waiting for their time to appear.

"It sure ain't every day you bury your employer," the old-timer puffed almost brought to tears, wiping his sweaty face with a soaked bandana. He unbuckled his faded denim breeches and buckled them shut again, glancing furtively around him. At some distance sufficiently far enough from the ranch, the old-timer and the bronco cracker had spent the rest of the evening digging in the dying light three holes where the corpses now were put to rest. The broncocracker stood the spade against the oak-tree that stood shadowing the tombs. He took a step closer to the massive trunk and indolently leaned his lean body against it and stood like he was thinking of an apt answer while catching his breath.

"In a matter…of seconds…eh…an' it was…all over with…" he returned and asked, pointing directly at the clogged hole that from now on should be Bill Buchanan's resting place, "Did you see that smile on his face? The smile of a murderer, huh?"

"I saw it, alright, but it ain't the word for it, son. It was a grin, a grinnin' corpse," the old-timer said gravely, pulling at a sleeve. He took off his greasy bowler and stood and held it with both hands in front of him, turning it in his grimy fingers like it were a rosary, his ragged unkempt hair, matted where the hat had compressed it, immobile in the breeze. Remaining in the shade of the tree the bronco cracker shifted his weight, his long arms hanging slack and idling along his sides. Other than the two of them, there was no other human being around. The sheriffs were headed home before the obsequies.

"When are you leavin'?" the broncocracker half shouted and swung open the door of the bunkhouse.

The old man halted behind him and dried his forehead with the heel of his dirty hand.

"Ain't leavin' till I get paid," he spat out and glanced out across the plain. He nodded at the graves and continued, "An'…he's not gonna pay us…an' we have a lotta' job ahead ropin' in those mustangs an' brand 'em. Two…eh, one an' a half horse's waitin' to be shod in that barn, remember," he added and pointed with a stained finger. He squinted and announced matter-of-factly, "One of 'em mares's givin' birth within short."

His young mate nodded, opening the door wider, eyes downcast. Slowly a grin formed, beginning in the corners of his eyes. He shrugged, favoring one leg.

"I reckon you can need a hand, bein' short of workfolks," he suggested laconically, and got a chuckle in return.

"You bet, sonny. Now we ain't cooped no more," the old man said with a shrewd grin, whistling quietly to himself.

"I guess yo're right, ol' bastard."

XXV

Sheriff Douglas Kimble was the first to rise. For nearly two weeks he had been kept in custody in his inhospitable basement jail cell, one six by twelve feet. The last three days had he been sitting silently at the table of the crammed courtroom, and now the critical moment had occurred, the moment when the chairman of the jury, Judge Patrick McCrea, was about to prescribe the verdict. From that moment and forward on, there would be no more cross-examinations, no more questions would be asked, no more answers would be expected. No more efforts to prolong the procedures would be considered, no more mitigating circumstances and loopholes no longer would be available, according to his counselor, the same lawyer who in clear language had expressed that in his opinion, the likelihood of a verdict of acquittal would be literally reduced to zilch. Kimble acknowledged the implication of all this. Nevertheless was he still trying to avoid any kind of emotional outbursts, although his entire body was fidgeting. During their first session together, his lawyer had predicted when they sat huddling in privacy thumbing through the paperwork, that if worse come to worse his client might be out of job when walking out, because basically they cannot bring forward anything compromising against you. If worse came to worse, he'd said. But that was before the moment when the prosecutor had presented the plaintiff's version. The prosecutor virtually had milled them down thoroughly, not to mention the jurors, who had been watching him, Douglas Kimble, carefully, frowning on his unsteadiness, his answers, most of which void of sufficient conviction and substance, and above all, void of truth. They had frowned on his darting and fluttering eyes, his scams at the poker table, and his amorous interludes had induced whisperings among the public severe enough to frighten them away, and consequently the outcome of their voting would be grieving, and the ultimate result would be that the jurors wouldn't be satisfied until they watched him get his neck stretched and hang in the gallows. Too many times during the sessions Sheriff Kimble and his lawyer had got thrown off tracks. And besides, the testifying had shown that the sheriff had taken no actions whatsoever to solve neither of the crimes being committed, manslaughter, deliberate assassinations of decent people out journeyed, out of whom one child, and so and so. No, Kimble had never been heroic in any way. Furthermore, the sheriff had been incapable of producing any kind of statement concerning his whereabouts on the days prior to and after the assassinations. He simply had no trustworthy alibi. He was unable to produce any. And Freeman, the cook at Buchanan's ranch, testified that Sheriff Douglas Kimble had de facto taken part in the coach hold-up. Another witness, and accomplice, had short before dying testified the same. As had also Kimble's vice sheriff and two witnesses that had overheard one of the murderers last words before dying. Kimble recalled what the prosecutor had said in his summing-up. "Your Honor, feelings may be transitory, but what I present here is facts, and nothing but facts, raw, cold facts." Gross negligence in duty. It was there it all started, and to this his lawyer could just nod in agreement. But soon things got worse and went off track when the prosecutor started asking questions about more precarious and sensitive details. Then the lawyer got wordless, and was taken aback one shrinkage in his argumentation, one following another, and to boot the admonitions from the judge became more and more customary over time, and the smug expression on Mr. Benson's face, the plaintiff's young Washington lawyer, grew more and more unendurable to him while one raw fact following another got presented to the jurors. Miss Süsskind, on the other hand often changed expression as time went by, efficacious and straight-faced initially, appreciative and almost maudlin at times, then again unbiased.

Judge Patrick McCrea, chairman of the proceedings, now had pronounced the verdict of the tribunal sessions held before the court of Casper, Wyoming on November 6th 1868. An abrupt silence settled on the courtroom while His Honor in plain terms in due solemnity declared the judicial decision. Willful murder 1:st degree, victim: Judge Ken Anderson. Two house painters and a black whore had, independent of one another, observed Sheriff Kimble in the vicinity of the venue prior to or shortly after the murder being committed, around 6 p.m. September 19th. 1868. His participation in the assault of the coach on August 15th was verified. There wasn't proved, however, that manslaughter was effected by him, Douglas Kimble, at the same location and time. He wasn't foully accused, he had in fact participated, and was involved in the murder of the judge, and was sentenced to be hanged by the neck until death on the 11th of November. Douglas Kimble had five more days to live.

He noticed that his lawyer hadn't moved. Slowly Douglas Kimble comprehended the implication of this fact. The game was over. There would be no second chance. There would be no restart which meant he was facing extinction. A family. Had he ever had any? A hand-off approach, a foundation for socializing when boredom set in. He had never been efficacious enough for such. He had been too effete, as had his father and probably his mother as well. Had he been too strict with himself? Five days from this very moment and he would be crooked and there was no one to apply to. Very slowly Douglas Kimble comprehended the implications of this. On this very occasion Daniel Heathcliff Freeman would climb the gallows together with him. He had heard the judge proclaiming the jury's view that in his defense there was no trustworthy substance whatsoever. He had also heard His Honor pronouncing the verdict and heard him rap the mallet against the top of the mahogany desk. A hollow bang, powerful and commanding. The same mallet had declared Senor Jimenez, the vaquero, not guilty of charge. There was no proof of him being present at the coach attack. He got banished from America, however, for the rest of his life, on the grounds of having discharged gunfire toward a lawman on duty. Judge McCrea had raised an angry finger in the air and told the man "never to show his ugly face in this country again," Kimble couldn't help but smile a little when hearing His Honor saying it. Much laughter were heard in the public as well.

No sooner had the judge slammed his mallet in the desk for the last time than a tipsy bailiff ordered everybody to rise. Half dizzy Douglas Kimble perked his head up, and two jailers brusquely ordered him up to his feet, then diligently handcuffed him. For the last time the former sheriff of Sioux Falls got retreated to his basement custody. He shot a glance over his shoulder and met the eyes of his legal adviser, where he was standing distantly, looking long after him, a briefcase in hand, ready for other battles to come. He looked neutral, expressionless of countenance. He had performed his stint. He had done what he should do as a defense lawyer. In his own opinion. Now he couldn't push this case further. Other cases were now to be considered in the near future. There would be other files for him to flip through. This he knew. He had, in his own view, performed his stint satisfactorily, considering the circumstances, and now other clients stood in wait. This case was closed for ever and there was no annexation left, no more loopholes. No, nothing more of that kind. This his defender soon would tell him in his unsentimental and scanty parlance. Kimble thought about this as he meanwhile listened to the dragging steps behind him. At dawn on the 11th of November, they would be heard again for the very last time.

Nearly a hundred people made their hasty exit from the stuffy courtroom and the entrance successively filled near the railing. Jeff and Hayden filed in anxious to hit the street in shortest time possible. Jeff glanced over some shoulders to see Birgit at some distance, her right arm shot upward, her lips forming the request "Wait for us outside!" "Us" included her lawyer Thomas Benson, who trying his best to avoid too much publicity, was forcing his way past an ocean of faces, half a dozen of whom belonging to reporters from different newspapers. Making occasional adjustments of his glasses, forcing now and again a brave smile, he slowly and very patiently in a gentlemanly manner pushed his way through the throng, briefcase in hand. Lying ahead was a post-trial dinner and then an arduous and long way back to Washington.

"I can see you guys are skippin' that pre-packed grub today, eh," Hayden said with a satisfied grin ogling at Birgit, who sat absorbed by the giant steaks lying on their plates. Without waiting for a reply, he then concentrated on his own serving, sliced it carefully, forked a piece and the first load rapidly disappeared under his groomed mustache. He chewed long and looked about the tasteful premises, decorated with antiques. The place was carefully selected by Birgit and occupied two floors of a concrete building of an antebellum edifice, situated in the very heart of town. An efficient-looking young waiter had escorted them to a small table in an out-of-the-way corner, where they could huddle without having to run the risk of getting eavesdropped.

When the waiter for the umpteenth time had asked if everything had proven satisfactorily, the small talk got brought to an end. When the second pot of coffee sat before them, Hayden bent forward and looking as if he were excavating his brains, started to grope for the proper words. Jeff lit a cigarette and glanced furtively to his side where Mr. Benson waited with his head cocked to one side, expectant. Birgit actually smiled. Jeff got the impression she somehow was in pain, though. Hayden leaned back in his chair and waited a moment then said, "Like I said before…in front of the court…I've been in close contact with 'em officials in Boston." His voice was so low they could barely hear it. He turned his head a bit to look over at Birgit, and said quietly, "Driscoll…Frank Driscoll's dead."

Birgit opened her mouth but no word left it.

Jeff quickly forestalled her, inquiring, "Does anybody else know 'bout this?"

"Just the judge an' the tribunal, an' 'em officials in Boston, of course," Hayden shared silently, his gaze still focused on Birgit.

"What happened?" Birgit wondered, staring past Hayden.

"He shot 'imself with his own little derringer in a shabby hotel room in Norfolk, Virginia. Well, it was pretty difficult for our men to spot 'im, cause he was disguised an' operatin' under a faked identity, you know. In fact he left a parting letter behind. Our men out there promised to dispatch it. It's due to arrive in a week or two," Hayden said.

Having disclosed this, Hayden secretively glanced at Birgit, who just nodded discretely. Thoughtfully Hayden sipped his tepid coffee and surveyed the bunch of rednecks at the bar desk, celebrating the aftermath of a wedding. He hoisted up a shoulder and from the side pocket of his jacket picked up a box of cigars, plucked out one and hunched his shoulders forward and lit it up. He took a draw on the cigar and shot another glance at the men encompassing the bar desk, then squinted at Birgit and Wolf behind the smoke and demanded professionally, "Miss Süsskind, did you know this man, Frank Driscoll?"

Birgit glanced toward Jeff and thought for a second, then shook her head in frustration, cleared her voice and said, her voice trembling a little, "I did not, Mr. Hayden. You see…Frank Driscoll was a very…sick man." She flushed and got silent and looked at her brother, then went on after a pause, "We got friends in a way you know, initially. This might sound cruel to you…but well…I knew of no way to get rid of him. Some year back my father invited him for dinner in our Boston residence, and well…he fell in love with me, and it was so it all began. I just, how shall I say, felt sorry for him, that's all."

Hayden leaned forward a bit, though not too close as though not having an intension to exclude the rest of the party. "So your father and Frank Driscoll were knowing each other?"

"They were, yes…since the war. I got the impression my father pitied him, too, and I also had the im…" Her voice trailed off and her cheeks reddened tremendously.

"Go ahead, Miss Süsskind," Hayden nudged, giving her an open face.

She swallowed hard, looking askance at Jeff and at the lawyer in turn. "Well, I...suspect...eh, had the impression that my father had his arms tightened in some way."

"In what way?" Hayden insisted, his voice hardened.

"I am not privy to that information, Mr. Hayden...Does it matter?" she demanded after a short pause.

Jeff waited for a moment to charge in, the lawyer forestalled him, though, Jeff seeing something in the man's body language, that got him on other thoughts, a sign in his eyes saying: "Let her unload." As for Hayden, he evidently could think of no quick response, so he just shrugged and withdrew, his arms slowly easing backward on the starched tablecloth, until they finally fell into his lap.

"Sorry, Miss Süsskind, my intention never was to get you flustered," he said apologetically, glancing at Jeff, looking as if he was tired of coaxing.

"It's alright, Mr. Hayden," Birgit answered friendly and released a little laughter while she ogled at Jeff, who now seemed to have slipped into another and better world. He simply couldn't take his eyes off her. Her creamy pale skin, her artistically beautiful face, the helmet of blonde-reddish hair, her carriage, her outward beauty as well as her internal, showing no trace of acrimony, her affection for her weak little brother, a genius in almost every aspect, alike his sister fragile, but yet so unbelievably strong, dedicated and forward-looking. The more he saw of them, the more he admired and liked them.

They left at six o'clock. They extended their hands and said their farewells. Pursuant to orders from above, Hayden was headed eastward, his destination Washington DC, where he was due to meet with some politicians from Wyoming at a brief summons. Some high officers from the army would also be around at the meetings, according to Hayden. Jeff nodded and rolled his eyes in utter disbelief when learning about it, grinning and saying something to the effect of, "Nice society, eh."

"You bet, I can't wait," Hayden answered with a grin.

Jeff turned to the lawyer, walking to his left, bowler on head, carrying his bulky briefcase in one hand, and a grip in the other.

"An' you are goin' west, Mr. Benson...ready for other battles?"

"Just Thomas will be fine…Yeah, Seattle, but incidentally I promised my father to stop by for a day or two. He's running a haulage in Clanston," he declared, his face slightly red.

Again they said their farewells and Hayden and the lawyer commenced their walk to the stage coach station four blocks away. Jeff and Birgit lingered by the curb to see the backs of the men disappear in the next intersection. Fifty or so steps in front of them, but still within view, Wolf walked in a stroll, paying the others no mind. A slight westerly wind rattled the almost bared elm overhead, and two leaves stiffly spiraled down and without a sound landed softly underfoot. Draped in her olive cardigan Birgit shivered a little. Jeff stuck his left hand into the pocket of his denim and side by side they started walking. A shudder of lust racked his body, and gingerly he put his free hand on her shoulder. She flinched somewhat, but she didn't protest. He asked her what the name of that song was she'd sung that evening long ago back at Mrs. Penn's, accompanying herself on the old Campbell piano. Birgit thought for a while, a furrow forming between her brows, then she said, "Oh, that time. Eh…either was it 'Liebesbotschaft' by Schubert or…"

"Or…?"

"Clara Schumann, 'Beim Abschied.' The poetry is Frederike Serre's…"

"Well, whichever it was, it was the most beautiful song I've heard ever…in all my life."

"Was it really?"

"Yes…eh, by the way Liebes…what does it mean in English…?"

"Liebesbotschaft means love message in English," she said earnestly, her eyes turned on him.

"And the other song, what does it mean…?"

"At the farewell."

"At the farewell…?"

"Yes."

XXVI

A week later in an acrid scent of shooting…

Slowly, trying to keep it as steady as he could, he angled out his arm and shut his left eye and fired five times, one shot coming hard upon the other. He lowered his arm slowly and with his free hand pushed his bowler back on his head, doubt detectable in his eyes.

"Great, Buster. You've improved quite a lot!" Jeff said encouragingly.

"Yeah, Russell an' me' we been practicin' an hour a day, sometimes more, you know, when yo' were off," the chubby boy shared proudly and crouched down for a better look, his breath condensed in the chilly air. His eyes quickly scanned the holes that just had penetrated the empty tin cans of some home-canned beans and old Arbuckle coffee boxes. Jeff looked down at his profile, the half of it hidden behind the turned-up collar of his white wool sheep winter coat. The boy slowly raised up and smiling happily faced Jeff who looked back down at him with his hand outstretched in a manner as to admonish him to hand him the reeking Colt. With fumbling hands, the boy unbuckled the gunbelt that sat tied around his roundish waist and passed it across with gun in it.

"You know, it's good bein' away from home…mama an' Betty are always fightin'," he said gloomily and turned at the sound of a wagon rattling by out the street.

"Is that a fact, eh?" Jeff managed. As if not knowing what more to say, he with gunbelt in one hand commenced his walk in a dawdle toward the gate of the corral, the boy slowly tagging along with diffidence, his footwear sucking in the mud.

"Listen Buster, do you have any idea why 'em fight?" Jeff said.

The boy stopped short and for an instant stood to study his heels, his freckled, true-hearted face all of a sudden turned very serious in the long core of light from the late low sun. He swallowed. Standing there leaning in the wind in his drooping badly hemmed-in and sweet-smelling jacket, a hand-me-down from his newly dead father, he steadily looked up at Jeff, but said nothing. After sometime he dropped his head and hunched in his jacket studied his muddy footwear some more, his hands jammed deep in his pockets. In an effort to appear dashing, he then said right-out like he'd got another thought up front, "Jeff."

"Yeah?"

"Will you do me a favor?"

A horse whinnied from out the street. Two foreign drovers from out the range by the look of them, strangers on their way in to town, were passing by, hollow-eyed and dusty, looking like they'd been on the road a long time. They were headed for the abattoirs in Abilene or Langtry with their seven, eight-hundred head transiting stock, hard-looking and brute-faced like thugs, armed men both with faces hardened by wind and sun, and with several days of stubble, looking when they'd spotted them their way without expression or gesture of recognition, their horses with breaths rising whitely dancing under them, casting their heads skittishly up and down. Jeff's eyes studiously watched the horsemen and the horses they rode during the period of their passing until they finally curbed and set the horses outside the livery stable and tied them to the bar. He then turned back to the kid and said, his voice all but lost in the breeze, "What favor, Buster…eh, what favor…?"

"I want so madly yo' be my father. Well…" He rubbed his hand over his face and proceeded, "Uh, yo' know, there ain't many good ones to look up to around…"

Listening to the wind, Jeff weighed the boy's words for a good while, then went closer to him and replied, "Look Buster, now yo' an' me are compeers right? Neither of us has no father. We are all powerless when it comes to our faiths…"

"Yeah, I guess."

"I was 'bout your age when I lost mine, an' same goes for Wolf. We're peers, right?"

The boy said nothing, just offered a precocious nod. From the smith's shop smoke rose and iron clang got heard. Outside it a young unsaddled dapple-gray horse stood tethered to a wagon wheel by a rope halter. A tall leather-aproned youngish boy, carrying a toolbox in one hand with quick pace and no hesitation backed up toward the steady-standing horse. He put down the box and stooped and lifted a hoof and yanked it his way and held it still, trapped between his knees. He reached down for a crowbar, then started to pray the old shoe off, his face pointed down. A high-pitched male voice from inside the shop sought its way outside. Then it got quiet. It was the proprietor of the smithy, Jonathan Morgan, a former dealer of slaves.

They'd stopped by the corral's gate at which the town's water wagon, and a black-painted prison coach with only one rear door stood parked, the same vehicle that had transferred his father from the courthouse in Casper to the gallows in Sioux Falls. Jeff's eyes wandered over the boy as clops of hooves got heard another time from the nearby street. Another entourage of cowboys, locals, from a ranch a ways out slowly rode past by twos and threes heading for the saloon with a dog running beside them barking. Outside the saloon two drovers sat on the tie rail waiting them, and yet two others of their kind stood waiting idle in the doorway. He turned to look and raised a hand at them in greeting and then dredged up his makings from different pockets of his apparel, and swiftly started rolling himself a cigarette. When he was done and had wet and licked shut the paper, he jutted his chin into the corral and addressed the boy saying, "Now yo' are learnin' how to use a gun. Then I get it yo' want to learn how to ride a horse?"

A happy smile lit up the boy's face.

"You sure ain't close-fisted, Jeff! That question nobody has never asked me before, sir!"

"I do now," Jeff said, firing up his cigarette.

The boy turned slowly and looked toward the dark shapes of the mountains as a cool wind came down from the north with gusts of wind blowing dust off the top of the ground, the place else empty around them.

"Jeff!"

"Yeah…what is it, Buster?"

The boy took off his battered bowler and thoughtfully scratched his unkempt hair.

"Then we can ride out somewheres after school, right…if I maintain my seat…?" He looked down at his large shineless boots as if woolgathering, turning the hat in his fingers inch by inch.

"Right," Jeff said and managed a warped smile.

"When do we get started?" the boy demanded expectantly and placed his right hand alongside his cheek, like he were in some dream. "Less than in a weeks' time…in case yo' got the time…?" he wondered excitingly.

Without answering, as if occupied with other thoughts, or hadn't he caught the kid's words, Jeff undid the latch, raised and swung the gate of the pen open.

"Look Buster..." he said, facing the kid when stepping out of the pen, "Fortunately we forget much things in life, but those special events, 'em we don't forget. Ain't that life, or what do you say?"

The boy stood for a while with his legs in a straddle, the heels of his mud-caked brogan boots sinking deeper into the clay underfoot. A deep wrinkle had formed between his eyebrows. Jeff was charging the Colt, the cigarette dangling in his mouth as kids voices got heard in the distant air.

"You mean...those we...remember...?" the boy said inquiringly, looking as though the subject prompted some memory in his inner.

"Yeah, sort of," Jeff said, blowing smoke from his nostrils.

"I guess yo' might be right, Jeff." He nodded his head severely, and said again, "I guess yo' might be right...Uh Jeff."

"Yeah?"

"Do I draw quick, yo' think?"

"Yo' draw quick, but yo' don't draw quick enough," Jeff said, seating the last ball.

"My aim is to draw quickern eye can follow if it comes to a showdown one day..." the kid said enthusiastically.

"Then yo' gotta practice some more," Jeff replied, capping the nipple and sliding the gun back into the holster.

"More...?"

"Yeah...a lot more before yo're a crackerjack..."

"Do yo' reckon it's a long way off...?"

"Yeah, I reckon...It depends on yo'. Yo're malleable."

"What does that mean...?" the boy wondered, looking square at Jeff, his brows furrowed.

"Yo' improve quick."

"Does it mean that?"

"Yeah, kinda...By the way, how tall are yo', Buster...?"

"Why...?"

"Yo've grown since I saw yo' last...an' yo' pad a pretty great punch..."

"Five foot eight, I reckon...Jeff..."

"Yeah?"

Rubbing one boot toe on the ground while looking off toward the abandoned street, the boy said, as if something just had occurred to him, "Uh, there was another thing…"

"What other thing, Buster…?"

"There are some other new card tricks I would like to show yo' firsthand…I bet yo' can't do 'em."

Jeff took a drag on his cigarette and expelling smoke from his nostrils said, "Come over tomorrow after school hours so can yo' show me, alright?"

"Alright."

It seemed like Wayne Seay was perpetually drunk, at least at those occasions when he approached Jeff at the sheriff's office. He was also wearing a different look. As far as Jeff could recall, this was his third visit this week. Last time was by noontimes yesterday. Either the man began to be forgetful, or was his strategy deliberately methodical in that sense that he literally squirted Jeff with standing and persuasive arguments, among which "Town needs a sheriff an' you're the man" and "Give it a thought…you ain't supposed to say yes today…give it another day…or two…" soon would turn out to be the most frequent. How many times hadn't Jeff heard those lines, and his answer had always been the same.

"Thanks, but I already have declined your offer, Wayne…I ain't runnin'…" How could he make himself clearer? he asked himself. On the desk ahead of him sat a substantial accumulation of paperwork, most of which reminders from Douglas Kimble's epoch in office. And here the old goat was standing again, upsetting the tranquility of the early evening. On the desk sat the rancher's dented tin mug, his favorite, drained to the lees. He never declined coffee. Black coffee with two huge spoons of sugar. More frazzled than ever he looked down at Jeff and loudly said, "I hope I won't be in the way, O'Halloran…but listen…frankly I ain't come here just for…social reasons…Yo' know how slim the pickings are. If we could get one who has been a deputy, so much the better."

He made a stop and leered for a long time. Jeff lent back in his swivel and tried to relax, putting one knee over the other, his hands folded behind the neck, studying the tobacco-stained ceiling. Neither looked at the other for a long while. Finally Jeff dropped his gaze and looked to where Seay stood in his hulking shape. He bent forward and took a sheet from the pile, flipped it, stood and walked away to the file cabinet. Halfway he stopped and looked blankly at the rancher over his shoulder and said, "Listen, Seay, my answers are neither warped nor belated, an' today it's still the same as last time you asked: I ain't runnin' for the election, you hear?"

He looked squarely at the rancher, wondering what he must be thinking. He scowled at Jeff and placed his meaty hands on his broad hips. Jeff turned back and approached the file cabinet and slid out a drawer. In the very same moment got heard two short solid knocks at the door that went open on squeaking hinges, and Birgit popped her head around it. Seeing Jeff and the rancher, she opened the door wider and hesitantly stepped inside. She was carrying an envelope in her hand. For a short while a slight bewilderment beleaguered the dingy office, until the stocky rancher touched the brim of his Stetson, his watery eyes drooling and yearning as Birgit walked by. He cleared his throat and sincerely droned out, standing swinging, feet spaced.

"Miss Süsskind! What a nice surprise meetin' you, as always!"

He smiled, then Birgit smiled. Jeff had returned to his chores, his face contorted in concentration.

"Maybe…you could help me…Miss Süss…kind…" Seay began cheerfully, hobbling around, slurring his words.

Jeff twisted around and went back and retook his seat behind his writing desk. He glanced up at the rancher, who already had an eye on him. Jeff already felt what was to come next.

"Help you, Mr. Seay? In what way?" Birgit demanded, her voice suddenly gone thick.

"Help me prove…that…man's ain't…in no funk," the rancher slurred and smiled thinly.

Jeff scowled at the man, but then he just got in return a wider smile. With growing concern Jeff said in a quiet voice, "That talk ain't goin' to help you, Wayne. Look, I ain't got nothin' more to say. You ain't sober, an' I ask you to get out. I've got other things to…"

"But I've…got a lotta things…to say!!" the rancher brawled and pulled off his hat and tossed it on the desk in front of Jeff then clawed his fingers through his thick gray hair. With eyes crazy-looking and mitts clipping and shoulders hoisted just like someone about to attempt a feat of strength, he took a step closer, blood beating in the arteries of his temples, small tics at his mouth's corner. The man seemed totally out of control and Jeff couldn't discern any sign of sense in his bloodshot puffy eyes incandesced with madness. He quickly glanced at Birgit who stood shaking her head in disgust, powerless, her eyes widened.

The rancher now moved with a remarkable velocity and Jeff realized there would be no way of preventing the catastrophe from taking place. A powerful clash came forth when he kicked his swivel backward into the wall right behind and raised himself up. He sucked in some air, and hooking low closed the small space between them and charged. He realized he wouldn't be given any second chance, seeing the maniac coming nearer. He lowered his head and feinted then placed a forceful uppercut in the man's solar plexus, then he rapidly re-loaded and discharged another one square in the man's face so hard he could hear the cartilage snap. Then he moved sideways, watching, marshaling himself for another swoop, fighting to keep still, then charged another time. The hit broke the rancher's nose and blood started to flow from the gash in his squishy nose and down his mouth and chin and all the way down the collar of his heavy flannel shirt. There was now nothing else in the rancher's wild eyes but hatred. No fear, no sign of surprise, just sheer hatred. Birgit hadn't budged, stood paralyzed, eyes downcast, shrieking over the entire gamut.

"Stop it, you hear!! Just stop it!! Mister Seay, get out of here, please!!"

The rancher wasn't likely to give up, though. He brushed a hand back over his head then wailed and sniveled a little, moved as quickly as ever before, not many sharp words uttered from him so far. He was all concentration, and the loss of blood didn't sap his power, not yet anyway. His breast heaved and the blood stained his shirt and bandana. Jeff moved on circling. Very rapidly the bear-alike giant clenched his right fist and tried desperately to whack Jeff over his neck, but the blow only hit plain air. Jeff feinted and charged and again landed a brutal shot to the man's nose, and one more to his right eyebrow. Warm blood immediately started oozing down the rancher's right half of face. Jeff proceeded to tag along as Seay meanwhile, passing a hand across his bleeding nose, was trying his best to focus his foggy eyes on him. He went on trashing about for a good while with his arm in level with Jeff's throat as though he was trying to get at it with his fingers, getting more frustrated seeing Jeff ducking out of the way. Jeff let the man flounder and open his face to him. Right then he struck with a punch that landed flush on the rancher's jaw. The giant let out a brawl and went down on all fours in a howl of fury and when down he suddenly exploded and tried to make a grab for Jeff's legs. He didn't appear to have much stamina left, though, and Jeff now began to understand that the end of the fight was in sight. Right then the man on shaky legs started to crawl to his feet.

"Yo' had enough…else we…go on for a while…" Jeff hissed out of puff.

The rancher's mouth cracked into a wry smile.

"I haven't…had enough…no way…not till…I've finished…yo' off…yo' hear!!" he groaned, the sentence culminating in a brawl.

Halfway to his feet, he extended both hands and using the off-edge of the desk as support he laboriously got up and stood rocking on his heels with blood dripping from his crashed nose, his face covered entirely with blood. Unexpectedly he as a last resort charged and was about to land a punch on Jeff's chin. Jeff prepared, parried and a dull sound came forth by the impact that got straight for the rancher's chin. A loud bang got heard and a moment later there was silence. The rancher lay lifeless with his bloody shirt sliced open at the front, bleeding from his nose, vanquished, a loop of spittle seeping in and out from his half-open mouth in time with his labored breathing.

Birgit had left the office, leaving the door open, and a small gathering of people stood grouped outside, alerted by the commotion. "What have you done with the man, sheriff? Clubbed 'im dead?" a female voice grumbled from out the street. Jeff stood for a short instant and blinked and peered out at the sun that was standing low in the west. He felt the demanding eyes from the assembly, all faces expectant-looking, prepared for a detailed explanation.

"Sheriff!! Sheriff!!" it came from a bunch of crying kids. "Can we come inside an'…?"

Jeff interrupted them in mid-sentence, shouting back at them, "He just fainted…he'll soon come to!!"

With his breath soaring he slowly turned around and looked about the place. Fatigue hit him and his feet felt heavy when he advanced on the motionless rancher. Feeling the rank smell of sweat whiffing from off him he stooped low and regarded him to see he was breathing hard. His thin lips were formed into a slight startled smile, and occasionally it almost looked like they were forming words, not friendly words, though, no merely taunts. He had come to. He made efforts to curl himself up, although in vain. Jeff hovered into and bent lower in the knees, and bowlegged for a better hold locked his arms about then with a low groan, applying all his strength, careful not to bloody himself, steadied himself and made a clutch at and got hold of the limp frame, and moving quickly began to drag his former assailant toward the doorstep without halting, his face twisted with exertion. It turned out to be a hardship, the burden growling, its nose now almost twice the normal size. Within the minute he was at the threshold where he halted. He turned to see what way to go, selecting a landmark. With his shoulders hoisted he dragged his limp burden outside and to the top of the stairs. Although quizzical eyes waited outside, not much was said when Jeff descended the footworn gritty stairs and finally dumped the rancher by the hitching rail but a few yards away next to a heap of horse dung, and there he lay shaking spasmodically, articulating laboriously his under jaw. The crowd out there now was in the act of breaking up, and what the deputy sheriff heard behind his back when retreating was just some spread "Thanks a lot, Jeff." Some harsh voice out there loudly said: "It was 'bout time someone took 'im down a peg or two, O'Halloran!" Some other voices loudly grunted their agreement.

As for Birgit, she wasn't to be seen out there, and somehow Jeff was contrite for not having paid more regard to her at the office. Why hadn't he asked her to go out when he began to understand a brawl was in the making? But on the other hand, she already knew there prevailed a lot of nasty rumors about Wayne Seay. Now the evidence of these allegations couldn't elude her. Wayne Seay was in fact a crazy man.

In the evening the atmosphere over dinner was remarkably different. Birgit, tired-looking and black about the eyes – she and her brother had most of the morning been rehearsing Mozart's last violin sonata, the one in A major K. 526 – ate less than usual, and had scarcely spoken in all day, and Jeff noted she had cried. The landlady also, alleging tiredness, excused herself and departed after the table was cleared and the dishes washed. Jeff knew he didn't have to speculate whether Mrs. Penn and Wolf were informed or not. They were, because she never kept them outside, and Jeff couldn't free himself from the impression the landlady and the young man deliberately had withdrawn, giving Jeff and Birgit some time to straighten things out together privately.

Birgit sat in the living room couch with her hands tucked under her chin. Before her on the table with family pictures on it right by with faces watching gravely, she had placed the letter. She looked long at Jeff when he with deliberateness approached, her look neutral, not reproachful, like some half hour before.

"Sorry," Jeff began, glancing around to see if anyone else was about.

"Sorry...?" she repeated questioningly, leaning on her elbows.

"Well, it was me or 'im, you know. People are a lot different out here, I reckon," Jeff grunted, trying a counteroffensive out of the tension. He offered a nod with his chin toward the letter.

"What have you got there?"

She retrieved the white sheet of paper and unfolded it. "You just dropped him in the muck, didn't you?"

"You mean…Seay…?"

"Yes," she said and nodded, as she pried the curves out of the paper.

"Well, you know…it just happened that way," he said and half turned then strolled to one of the windows and stood and looked out, waiting for more to come. Rain was falling in sheets along the street.

She continued, "I got this letter this morning. It's from Frank…Frank Driscoll. Can I read it to you? In parts I mean, because it's extremely personal, private one might say."

He turned around and looked at her. She had raised her chin and sat frowning at him, her eyes almost wet. "Would it be…alright if I read it to you?" she asked again and swallowed as he met her eyes.

"Why not?" he replied, sounding only mildly curious.

"In parts, then?" she wondered, head cocked.

"Yeah."

She again lifted the letter from the table, then laid it back and leaned forward on both elbows, paused for effect, then said, "You have been thinking a lot about the violin, haven't you, Jeff?"

"The violin? Yeah?" He stuffed his hands in the pockets of his denim and waited, his eyes bearing down on her.

"Frank…Driscoll claims there is a map hidden in it, a map which leads to a tremendous fortune. Actually he uses that word…tremendous," she said, her voice soft and urgent.

Jeff sauntered a bit closer to where she sat and finally took a seat in the sofa not far from her.

"Alright, I'm listenin'…tell me more, well, it's hard to believe, but…" he said and looked at her apprehensively. He enjoyed the closeness and the privacy of their chat.

"Well, I've read it many times…" she mumbled as if intervening, "And as you know my father was a doctor and for some years he served as a military doctor, a surgeon...and Frank Driscoll was his, well, assistant during that time."

"Yeah, I know of that...go ahead. By the way..." he went on, "That Driscoll, what's he like?"

She leaned back and released a long breath, her features tightened, head thrown back. He studied her profile and her beautifully modeled hands, a perfect combination of strength and suppleness.

"Well, he is...was perverse in some sense, you know...a complicated character. Not many men looked after his clothes the way he did and..."

"But you had an affair with 'im, ain't it so?" Jeff objected defensively, still studying her hands that lightly rested on her thighs.

"A very brief one. In fact it was no affair," she protested, her cheeks turning red, her head tilted toward the chest.

"Alright...I'm sorry...I've no intension to embarrass you...Go ahead," he said, almost mocking.

She flashed a morose eye in his direction, then said, "One day my father's cavalry squad rode upon an Apache camp that had a sick child. My father went to see it and gave it some treatment and as a pay the chief, who knew a little English, offered my father that violin. He declined, but the chief prevailed upon him, climbed to be offended if he declined, considered it an honor to give my father the instrument. If you open it, you will find a map to a fortune, the chief told him," she explained, trying to keep the voice hushed.

"That conversation was overheard by Frank Driscoll, right?" Jeff asked quietly.

"Yes, that's what he is alleging."

"What do YOU think? Do YOU believe that story?"

She gave the question some thought, her breath short for a while then said, "Well, in all essentials I don't know what to think. Honestly I don't."

Jeff clenched his eyes shut, giving her some opportunity to compose herself. Finally he said, "Why don't you just open it? An' another thing, why didn't your father tell 'bout that map? Or maybe he did?"

"Of course he didn't. In fact I have been asking myself the same question all day. Maybe he didn't believe there was a map, or he wanted the instrument to stay intact. It's an extremely precious object, you know...built in Italy."

Jeff quickly stood, and zigzagging between the furniture made his way to his room where he drew out the bottom drawer of the bureau of walnut. He reached into and picked up the violin, wrapped-up in a clean black cotton shirt. Having removed the wrapping, he briefly studied the instrument. He weighed it in his hand. It didn't weigh much. He looked at himself in the mirror. His suspicions quickly got confirmed. His lip was split and the corner of his right eye was remarkably swollen with a discoloration forming underneath it. He again regarded the violin for some long minute. Deep in thoughts he made his way back to the living room, holding in a firm keep the instrument by the neck, one weighty inquiry running through his head. Basically was he doubtful it ever would be answered. He stepped in close to the young woman. She looked up into his face, then at the violin. She said in disbelieve, "How could one get that map into this thing? As far as I'm concerned, there's no evidence of it ever havin' been opened."

She looked up at him with eyes that comprehended nothing. He gestured with his chin at the violin and handed it down to her. She grabbed it by the neck and set about to scrutinize it from all angels, then stared up into his face for a long time, as if she tried to find the words. She then dropped her head and looked down at the smooth object again and sank it to her lap in a helpless gesture.

"The only way to find out is by cracking it, I presume," she finally said. She straightened her back and violin in hand suddenly jumped to her feet and impulsively said, "I go out in the kitchen and get us some coffee."

She lowered the artifact to the table and got erect and stood and looked at him. He noted that her eyes now were clearing.

"Would you latch up to such an idea?" he inquired, sounding genuinely surprised.

"You mean…crushing it?"

"Yeah?"

She just gave a slight shrug as if that were reasonable, then withdrew. Shortly afterward he heard her light footfalls again.

"What do YOU say, Jeff?" she chirped coming back from the kitchen, carrying two cups and two saucers.

"Well, it's up to you to decide…I don't mind."

She retook her seat and looked out the semidarkness of the almost level room. She twisted her head a little so he could see her in full face, the pronounced cheekbones now more emphasized in the dim light. A beautifully sculptured face. "A very nice piece..." she began, her gaze lowered to the table.

Jeff's reply came quickly, "Yeah...too nice to get cracked."

"Jeff."

"Yeah?"

"Can you promise me one thing?" she demanded, her voice somewhat taut.

"Sure."

"Can you promise to keep all this between the two of us?"

"Absolutely."

"You know, even if there was a way to open it, I doubt I would do."

Her voice almost trailed off in uttering these words. Along the day the sun had tried its best peeking through the clouds. Now it was raining, heavy at times, and the wind was gusting up. They sat in silence, listening to the rain smattering, watching the beads of water trickling downward on the windows as the clock chimed, telling the time to be six. Jeff stood and stretched then sauntered to the rain-bleared window. He stood and looked into the encroaching darkness from one end of the dirt street to the other. The street, the one that led out of town northward, rutted with wagon tracks and imprints of horse feet, was quiet. No one in sight in the hushed emptiness. No. It was starless and cold and raining lightly. Puddles of rain dotted the gritty and rut driveway, reminding Jeff of other puddles, waiting on the plank floor of the sheriff's office. In the building right across the street, dimly defined behind the glass, a solitary old woman stood in a hump, tending plants. He looked skyward. Sketched against the autumn heaven the moon hung whitish in a blurred daze.

"Jeff!"

"Yeah?" he responded without turning.

"I need to cleanse my soul," she said, sounding like she was weighing every word.

He turned to study her. He was about to answer something when her question hit him.

"Are you cold?"

"Cold? No...how so?" he said.

"Do you mind...if I light a fire?"

"I can't stop you. Listen...what 'bout that coffee?"

"Coming," she assured and stood up from the couch with the violin in one hand and the letter in the other. At a leisurely pace she crossed straight to the fireplace. Undaunted she bent down and slightly yanked open the golden door with caution so as to prevent hot embers from falling out. She took a hesitant step forward then pitched the objects inside one at a time, then straightened her back and stood hands on hips glaring down into, as though she was having second thoughts. Jeff decided to bear and wear. Very slowly, almost ritualistically, she took a sulfur stick from the mantel and scraped it to the striking surface of the box. She gingerly pitched the stick into and withdrew. A flurry of sparks ascended and a moment later the letter curled and blackened and was transformed into ash, and the fire took with flames calmly raising and snaking up along the sides. Sometime later the violin was swallowed by flames springing back to life, illuminating for a short while the room from wall to wall with crackling sounds ablaze in an orange light, and after yet sometime the fire lost by and by. And after yet a while there was nothing left to see but for a single sheet of flame that slowly died and subsided into ultimate nothingness. Then she reached inside and held her hands to the fleeting warmth as if in a gesture of benediction. Taking a breath, she retreated a step or two.

"I feel like being at a juncture," she announced solemnly, giving Jeff an imperious eye where he stood in silhouette toward the black window-glass, tall and lean-hipped and heavy-lidded, his face in half shadow crusted with blood. Not knowing whether he'd been watching her or not, she said, "Now I'm free to move on, you know…at last."

"So you're cleansed?" he said and looked down at his scarred knuckles.

Slowly she turned to him and looked at him directly. "Now I am cleansed. I am no longer a martyr…I have gained control" she said and smiled bravely. "Do you understand what that means?" She slowly made it back to the stove and reached down her hands and looked straight into the settling dying glows with frank indifference and held them there for the warmth of them.

It didn't take long for him to consider his answer. He understood and he sensed a thrill for being the only one alive to acknowledge how beautiful she was in this very moment. Her hair with ruddy strokes in it that seemed to come and vanish in varying light, her features so beautifully sculptured, her body and carriage and face so void of flaws, her breasts peeking from the white blouse, her teeth so well-tended and white, her hide so pale, the unadorned lips so sensitive, her arms and hands so well-muscled and strong-looking and yet so gracious, her neckline so consummate in her open-necked white blouse, her eyes so kind and so full of expression, her voice so resonant. He felt a sudden urge to draw her into his arms. Before doing he went to her and standing by her side quietly said into her ear, "Now sing those songs for me, will yo' Birgit…"

With a sudden blush risen on her face she flashed him a quick smile and responded while she dawdling started for the old piano, "Oh, those songs?…Eh, shall I sing them both…?"

He looked longest after her and said, his voice so low it was almost inaudible, "Yes, do, please…Sing both."

Outside the fogged windows the day was gone completely. The nightlights were on, and the heavens were all black. In a holding pen by the livery a horse whinnied long, and from somewhere down the depopulated street two dogs slapped tongue aggressively at an empty wagon that rattled by in a dull creak of wheels.

CPSIA information can be obtained
at www.ICGtesting.com
Printed in the USA
BVHW052308270522
638313BV00003B/27

9 781685 621087